Hans Christian Andersen

German Fairy Tales

Hans Christian Andersen

German Fairy Tales

ISBN/EAN: 9783743307544

Manufactured in Europe, USA, Canada, Australia, Japa

Cover: Foto ©ninafisch / pixelio.de

Manufactured and distributed by brebook publishing software
(www.brebook.com)

Hans Christian Andersen

German Fairy Tales

CONTENTS.

	PAGE
What the Moon Saw	9
The Story of the Year	50
She was Good for Nothing	60
"There is a Difference"	69
Every Thing in its Right Place	74
The Goblin and the Huckster	84
In a Thousand Years	88
The Bond of Friendship	91
Jack the Dullard. An Old Story told Anew	102
Something	108
Under the Willow-tree	116
The Beetle	135
What the Old Man does is Always Right	145
The Wind tells about Waldemar Daa and his Daughters	151
Ib and Christine	165
Ole the Tower-Keeper	180
The Bottle-Neck	192
Good Humor	205

6 CONTENTS.

PAGE

A Leaf from the Sky.................................... 209

The Dumb Book 213

The Jewish Girl.. 215

The Thorny Road of Honor............................. 221

The Old Gravestone.................................... 226

The Old Bachelor's Nightcap 230

The Marsh King's Daughter............................ 246

The Last Dream of the Old Oak-tree. A Christmas Tale. 292

The Bell-deep 299

The Puppet Showman................................... 303

The Pigs 308

A Story from the Sand-dunes 311

The Bishop of Börglum and his Warriors 352

The Snow Man... 360

Two Maidens.. 366

The Farmyard Cock and the Weathercock.............. 369

The Pen and Inkstand.................................. 372

The Child in the Grave................................. 375

INTRODUCTION.

It is a strange thing, that when I feel most fervently and most deeply, my hands and my tongue seem alike tied, so that I cannot rightly describe or accurately portray the thoughts that are rising within me; and yet I am a painter: my eye tells me as much as that, and all my friends who have seen my sketches and fancies say the same.

I am a poor lad, and live in one of the narrowest of lanes; but I do not want for light, as my room is high up in the house, with an extensive prospect over the neighboring roofs. During the first few days I went to live in the town, I felt low-spirited and solitary enough. Instead of the forest and the green hills of former days, I had here only a forest of chimney-pots to look out upon. And then I had not a single friend; not one familiar face greeted me.

So one evening I sat at the window, in a desponding mood; and presently I opened the casement and looked out. Oh, how my heart leaped up with joy! Here was a well-known face at last—a round, friendly countenance, the face of a good friend I had known at home. In fact, it was the Moon that looked in upon me. He was quite unchanged, the dear old Moon, and had the same face exactly that he used to show when he peered down upon me through the willow-trees on the moor. I kissed my hand to him over and over again, as he shone far into my little room; and he, for his part, promised me that every evening, when he came abroad, he would look in upon me for a few moments. This promise he has faithfully kept. It is a pity that he can only stay such a short time when he comes. Whenever he appears, he tells me of one thing or another that he has seen on the previous night, or on that same evening. "Just paint the scenes I describe to you"—this is what he said to me—"and you will have a very pretty picture-book." I have followed his injunction for many evenings. I could make up a new "Thousand and One Nights," in my own way, out of these pictures, but the number might be too great, after all. The pictures I have here given have not been chosen at random, but follow in their proper order, just as they were described to me. Some great gifted painter, or some poet or musician, may make something more of them, if he likes; what I have given here are only hasty sketches, hurriedly put upon the paper, with some of my own thoughts interspersed; for the Moon did not come to me every evening —a cloud sometimes hid his face from me.

ANDERSEN'S TALES.

WHAT THE MOON SAW.

First Evening.

"Last night"—I am quoting the Moon's own words—
"last night I was gliding through the cloudless Indian sky.
My face was mirrored in the waters of the Ganges, and my
beams strove to pierce through the thick intertwining
boughs of the bananas, arching beneath me like the tor-
toise's shell. Forth from the thicket tripped a Hindoo maid,
light as a gazelle, beautiful as Eve. Airy and etherial as a
vision, and yet sharply defined among the shadows, stood
this daughter of Hindostan : I could read on her delicate
brow the thought that had brought her thither. The thorny
creeping plants had torn her sandals, but for all that she
came rapidly forward. The deer that had come down to
the river to quench their thirst, sprang by with a startled
bound, for in her hand the maiden bore a lighted lamp. I
could see the blood in her delicate finger tips, as she spread
them for a screen before the dancing flame. She came
down to the stream, and set the lamp upon the water, and
let it float away. The flame flickered to and fro, and seemed
ready to expire ; but still the lamp burned on, and the girl's
black sparkling eyes, half veiled behind her long silken

1*

lashes, followed it with a gaze of earnest intensity. She knew that if the lamp continued to burn so long as she could keep it in sight, her betrothed was still alive ; but if the lamp was suddenly extinguished, he was dead. And the lamp burned bravely on, and she fell on her knees and prayed. Near her in the grass lay a speckled snake, but she heeded it not—she thought only of Bramah and her betrothed. ' He lives !' she shouted joyfully, ' he lives !' And from the mountains the echo came back upon her, ' he lives !' "

Second Evening.

" Yesterday," said the Moon to me, " I looked down upon a small courtyard surrounded on all sides by houses. In the courtyard sat a clucking hen with eleven chickens ; and a pretty little girl was running and jumping around them. The hen was frightened, and screamed, and spread out her wings over the little brood. Then the girl's father came out and scolded her ; and I glided away and thought no more of the matter.

" But this evening, only a few minutes ago, I looked down into the same courtyard. Every thing was quiet. But presently the little girl came forth again, crept quietly to the hen-house, pushed back the bolt, and slipped into the apartment of the hen and chickens. They cried out loudly, and came fluttering down from their perches, and ran about in dismay, and the little girl ran after them. I saw it quite plainly, for I looked through a hole in the hen-house wall. I was angry with the wilful child, and felt glad when her father came out and scolded her more violently than yesterday, holding her roughly by the arm : she held down her head, and her blue eyes were full of large tears. ' What are you about here?' he asked. She wept and said, 'I wanted to kiss the hen and beg her pardon for frightening her yesterday ; but I was afraid to tell you.'

" And the father kissed the innocent child's forehead, and I kissed her on the mouth and eyes."

Third Evening.

" In the narrow street round the corner yonder—it is so narrow that my beams can only glide for a minute along the walls of the house, but in that minute I see enough to learn what the world is made of—in that narrow street I saw a woman. Sixteen years ago that woman was a child, playing in the garden of the old parsonage, in the country. The hedges of rose-bush were old, and the flowers were faded. They straggled wild over the paths, and the ragged branches grew up among the boughs of the apple-trees ; here and there were a few roses still in bloom—not so fair as the queen of flowers generally appears, but still they had color, and scent too. The clergyman's little daughter appeared to me a far lovelier rose, as she sat on her stool under the straggling hedge, hugging and caressing her doll with the battered pasteboard cheeks.

" Ten years afterwards I saw her again. I beheld her in a splendid ballroom : she was the beautiful bride of a rich merchant. I rejoiced at her happiness, and sought her on calm quiet evenings—ah, nobody thinks of my clear eye and my silent glance ! Alas ! my rose ran wild, like the rose-bushes in the garden of the parsonage. There are tragedies in every-day life, and to-night I saw the last act of one.

" She was lying in bed in a house in that narrow street : she was sick unto death, and the cruel landlord came up, and tore away the thin coverlet, her only protection against the cold. 'Get up!' said he; 'your face is enough to frighten one. Get up and dress yourself, give me money, or I'll turn you out into the street! Quick—get up!' She answered, 'Alas! death is gnawing at my heart. Let me rest.' But he forced her to get up and bathe her face, and put a wreath of roses in her hair; and he placed her in a chair at the window, with a candle burning beside her, and went away.

"I looked at her, and she was sitting motionless, with her hands in her lap. The wind caught the open window and shut it with a crash, so that a pane came clattering down in fragments; but still she never moved. The curtain caught fire, and the flames played about her face; and I saw that she was dead. There at the open window sat the dead woman, preaching a sermon against *sin*—my poor faded rose out of the parsonage garden!"

Fourth Evening.

"This evening I saw a German play acted," said the Moon. "It was in a little town. A stable had been turned into a theatre; that is to say, the stable had been left standing, and had been turned into private boxes, and all the timber work had been covered with colored paper. A little iron chandelier hung beneath the ceiling, and that it might be made to disappear into the ceiling, as it does in great theatres, when the *ting-ting* of the prompter's bell is heard, a great inverted tub had been placed just above it.

"*Ting-ting!* and the little iron chandelier slowly rose at least half a yard and disappeared in the tub; and that was the sign that the play was going to begin. A young nobleman and his lady, who happened to be passing through the little town, were present at the performance, and conse quently the house was crowded. But under the chandelier was a vacant space like a little crater ; not a single soul sat there, for the tallow was dripping, drip, drip ! I saw every thing, for it was so warm in there that every loop-hole had been opened. The male and female servants stood outside, peeping through the chinks, although a real police-man was inside, threatening them with a stick. Close by the orchestra could be seen the noble young couple in two old armchairs, which were usually occupied by his worship the mayor and his lady ; but these latter were to-day obliged to content themselves with wooden forms, just as if they had been ordinary citizens ; and the lady observed quietly to herself, ' One sees, now, that there is rank above rank ;' and this incident gave an air of extra festivity to the whole proceedings. The chandelier gave little leaps, the crowd got their knuckles rapped, and I, the Moon, was present at the performance from beginning to end."

Fifth Evening.

" Yesterday," began the Moon, " I looked down upon the turmoil of Paris. My eye penetrated into an apartment of the Louvre. An old grandmother, poorly clad—she belonged to the working class—was following one of the under-ser-vants into the great empty throne-room, for this was the apartment she wanted to see—that she was resolved to see ; it had cost her many a little sacrifice, and many a coaxing word, to penetrate thus far. She folded her thin hands, and looked round with an air of reverence, as if she had been in a church.

" ' Here it was,' she said, ' here!' And she approached the throne, from which hung the rich velvet fringed with gold lace. ' There,' she exclaimed, ' there !' and she knelt and kissed the purple carpet. I think she was actually weeping.

"'But it was not *this very* velvet!' observed the footman, and a smile played about his mouth. 'True, but it was this very place,' replied the woman, 'and it must have looked just like this.' 'It looked so, and yet it did not,' observed the man: 'the windows were beaten in, and the doors were off their hinges, and there was blood upon the floor.' 'But for all that you can say, my grandson died upon the throne of France. Died!' mournfully repeated the old woman. I do not think another word was spoken, and they soon quitted the hall. The evening twilight faded, and my light shone doubly vivid upon the rich velvet that covered the throne of France.

"Now who do you think this poor woman was? Listen, I will tell you a story.

"It happened in the Revolution of July, on the evening of the most brilliantly victorious day, when every house was a fortress, every window a breastwork. The people stormed the Tuileries. Even women and children were to be found among the combatants. They penetrated into the apartments and halls of the palace. A poor half-grown boy in a ragged blouse fought among the older insurgents. Mortally wounded with several bayonet thrusts, he sank down. This happened in the throne-room. They laid the bleeding youth upon the throne of France, wrapped the velvet around his wounds, and his blood streamed forth upon the imperial purple. There was a picture! the splendid hall, the fighting groups! A torn flag lay upon the ground, the tricolor was waving above the bayonets, and on the throne lay the poor lad with the pale glorified countenance, his eyes turned towards the sky, his limbs writhing in the death-agony, his breast bare, and his poor tattered clothing half hidden by the rich velvet embroidered with silver lilies. At the boy's cradle a prophecy had been spoken : 'He will die on the throne of France !' The mother's heart dreamt of a second Napoleon.

"My beams have kissed the wreath of *immortelles* on his grave ; and this night they kissed the forehead of the old grandame, while in a dream the picture floated before her which thou mayst draw—the poor boy on the throne of France."

Sixth Evening.

"I've been in Upsala," said the Moon : "I looked down upon the great plain covered with coarse grass, and upon the barren fields. I mirrored my face in the Tyris river, while the steamboat drove the fish into the rushes. Beneath me floated the waves, throwing long shadows on the so-called graves of Odin, Thor, and Friga. In the scanty turf that covers the hill-side names have been cut.* There is no monument here, no memorial on which the traveller can have his name carved, no rocky wall on whose surface he can get it painted ; so visitors have the turf cut away for that purpose. The naked earth peers through in the form of great letters and names ; these form a network over the whole hill. Here is an immortality, which lasts till the fresh turf grows !

"Upon the hill stood a man, a poet. He emptied the mead horn with the broad silver rim, and murmured a name. He begged the winds not to betray him, but I heard the name. I knew it. A count's coronet sparkles above it, and

---

* Travellers on the Continent have frequent opportunities of seeing how universally this custom prevails among travellers. In some places on the Rhine, pots of paint and brushes are offered by the natives to the traveller desirous of "immortalizing" himself.

therefore he did not speak it out. I smiled, for I knew that a poet's crown adorns his own name. The nobility of Eleanora d'Este is attached to the name of Tasso. And I also know where the Rose of Beauty blooms!"

Thus spake the Moon, and a cloud came between us. May no cloud separate the poet from the rose.

Seventh Evening.

"Along the margin of the shore stretches a forest of firs and beeches : and fresh and fragrant is this wood ; hundreds of nightingales visit it every spring. Close beside is the sea, the ever-changing sea, and between the two is placed the broad high-road. One carriage after another rolls over it ; but I did not follow them, for my eye loves best to rest upon one point. A Hun's Grave* lies there, and the sloe and blackthorn grow luxuriantly among the stones. Here is true poetry in nature.

"And how do you think men appreciate this poetry? I will tell you what I heard there last evening and during the night.

"First, two rich landed proprietors came driving by. 'Those are glorious trees!' said the first. 'Certainly ; there are ten loads of firewood in each,' observed the other: 'it will be a hard winter, and last year we got fourteen dollars a load'—and they were gone. 'The road here is wretched,' observed another man who drove past. 'That's the fault of those horrible trees,' replied his neighbor ; 'there is no free current of air ; the wind can only come from the sea'—and they were gone. The stage coach went rattling past. All the passengers were asleep at this beau-

---

* Large mounds, similar to the " barrows " found in Britain, are thus designated in Germany and the North.

tiful spot. The postillion blew his horn, but he only thought, 'I can play capitally. It sounds well here. I wonder if those in there like it?'—and the stage-coach vanished. Then two young fellows came galloping up on horseback. There's youth and spirit in the blood here! thought I; and, indeed, they looked with a smile at the moss-grown hill and thick forest. 'I should not dislike a walk here with the miller's Christine,' said one—and they flew past.

"The flowers scented the air; every breath of air was hushed: it seemed as if the sea were a part of the sky that stretched above the deep valley. A carriage rolled by. Six people were sitting in it. Four of them were asleep; the fifth was thinking of his new summer coat, which would suit him admirably; the sixth turned to the coachman and asked him if there were any thing remarkable connected with yonder heap of stones. 'No,' replied the coachman, 'it's only a heap of stones; but the trees are remarkable.' 'How so?' 'Why, I'll tell you how they are very remarkable. You see, in winter, when the snow lies very deep, and has hidden the whole road so that nothing can be seen, those trees serve me for a landmark. I steer by them, so as not to drive into the sea; and you see that is why the trees are remarkable.'

"Now came a painter. He spoke not a word, but his eyes sparkled. He began to whistle. At this the nightingales sang louder than ever. 'Hold your tongues!' he cried testily; and he made accurate notes of all the colors and transitions—blue, and lilac, and dark brown. 'That will make a beautiful picture,' he said. He took it in just as a mirror takes in a view; and as he worked he whistled a march of Rossini. And last of all came a poor girl. She laid aside the burden she carried, and sat down to rest upon the Hun's Grave. Her pale, handsome face was bent in a listening attitude towards the forest. Her eyes brightened, she gazed earnestly at the sea and the sky, her hands were folded, and I think she prayed, 'Our Father.' She herself could not understand the feeling that swept through her, but I know that this minute, and the beautiful natural scene, will live within her memory for years, far more vividly and more truly than the painter could portray it with his colors on paper. My rays followed her till the morning dawn kissed her brow."

Eighth Evening.

Heavy clouds obscured the sky, and the Moon did not make his appearance at all. I stood in my little room, more lonely than ever, and looked up at the sky where he ought to have shown himself. My thoughts flew far away, up to my great friend, who every evening told me such pretty tales, and showed me pictures. Yes, he has had an experience indeed. He glided over the waters of the Deluge, and smiled on Noah's ark just as he lately glanced down upon me, and brought comfort and promise of a new world that was to spring forth from the old. When the Children of Israel sat weeping by the waters of Babylon, he glanced mournfully upon the willows where hung the silent harps. When Romeo climbed the balcony, and the promise of true love fluttered like a cherub towards heaven, the round Moon hung, half hidden among the dark cypresses, in the lucid air. He saw the captive giant at St. Helena, looking from the lonely rock across the wide ocean, while great thoughts swept through his soul! Ah! what tales the Moon can tell. Human life is like a story to him. To-night I shall not see thee again, old friend. To-night I can draw no picture of the memories of thy visit. And as I looked dreamily towards the clouds, the sky became bright. There was a glancing light, and a beam from the Moon fell upon me. It vanished again, and dark clouds flew past : but still it was a greeting, a friendly good-night offered to me by the Moon.

NINTH EVENING.

The air was clear again. Several evenings had passed, and the Moon was in the first quarter. Again he gave me an outline for a sketch. Listen to what he told me.

" I have followed the polar bird and the swimming whale to the eastern coast of Greenland. Gaunt ice-covered rocks and dark clouds hung over a valley, where dwarf willows and barberry bushes stood clothed in green. The blooming lychnis exhaled sweet odors. My light was faint, my face pale as the water-lily that, torn from its stem, has been drifting for weeks with the tide. The crown-shaped Northern Light burned fiercely in the sky. Its ring was broad, and from its circumference the rays shot like whirling shafts of fire across the whole sky, flashing in changing radiance from green to red. The inhabitants of that icy region were assembling for dance and festivity ; but accustomed to this glorious spectacle, they scarcely deigned to glance at it. ' Let us leave the souls of the dead to their ball-play with the heads of the walruses,' they thought in their superstition, and they turned their whole attention to the song and dance. In the midst of the circle, and divested of his furry cloak, stood a Greenlander, with a small pipe, and he played and sang a song about catching the seal, and the chorus around him chimed in with ' *Eia, Eia, Ah.*' And in their white furs they danced about in the circle, till you might fancy it was a polar bear's ball.

" And now a Court of Judgment was opened. Those Greenlanders who had quarrelled stepped forward, and the offended person chanted forth the faults of his adversary in an extempore song, turning them sharply into ridicule, to the sound of the pipe and the measure of the dance. The defendant replied with a satire as keen, while the audience laughed, and gave their verdict. The rocks heaved, the glaziers melted, and great masses of ice and snow came crashing down, shivering to fragments as they fell : it was a glorious Greenland summer night. A hundred paces away, under the open tent of hides, lay a sick man. Life still flowed through his warm blood, but still he was to die —he himself felt it, and all who stood around him knew it also ; therefore his wife was already sewing round him the shroud of furs, that she might not afterwards be obliged to touch the dead body. And she asked, 'Wilt thou be buried on the rock, in the firm snow ? I will deck the spot with thy *kayak*, and thy arrows, and the *angekokk* shall dance over it. Or wouldst thou rather be buried in the sea?' 'In the sea,' he whispered, and nodded with a mournful smile. 'Yes, it is a pleasant summer tent, the sea,' observed the wife. 'Thousands of seals sport there, the walrus shall lie at thy feet, and the hunt will be safe and merry !' And the yelling children tore the outspread hide from the window-hole, that the dead man might be carried to the ocean, the billowy ocean, that had given him food in life, and that now, in death, was to afford him a place of rest. For his monument, he had the floating, ever-changing icebergs, whereon the seal sleeps, while the storm-bird flies round their gleaming summits !"

Tenth Evening

"I knew an old maid," said the Moon. "Every winter she wore a wrapper of yellow satin, and it always remained new, and was the only fashion she followed. In summer she always wore the same straw hat, and I verily believe the very same gray-blue dress.

"She never went out, except across the street to an old female friend ; and in later years she did not even take this walk, for the old friend was dead. In her solitude my old maid was always busy at the window, which was adorned in summer with pretty flowers, and in winter with cress, grown upon felt. During the last months I saw her no more at the window, but she was still alive. I knew that, for I had not yet seen her begin the 'long journey,' of which she often spoke with her friend. 'Yes, yes,' she was in the habit of saying, ' when I come to die, I shall take a longer journey than I have made my whole life long. Our family vault is six miles from here. I shall be carried there, and shall sleep there among my family and relatives.' Last night a van stopped at the house. A coffin was carried out, and then I knew that she was dead. They placed straw round the coffin, and the van drove away. There slept the quiet old lady, who had not gone out of her house once for the last year. The van rolled out through the town-gate as briskly as if it were going for a pleasant excursion. On the high-road the pace was quicker yet. The coachman looked nervously around every now and then—I fancy he half expected to see her sitting on the coffin, in her yellow satin wrapper. And because he was startled, he foolishly lashed his horses, while he held the reins so tightly that the poor beasts were in a foam : they were young and fiery. A hare jumped across the road and startled them, and they fairly ran away. The old sober maiden, who had for years and years moved quietly round and round in a dull circle, was now, in death, rattled over stock and stone on the public highway The coffin in its covering of straw tumbled out of the van, and was left on the high-road, while horses, coachman, and carriage flew past in wild career. The lark rose up carolling from the field, twittering her morning lay over the coffin, and presently perched upon it, picking with her beak at the straw covering, as though she would tear it up. The lark rose up again, singing gayly, and I withdrew behind the red morning clouds."

Eleventh Evening.

"I will give you a picture of Pompeii," said the Moon. "I was in the suburb in the Street of Tombs, as they call it, where the fair monuments stand, in the spot where, ages ago, the merry youths, their temples bound with rosy wreaths, danced with the fair sisters of Laïs. Now, the stillness of death reigned around. German mercenaries, in the Neapolitan service, kept guard, played cards, and diced; and a troop of strangers from beyond the mountains came into the town, accompanied by a sentry. They wanted to see the city that had risen from the grave illumined by my beams; and I showed them the wheel-ruts in the streets paved with broad lava-slabs; I showed them the names on the doors, and the signs that hung there yet: they saw in the little courtyard the basins of the fountains, ornamented with shells; but no jet of water gushed upward, no songs sounded forth from the richly painted chambers, where the bronze dog kept the door.

"It was the City of the Dead; only Vesuvius thundered forth his everlasting hymn, each separate verse of which is called by men an eruption. We went to the temple of Venus, built of snow-white marble, with its high altar in front of the broad steps, and the weeping-willows sprouting freshly forth among the pillars. The air was transparent and blue, and black Vesuvius formed the background, with fire ever shooting forth from it, like the stem of the pine-tree. Above it stretched the smoky cloud in the silence of the night, like the crown of the pine, but in a blood-red illumination. Among the company was a lady singer, a real and great singer. I have witnessed the homage paid to her in the greatest cities of Europe. When they came to the tragic theatre, they all sat down on the amphitheatre steps, and thus a small part of the house was occupied by an audience, as it had been many centuries ago. The stage still stood unchanged, with its walled side-scenes, and the two arches in the background, through which tho beholders saw the same scene that had been exhibited in the old times—a scene painted by nature herself, namely, the mountains between Sorento and Amalfi. The singer gayly mounted the ancient stage, and sang. The place inspired her, and she reminded me of a wild Arab horse, that rushes headlong on with snorting nostrils and flying mane—her song was so light and yet so firm. Anon I thought of the mourning mother beneath the cross at Golgotha, so deep was the expression of pain. And, just as it had done thousands of years ago, the sound of applause and delight now filled the theatre. 'Happy, gifted creature!' all the hearers exclaimed. Five minutes more, and the stage was empty, the company had vanished, and not a sound more was heard—all was gone. But the ruins stood unchanged, as they will stand when centuries shall have gone by, and when none shall know of the momentary applause and of the triumph of the fair songstress; when all will be forgotten and gone, and even for me this hour will be but a dream of the past."

Twelfth Evening.

"I looked through the windows of an editor's house," said the Moon. "It was somewhere in Germany. I saw handsome furniture, many books, and a chaos of newspapers. Several young men were present: the editor himself stood at his desk, and two little books, both by young authors, were to be noticed. 'This one has been sent to me,' said he. 'I have not read it yet; what think *you* of the contents?' 'Oh,' said the person addressed—he was a poet himself—'it is good enough; a little broad certainly; but, you see, the author is still young. The verses might be better, to be sure; the thoughts are sound, though there is certainly a good deal of common-place among them. But what will you have? You can't be always getting something new. That he'll turn out any thing great I don't believe, but you may safely praise him. He is well read, a remarkable Oriental scholar, and has a good judgment. It was he who wrote that nice review of my 'Reflections on Domestic Life.' We must be lenient towards the young man.'

"'But he is a complete hack!' objected another of the gentlemen. 'Nothing is worse in poetry than mediocrity, and he certainly does not go beyond this.'

"'Poor fellow,' observed a third, 'and his aunt is so happy about him. It was she, Mr. Editor, who got together so many subscribers for your last translation.'

"'Ah, the good woman! Well, I have noticed the book briefly. Undoubted talent—a welcome offering—a flower in the garden of poetry—prettily brought out—and so on. But this other book—I suppose the author expects me to purchase it? I hear it is praised. He has genius, certainly: don't you think so?'

"'Yes, all the world declares as much,' replied the poet, 'but it has turned out rather wildly. The punctuation of the book, in particular, is very eccentric.'

"'It will be good for him if we pull him to pieces, and anger him a little, otherwise he will get too good an opinion of himself.'

"'But that would be unfair,' objected the fourth. 'Let us not carp at little faults, but rejoice over the real and abundant good that we find here : he surpasses all the rest.'

"'Not so. If he is a true genius, he can bear the sharp voice of censure. There are people enough to praise him. Don't let us quite turn his head.'

"'Decided talent,' wrote the editor, 'with the usual carelessness. That he can write incorrect verses may be seen in page 25, where there are two false quantities. We recommend him to study the ancients,' etc.

"I went away," continued the Moon, "and looked through the windows in the aunt's house. There sat the bepraised poet, the *tame* one; all the guests paid homage to him, and he was happy.

"I sought the other poet out, the *wild* one; him also I found in a great assembly at his patron's, where the tame poet's book was being discussed.

"I shall read yours also," said Mæcenas; "but to speak honestly—you know I never hide my opinion from you—I don't expect much from it, for you are much too wild, too fantastic. But it must be allowed that, as a man, you are highly respectable."

"A young girl sat in a corner; and she read in a book these words :

"'In the dust lies genius and glory,
But ev'ry-day talent will *pay*.
It's only the old, old story,
But the piece is repeated each day.'"

2

THIRTEENTH EVENING.

The Moon said, "Beside the woodland path there are two small farm-houses. The doors are low, and some of the windows are placed quite high, and others close to the ground; and whitethorn and barberry bushes grow around them. The roof of each house is overgrown with moss and with yellow flowers and houseleek. Cabbage and potatoes are the only plants cultivated in the gardens, but out of the hedge there grows a willow-tree, and under this willow-tree sat a little girl, and she sat with her eyes fixed upon the old oak-tree between the two huts.

"It was an old withered stem. It had been sawn off at the top, and a stork had built his nest upon it ; and he stood in this nest clapping with his beak. A little boy came and stood by the girl's side : they were brother and sister.

"'What are you looking at ?' he asked.

"'I'm watching the stork,' she replied : "our neighbors told me that he would bring us a little brother or sister to-day; let us watch to see it come !"

"'The stork brings no such things,' the boy declared, 'you may be sure of that. Our neighbor told me the same thing, but she laughed when she said it, and so I asked her if she could say 'On my honor,' and she could not; and I knew by that that the story about the storks is not true, and that they only tell it to us children for fun.'

"'But where do the babies come from, then ?' asked the girl.

"'Why, an angel from heaven brings them under his cloak: but no man can see him; and that's why we never know when he brings them.'

"At that moment there was a rustling in the branches of

the willow-tree, and the children folded their hands and looked at one another: it was certainly the angel coming with the baby. They took each other's hand, and at that moment the door of one of the houses opened, and the neighbor appeared.

" 'Come in, you two,' she said. 'See what the stork has brought. It is a little brother.'

"And the children nodded gravely at one another, for they had felt quite sure already that the baby was come."

FOURTEENTH EVENING.

" I was gliding over the Lüneburg Heath," the Moon said. " A lonely hut stood by the wayside, a few scanty bushes grew near it, and a nightingale who had lost his way sang sweetly. He died in the coldness of the night: it was his farewell song that I heard.

"The morning dawn came glimmering red. I saw a caravan of emigrant peasant families who were bound to Hamburgh, there to take ship for America, where fancied prosperity would bloom for them. The mothers carried their little children at their backs, the elder ones tottered by their sides, and a poor starved horse tugged at a cart that bore their scanty effects. The cold wind whistled, and therefore the little girl nestled closer to her mother, who, looking up at my decreasing disk, thought of the bitter want at home, and spoke of the heavy taxes they had not been able to raise. The whole caravan thought of the same thing; therefore, the rising dawn seemed to them a message from the sun, of fortune that was to gleam brightly upon them. They heard the dying nightingale sing: it was no false prophet, but a harbinger of fortune. The wind whistled, therefore they did not understand that the night-i.gale sung, 'Fare away over the sea ! Thou hast paid the long passage with all that was thine, and poor and helpless shalt thou enter Canaan. Thou must sell thyself, thy wife, and thy children. But your griefs shall not last long. Behind the broad fragrant leaves lurks the goddess of Death, and her welcome kiss shall breathe fever into thy blood. Fare away, fare away, over the heaving billows.' And the caravan listened well pleased to the song of the nightingale, which seemed to promise good fortune. Day broke through the light clouds ; country people went across the heath to church ; the black-gowned women with their white head-dresses looked like ghosts that had stepped forth from the church pictures. All around lay a wide dead plain, covered with faded brown heath, and black charred spaces between the white sand-hills. The women carried hymn-books, and walked into the church. Oh, pray, pray for those who are wandering to find graves beyond the foaming billows."

Fifteenth Evening.

"I know a Pulcinella,"* the Moon told me. "The public applaud vociferously directly they see him. Every one of his movements is comic, and is sure to throw the house into convulsions of laughter ; and yet there is no art in it all—it is complete nature. When he was yet a little boy, playing about with other boys, he was already Punch Nature had intended him for it, and had provided him with a hump on his back, and another on his breast ; but his inward man, his mind, on the contrary, was richly furnished Not one could surpass him in depth of feeling or in readi-

---

* The comic or grotesque character of the Italian ballet, from which English "Punch" takes his origin.

ness of intellect. The theatre was his ideal world. If he had possessed a slender, well-shaped figure, he might have been the first tragedian on any stage: the heroic, the great, filled his soul; and yet he had to become a Pulcinella. His very sorrow and melancholy did but increase the comic dryness of his sharply cut features, and increased the laughter of the audience, who showered plaudits on their favorite. The lovely Columbine was indeed kind and cordial to him; but she preferred to marry the Harlequin. It would have been too ridiculous if beauty and ugliness had in reality paired together.

"When Pulcinella was in very bad spirits, she was the only one who could force a hearty burst of laughter, or even a smile from him; first she would be melancholy with him, then quieter, and at last quite cheerful and happy. 'I know very well what is the matter with you,' she said; 'yes, you're in love!' And he could not help laughing. 'I and Love!' he cried, 'that would have an absurd look. How the public would shout!' 'Certainly you are in love,' she continued; and added with a comic pathos, 'and I am the person you are in love with.' You see, such a thing may be said when it is quite out of the question—and, indeed, Pulcinella burst out laughing, and gave a leap into the air, and his melancholy was forgotten.

"And yet she had only spoken the truth. He *did* love her, love her adoringly, as he loved what was great and lofty in art. At her wedding he was the merriest among the guests, but in the stillness of night he wept: if the public had seen his distorted face then, they would have applauded rapturously.

"And a few days ago Columbine died. On the day of the funeral Harlequin was not required to show himself on the boards, for he was a disconsolate widower. The director had to give up a very merry piece, that the public might not too painfully miss the pretty Columbine and the agile Harlequin. Therefore Pulcinella had to be more boisterous and extravagant than ever; and he danced and capered, with despair in his heart; and the audience yelled, and shouted '*Bravo, bravissimo!*' Pulcinella was actually called before the curtain. He was pronounced inimitable.

"But last night the hideous little fellow went out of town, quite alone, to the deserted churchyard. The wreath of flowers on Columbine's grave was already faded, and he sat down there. It was a study for a painter. As he sat with his chin on his hands, his eyes turned up towards me, he looked like a grotesque monument—a Punch on a grave —peculiar and whimsical! If the people could have seen their favorite, they would have cried as usual, '*Bravo, Pulcinella; bravo, bravissimo!*'"

Sixteenth Evening.

Hear what the Moon told me. "I have seen the cadet who had just been made an officer put on his handsome uniform for the first time; I have seen the young bride in her wedding-dress, and the princess girl-wife happy in her gorgeous robes; but never have I seen a felicity equal to that of a little girl of four years old, whom I watched this evening. She had received a new blue dress, and a new pink hat; the splendid attire had just been put on, and all were calling for a candle, for my rays, shining in through the windows of the room, were not bright enough for the occasion, and further illumination was required. There stood the little maid, stiff and upright as a doll, her arms stretched painfully straight out away from her dress, and her fingers apart; and oh, what happiness beamed from her whole countenance ! 'To-morrow you shall go out in your new clothes,' said her mother; and the little one looked up at her hat, and down at her frock, and smiled brightly. 'Mother,' she cried, 'what will the little dogs think, when they see me in these splendid new things ?'"

Seventeenth Evening.

"I have spoken to you of Pompeii," said the Moon—"that corpse of a city, exposed in the view of living towns. I know another sight still more strange; and this is not the corpse, but the spectre of a city. Whenever the jetty fountains splash into the marble basins, they seem to me to be telling the story of the floating city. Yes, the spouting water may tell of her, the waves of the sea may sing of her fame ! On the surface of the ocean a mist often rests, and that is her widow's veil. The bridegroom of the sea is dead, his palace and his city are his mausoleum ! Dost thou know this city ? She has never heard the rolling of wheels or the hoof-tread of horses in her streets, through which the fish swim, while the black gondola glides spectrally over the green water. I will show you the place," continued the Moon, "the largest square in it, and you will fancy yourself transported into the city of a fairy tale. The grass grows rank among the broad flagstones, and in the morning twilight thousands of tame pigeons flutter around the solitary lofty tower. On three sides you find yourself surrounded by cloistered walks. In these the silent Turk sits smoking his long pipe, the handsome Greek leans against the pillar and gazes at the upraised trophies and lofty masts, memorials of power that is gone. The flags hang down like mourning scarfs. A girl rests there : she has put down her heavy pails filled with water; the yoke with which she has carried them rests on one of her shoulders, and she leans against the mast of victory. That is not a fairy palace you see before you yonder, but a church : the gilded domes and shining orbs flash back my beams ; the glorious bronze horses up yonder have made journeys, like the bronze horse in the fairy tale : they have come hither, and gone hence, and have returned again. Do you notice the variegated splendor of the walls and windows ? It looks as if Genius had followed the caprices of a child, in the adornment of these singular temples. Do you see the winged lion on the pillar ? The gold glitters still, but his wings are tied—the lion is dead, for the king of the sea is dead; the great halls stand desolate, and where gorgeous paintings hung of yore the naked wall now peers through. The *lazzarone* sleeps under the arcade, whose pavement in old times was to be trodden only by the feet of high nobility. From the deep wells, and perhaps from the prisons by the Bridge of Sighs, rise the accents of woe, as at the time when the tambourine was heard in the gay gondolas, and the golden ring was cast from the *Bucentaur* to Adria, the queen of the seas. Adria ! shroud thyself in the mists; let the veil of thy widowhood shroud thy form, and clothe in the weeds of woe the mausoleum of thy bridegroom—the marble, spectral Venice."

Eighteenth Evening.

"I looked down upon a great theatre," said the Moon. "The house was crowded, for a new actor was to make his first appearance that night. My rays glided over a little window in the wall, and I saw a painted face with the forehead pressed against the panes. It was the hero of the evening. The knightly beard curled crisply about the chin; but there were tears in the man's eyes, for he had been hissed off, and indeed with reason. The poor Incapable! But Incapables cannot be admitted into the empire of Art. He had deep feeling, and loved his art enthusiastically, but the art loved not him. The prompter's bell sounded; '*the hero enters with a determined air,*' so ran the stage direction in his part, and he had to appear before an audience who turned him into ridicule. When the piece was over, I saw a form wrapped in a mantle, creeping down the steps: it was the vanquished knight of the evening. The scene-shifters whispered to one another, and I followed the poor fellow home to his room. To hang one's self is to die a mean death, and poison is not always at hand, I know; but he thought of both. I saw how he looked at his pale face in the glass, with eyes half closed, to see if he should look well as a corpse. A man may be very unhappy, and yet exceedingly affected. He thought of death, of suicide; I believe he pitied himself, for he wept bitterly, and when a man has had his cry out he doesn't kill himself.

" Since that time a year had rolled by. Again a play was to be acted, but in a little theatre, and by a poor strolling company. Again I saw the well-remembered face, with the painted cheeks and the crisp beard. He looked up at me and smiled; and yet he had been hissed off only a minute before—hissed off from a wretched theatre, by a miserable audience. And to-night a shabby hearse rolled out of the town-gate. It was a suicide—our painted, despised hero. The driver of the hearse was the only person present, for no one followed except my beams. In a corner of the churchyard the corpse of the suicide was shovelled into the earth, and nettles will soon be growing rankly over his grave, and the sexton will throw thorns and weeds from the other graves upon it."

Nineteenth Evening.

"I come from Rome," said the Moon. "In the midst of the city, upon one of the seven hills, lie the ruins of the imperial palace. The wild fig-tree grows in the clefts of the wall, and covers the nakedness thereof with its broad gray-green leaves; trampling among heaps of rubbish, the ass treads upon green laurels, and rejoices over the rank thistles. From this spot, whence the eagles of Rome once flew abroad, whence they 'came, saw, and conquered,' our door leads into a little mean house, built of clay between two pillars; the wild-vine hangs like a mourning garland over the crooked window. An old woman and her little grand-daughter live there : they rule now in the palace of the Cæsars, and show to strangers the remains of its past glories. Of the splendid throne-hall only a naked wall yet stands, and a black cypress throws its dark shadow on the spot where the throne once stood. The dust lies several feet deep on the broken pavement; and the little maiden, now the daughter of the imperial palace, often sits there on her stool when the evening bells ring. The keyhole of the door close by she calls her turret window; through this she can see half Rome, as far as the mighty cupola of St. Peter's.

"On this evening, as usual, stillness reigned around; and in the full beam of my light came the little grand-daughter. On her head she carried an earthen pitcher of antique shape, filled with water. Her feet were bare, her short frock and white sleeves were torn. I kissed her pretty round shoulders, her dark eyes, and black shining hair. She mounted the stairs; they were steep, having been made up of rough blocks of broken marble and the capital of a fallen pillar. The colored lizards slipped away, startled, from before her feet, but she was not frightened at them. Already she lifted her hand to pull the door-bell— a hare's foot fastened to a string formed the bell-handle of the imperial palace. She paused for a moment—of what might she be thinking? Perhaps of the beautiful Christ-child, dressed in gold and silver, which was down below in the chapel, where the silver candlesticks gleamed so bright, and where her little friends sung the hymns in which she also could join? I know not. Presently she moved again —she stumbled; the earthen vessel fell from her head, and broke on the marble steps. She burst into tears. The beautiful daughter of the imperial palace wept over the worthless broken pitcher; with her bare feet she stood there weeping, and dared not pull the string, the bell-rope of the imperial palace!"

Twentieth Evening.

It was more than a fortnight since the Moon had shone. Now he stood once more, round and bright, above the clouds, moving slowly onward. Hear what the Moon told me.

"From a town in Fezzan I followed a caravan. On the margin of the sandy desert, in a salt plain, that shone like a frozen lake, and was only covered in spots with light drifting sand, a halt was made. The eldest of the company —the water-gourd hung at his girdle, and on his head was a little bag of unleavened bread—drew a square in the sand with his staff, and wrote in it a few words out of the Koran,

and then the whole caravan passed over the consecrated
spot. A young merchant, a child of the East, as I could
tell by his eye and his figure, rode pensively forward on his
white snorting steed. Was he thinking, perchance, of his
fair young wife? It was only two days ago that the camel,
adorned with furs and with costly shawls, had carried her,
the beauteous bride, round the walls of the city, while
drums and cymbals had sounded, the women sang, and
festive shots, of which the bridegroom fired the greatest
number, resounded round the camel ; and now he was
journeying with the caravan across the desert.

" For many nights I followed the train. I saw them rest
by the well-side among the stunted palms ; they thrust the
knife into the breast of the camel that had fallen, and roasted
its flesh by the fire. My beams cooled the glowing sands,
and showed them the black rocks, dead islands in the immense ocean of sand. No hostile tribes met them in their
pathless route, no storms arose, no columns of sand whirled
destruction over the journeying caravan. At home the
beautiful wife prayed for her husband and her father. ' Are
they dead ?' she asked of my golden crescent ; ' Are they
dead ?' she cried to my full disk. Now the desert lies behind them. This evening they sit beneath the lofty palm-
trees, where the crane flutters round them with its long
wings, and the pelican watches from the branches of the
mimosa. The luxuriant herbage is trampled down, crushed
by the feet of elephants. A troop of negroes are returning
from a market in the interior of the land : the women, with
copper buttons in their black hair, and decked out in clothes
dyed with indigo, drive the heavily laden oxen, on whose
backs slumber the naked black children. A negro leads a
young lion, which he has bought, by a string. They
approach the caravan ; the young merchant sits pensive

and motionless, thinking of his beautiful wife, dreaming, in
the land of the blacks, of his white fragrant lily beyond
the desert. He raises his head, and—" But at this moment a cloud passed before the Moon, and then another.
I heard nothing more from him this evening.

TWENTY-FIRST EVENING.

"I saw a little girl weeping," said the Moon; "she was
weeping over the depravity of the world. She had received
a most beautiful doll as a present. Oh, that was a glorious
doll, so fair and delicate! She did not seem created for
the sorrows of this world. But the brothers of the little
girl, those great naughty boys, had set the doll high up in
the branches of a tree, and had run away.

"The little girl could not reach up to the doll, and could
not help her down, and that is why she was crying. The
doll must certainly have been crying too; for she stretched
out her arms among the green bushes, and looked quite
mournful. Yes, these are the troubles of life of which the
little girl had often heard tell. Alas, poor doll! it began
to grow dark already; and suppose night were to come on
completely! Was she to be left sitting there alone on the
bough all night long? No, the little maid could not make
up her mind to that. 'I will stay with you,' she said, although she felt any thing but happy in her mind. She
could almost fancy she distinctly saw little gnomes, with
their high-crowned hats, sitting in the bushes; and further
back in the long walk, tall spectres appeared to be dancing
They came nearer and nearer, and stretched out their hands
towards the tree on which the doll sat; they laughed scornfully, and pointed at her with their fingers. Oh, how frightened the little maid was! 'But if one has not done any

thing wrong,' she thought, 'nothing evil can harm one. I wonder if I have done any thing wrong?' And she considered. 'Oh, yes! I laughed at the poor duck with the red rag on her leg; she limped along so funnily, I could not help laughing; but it's a sin to laugh at animals.' And she looked up at the doll. 'Did you laugh at the duck too?' she asked; and it seemed as if the doll shook her head.

Twenty-second Evening.

"I looked down upon Tyrol," said the Moon, "and my beams caused the dark pines to throw long shadows upon the rocks. I looked at the pictures of St. Christopher carrying the Infant Jesus that are painted there upon the walls of the houses, colossal figures reaching from the ground to the roof. St. Florian was represented pouring water on the burning house, and the Lord hung bleeding on the great cross by the wayside. To the present generation these are old pictures, but I saw when they were put up, and marked how one followed the other. On the brow of the mountain yonder is perched, like a swallow's nest, a lonely convent of nuns. Two of the sisters stood up in the tower tolling the bell; they were both young, and therefore their glances flew over the mountain out into the world. A travelling coach passed by below; the postillion wound his horn, and the poor nuns looked after the carriage for a moment with a mournful glance, and a tear gleamed in the eyes of the younger one. And the horn sounded faint and more faintly, and the convent-bell drowned its expiring echoes."

Twenty-third Evening.

Hear what the Moon told me. "Some years ago, here in Copenhagen, I looked through the window of a mean little room. The father and mother slept, but the little son was not asleep. I saw the flowered cotton curtains of the bed move, and the child peep forth. At first I thought he was looking at the great clock, which was gayly painted in red and green. At the top sat a cuckoo, below hung the heavy leaden weights, and the pendulum with the polished disk of metal went to and fro, and said 'tick, tick.' But no, he was not looking at the clock, but at his mother's spinning-wheel, that stood just underneath it. That was the boy's favorite piece of furniture, but he dared not touch it, for if he meddled with it he got a rap on the knuckles. For hours together, when his mother was spinning, he would sit quietly by her side, watching the murmuring spindle and the revolving wheel, and as he sat he thought of many things. Oh, if he might only turn the wheel himself! Father and mother were asleep; he looked at them, and looked at the spinning-wheel, and presently a little naked foot peered out of bed, and then a second foot, and then two little white legs. There he stood. He looked round once more to see if father and mother were still asleep—yes, they slept; and now he crept *softly, softly,* in his short little nightgown, to the spinning-wheel, and began to spin. The thread flew from the wheel, and the wheel whirled faster and faster. I kissed his fair hair and his blue eyes, it was such a pretty picture.

"At that moment the mother awoke. The curtain shook, she looked forth, and fancied she saw a gnome or some other kind of little spectre. 'In Heaven's name!' she cried, and aroused her husband in a frightened way. He opened his eyes, rubbed them with his hands, and looked at the brisk little lad. 'Why, that is Bertel,' said he. And my eye quitted the poor room, for I have so much to see. At the same moment I looked at the halls of the Vatican, where the marble gods are enthroned. I shone upon the group of the Laocoon; the stone seemed to sigh. I pressed a silent kiss on the lips of the Muses, and they seemed to stir and move. But my rays lingered longest on the Nile group with the colossal god. Leaning against the Sphinx, he lies there thoughtful and meditative, as if he were thinking on the rolling centuries; and little love-gods sport with him and with the crocodiles. In the horn of plenty sat with folded arms a little tiny love-god, contemplating the great solemn river-god, a true picture of the boy at the spinning wheel—the features were exactly the same. Charming and life-like stood the little marble form, and yet the wheel of the year has turned more than a thousand times since the time when it sprang forth from the stone. Just as often as the boy in the little room turned the spinning wheel had the great wheel murmured, before the age could again call forth marble gods equal to those he afterwards formed.

"Years have passed since all this happened," the Moon went on to say. "Yesterday I looked upon a bay on the eastern coast of Denmark. Glorious woods are there; and high trees, an old knightly castle with red walls, swans floating in the ponds, and in the background appears, among orchards, a little town with a church. Many boats, the crews all furnished with torches, glided over the silent expanse—but these fires had not been kindled for catching fish, for every thing had a festive look. Music sounded, a song was sung, and in one of the boats the man stood erect to whom homage was paid by the rest, a tall sturdy man, wrapped in a cloak. He had blue eyes and long white hair. I knew him, and thought of the Vatican, and of the group of the Nile, and the old marble gods. I thought of the simple little room where little Bertel sat in his night-shirt by the spinning-wheel. The wheel of time has turned, and new gods have come forth from the stone. From the boats there arose a shout: 'Hurrah, hurrah for Bertel Thorwaldsen!'"

Twenty-fourth Evening.

"I will now give you a picture from Frankfort," said the Moon. "I especially noticed one building there. It was not the house in which Goethe was born, nor the old Council House, through whose grated windows peered the horns of the oxen that were roasted and given to the people when the emperors were crowned. No, it was a private house, plain in appearance, and painted green. It stood near the old Jews' Street. It was Rothschild's house.

"I looked through the open door. The staircase was brilliantly lighted: servants carrying wax candles in massive silver candlesticks stood there, and bowed low before an old woman, who was being brought down-stairs in a litter. The proprietor of the house stood bareheaded, and respectfully imprinted a kiss on the hand of the old woman. She was his mother. She nodded in a friendly manner to him and to the servants, and they carried her into the dark narrow street, into a little house, that was her dwelling. Here her children had been born, from hence the fortune of the family had arisen. If she deserted the despised street and the little house, fortune would also desert her children. That was her firm belief."

The Moon told me no more; his visit this evening was far too short. But I thought of the old woman in the narrow despised street. It would have cost her but a word, and a brilliant house would have arisen for her on the banks of the Thames—a word, and a villa would have been prepared in the Bay of Naples.

"If I deserted the lowly house, where the fortunes of my sons first began to bloom, fortune would desert them!" It was a superstition, but a superstition of such a class, that he who knows the story and has seen this picture, need have only two words placed under the picture to make him understand it ; and these two words are : "A mother."

TWENTY-FIFTH EVENING.

"It was yesterday, in the morning twilight"—these are the words the Moon told me—"in the great city no chimney was yet smoking—and it was just at the chimneys that I was looking. Suddenly a little head emerged from one of them, and then half a body, the arms resting on the rim of the chimney-pot. 'Ya-hip ! ya-hip !' cried a voice. It was the little chimney-sweeper, who had for the first time in his life crept through a chimney, and stuck out his head at the top. 'Ya-hip ! ya-hip !' Yes, certainly that was a very different thing to creeping about in the dark narrow chimneys ! the air blew so fresh, and he could look over the whole city towards the green wood. The sun was just rising. It shone round and great, just in his face, that beamed with triumph, though it was very prettily blacked with soot.

"'The whole town can see me now,' he exclaimed, 'and the moon can see me now, and the sun too. Ya-hip ! ya-hip !' And he flourished his broom in triumph."

Twenty-sixth Evening.

"Last night I looked down upon a town in China," said the Moon. "My beams irradiated the naked walls that form the streets there. Now and then, certainly, a door is seen; but it is locked, for what does the Chinaman care about the outer world? Close wooden shutters covered the windows behind the walls of the houses; but through the windows of the temple a faint light glimmered. I looked in, and saw the quaint decorations within. From the floor to the ceiling pictures are painted, in the most glaring colors, and richly gilt—pictures representing the deeds of the gods here on earth. In each niche statues are placed, but they are almost entirely hidden by the colored drapery and the banners that hang down. Before each idol (and they are all made of tin) stood a little altar of holy water, with flowers and burning wax-lights on it. Above all the rest stood Fo, the chief deity, clad in a garment of yellow silk, for yellow is here the sacred color. At the foot of the altar sat a living being, a young priest. He appeared to be praying, but in the midst of his prayer he seemed to fall into deep thought, and this must have been wrong, for his cheeks glowed and he held down his head. Poor Soui-hong! Was he, perhaps, dreaming of working in the little flower-garden behind the high street wall? And did that occupation seem more agreeable to him than watching the wax-lights in the temple? Or did he wish to sit at the rich feast, wiping his mouth with silver paper between each course? Or was his sin so great that, if he dared utter it, the Celestial Empire would punish it with death? Had his thoughts ventured to fly with the ships of the barbarians, to their homes in far distant England? No, his thoughts did not fly so far, and yet they were sinful, sinful as thoughts born of young hearts, sinful here in the temple, in the presence of Fo and the other holy gods.

"I know whither his thoughts had strayed. At the further end of the city, on the flat roof paved with porcelain, on which stood the handsome vases covered with painted flowers, sat the beauteous Pu, of the little roguish eyes, of the full lips, and of the tiny feet. The tight shoe pained her, but her heart pained her still more. She lifted her graceful round arm, and her satin dress rustled. Before her stood a glass bowl containing four gold-fish. She stirred the bowl carefully with a slender lacquered stick, very slowly, for she, too, was lost in thought. Was she thinking, perchance, how the fishes were richly clothed in gold, how they lived calmly and peacefully in their crystal world, how they were regularly fed, and yet how much happier they might be if they were free? Yes, that she could well understand, the beautiful Pu. Her thoughts wandered away from her home, wandered to the temple, but not for the sake of holy things. Poor Pu! Poor Soui-hong!

"Their earthly thoughts met, but my cold beam lay between the two, like the sword of the cherub."

TWENTY-SEVENTH EVENING.

"The air was calm," said the Moon; "the water was transparent as the purest ether through which I was gliding, and deep below the surface I could see the strange plants that stretched up their long arms towards me like the gigantic trees of the forest. The fishes swam to and fro above their tops. High in the air a flight of wild swans were winging their way, one of which sank lower and lower, with wearied pinions, his eyes following the airy caravan, that melted further and further into the distance. With out-spread wings he sank slowly, as a soap-bubble sinks in the still air, till he touched the water. At length his head lay back between his wings, and silently he lay there, like white lotus-flower upon the quiet lake. And a gentle wind arose, and crisped the quiet surface, which gleamed like the clouds that poured along in great broad waves ; and the swan raised his head, and the glowing water splashed like blue fire over his breast and back. The morning dawn illuminated the red clouds, the swan rose strengthened, and flew towards the rising sun, towards the bluish coast whither the caravan had gone ; but he flew alone, with a longing in his breast. Lonely he flew over the blue swelling billows."

Twenty-eighth Evening.

"I will give you another picture of Sweden," said the Moon. "Among dark pine woods, near the melancholy banks of the Stoxen, lies the old convent church of Wreta. My rays glided through the grating into the roomy vaults, where kings sleep tranquilly in great stone coffins. On the wall, above the grave of each, is placed the emblem of earthly grandeur, a kingly crown; but it is made only of wood, painted and gilt, and is hung on a wooden peg driven into the wall. The worms have gnawed the gilded wood, the spider has spun her web from the crown down to the sand, like a mourning banner, frail and transient as the grief of mortals. How quietly they sleep ! I can remember them quite plainly. I still see the bold smile on their lips, that so strongly and plainly expressed joy or grief. When the steamboat winds along like a magic snail over the lakes, a stranger often comes to the church, and visits the burial vault; he asks the names of the kings, and they have a dead and forgotten sound. He glances with a smile at the worm-eaten crowns, and if he happens to be a pious, thoughtful man, something of melancholy mingles with the smile. Slumber on, ye dead ones! The Moon thinks of you, the Moon at night sends down his rays into your silent kingdom, over which hangs the crown of pine wood."

Twenty-ninth Evening.

"Close by the high-road," said the Moon, "is an inn, and opposite to it is a great wagon-shed, whose straw roof was just being re-thatched. I looked down between the bare rafters and through the open loft into the comfortless space below. The turkey-cock slept on the beam, and the saddle rested in the empty crib. In the middle of the shed stood a travelling carriage; the proprietor was inside, fast asleep, while the horses were being watered. The coachman stretched himself, though I am very sure that he had been most comfortably asleep half the last stage. The door of the servants' room stood open, and the bed looked as if it had been turned over and over; the candle stood on the floor, and had burnt deep down into the socket. The wind blew cold through the shed: it was nearer the dawn than to midnight. In the wooden frame on the ground slept a wandering family of musicians. The father and mother seemed to be dreaming of the burning liquor that remained in the bottle. The little pale daughter was dreaming too, for her eyes were wet with tears. The harp stood at their heads, and the dog lay stretched at their feet."

Thirtieth Evening.

"It was in a little provincial town," the Moon said; "it certainly happened last year, but that has nothing to do with the matter. I saw it quite plainly. To-day I read about it in the papers, but there it was not half so clearly expressed. In the taproom of the little inn sat the bear leader, eating his supper; the bear was tied up outside, behind the wood-pile—poor Bruin, who did nobody any harm, though he looked grim enough. Up in the garret three little children were playing by the light of my beams; the eldest was perhaps six years old, the youngest certainly not more than two. 'Tramp, tramp'—somebody was coming upstairs: who might it be? The door was thrust open —it was Bruin, the great, shaggy Bruin! He had got tired of waiting down in the courtyard, and had found his way to the stairs. I saw it all," said the Moon. "The children were very much frightened at first at the great shaggy animal; each of them crept into a corner, but he found them all out, and smelt at them, but did them no harm. 'This must be a great dog,' they said, and began to stroke him. He lay down upon the ground, the youngest boy clambered on his back, and bending down a little head of golden curls, played at hiding in the beast's shaggy skin. Presently the eldest boy took his drum, and beat upon it till it rattled again; the bear rose upon his hind legs, and began to dance. It was a charming sight to behold. Each boy now took his gun, and the bear was obliged to have one too, and he held it up quite properly. Here was a capital playmate they had found; and they began marching—one, two; one, two.

"Suddenly some one came to the door, which opened, and the mother of the children appeared. You should have seen her in her dumb terror, with her face as white as chalk, her mouth half open, and her eyes fixed in a horrified stare. But the youngest boy nodded to her in great glee, and called out in his infantile prattle, 'We're playing at soldiers·' And then the bear leader came running up."

Thirty-first Evening.

The wind blew stormy and cold, the clouds flew hurriedly past; only for a moment now and then did the Moon become visible. He said, " I looked down from the silent sky upon the driving clouds, and saw the great shadows chasing each other across the earth. I looked upon a prison. A closed carriage stood before it; a prisoner was to be carried away. My rays pierced through the grated window towards the wall : the prisoner was scratching a few lines upon it, as a parting token; but he did not write words, but a melody, the outpouring of his heart. The door was opened, and he was led forth, and fixed his eyes upon my round disk. Clouds passed between us, as if he were not to see my face, nor I his. He stepped into the carriage, the door was closed, the whip cracked, and the horses galloped off into the thick forest, whither my rays were not able to follow him; but as I glanced through the grated window, my rays glided over the notes, his last farewell engraved on the prison wall—where words fail, sounds can often speak. My rays could only light up isolated notes, so the greater part of what was written there will ever remain dark to me. Was it the death-hymn he wrote there? Were these the glad notes of joy? Did he drive away to meet death, or hasten to the embraces of his beloved? The rays of the Moon do not read all that is written by mortals."

Thirty-second Evening.

" I love the children," said the Moon, "especially the quiet little ones—they are so droll. Sometimes I peep into the room, between the curtain and the window frame, when they are not thinking of me. It gives me pleasure to see them dressing and undressing. First, the little round naked shoulder comes creeping out of the frock, then the arm; or I see how the stocking is drawn off, and a plump little white leg makes its appearance, and a white little foot that is fit to be kissed ; and I kiss it too.

"But about what I was going to tell you. This evening I looked through a window, before which no curtain was drawn, for nobody lives opposite. I saw a whole troop of little ones, all of one family, and among them was a little sister. She is only four years old, but can say her prayers as well as any of the rest. The mother sits by her bed every evening, and hears her say her prayers; and then she has a kiss, and the mother sits by the bed till the little one has gone to sleep, which generally happens as soon as ever she can close her eyes.

"This evening the two elder children were a little boisterous. One of them hopped about on one leg in his long white nightgown, and the other stood on a chair surrounded by the clothes of all the children, and declared he was acting Grecian statues. The third and fourth laid the clean linen carefully in the box, for that is a thing that has to be done; and the mother sat by the bed of the youngest, and announced to all the rest that they were to be quiet, for little sister was going to say her prayers.

"I looked in, over the lamp, into the little maiden's bed, where she lay under the neat white coverlet, her hands folded demurely and her little face quite grave and serious. She was praying the Lord's Prayer aloud. But her mother interrupted her in the middle of her prayer. 'How is it,' she asked, ' that when you have prayed for daily bread, you always add something I cannot understand? You must tell me what that is.' The little one lay silent, and looked at her mother in embarrassment. 'What is it you say after *our daily bread?*' 'Dear mother, don't be angry : I only said, *and plenty of butter on it.*'"

<hr>

THE STORY OF THE YEAR.

It was far in January, and a terrible fall of snow was pelting down. The snow eddied through the streets and lanes; the window-panes seemed plastered with snow on the outside; snow plumped down in masses from the roofs ; and a sudden hurry had seized on the people, for they ran, and flew, and fell into each others' arms, and as they clutched each other fast for a moment, they felt that they were safe at least for that length of time. Coaches and horses seemed frosted with sugar. The footmen stood with their backs against the carriages, so as to turn their faces from the wind. The foot-passengers kept in the shelter of the carriages, which could only move slowly on in the deep snow; and when the storm at last abated, and a narrow path was swept clean alongside the houses, the people stood still in this path when they met, for none liked to take the first step aside into the deep snow to let the other pass him. Thus they stood silent and motionless, till, as if by tacit consent, each sacrificed one leg, and stepping aside, buried it in the deep snow-heap.

Towards evening it grew calm. The sky looked as if it had been swept, and had become more lofty and transparent. The stars looked as if they were quite new, and some of them were amazingly bright and pure. It froze so hard that the snow creaked, and the upper rind of snow might well have grown hard enough to bear the sparrows in the morning dawn. These little birds hopped up and down where the sweeping had been done; but they found very little food, and were not a little cold.

"Piep!" said one of them to another; "they call this a new year, and it is worse than the last! We might just as well have kept the old one. I'm dissatisfied, and I've a right to be so."

"Yes; and the people ran about and fired off shots to celebrate the new year," said a little shivering sparrow; "and they threw pans and pots against the doors, and were quite boisterous with joy, because the old year was gone. I was glad of it too, because I hoped we should have had warm days; but that has come to nothing—it freezes much harder than before. People have made a mistake in reckoning the time!"

"That they have!" a third put in, who was old, and had a white poll; "they've something they call the calendar— it's an invention of their own—and every thing is to be arranged according to that; but it won't do. When Spring comes, then the year begins, and I reckon according to that."

"But when will Spring come?" the others inquired.

"It will come when the stork comes back. But his movements are very uncertain, and here in towns no one knows any thing about it: in the country they are better informed. Shall we fly out there and wait? There, at any rate, we shall be nearer to Spring."

"Yes, that may be all very well," observed one of the sparrows, who had been hopping about for a long time, chirping, without saying any thing decided. "I've found a few comforts here in town, which I'm afraid I should miss out in the country. Near this neighborhood, in a courtyard, there lives a family of people, who have taken the very sensible notion of placing three or four flower-pots against the wall, with their mouths all turned inwards, and the bottom of each pointing outwards. In each flower-pot a hole has been cut, big enough for me to fly in and out at it. I and my husband have built a nest in one of those pots, and have brought up our young family there. The family of people, of course, made the whole arrangement that they might have the pleasure of seeing us, or else they would not have done it. To please themselves they also strew crumbs of bread; and so we have food, and are in a manner provided for. So I think my husband and I will stay where we are, although we are very dissatisfied—but we shall stay."

"And we will fly into the country to see if Spring is not coming!" And away they flew.

Out in the country it was hard Winter, and the glass was a few degrees lower than in the town. The sharp winds swept across the snow-covered fields. The farmer, muffled in warm mittens, sat in his sledge, and beat his arms across his breast to warm himself, and the whip lay across his knees. The horses ran till they smoked again. The snow creaked, and the sparrows hopped about in the ruts, and shivered, "Piep! when will Spring come? it is very long in coming!"

"Very long," sounded from the next snow-covered hill, far over the field. It might be the echo which was heard; or perhaps the words were spoken by yonder wonderful old man, who sat in wind and weather high on a heap of snow. He was quite white, attired like a peasant in a coarse white coat of frieze; he had long white hair, and was quite pale, with big blue eyes.

"Who is that old man yonder?" asked the sparrows.

"I know who he is," quoth an old raven, who sat on the

fence-rail, and was condescending enough to acknowledge that we are all like little birds in the sight of Heaven, and therefore was not above speaking to the sparrows, and giving them information. "I know who the old man is. It is Winter, the old man of last year. He is not dead, as the calendar says, but is guardian to little Prince Spring, who is to come. Yes, Winter bears sway here. Ugh! the cold makes you shiver, does it not, you little ones?"

"Yes. Did I not tell the truth?" said the smallest sparrow: "the calendar is only an invention of man, and is not arranged according to nature! They ought to leave these things to us, who are born cleverer than they."

And one week passed away, and two passed away. The frozen lake lay hard and stiff, looking like a sheet of lead, and damp icy mists lay brooding over the land; the great black crows flew about in long rows, but silently; and it seemed as if nature slept. The sunbeam glided along over the lake, and made it shine like burnished tin. The snowy covering on the field and on the hill did not glitter as it had done; but the white form, Winter himself, still sat there, his gaze fixed unswervingly upon the south. He did not notice that the snowy carpet seemed to sink as it were into the earth, and that here and there a little grass-green patch appeared, and that all these patches were crowded with sparrows.

"Kee-wit! kee-wit! Is Spring coming now?"

"Spring!" The cry resounded over field and meadow, and through the black-brown woods, where the moss still glimmered in bright green upon the tree-trunks; and from the south the first two storks came flying through the air. On the back of each sat a pretty little child—one was a girl and the other a boy. They greeted the earth with a kiss, and wherever they set their feet, white flowers grew up from beneath the snow. Then they went hand in hand to the old ice-man, Winter, clung to his breast embracing him, and in a moment they, and he, and all the region around were hidden in a thick damp mist, dark and heavy, that closed over all like a veil. Gradually the wind rose, and now it rushed roaring along, and drove away the mist with heavy blows, so that the sun shone warmly forth, and Winter himself vanished, and the beautiful children of Spring sat upon the throne of the year.

"That's what I call Spring," cried each of the sparrows. "Now we shall get our rights, and have amends for the stern Winter."

Wherever the two children turned, green buds burst forth on bushes and trees, the grass shot upwards, and the cornfields turned green and became more and more lovely And the little maiden strewed flowers all around. Her apron, which she held up before her, was always full of them; they seemed to spring up there, for her lap continued full, however zealously she strewed the blossoms around; and in her eagerness she scattered a snow of blossoms over apple-trees and peach-trees, so that they stood in full beauty before their green leaves had fairly come forth.

And she clapped her hands, and the boy clapped his, and then flocks of birds came flying up, nobody knew whence, and they all twittered and sang, "Spring has come !"

That was beautiful to behold. Many an old granny crept forth over the threshold into the sunshine, and tripped glee-fully about, casting a glance at the yellow flowers which shone everywhere in the fields, just as they used to do when she was young. The world grew young again to her, and she said, "It is a blessed day out here to-day !"

The forest still wore its brown-green dress, made of buds; but the thyme was already there, fresh and fragrant; there were violets in plenty, anemones and primroses came forth, and there was sap and strength in every blade of grass. That was certainly a beautiful carpet, on which no one could resist sitting down, and there accordingly the young spring pair sat hand in hand, and sang and smiled, and grew on.

A mild rain fell down upon them from the sky, but they did not notice it, for the rain-drops were mingled with their own tears of joy. They kissed each other, and were betrothed as people that should marry, and in the same moment the verdure of the woods was unfolded, and when the sun rose, the forest stood arrayed in green.

And hand in hand the betrothed pair wandered under the fresh pendent ocean of leaves, where the rays of the sun gleamed through the interstices in lovely, changing hues. What virgin purity, what refreshing balm in the delicate leaves! The brooks and streams rippled clearly and merrily among the green velvety rushes and over the colored pebbles. All nature seemed to say, " There is plenty, and there shall be plenty always!" And the cuckoo sang and the lark carolled : it was a charming Spring; but the willows had woolly gloves over their blossoms : they were desperately careful, and that is wearisome.

And days went by and weeks went by, and the heat came as it were whirling down. Hot waves of air came through the corn, that became yellower and yellower. The white water-lily of the north spread its great green leaves over the glassy mirror of the woodland lakes, and the fishes sought out the shady spots beneath; and at the sheltered side of the wood, where the sun shone down upon the walls of the farmhouse, warming the blooming roses, and the cherry-trees, which hung full of juicy black berries, almost hot with the fierce beams, there sat the lovely wife of Sum-

mer, the same being whom we have seen as a child and as
a bride; and her glance was fixed upon the black gathering
clouds, which in wavy outlines—blue-black and heavy—
were piling themselves up, like mountains, higher and
higher. They came from three sides, and growing like a
petrified sea, they came swooping towards the forest, where
every sound had been silenced as if by magic. Every
breath of air was hushed, every bird was mute. There was
a seriousness—a suspense throughout all nature; but in the
highways and lanes, foot-passengers, and riders, and men in
carriages were hurrying on to get under shelter. Then suddenly there was a flashing of light, as if the sun were burst
forth— flaming, burning, all-devouring ! And the darkness
returned amid a rolling crash. The rain poured down in
streams, and there was alternate darkness and blinding
light; alternate silence and deafening clamor. The young,
brown, feathery reeds on the moor moved to and fro in long
waves, the twigs of the woods were hidden in a mist of
waters, and still came darkness and light, and still silence
and roaring followed one another ; grass and corn lay
beaten down and swamped, looking as though they could
never raise themselves again. But soon the rain fell only in
gentle drops, the sun peered through the clouds, the water-
drops glittered like pearls on the leaves, the birds sang, the
fishes leaped up from the surface of the lake, the gnats
danced in the sunshine, and yonder on the rock, in the salt,
heaving sea-water, sat Summer himself—a strong man with
sturdy limbs and long dripping hair—there he sat, strengthened by the cool bath, in the warm sunshine. All nature
round about was renewed, every thing stood luxuriant,
strong, and beautiful; it was Summer, warm, lovely Summer.

And pleasant and sweet was the fragrance that streamed
upwards from the rich clover-field, where the bees swarmed

round the old ruined place of meeting : the bramble wound itself around the altar-stone, which, washed by the rain, glittered in the sunshine; and thither flew the queen-bee with her swarm, and prepared wax and honey. Only Summer saw it, he and his strong wife; for them the altar-table stood covered with the offerings of nature.

And the evening sky shone like gold, shone as no church dome can shine; and in the interval between the evening and the morning red, there was moonlight : it was Summer.

And days went by, and weeks went by. The bright scythes of the reapers gleamed in the cornfields; the branches of the apple-trees bent down, heavy with red-and-yellow fruit. The hops smelt sweetly, hanging in large clusters; and under the hazel-bushes where hung great bunches of nuts, rested a man and woman—Summer and his quiet consort.

"What wealth !" exclaimed the woman : "all around a blessing is diffused, everywhere the scene looks homelike and good; and yet—I know not why—I long for peace and rest—I know not how to express it. Now they are already ploughing again in the field. The people want to gain more and more. See, the storks flock together, and follow at a little distance behind the plough—the bird of Egypt that carried us through the air. Do you remember how we came as children to this land of the North? We brought with us flowers, and pleasant sunshine, and green to the woods; the wind has treated them roughly, and they have become dark and brown like the trees of the South, but they do not, like them, bear fruit."

"Do you wish to see the golden fruit?" said the man : "then rejoice." And he lifted his arm, and the leaves of the forest put on hues of red and gold, and beauteous tints spread over all the woodland. The rose-bush gleamed with scarlet hips ; the elder-branches hung down with great heavy bunches of dark berries; the wild chestnuts fell ripe from their dark husks; and in the depths of the forests the violets bloomed for the second time.

But the Queen of the Year became more and more silent, and paler and paler. "It blows cold," she said, "and night brings damp mists. I long for the land of my childhood."

And she saw the storks fly away, one and all; and she stretched forth her hands towards them. She looked up at the nests, which stood empty. In one of them the long-stalked cornflower was growing; in another, the yellow mustard-seed, as if the nest were only there for its protection and comfort; and the sparrows were flying up into the storks' nests.

"Piep! where has the master gone? I suppose he can't bear it when the wind blows, and that therefore he has left the country. I wish him a pleasant journey!"

The forest leaves became more and more yellow, leaf fell down upon leaf, and the stormy winds of autumn howled. The year was far advanced, and the Queen of the Year reclined upon the fallen yellow leaves, and looked with mild eyes at the gleaming star, and her husband stood by her. A gust swept through the leaves; they fell again in a shower, and the Queen was gone, but a butterfly, the last of the season, flew through the cold air.

The wet fogs came, an icy wind blew, and the long dark nights drew on apace. The Ruler of the Year stood there with locks white as snow, but he knew not it was his hair that gleamed so white—he thought snow-flakes were falling from the clouds; and soon a thin covering of snow was spread over the fields.

And then the church bells rang for the Christmas time.

"The bells ring for the new-born," said the Ruler of the Year. "Soon the new king and queen will be born; and

I shall go to rest, as my wife has done—to rest in the gleaming star."

And in the fresh green fir-wood, where the snow lay, stood the Angel of Christmas, and consecrated the young trees that were to adorn his feast.

"May there be joy in the room, and under the green boughs," said the Ruler of the Year. In a few weeks he had become a very old man, white as snow. "My time for rest draws near, and the young pair of the year shall now receive my crown and sceptre."

"But the might is still thine," said the Angel of Christmas; "the might and not the rest. Let the snow lie warmly upon the young seed. Learn to bear it, that another receives homage while thou yet reignest. Learn to bear being forgotten while thou art yet alive. The hour of thy release will come when Spring appears."

"And when will Spring come?" asked Winter.

"It will come when the stork returns."

And with white locks and snowy beard, cold, bent, and hoary, but strong as the wintry storm, and firm as ice, old Winter sat on the snowy drift on the hill, looking towards the south, where he had before sat and gazed. The ice cracked, the snow creaked, the skaters skimmed to and fro on the smooth lakes, ravens and crows contrasted picturesquely with the white ground, and not a breath of wind stirred. And in the quiet air old Winter clenched his fists, and the ice was fathoms thick between land and land.

Then the sparrows came again out of the town, and asked "Who is that old man yonder?" And the raven sat there again, or a son of his, which comes to quite the same thing, and answered them and said, "It is Winter, the old man of last year. He is not dead, as the almanac says, but he is the guardian of Spring, who is coming."

"When will Spring come?" asked the sparrows. "Then we shall have good times, and a better rule. The old one was worth nothing."

And Winter nodded in quiet thought at the leafless forest, where every tree showed the graceful form and bend of its twigs; and during the Winter sleep the icy mists of the clouds came down, and the ruler dreamed of his youthful days, and of the time of his manhood; and towards the morning dawn the whole wood was clothed in glittering hoar-frost. That was the summer dream of Winter, and the sun scattered the hoar-frost from the boughs.

"When will Spring come?" asked the sparrows.

"The Spring!" sounded like an echo from the hills on which the snow lay. The sun shone warmer, the snow melted, and the birds twittered, "Spring is coming!"

And aloft through the air came the first stork, and the second followed him. A lovely child sat on the back of each, and they alighted on the field, kissed the earth, and kissed the old silent man, and he disappeared, shrouded in the cloudy mist. And the story of the year was done.

"That is all very well," said the sparrows; "it is very beautiful too, but it is not according to the almanac, and therefore it is irregular."

SHE WAS GOOD FOR NOTHING.

THE mayor stood at the open window. His shirt-frill was very fine, and so were his ruffles; he had a breast-pin stuck in his frill, and was uncommonly smooth-shaven—all his own work; certainly he had given himself a slight cut, but

TEE MAYOR AND THE WASHERWOMAN'S SON.

he had stuck a bit of newspaper on the place. "Hark 'ee, youngster!" he cried.

The youngster in question was no other than the son of the poor washerwoman, who was just going past the house; and he pulled off his cap respectfully. The peak of the said cap was broken in the middle, for the cap was arranged so that it could be rolled up and crammed into his pocket. In his poor, but clean and well-mended attire, with heavy wooden shoes on his feet, the boy stood there, as humble and abashed as if he stood opposite the king himself.

"You're a good boy," said Mr. Mayor. "You're a civil boy. I suppose your mother is rinsing clothes yonder in the river? I suppose you are to carry that thing to your mother that you have in your pocket? That's a bad affair with your mother. How much have you got in it?"

"Half a quartern," stammered the boy, in a frightened voice.

"And this morning she had just as much," the mayor continued.

"No," replied the boy, "it was yesterday."

"Two halves make a whole. She's good for nothing! It's a sad thing with that kind of people! Tell your mother she ought to be ashamed of herself; and mind you don't become a drunkard—but you will become one, though. Poor child—there, go!"

Accordingly the boy went on his way. He kept his cap in his hand, and the wind played with his yellow hair, so that great locks of it stood up straight. He turned down by the street corner, into the little lane that led to the river, where his mother stood by the washing bench, beating the heavy linen with the mallet. The water rolled quickly along, for the flood-gates at the mill had been drawn up, and the sheets were caught by the stream, and threatened to overturn the bench. The washerwoman was obliged to lean against the bench, to support it.

"I was very nearly sailing away," she said. "It is a good thing that you are come, for I have need to recruit my strength a little. For six hours I've been standing in the water. Have you brought any thing for me?"

The boy produced the bottle, and the mother put it to her mouth, and took a little.

"Ah, how that revives one!" she said: "how it warms! It is as good as a hot meal, and not so dear. And you, my boy! you look quite pale. You are shivering in your thin clothes—to be sure it is autumn. Ugh! how cold the water is! I hope I shall not be ill. But no, I shall not be that! Give me a little more, and you may have a sip too, but only a little sip, for you must not accustom yourself to it, my poor dear child!"

And she stepped up to the bridge on which the boy stood, and came ashore. The water dripped from the straw matting she had wound round her, and from her gown.

"I work and toil as much as ever I can," she said, "but I do it willingly, if I can only manage to bring you up honestly and well, my boy."

As she spoke, a somewhat older woman came towards them. She was poor enough to behold, lame of one leg, with a large false curl hanging down over one of her eyes, which was a blind one. The curl was intended to cover the eye, but it only made the defect more striking. This was a friend of the laundress. She was called among the neighbours, "Lame Martha with the curl."

"Oh, you poor thing! How you work, standing there in the water!" cried the visitor. "You really require something to warm you; and yet malicious folks cry out about the few drops you take!" And in a few minutes' time the mayor's late speech was reported to the laundress; for Martha had heard it all, and she had been angry that a man could speak as he had done to a woman's own child, about the few drops the mother took ; and she was the more angry, because the mayor on that very day was giving a great feast, at which wine was drunk by the bottle—good wine, strong wine. "A good many will take more than they need —but that's not called drinking. *They* are good; but *you* are good for nothing !" cried Martha, indignantly.

"Ah, so he spoke to you, my child?" said the washer-woman; and her lips trembled as she spoke. "So he says you have a mother who is good for nothing? Well, perhaps he's right, but he should not have said it to the child. Still, I have had much misfortune from that house."

"You were in service there when the mayor's parents were alive, and lived in that house. That is many years ago : many bushels of salt have been eaten since then, and we may well be thirsty;" and Martha smiled. "The mayor has a great dinner-party to-day. The guests were to have been put off, but it was too late, and the dinner was already cooked. The footman told me about it. A letter came a little while ago, to say that the younger brother had died in Copenhagen."

"Died !" repeated the laundress—and she became pale as death.

"Yes, certainly," said Martha. "Do you take that so much to heart? Well, you must have known him years ago, when you were in service in the house."

"Is he dead? He was such a good, worthy man ! There are not many like him." And the tears rolled down her cheeks. "Good heavens ! every thing is whirling around me—it was too much for me. I feel quite ill." And she leaned against the plank.

"Good heavens, you are ill indeed!" exclaimed the other woman. "Come, come, it will pass over presently. But no, you really look seriously ill. The best thing will be for me to lead you home."

"But my linen yonder—"

"I will take care of that. Come, give me your arm. The boy can stay here and take care of it, and I'll come back and finish the washing ; that's only a trifle."

The laundress's limbs shook under her. "I have stood too long in the cold water," she said faintly, "and I have eaten and drunk nothing since this morning. The fever is in my bones. O kind Heaven, help me to get home ! My poor child !" and she burst into tears. The boy wept too, and soon he was sitting alone by the river, beside the damp linen. The two women could make only slow progress. The laundress dragged her weary limbs along, and tottered through the lane and round the corner into the street where stood the house of the mayor; and just in front of his mansion she sank down on the pavement. Many people assembled round her, and Lame Martha ran into the house to get help. The mayor and his guests came to the window.

"That's the washerwoman !" he said. "She has taken a glass too much. She is good for nothing. It's a pity for the pretty son she has. I really like the child very well; but the mother is good for nothing."

Presently the laundress came to herself, and they led her into her poor dwelling, and put her to bed. Kind Martha heated a mug of beer for her, with butter and sugar, which she considered the best medicine ; and then she hastened to the river, and rinsed the linen—badly enough, though her will was good. Strictly speaking, she drew it ashore, wet as it was, and laid it in a basket.

Towards evening she was sitting in the poor little room with the laundress. The mayor's cook had given her some roasted potatoes and a fine fat piece of ham, for the sick woman, and Martha and the boy discussed these viands while the patient enjoyed the smell, which she pronounced very nourishing.

And presently the boy was put to bed, in the same bed in which his mother lay; but he slept at her feet, covered with an old quilt made up of blue and white patches.

Soon the patient felt a little better. The warm beer had strengthened her, and the fragrance of the provisions pleased her also. "Thanks, you kind soul," she said to Martha. "I will tell you all when the boy is asleep. I think he has dropped off already. How gentle and good he looks, as he lies there with his eyes closed! He does not know what his mother has suffered, and Heaven grant he may never know it. I was in service at the councillor's, the father of the mayor. It happened that the youngest of the sons, the student, came home. I was young then, a wild girl, but honest—that I may declare in the face of Heaven. The student was merry and kind, good and brave. Every drop of blood in him was good and honest. I have not seen a better man on this earth. He was the son of the house, and I was only a maid, but we formed an attachment to each other, honestly and honorably. And he told his mother of it, for she was in his eyes as a Deity on earth; and she was wise and gentle. He went away on a journey, but before he started he put his gold ring on my finger; and directly he was gone my mistress called me. With a firm yet gentle seriousness she spoke to me, and it seemed as if Wisdom itself were speaking. She showed me clearly, in spirit and in truth, the difference there was between him and me.

"'Now he is charmed with your pretty appearance,' she said, 'but your good looks will leave you. You have not been educated as he has. You are not equals in mind, and there is the misfortune. I respect the poor,' she continued; 'in the sight of God they may occupy a higher place than many a rich man can fill; but here on earth we must beware of entering a false track as we go onward, or our carriage is upset, and we are thrown into the road. I know that a worthy man wishes to marry you—an artisan—I mean Erich the glovemaker. He is a widower without children, and is well to do. Think it over.'

"Every word she spoke cut into my heart like a knife, but I knew that my mistress was right, and that knowledge weighed heavily upon me. I kissed her hand, and wept bitter tears, and I wept still more when I went into my room and threw myself on my bed. It was a heavy night that I had to pass through. Heaven knows what I suffered and how I wrestled! The next Sunday I went to the Lord's house, to pray for strength and guidance. It seemed like a Providence, that as I stepped out of church Erich came towards me. And now there was no longer a doubt in my mind. We were suited to each other in rank and in means, and he was even then a thriving man. Therefore I went up to him, took his hand, and said, 'Are you still of the same mind towards me?' 'Yes, ever and always,' he replied. 'Will you marry a girl who honors and respects, but who does not love you—though that may come later?' I asked again. 'Yes, it will come!' he answered; and upon this we joined hands. I went home to my mistress. I wore the gold ring that the son had given me at my heart. I could not put it on my finger in the daytime, but only in the evening when I went to bed. I kissed the ring again and again, til' my lips almost bled, and then I gave it to my mistress, and told her the banns were to be put up next week for me and the glovemaker. Then my mistress put her arms round me and kissed me. *She* did not say that *I* was good for nothing; but perhaps I was better then than I am now, though the misfortunes of life had not yet found me out. In a few weeks we were married; and for the first year the world went well with us: we had a journeyman and an apprentice, and you, Martha, lived with us as our servant."

"Oh, you were a dear, good mistress," cried Martha. "Never shall I forget how kind you and your husband were!"

"Yes, those were our good years, when you were with us. We had not any children yet. The student I never saw again. Yes, though, I saw him, but he did not see me. He was here at his mother's funeral. I saw him stand by the grave. He was pale as death, and very downcast, but that was for his mother; afterwards, when his father died, he was away in a foreign land, and did not come back hither. I know that he never married; I believe he became a lawyer. He had forgotten me; and even if he had seen me again, he would not have known me, I look so ugly. And that is very fortunate."

And then she spoke of her days of trial, and told how misfortune had come, as it were swooping down upon them.

"We had five hundred dollars," she said; "and as there was a house in the street to be bought for two hundred, and it would pay to pull it down and build a new one, it was bought. The builder and carpenter calculated the expense, and the new house was to cost ten hundred and twenty. Erich had credit, and borrowed the money in the chief town, but the captain who was to bring it was shipwrecked, and the money was lost with him.

"Just at that time my dear sweet boy who is sleeping yonder was born. My husband was struck down by a long heavy illness : for three quarters of a year I was compelled to dress and undress him. We went back more and more, and fell into debt. All that we had was sold, and my husband died. I have worked, and toiled, and striven, for the sake of the child, and scrubbed staircases, washed linen, clean and coarse alike, but I was not to be better off, such was God's good will. But He will take me to Himself in His own good time, and will not forsake my boy." And she fell asleep.

Towards morning she felt much refreshed, and strong enough, as she thought, to go back to her work. She had just stepped again into the cold water, when a trembling and faintness seized her : she clutched at the air with her hand, took a step forward, and fell down. Her head rested on the bank, and her feet were still in the water : her wooden shoes, with a wisp of straw in each, which she had worn, floated down the stream, and thus Martha found her on coming to bring her some coffee.

In the mean time a messenger from the mayor's house had been dispatched to her poor lodging, to tell her " to come to the mayor immediately, for he had something to tell her." It was too late ! A barber-surgeon was brought to open a vein in her arm; but the poor woman was dead.

" She has drunk herself to death !" said the mayor.

In the letter that brought the news of his brother's death the contents of the will had been mentioned, and it was a legacy of six hundred dollars to the glovemaker's widow who had once been his mother's maid. The money was to be paid, according to the mayor's discretion, in large or smaller sums, to her or to her child.

" There was some fuss between my brother and her," said

the mayor. "It's a good thing that she's dead ; for now the boy will have the whole, and I will get him into a house among respectable people. He may turn out a reputable working-man."

And Heaven gave its blessing to these words.

So the mayor sent for the boy, promised to take care of him, and added that it was a good thing the lad's mother was dead, inasmuch as she had been good for nothing.

They bore her to the churchyard, to the cemetery of the poor, and Martha strewed sand upon her grave, and planted a rose tree upon it, and the boy stood beside her.

"My dear mother !" he cried, as the tears fell fast. Is it true what they said—that she was good for nothing ?" "No, she was good for much !" replied the old servant, and she looked up indignantly. "I knew it many a year ago, and more than all since last night. I tell you she was worth much, and the Lord in heaven knows it is true, let the world say as much as it chooses, 'She was good for nothing.' "

◆◆◆

"THERE IS A DIFFERENCE."

It was in the month of May. The wind still blew cold, but bushes and trees, field and meadow, all alike said the spring had come. There was store of flowers even in the wild hedges ; and there spring carried on his affairs, and preached from a little apple-tree, where one branch hung fresh and blooming, covered with delicate pink blossoms that were just ready to open. The apple-tree branch knew well enough how beautiful he was, for the knowledge is

inherent in the leaf as well as in the blood ; and consequently the branch was not surprised when a nobleman's
carriage stopped opposite to him on the road, and the young
countess said that an apple branch was the loveliest thing
one could behold, a very emblem of spring in its most
charming form. And the branch was most carefully broken
off, and she held it in her delicate hand, and sheltered it
with her silk parasol. Then they drove to the castle, where-
there were lofty halls and splendid apartments. Pure white
curtains fluttered round the open windows, and beautiful
flowers stood in shining transparent vases ; and in one of
these, which looked as if it had been cut out of fresh-fallen
snow, the apple branch was placed among some fresh light
twigs of beech. It was charming to behold.

But the branch became proud ; and this was quite like
human nature.

People of various kinds came through the room, and
according to their rank they might express their admiration. A few said nothing at all, and others again said too
much, and the apple-tree branch soon got to understand
that there was a difference among plants. "Some are
created for beauty, and some for use ; and there are some
which one can do without altogether," thought the apple
branch ; and as he stood just in front of the open window,
from whence he could see into the garden and across the
fields, he had flowers and plants enough to contemplate and
to think about, for there were rich plants and humble plants
—some very humble indeed.

"Poor despised herbs !" said the apple branch. "There
is certainly a difference ! And how unhappy they must
feel, if indeed that kind *can* feel like myself and my equals.
Certainly there is a difference, and distinctions must be
made, or we should all be equal."

And the apple branch looked down with a species of pity, especially upon a certain kind of flower of which great numbers are found in the fields and ditches. No one bound them into a nosegay, they were too common ; for they might be found even among the paving-stones, shooting up everywhere like the rankest weeds, and they had the ugly name of "dandelion," or "dog-flower."

"Poor despised plants !" said the apple branch. "It is not your fault that you received the ugly name you bear. But it is with plants as with men—there must be a difference !"

"A difference ?" said the sunbeam ; and he kissed the blooming apple branch, and saluted in like manner the yellow dandelions out in the field—all the brothers of the sunbeam kissed them, the poor flowers as well as the rich.

Now the apple branch had never thought of the boundless beneficence of Providence in creation towards every thing that lives and moves and has its being ; he had never thought how much that is beautiful and good may be hidden, but not forgotten ; but that, too, was quite like human nature.

The sunbeam, the ray of light, knew better ; and said, "You don't see far, and you don't see clearly. What is the despised plant that you especially pity ?"

"The dandelion," replied the apple branch. "It is never received into a nosegay; it is trodden under foot There are too many of them ; and when they run to seed, they fly away like little pieces of wool over the roads, and hang and cling to people's dress. They are nothing but weeds—but it is right there should be weeds too. Oh, I'm really very thankful that I was not created one of those flowers."

But there came across the fields a whole troop of children ; the youngest of whom was so small that it was carried by the rest, and when it was set down in the grass among the yellow flowers it laughed aloud with glee, kicked out with its little legs, rolled about and plucked the yellow flowers, and kissed them in its pretty innocence. The elder children broke off the flowers with their tall stalks, and bent the stalks round into one another, link by link, so that a whole chain was made; first a necklace, and then a scarf to hang over their shoulders and tie round their waists, and then a chaplet to wear on the head : it was quite a gala of green links and yellow flowers. The eldest children carefully gathered the stalks on which hung the white feathery ball, formed by the flowers that had run to seed ; and this loose, airy wool-flower, which is a beautiful object, looking like the finest snowy down, they held to their mouths, and tried to blow away the whole head at one breath : for their grandmother had said that whoever could do this would be sure to get new clothes before the year was out. So on this occasion the despised flower was actually raised to the rank of a prophet or augur.

"Do you see?" said the sunbeam. "Do you see the beauty of those flowers? do you see their power?"

"Yes, over the children," replied the apple branch.

And now an old woman came into the field, and began to dig with a blunt shapeless knife round the root of the dandelion plant, and pulled it up out of the ground. With some of the roots she intended to make tea for herself; others she was going to sell for money to the druggist.

"But beauty is a higher thing!" said the apple-tree branch. "Only the chosen few can be admitted into the realm of beauty. There is a difference among plants, just as there is a difference among men."

And then the sunbeam spoke of the boundless love of the

Creator, as manifested in the creation, and of the just distribution of things in time and in eternity.

"Yes, yes, that is your opinion," the apple branch persisted.

But now some people came into the room, and the beautiful young countess appeared, the lady who had placed the apple branch in the transparent vase in the sunlight. She carried in her hand a flower, or something of the kind. The object, whatever it might be, was hidden by three or four great leaves, wrapped round it like a shield, that no draught or gust of wind should injure it ; and it was carried more carefully than the apple bough had ever been. Very gently the large leaves were now removed, and lo, there appeared the fine feathery seed crown of the despised dandelion ! This it was that the lady had plucked with the greatest care, and had carried home with every precaution, so that not one of the delicate feathery darts that form its downy ball should be blown away. She now produced it, quite uninjured, and admired its beautiful form, its peculiar construction, and its airy beauty, which was to be scattered by the wind.

"Look, with what singular beauty Providence has invested it !" she said. "I will paint it, together with the apple branch, whose beauty all have admired; but this humble flower has received just as much from Heaven in a different way; and, various as they are, both are children of the kingdom of beauty."

And the sunbeam kissed the humble flower, and he kissed the blooming apple branch, whose leaves appeared covered with a roseate blush.

EVERY THING IN ITS RIGHT PLACE.

IT is more than a hundred years ago.

Behind the wood, by the great lake, stood the old baronial mansion. Round about it lay a deep moat, in which grew reeds and grass. Close by the bridge, near the entrance-gate, rose an old willow-tree that bent over the reeds.

Up from the hollow lane sounded the clang of horns and the trampling of horses; therefore the little girl who kept the geese hastened to drive her charges away from the bridge, before the hunting company should come galloping up. They drew near with such speed that the girl was obliged to climb up in a hurry, and perch herself on the coping-stone of the bridge, lest she should be ridden down. She was still half a child, and had a pretty light figure, and a gentle expression in her face, with two clear blue eyes. The noble baron took no note of this, but as he galloped past the little goose-herd he reversed the whip he held in his hand, and in rough sport gave her such a push in the chest with the butt-end, that she fell backwards into the ditch.

"Every thing in its place," he cried; "into the puddle with you!" And he laughed aloud, for this was intended for wit, and the company joined in his mirth: the whole party shouted and clamored, and the dogs barked their loudest.

Fortunately for herself, the poor girl in falling seized one of the hanging branches of the willow-tree, by means of which she kept herself suspended over the muddy water, and as soon as the baron and his company had disappeared through the castle-gate, the girl tried to scramble up again;

but the bough broke off at the top, and she would have fallen backward among the reeds, if a strong hand from above had not at that moment seized her. It was the hand of a pedler, who had seen from a short distance what had happened, and who row hurried up to give aid.

"Every thing in its right place," he said, mimicking the gracious baron; and he drew the little maiden up to the firm ground. He would have restored the broken branch to the place from which it had been torn, but "every thing in its place" cannot always be managed, and therefore he stuck the piece in the ground. "Grow and prosper till you can furnish a good flute for them up yonder," he said; for he would have liked to play the "rogue's march" for my lord the baron, and my lord's whole family. And then he betook himself to the castle, but not into the ancestral hall, he was too humble for that! He went to the servants' quarters, and the men and maids turned over his stock of goods, and bargained with him; and from above, where the guests were at table, came a sound of roaring and screaming that was intended for song, and indeed they did their best. Loud laughter, mingled with the barking and howling of dogs, sounded through the windows, for there was feasting and carousing up yonder. Wine and strong old ale foamed in the jugs and glasses, and the dogs sat with their masters and dined with them. They had the pedler summoned upstairs, but only to make fun of him. The wine had mounted into their heads, and the sense had flown out. They poured wine into a stocking, that the pedler might drink with them, but that he must drink quickly; that was considered a rare jest, and was a cause of fresh laughter. And then whole farms, with oxen and peasants too, were staked on a card, and won and lost.

"Every thing in its right place!" said the pedler, when

he had at last made his escape out of what he called "the Sodom and Gomorrah up yonder." "The open high-road is my right place," he said; "I did not feel at all happy there." And the little maiden who sat keeping the geese nodded at him in a friendly way, as he strode along beside the hedges.

And days and weeks went by; and it became manifest that the willow branch which the pedler had stuck into the ground by the castle moat remained fresh and green, and even brought forth new twigs. The little goose-girl saw that the branch must have taken root, and rejoiced greatly at the circumstance; for this tree, she said, was now her tree.

The tree certainly came forward well; but every thing else belonging to the castle went very rapidly back, what with feasting and gambling—for these two things are like wheels, upon which no man can stand securely.

Six years had not passed away before the noble lord passed out of the castle-gate, a beggared man, and the mansion was bought by a rich dealer; and this purchaser was the very man who had once been made a jest of there, for whom wine had been poured into a stocking; but honesty and industry are good winds to speed a vessel; and now the dealer was possessor of the baronial estate. But from that hour no more card-playing was permitted there. "That is bad reading," said he: "when the Evil One saw a Bible for the first time, he wanted to put a bad book against it, and invented card-playing."

The new proprietor took a wife; and who might that be but the goose-girl, who had always been faithful and good, and looked as beautiful and fine in her new clothes as if she had been born a great lady. And how did all this come about? That is too long a story for our busy time, but it really happened, and the most important part is to come.

It was a good thing now to be in the old mansion. The mother managed the domestic affairs, and the father superintended the estate, and it seemed as if blessings were streaming down. Where rectitude enters in, prosperity is sure to follow. The old house was cleaned and painted, the ditches were cleared and fruit-trees planted. Every thing wore a bright cheerful look, and the floors were as polished as a draught-board. In the long winter evenings the lady sat at the spinning-wheel with her maids, and every Sunday evening there was a reading from the Bible, by the Councillor of Justice himself—this title the dealer had gained, though it was only in his old age. The children grew up—for children had come—and they received the best education, though all had not equal abilities, as we find indeed in all families.

In the mean time the willow branch at the castle-gate had grown to be a splendid tree, which stood there free and self-sustained. "That is our genealogical tree," the old people said, and the tree was to be honored and respected—so they told all the children, even those who had not very good heads.

And a hundred years rolled by.

It was in our own time. The lake had been converted to moorland, and the old mansion had almost disappeared. A pool of water and the ruins of some walls, this was all that was left of the old baronial castle, with its deep moat; and here stood also a magnificent old willow, with pendent boughs, which seemed to show how beautiful a tree may be if left to itself. The main stem was certainly split from the root to the crown, and the storm had bowed the noble tree a little; but it stood firm for all that, and from every cleft into which wind and weather had carried a portion of earth, grasses and flowers sprang forth : espe-

cially near the top, where the great branches parted, a sort
of hanging-garden had been formed of wild raspberry bush,
and even a small quantity of mistletoe had taken root, and
stood, slender and graceful, in the midst of the old willow
which was mirrored in the dark water. A field-path led
close by the old tree.

High by the forest hill, with a splendid prospect in every
direction, stood the new baronial hall, large and magnificent, with panes of glass so clearly transparent, that it
looked as if there were no panes there at all. The grand
flight of steps that led to the entrance looked like a bower
of roses and broad-leaved plants. The lawn was as freshly
green as if each separate blade of grass were cleaned
morning and evening. In the hall hung costly pictures;
silken chairs and sofas stood there, so easy that they looked
almost as if they could run by themselves ; there were
tables of great marble slabs, and books bound in morocco
and gold. Yes, truly, wealthy people lived here, people of
rank—the baron with his family.

All things here corresponded with each other. The motto
was still, " Every thing in its right place;" and therefore all
the pictures which had been put up in the old house for
honor and glory hung now in the passage that led to the
servants' hall : they were considered as old lumber, and
especially two old portraits, one representing a man in a
pink coat and powdered wig, the other a lady with powdered
hair and holding a rose in her hand, and each surrounded
with a wreath of willow leaves. These two pictures were
pierced with many holes, because the little barons were in
the habit of setting up the old people as a mark for their
cross-bows. The pictures represented the Councillor of
Justice and his lady, the founders of the present family.

" But they did not properly belong to our family," said

one of the little barons. "He was a dealer, and she had kept the geese. They were not like papa and mamma."

The pictures were pronounced to be worthless; and as the motto was "Every thing in its right place," the great-grandmother and great-grandfather had been sent into the passage that led to the servants' hall.

The son of the neighboring clergyman was tutor in the great house. One day he was out walking with his pupils, the little barons and their eldest sister, who had just been confirmed; they came along the field-path, past the old willow, and as they walked on the young lady bound a wreath of field flowers, "Every thing in its right place," and the flowers formed a pretty whole. At the same time she heard every word that was spoken, and she liked to hear the clergyman's son talk of the power of nature and of the great men and women in history. She had a good hearty disposition, with true nobility of thought and soul, and a heart full of love for all that God hath created.

The party came to a halt at the old willow-tree. The youngest baron insisted on having such a flute cut for him from it as he had made of other willows. Accordingly the tutor broke off a branch.

"Oh, don't do that !" cried the young baroness ; but it was done already. "That is our famous old tree," he continued, " and I love it dearly. They laugh at me at home for this, but I don't mind. There is a story attached to this tree."

And she told what we all knew about the tree, about the old mansion, the pedler and the goose-girl, who had met for the first time in this spot, and had afterwards become the founders of the noble family to which the young barons belonged.

"They would not be ennobled, the good old folks !" she

said. "They kept to the motto, 'Every thing in its right place;' and accordingly they thought it would be out of place for them to purchase a title with money. My grandfather, the first baron, was their son : he is said to have been a very learned man, very popular with princes and princesses, and a frequent guest at the court festivals. The others at home love him best; but, I don't know how, there seems to me something about that first pair that draws my heart towards them. How comfortable, how patriarchal it must have been in the old house, where the mistress sat at the spinning-wheel among her maids, and the old master read aloud from the Bible!"

"They were charming, sensible people," said the clergyman's son ; and with this the conversation naturally fell upon nobles and citizens. The young man scarcely seemed to belong to the citizen class, so well did he speak concerning the purpose and meaning of nobility. He said :

"It is a great thing to belong to a family that has distinguished itself, and thus to have, as it were, in one's blood, a spur that urges one on to make progress in all that is good. It is delightful to have a name that serves as a card of admission into the highest circles. Nobility means that which is great and noble : it is a coin that has received a stamp to indicate what it is worth. It is the fallacy of the time, and many poets have frequently maintained this fallacy, that nobility of birth is accompanied by foolishness, and that the lower you go among the poor, the more does everything around shine. But that is not my view, for I consider it entirely false. In the higher classes many beautiful and kindly traits are found. My mother told me one of this kind, and I could tell you many others.

"My mother was on a visit to a great family in town. My grandmother, I think, had been housekeeper to the count's mother. The great nobleman and my mother were alone in the room, when the former noticed that an old woman came limping on crutches into the courtyard. In deed, she was accustomed to come every Sunday, and carry away a gift with her. ' Ah, there is the poor old lady,' said the nobleman: ' walking is a great toil to her ;' and before my mother understood what he meant, he had gone out of the room and run down the stairs, to save the old woman the toilsome walk, by carrying to her the gift she had come to receive.

" Now, that was only a small circumstance, but, like the widow's two mites in the Scripture, it has a sound that finds an echo in the depths of the heart in human nature ; and these are the things the poet should show and point out ; especially in these times should he sing of it, for that does good, and pacifies and unites men. But where a bit of mortality, because it has a genealogical tree and a coat of arms, rears up like an Arabian horse, and prances in the street, and says in the room, ' People out of the street have been here,' when a commoner has been—that is nobility in decay, and become a mere mask—a mask of the kind that Thespis created ; and people are glad when such a one is turned into satire."

This was the speech of the clergyman's son. It was certainly rather long, but then the flute was being finished while he made it.

At the castle there was a great company. Many guests came from the neighborhood and from the capital. Many ladies, some tastefully and others tastelessly dressed, were there, and the great hall was quite full of people. The clergymen from the neighborhood stood respectfully congregated in a corner, which made it look almost as if there were to be a burial there. But it was not so, for this was a party of pleasure, only that the pleasure had not yet begun.

A great concert was to be performed, and consequently the little baron had brought in his willow flute; but he could not get a note out of it, nor could his papa, and therefore the flute was worth nothing. There was instrumental music and song, both of the kind that delight the performers most —quite charming !

"You are a performer ?" said a cavalier—his father's son and nothing else—to the tutor. "You play the flute and make it too—that's genius. That should command, and should have the place of honor !"

" No indeed," replied the young man, "I only advance with the times, as every one is obliged to do."

" Oh, you will enchant us with the little instrument, will you not ?" And with these words he handed to the clergyman's son the flute cut from the willow-tree by the pool, and announced aloud that the tutor was about to perform a solo on that instrument.

Now, they only wanted to make fun of him, that was easily seen ; and therefore the tutor would not play, though indeed he could do so very well ; but they crowded round him and importuned him so strongly, that at last he took the flute and put it to his lips.

That was a wonderful flute ! A sound, as sustained as that which is emitted by the whistle of a steam-engine, and much stronger, echoed far over courtyard, garden, and wood, miles away into the country ; and simultaneously with the tone came a rushing wind that roared, "Every thing in its right place !" And papa flew as if carried by the wind straight out of the hall and into the shepherd's cot ; and the shepherd flew, not into the hall, for there he could not come—no, but into the room of the servants, among the

smart lacqueys who strutted about there in silk stockings :
and the proud servants were struck motionless with horror
at the thought that such a personage dared to sit down to
table with them.

But in the hall the young baroness flew to the place of
honor at the top of the table, where she was worthy to sit ;
and the young clergyman's son had a seat next to her ; and
there the two sat as if they were a newly married pair. An
old count of one of the most ancient families in the country
remained untouched in his place of honor ; for the flute
was just, as men ought to be. The witty cavalier, the son
of his father and nothing else, who had been the cause of
the flute-playing, flew head-over-heels into the poultry-house
—but not alone.

For a whole mile round about the sounds of the flute
were heard, and singular events took place. A rich banker's
family, driving along in a coach and four, was blown quite
out of the carriage, and could not even find a place on the
footboard at the back. Two rich peasants, who in our times
had grown too high for their cornfields, were tumbled into
the ditch. It was a dangerous flute, that : luckily it burst
at the first note, and that was a good thing, for then it was
put back into the owner's pocket. "Every thing in its right
place."

The day afterwards not a word was said about this marvellous event ; and thence has come the expression "pocket-
ing the flute." Every thing was in its usual order, only
that the two old portraits of the dealer and the goose-gir
hung on the wall in the banqueting hall. They had been
blown up yonder, and as one of the real connoisseurs said
they had been painted by a master's hand, they remained
where they were, and were restored. "Every thing in its
right place."

And to that it will come ; for *hereafter* is long—longer than this story.

—————◆•◆—————

THE GOBLIN AND THE HUCKSTER.

THERE was once a regular student : he lived in a garret, and nothing at all belonged to him. But there was also once a regular huckster : he lived on the ground-floor, and the whole house was his ; and the goblin kept with him, for on the huckster's table on Christmas Eve there was always a dish of plum-porridge, with a great piece of butter floating in the middle. The huckster could accomplish that ; and consequently the goblin stuck to the huckster's shop, and that was very interesting.

One evening the student came through the back door to buy candles and cheese for himself. He had no one to send, and that's why he came himself. He procured what he wanted and paid for it, and the huckster and his wife both nodded a "good-evening" to him; and the woman was one who could do more than merely nod—she had an immense power of tongue ! And the student nodded too, and then suddenly stood still, reading the sheet of paper in which the cheese had been wrapped. It was a leaf torn out of an old book, a book that ought not to have been torn up, a book that was full of poetry.

"Yonder lies some more of the same sort," said the huckster : "I gave an old woman a little coffee for the books; give me two groschen, and you shall have the remainder."

"Yes," said the student, "give me the book instead of the cheese : I can eat my bread and butter without cheese.

It would be a sin to tear the book up entirely. You are a capital man, a practical man, but you understand no more about poetry than does that cask yonder."

Now, that was an insulting speech, especially towards the cask; but the huckster laughed and the student laughed, for it was only said in fun. But the goblin was angry that any one should dare to say such things to a huckster who lived in his own house and sold the best butter.

When it was night, and the shop was closed and all were in bed, the goblin came forth, went into the bedroom, and took away the good lady's tongue; for she did not want that while she was asleep; and whenever he put this tongue upon any object in the room, the said object acquired speech and language, and could express its thoughts and feelings as well as the lady herself could have done; but only one object could use it at a time, and that was a good thing, otherwise they would have interrupted each other.

And the goblin laid the tongue upon the cask in which the old newspapers were lying.

"Is it true," he asked, "that you don't know what poetry means?"

"Of course I know it," replied the cask: "poetry is something that always stands at the foot of a column in the newspapers, and is sometimes cut out. I dare swear I have more of it in me than the student, and I'm only a poor tub compared to the huckster."

Then the goblin put the tongue upon the coffee-mill, and, mercy! how it began to go! And he put it upon the butter-cask, and on the cash-box: they were all of the waste-paper cask's opinion, and the opinion of the majority must be respected.

"Now I shall tell it to the student!" And with these words the goblin went quietly up the back stairs to the garret where the student lived. The student had still a candle burning, and the goblin peeped through the key-hole, and saw that he was reading in the torn book that he had carried up out of the shop down-stairs.

But how light it was in his room! Out of the book shot a clear beam, expanding into a thick stem, and into a mighty tree, which grew upward and spread its branches far over the student. Each leaf was fresh, and every blossom was a beautiful female head, some with dark sparkling eyes, others with wonderfully clear blue orbs; every fruit was a gleaming star, and there was a glorious sound of song in the student's room.

Never had the little goblin imagined such splendor, far less had he ever seen or heard any thing like it. He stood still on tiptoe, and peeped in till the light went out in the student's garret. Probably the student blew it out, and went to bed; but the little goblin remained standing there nevertheless, for the music still sounded on, soft and beautiful—a splendid cradle-song for the student, who had lain down to rest.

"This is an incomparable place," said the goblin : "I never expected such a thing ! I should like to stay here with the student." And then the little man thought it over —and he was a sensible little man too—but he sighed, "The student has no porridge !" And then he went down again to the huckster's shop : and it was a very good thing that he got down there again at last, for the cask had almost worn out the good woman's tongue, for it had spoken out at one side every thing that was contained in it, and was just about turning itself over, to give it out from the other side also, when the goblin came in, and restored the tongue to its owner. But from that time forth the whole shop, from the cash-box down to the firewood, took its tone from the cask, and paid him such respect, and thought so much of him, that when the huckster afterwards read the critical articles on theatricals and art in the newspaper, they were all persuaded the information came from the cask itself.

But the goblin could no longer sit quietly and contentedly listening to all the wisdom down there: so soon as the light glimmered from the garret in the evening he felt as if the rays were strong cables drawing him up, and he was obliged to go and peep through the keyhole; and there a feeling of greatness rolled around him, such as we feel besides the ever-heaving sea when the storm rushes over it, and he burst into tears! He did not know himself why he was weeping, but a peculiar feeling of pleasure mingled with his tears. How wonderfully glorious it must be to sit with the student under the same tree! But that might not be, he was obliged to be content with the view through the keyhole, and to be glad of that. There he stood on the cold landing-place, with the autumn wind blowing down from the loft-hole: it was cold, very cold; but the little mannikin only felt that when the light in the room was extinguished, and the tones in the tree died away. Ha! then he shivered, and crept down again to his warm corner, where it was homely and comfortable.

And when Christmas came, and brought with it the porridge and the great lump of butter, why, then he thought the huckster the better man.

But in the middle of the night the goblin was awaked by a terrible tumult and beating against the window-shutters. People rapped noisily without, and the watchman blew his horn, for a great fire had broken out—the whole street was full of smoke and flame. Was it in the house itself, or at a neighbor's? Where was it? Terror seized on all. The huckster's wife was so bewildered that she took her gold earrings out of her ears and put them in her pocket, that at any rate she might save something; the huckster ran for his share-papers; and the maid for her black silk mantilla, for she had found means to purchase one. Each one wanted to save the best thing they had; the goblin wanted to do the same thing, and in a few leaps he was up the stairs, and into the room of the student, who stood quite quietly at the open window, looking at the conflagration that was raging in the house of the neighbor opposite. The goblin seized upon the wonderful book which lay upon the table, popped it into his red cap, and held the cap tight with both hands. The great treasure of the house was saved; and now he ran up and away, quite on to the roof of the house, on to the chimney. There he sat, illuminated by the flames of the burning house opposite, both hands pressed tightly over his cap, in which the treasure lay; and now he knew the real feelings of his heart, and knew to whom it really belonged. But when the fire was extinguished, and the goblin could think calmly again, why, then .   .   .   .   .

"I must divide myself between the two," he said; "I can't quite give up the huckster, because of the porridge

Now, that was spoken quite like a human creature. We all of us visit the huckster, for the sake of the porridge.

IN A THOUSAND YEARS.

Yes, in a thousand years people will fly on the wings of steam through the air, over the ocean ! The young inhabitants of America will become visitors of old Europe. They will come over to see the monuments and the great cities, which will then be in ruins, just as we in our time make pilgrimages to the tottering splendors of Southern Asia. In a thousand years they will come !

The Thames, the Danube, and the Rhine still roll their course, Mont Blanc stands firm with its snow-capped summit, and the Northern Lights gleam over the lands of the North; but generation after generation has become dust, whole rows of the mighty of the moment are forgotten, like those who already slumber under the hill on which the rich trader whose ground it is has built a bench, on which he can sit and look out across his waving cornfields.

"To Europe !" cry the young sons of America; "to the land of our ancestors, the glorious land of monuments and fancy—to Europe !"

The ship of the air comes. It is crowded with passengers, for the transit is quicker than by sea. The electro-magnetic wire under the ocean has already telegraphed the number of the aërial caravan. Europe is in sight : it is the coast of Ireland that they see, but the passengers are still asleep; they will not be called till they are exactly over England. There they will first step upon European shore, the land of Shakspeare, as the educated call it; in the land of politics, the land of machines, as it is called by others.

Here they stay a whole day. That is all the time the busy race can devote to the whole of England and Scotland. Then the journey is continued through the tunnel under the English Channel, to France, the land of Charlemagne and Napoleon. Moliere is named : the learned men talk of the classic school of remote antiquity : there is rejoicing and shouting for the names of heroes, poets, and men of science, whom our time does not know, but who will be born after our time in Paris, the crater of Europe.

The air steamboat flies over the country whence Colum

bus went forth, where Cortes was born, and where Calderon sang dramas in sounding verse. Beautiful black-eyed women live still in the blooming valleys, and the oldest songs speak of the Cid and the Alhambra.

Then through the air, over the sea, to Italy, where once lay old, everlasting Rome. It has vanished! The Campagna lies desert: a single ruined wall is shown as the remains of St. Peter's, but there is a doubt if this ruin be genuine.

Next to Greece, to sleep a night in the grand hotel at the top of Mount Olympus, to say that they have been there; and the journey is continued to the Bosphorus, to rest there a few hours, and see the place where Byzantium lay; and where the legend tells that the harem stood in the time of the Turks, poor fishermen are now spreading their nets.

Over the remains of mighty cities on the broad Danube, cities which we in our time know not, the travellers pass; but here and there, on the rich sites of those that time will bring forth, the caravan sometimes descends, and departs again.

Down below lies Germany, that was once covered with a close net of railways and canals, the region where Luther spoke, where Goethe sang, and Mozart once held the sceptre of harmony! Great names shine there, in science and in art, names that are unknown to us. One day devoted to seeing Germany, and one for the North, the country of Oersted and Linnæus, and for Norway, the land of the old heroes and the young Normans. Iceland is visited on the journey home: the geysers burn no more, Hecla is an extinct volcano, but the rocky island is still fixed in the midst of the foaming sea, a continual monument of legend and poetry.

"There is really a great deal to be seen in Europe," says the young American, "and we have seen it in a week, according to the directions of the great traveller" (and here he mentions the name of one of his contemporaries) "in his celebrated work, 'How to see all Europe in a Week.'"

THE BOND OF FRIENDSHIP.

WE have just taken a little journey, and already we want to take a longer one. Whither? To Sparta, to Mycene, to Delphi? There are a hundred places at whose names the heart beats with the desire of travel. On horseback we go up the mountain paths, through brake and through brier. A single traveller makes an appearance like a whole caravan. He rides forward with his guide, a pack-horse carries trunks, a tent, and provisions, and a few armed soldiers follow as a guard. No inn with warm beds awaits him at the end of his tiring day's journey : the tent is often his dwelling-place. In the great wild region the guide cooks him a pillau of rice, fowls, and curry for his supper. A thousand gnats swarm round the tent. It is a boisterous night, and to-morrow the way will lead across swollen streams; take care you are not washed away !

What is your reward for undergoing these hardships? The fullest, richest reward. Nature manifests herself here in all her greatness; every spot is historical, and the eye and the thoughts are alike delighted. The poet may sing it, the painter portray it in rich pictures; but the air of reality which sinks deep into the soul of the spectator, and remains there, neither painter nor poet can produce.

In many little sketches I have endeavored to give an idea of a small part of Athens and its environs; but how colorless the picture seems! How little does it exhibit Greece, the mourning genius of beauty, whose greatness and whose sorrow the stranger never forgets!

The lonely herdsman yonder on the hills would, perhaps, by a simple recital of an event in his life, better enlighten the stranger who wishes in a few features to behold the land of the Hellenes, than any picture could do.

"Then," says my Muse, "let him speak." A custom, a good, peculiar custom, shall be the subject of the mountain shepherd's tale. It is called

THE BOND OF FRIENDSHIP.

Our rude house was put together of clay; but the door-posts were columns of fluted marble found near the spot where the house was erected. The roof reached almost down to the ground. It was now dark brown and ugly, but it had originally consisted of blooming olive and fresh laurel branches brought from beyond the mountain. Around our dwelling was a narrow gorge, whose walls of rock rose steeply upwards, and showed naked and black, and round their summits often hung clouds, like white living figures. Never did I hear a singing bird there, never did the men there dance to the sound of the bagpipe; but the spot was sacred from the old times; even its name reminded of this, for it was called Delphi! The dark solemn mountains were all covered with snow; the highest, which gleamed the longest in the red light of evening, was Parnassus; the brook which rolled from it near our house was once sacred also. Now the ass sullies it with its feet, but the stream rolls on and on, and becomes clear again. How I can remember every spot in the deep, holy solitude! In the midst of the hut a fire was kindled, and when the hot ashes lay there red and glowing, the bread was baked in them. When the snow was piled so high around our hut as almost to hide it, my mother appeared most cheerful: then she would hold my head between her hands, and sing the songs she never sang at any other times, for the Turks our masters would not allow it. She sang:

"On the summit of Olympus, in the forest of dwarf firs, lay an old stag. His eyes were heavy with tears; he wept blue and even red tears; and there came a roebuck by, and said, 'What ails thee, that thou weepest those blue and red tears?' And the stag answered, 'The Turk has come to our city: he has wild dogs for the chase, a goodly pack.' 'I will drive them away across the islands,' cried the young roebuck, 'I will drive them away across the islands into the deep sea!' But before evening sunk down the roebuck was slain, and before night the stag was hunted and dead."

And when my mother sang thus, her eyes became moist, and on the long eyelashes hung a tear; but she hid it, and baked her black bread in the ashes. Then I would clench my fist and cry, "We will kill the Turks!" but she repeated from the song the words, "I will drive them across the islands into the deep sea. But before evening sank down the roebuck was slain, and before the night came the stag was hunted and dead."

For several days and nights we had been lonely in our hut, when my father came home. I knew he would bring me shells from the Gulf of Lepanto, or perhaps even a bright gleaming knife. This time he brought us a child, a little half-naked girl, that he brought under his sheepskin cloak. It was wrapped in fur, and all that the little creature possessed when this was taken off, and she lay in my mother's lap, were three silver coins, fastened in her dark hair. My father told us that the Turks had killed the child's parents; and he told so much about them, that I dreamed of the Turks all night. He himself had been wounded, and my mother bound up his arm. The wound was deep, and the thick sheepskin was stiff with frozen blood. The little maiden was to be my sister. How radiantly beautiful she looked! Even my mother's eyes were not more gentle than hers. Anastasia, as she was called, was to be my sister, because her father had been united to mine by the old custom which we still kept. They had sworn brotherhood in their youth, and chosen the most beautiful and virtuous girl in the neighborhood to consecrate their bond of friendship. I often heard of the strange good custom.

So now the little girl was my sister. She sat in my lap, and I brought her flowers and the feathers of the mountain birds : we drank together of the waters of Parnassus, and dwelt together for many a year under the laurel roof of the hut, while my mother sang winter after winter of the stag who wept red tears. But as yet I did not understand that it was my own countrymen whose many sorrows were mirrored in those tears.

One day there came three Frankish men. Their dress was different from ours. They had tents and beds with them on their horses, and more than twenty Turks, all armed with swords and muskets, accompanied them; for they were friends of the pacha, and had letters from him commanding an escort for them. They only came to see our mountains, to ascend Parnassus amid the snow and the clouds, and to look at the strange black steep rock near our hut. They could not find room in it, nor could they endure the smoke that rolled along the ceiling and found its way out at the low door; therefore they pitched their tents on the small space outside our dwelling, roasted lambs and birds, and poured out strong sweet wine, of which the Turks were not allowed to partake.

When they departed, I accompanied them for some distance, carrying my little sister Anastasia, wrapped in a goatskin, on my back. One of the Frankish gentlemen made me stand in front of a rock, and drew me, and her too, as we stood there, so that we looked like one creature. I never thought of it; but Anastasia and I were really one. She was always sitting in my lap or riding in the goatskin at my back; and when I dreamed, she appeared in my dreams.

Two nights afterwards, other men, armed with knives and muskets, came into our tent. They were Albanians, brave men, my mother told me. They only stayed a short time. My sister Anastasia sat on the knee of one of them, and when they were gone she had not three, but only two silver coins in her hair. They wrapped tobacco in strips of paper and smoked it. I remember they were undecided as to the road they were to take.

But they had to make a choice. They went, and my father went with them. Soon afterwards we heard the sound of firing. The noise was renewed, and soldiers rushed into our hut, and took my mother, and myself, and my sister Anastasia prisoners. They declared that the robbers had been entertained by us, and that my father had acted as the robbers' guide, and therefore we must go with them. Presently I saw the corpses of the robbers brought in; I saw my father's corpse too. I cried and cried till I fell asleep. When I awoke, we were in prison, but the room was not worse than ours in our own house. They gave me onions to eat, and musty wine poured from a tarry cask, but we had no better fare at home.

How long we were kept prisoners I do not know; but many days and nights went by. When we were set free it was the time of the holy Easter feast. I carried Anastasia on my back, for my mother was ill, and could only move slowly, and it was a long way till we came down to the sea, to the Gulf of Lepanto. We went into a church that gleamed with pictures painted on a golden ground. They were pictures of angels, and very beautiful; but it seemed to me that our little Anastasia was just as beautiful. In the middle of the floor stood a coffin filled with roses. "The Lord Christ is pictured there in the form of a beautiful rose," said my mother; and the priest announced, "Christ is risen!" All the people kissed each other : each one had a burning taper in his hand, and I received one myself, and so did little Anastasia. The bagpipes sounded, men danced hand in hand from the church, and outside the women were roasting the Easter lamb. We were invited to partake, and I sat by the fire; a boy, older than myself, put his arms round my neck, kissed me, and said, "Christ is risen!" and thus it was that for the first time I met Aphtanides.

My mother could make fishermen's nets, for which there was a good demand here in the bay, and we lived a long time by the side of the sea, the beautiful sea, that tasted like tears, and in its colors reminded me of the song of the stag that wept—for sometimes its waters were red, and sometimes green or blue.

Aphtanides knew how to manage our boat, and I often sat in it, with my little Anastasia, while it glided on through the water, swift as a bird flying through the air. Then, when the sun sank down, the mountains were tinted with a deeper and deeper blue; one range seemed to rise behind the other, and behind them all stood Parnassus, with its snow-crowned summit. The mountain-top gleamed in the evening rays like glowing iron, and it seemed as though the light came from within it; for long after the sun had set, the mountain still shone through the clear blue air. The white water-birds touched the surface of the sea with their wings, and all here was as calm and quiet as among the black rocks at Delphi. I lay on my back in the boat, Anastasia leaned against me, and the stars above us shone brighter than the lamps in our church. They were the same stars, and they stood exactly in the same positions above me, as when I had sat in front of our hut at Delphi; and at last I almost fancied I was there. Suddenly there was a splash in the water, and the boat rocked violently. I cried out in horror, for Anastasia had fallen into the water: but in a moment Aphtanides had sprung in after her, and was holding her up to me! We dried her clothes as well as we could, remaining on the water till they were dry; for no one was to know what a fright we had had for our little adopted sister, in whose life Aphtanides now had a part.

The summer came. The sun burned so hot that the leaves turned yellow on the trees. I thought of our cool mountains, and of the fresh water they contained; my mother, too, longed for them; and one evening we wandered home. What peace, what silence! We walked on through the thick thyme, still fragrant though the sun had scorched its leaves. Not a single herdsman did we meet, not one solitary hut did we pass. Every thing was quiet and deserted; but a shooting star announced that in heaven there was yet life. I know not if the clear blue air gleamed with light of its own, or if the radiance came from the stars; but we could see the outlines of the mountains quite plainly. My mother lighted a fire, roasted some roots she had brought with her, and I and my little sister slept among the thyme, without fear of the ugly Smidraki,* from whose throat fire spurts forth, or of the wolf and jackal; for my mother sat beside us, and I considered her presence protection enough for us.

We reached our old home; but the hut was a heap of ruins, and a new one had to be built. A few women lent my mother their aid, and in a few days walls were raised, and covered with a new roof of olive branches. My mother made many bottle-cases of bark and skins; I kept the little flock of the priests,† and Anastasia and the little tortoises were my playmates.

Once we had a visit from our beloved Aphtanides, who said he had greatly longed to see us, and who stayed with us two whole happy days.

A month afterwards he came again, and told us that he was going in a ship to Corfu and Patras, but must bid us good-by first; and he had brought a large fish for our mother. He had a great deal to tell, not only of the fishermen yonder in the Gulf of Lepanto, but also of kings and heroes, who had once possessed Greece, just as the Turks possess it now.

I have seen a bud on a rose-bush gradually unfold in days and weeks, till it became a rose, and hung there in its beauty, before I was aware how large and beautiful and red it had become; and the same thing I now saw in Anastasia. She was now a beautiful, grown girl, and I had become a stout stripling. The wolf-skin that covered my

---

* According to the Greek superstition, this is a monster generated from the unopened entrails of slaughtered sheep, which are thrown away in the fields.

† A peasant who can read often becomes a priest; he is then called " very holy Sir," and the lower orders kiss the ground on which he has stepped.

mother's and Anastasia's bed, I had myself taken from wolves that had fallen beneath my shots.

Years had gone by, when one evening Aphtanides came in, slender as a reed, strong and brown. He kissed us all, and had much to tell of the fortifications of Malta, of the great ocean, and of the marvellous sepulchres of Egypt. It sounded strange as a legend of the priests, and I looked up to him with a kind of veneration.

"How much you know!" I exclaimed; "what wonders you can tell of!"

"But you have told me the finest thing, after all," he replied. "You told me of a thing that has never been out of my thoughts—of the good old custom of the bond of friendship, a custom I should like to follow. Brother, let you and I go to church, as your father and Anastasia's went before us: your sister Anastasia is the most beautiful and most innocent of girls; she shall consecrate us! No people has such grand old customs as we Greeks."

Anastasia blushed like a young rose, and my mother kissed Aphtanides.

A couple of miles from our house there, where loose earth lies on the hill, and a few scattered trees give a shelter, stood the little church; a silver lamp hung in front of the altar.

I had put on my best clothes: the white fustanella fell in rich folds around my hips, the red jacket fitted tight and close, the tassel on my fez cap was silver, and in my girdle gleamed a knife and my pistols. Aphtanides was clad in the blue garb worn by the Greek sailors; on his chest hung a silver plate with the figure of the Virgin Mary; his scarf was as costly as those worn by rich lords. Every one could see that we were about to go through a solemn ceremony. We stepped into the little simple church, where the evening

sunlight, streaming through the door, gleamed on the burn
ing lamp and the pictures on golden ground. We kneel
down on the altar steps, and Anastasia came before us. A
long white garment hung loose over her graceful form; on
her white neck and bosom hung a chain, covered with old
and new coins, forming a kind of collar. Her black hair
was fastened in a knot, and confined by a head-dress
made of silver and gold coins that had been found in an
old temple. No Greek girl had more beautiful ornaments
than she. Her countenance glowed, and her eyes were like
two stars.

We all three prayed silently; and then she said to us,
"Will you be friends in life and in death?" "Yes," we
replied. "Will you, whatever may happen, remember this:
my brother is part of myself. My secret is his, my happiness is his. Self-sacrifice, patience—every thing in me
belongs to him as to me?" And we again answered,
"Yes."

Then she joined our hands and kissed us on the forehead, and we again prayed silently. Then the priest came
through the door near the altar, and blessed us all three;
and a song, sung by the other holy men, sounded from behind the altar-screen, and the bond of eternal friendship was
concluded. When we rose, I saw my mother standing by
the church door weeping heartily.

"How cheerful it was now, in our little hut, and by the
springs of Delphi! On the evening before his departure,
Aphtanides sat thoughtful with me on the declivity of a
mountain; his arm was flung round my waist, and mine
was round his neck: we spoke of the sorrows of Greece,
and of the men whom the country could trust. Every
thought of our souls lay clear before each of us, and I seized
his hand.

"One thing thou must know, one thing that till now has been a secret between myself and Heaven. My whole soul is filled with love! with a love stronger than the love I bear to my mother and to thee!"

"And whom do you love?" asked Aphtanides, and his face and neck grew red as fire.

"I love Anastasia," I replied—and his hand trembled in mine, and he became pale as a corpse. I saw it; I understood the cause; and I believe *my* hand trembled. I bent towards him, kissed his forehead, and whispered, "I have never spoken of it to her, and perhaps she does not love me. Brother, think of this: I have seen her daily; she has grown up beside me, and has become a part of my soul!"

"And she shall be thine!" he exclaimed, "thine! I may not deceive thee, nor will I do so. I also love her; but to-morrow I depart. In a year we shall see each other once more, and then you will be married, will you not? I have a little gold of my own: it shall be thine. Thou must, thou shalt take it."

And we wandered home silently across the mountains. It was late in the evening when we stood at my mother's door.

Anastasia held the lamp upwards as we entered; my mother was not there. She gazed at Aphtanides with a beautifully mournful gaze. "To-morrow you are going from us," she said: "I am very sorry for it."

"Sorry!" he repeated, and in his voice there seemed a trouble as great as the grief I myself felt. I could not speak, but he seized her hand and said, "Our brother yonder loves you, and he is dear to you, is he not? His very silence is proof of his affection."

Anastasia trembled and burst into tears. Then I saw no one but her, thought of none but her, and threw my arms

round her, and said, " I love thee !" She pressed her lips
to mine, and flung her arms around my neck ; but the lamp
had fallen to the ground, and all was dark around us—dark
as in the heart of poor Aphtanides.

Before daybreak he rose, kissed us all, said farewell, and
went away. He had given all his money to my mother for
us. Anastasia was my betrothed, and in a few days afterwards she became my wife.

———◆◆———

JACK THE DULLARD.

AN OLD STORY TOLD ANEW.

FAR in the interior of the country lay an old baronial hall,
and in it lived an old proprietor, who had two sons, which
two young men thought themselves too clever by half.
They wanted to go out and woo the king's daughter ; for
the maiden in question had publicly announced that she
would choose for her husband that youth who could arrange
his words best.

So these two geniuses prepared themselves a full week
for the wooing—this was the longest time that could be
granted them ; but it was enough, for they had had much
preparatory information, and everybody knows how useful
that is. One of them knew the whole Latin dictionary
by heart, and three whole years of the daily paper of the
little town into the bargain ; and so well, indeed, that he
could repeat it all either backwards or forwards, just as
he chose. The other was deeply read in the corporation
laws, and knew by heart what every corporation ought to

know ; and accordingly he thought he could talk of affairs of state, and put his spoke in the wheel in the council. And he knew one thing more : he could embroider braces with roses and other flowers, and with arabesques, for he was a tasty, light-fingered fellow.

"I shall win the princess !" So cried both of them. Therefore their old papa gave to each a handsome horse. The youth who knew the dictionary and newspaper by heart had a black horse, and he who knew all about the corporation laws received a milk-white steed. Then they rubbed the corners of their mouths with fish-oil, so that they might become very smooth and glib. All the servants stood below in the courtyard, and looked on while they mounted their horses ; and just by chance the third son came up. For the proprietor had really three sons, though nobody counted the third with his brothers, because he was not so learned as they, and indeed he was generally known as " Jack the Dullard."

" Hallo !" said Jack the Dullard, " where are you going ? I declare you have put on your Sunday clothes !"

" We're going to the king's court, as suitors to the king's daughter. Don't you know the announcement that has been made all through the country ?" And they told him all about it.

"My word ! I'll be in it too !" cried Jack the Dullard ; and his two brothers burst out laughing at him, and rode away.

" Father dear," said Jack, "I must have a horse too. I I do feel so desperately inclined to marry ! If she accepts me, she accepts me ; and if she wont have me, I'll have her ; but she *shall* be mine !"

" Don't talk nonsense," replied the old gentleman. " You shall have no horse from me. You don't know how to speak

—you can't arrange your words. Your brothers are very, very different fellows from you."

" Well," quoth Jack the Dullard, " if I can't have a horse, I'll take the billy-goat, who belongs to me, and he can carry me very well !"

And so said, so done. He mounted the billy-goat, pressed his heels into its sides, and galloped down the high street like a hurricane.

" Hei, houp ! that was a ride ! Here I come !" shouted Jack the Dullard, and he sang till his voice echoed far and wide.

But his brothers rode slowly on in advance of him. They spoke not a word, for they were thinking about all the fine extempore speeches they would have to bring out, and all these had to be cleverly prepared beforehand.

" Hallo !" shouted Jack the Dullard. " Here am I ! Look what I have found on the high-road." And he showed them what it was; and it was a dead crow.

" Dullard !" exclaimed the brothers, " what are you going to do with that ?"

" With the crow ? why, I am going to give it to the princess."

" Yes, do so," said they ; and they laughed and rode on.

" Hallo, here I am again ! Just see what I have found now : you don't find that on the high-road every day !"

And the brothers turned round to see what he could have found now.

" Dullard !" they cried, " that is only an old wooden shoe, and the upper part is missing into the bargain; are you going to give that also to the princess ?"

" Most certainly I shall," replied Jack the Dullard; and again the brothers laughed and rode on, and thus they got far in advance of him; but—

"Hallo—hop rara!" and there was Jack the Dullard again. "I is getting better," he cried. "Hurrah! it is quite famous."

"Why, what have you found this time?" inquired the brothers.

"Oh," said Jack the Dullard, "I can hardly tell you How glad the princess will be!"

"Bah!" said the brothers; "that is nothing but clay out of the ditch."

"Yes, certainly it is," said Jack the Dullard; "and clay of the finest sort. See, it is so wet, it runs through one's fingers." And he filled his pocket with the clay.

But his brothers galloped on till the sparks flew, and consequently they arrived a full hour earlier at the town-gate than could Jack. Now at the gate each suitor was provided with a number, and all were placed in rows immediately on their arrival, six in each row, and so closely packed together that they could not move their arms; and that was a prudent arrangement, for they would certainly have come to blows, had they been able, merely because one of them stood before the other.

All the inhabitants of the country round about stood in great crowds around the castle, almost under the very windows, to see the princess receive the suitors; and as each stepped into the hall, his power of speech seemed to desert him, like the light of a candle that is blown out. Then the princess would say, "He is of no use! away with him out of the hall!"

At last the turn came for that brother who knew the dictionary by heart; but he did not know it now; he had absolutely forgotten it altogether; and the boards seemed to re-echo with his footsteps, and the ceiling of the hall was made of looking-glass, so that he saw himself standing on his head; and at the window stood three clerks and a head clerk, and every one of them was writing down every single word that was uttered, so that it might be printed in the newspapers, and sold for a penny at the street corners. It was a terrible ordeal, and they had moreover made such a fire in the stove, that the room seemed quite red-hot.

"It is dreadfully hot here!" observed the first brother.

"Yes," replied the princess, "my father is going to roast young pullets to-day."

"Baa!" there he stood like a baa-lamb. He had not been prepared for a speech of this kind; and had not a word to say, though he intended to say something witty. "Baa!"

"He is of no use!" said the princess. "Away with him!"

And he was obliged to go accordingly. And now the second brother came in.

"It is terribly warm here!" he observed.

"Yes, we're roasting pullets to-day," replied the princess.

"What—what were you—were you pleased to ob——" stammered he—and all the clerks wrote down, "pleased to ob——"

"He is of no use!" said the princess. "Away with him!"

Now came the turn of Jack the Dullard. He rode into the hall on his goat.

"Well, it's most abominably hot here."

"Yes, because I'm roasting young pullets," replied the princess.

"Ah, that's lucky!" exclaimed Jack the Dullard, "for I suppose you'll let me roast my crow at the same time?"

"With the greatest pleasure," said the princess. "But have you any thing you can roast it in? for I have neither pot nor pan."

"Certainly I have!" said Jack. "Here's a cooking utensil with a tin handle." And he brought out the old wooden shoe, and put the crow into it.

"Well, that *is* a famous dish!" said the princess. "But what shall we do for sauce?"

"Oh, I have that in my pocket," said Jack: "I have so much of it, that I can afford to throw some away;" and he poured some of the clay out of his pocket.

"I like that!" said the princess. "You can give an answer, and you have something to say for yourself, and so you shall be my husband. But are you aware that every word we speak is being taken down, and will be published in the paper to-morrow? Look yonder, and you will see in every window three clerks and a head clerk; and the old head clerk is the worst of all, for he can't understand any thing." But she only said this to frighten Jack the Dullard: and the clerks gave a great crow of delight, and each one spurted a blot out of his pen on to the floor.

"Oh, those are the gentlemen, are they?" said Jack; "then I will give the best I have to the head clerk." And he turned out his pockets, and flung the wet clay full in the head clerk's face.

"That was very cleverly done," observed the princess. "I could not have done that; but I shall learn in time."

And accordingly Jack the Dullard was made a king, and received a crown and a wife, and sat upon a throne. And this report we have wet from the press of the head clerk and the corporation of printers—but they are not to be depended upon in the least!

SOMETHING.

"I want to be something !" said the eldest of **five**
rothers. "I want to do something in the world. I don't
care how humble my position may be in society, if I only
effect some good, for that will really be something. I'll
make bricks, for they are quite indispensable things, and
then I shall truly have done something."

"But that *something* will not be enough !" quoth the
second brother. "What you intend doing is just as much
as nothing at all. It is journeyman's work, and can be
done by a machine. No, I would rather be a bricklayer at
once, for that *is* something real; and that's what I will be.
That brings rank : as a bricklayer, one belongs to a guild,
and is a citizen, and has one's own flag and one's own house
of call. Yes, and if all goes well, I will keep journeymen.
I shall become a master bricklayer, and my wife will be a
master's wife—that is what *I* call something."

"That's nothing at all !" said the third. "That is beyond
the pale of the guild, and there are many of those in a
town that stand far above the mere master artisan. You
may be an honest man; but as a 'master' you will after all
only belong to those who are ranked among common men.
I know something better than that. I will be an architect,
and will thus enter into the territory of art and speculation.
I shall be reckoned among those who stand high in point of
intellect. I shall certainly have to serve up from the pick-
axe, so to speak; so I must begin as a carpenter's apprentice, and must go about as an assistant, in a cap, though I
am accustomed to wear a silk hat. I shall have to fetch
beer and spirits for the common journeymen, and they will

call me 'thou,' and that is insulting! But I shall imagine to myself that the whole thing is only acting, and a kind of masquerade. To-morrow—that is to say, when I have served my time—I shall go my own way, and the others will be nothing to me. I shall go to the academy, and get instructions in drawing, and shall be called an architect. *That's something!* I may get to be called 'sir,' and even 'worshipful sir,' or even get a handle at the front or at the back of my name, and shall go on building and building, just as those before me have built. That will always be a thing to remember, and that's what *I* call something!"

"But I don't care at all for *that* something," said the fourth. "*I* won't sail in the wake of others, and be a copyist. I will be a genius; and will stand up greater than all the rest of you together. I shall be the creator of a new style, and will give the plan of a building suitable to the climate and the material of the country, for the nationality of the people, for the development of the age—and an additional story for my own genius."

"But supposing the climate and the material are bad," said the fifth, "that would be a disastrous circumstance, for these two exert a great influence! Nationality, moreover, may expand itself until it becomes affectation, and the development of the century may run wild with your work, as youth often runs wild. I quite realize the fact that none of you will be any thing real, however much you may believe in yourselves. But, do what you like, I will not resemble you: I shall keep on the outside of things, and criticise whatever you produce. To every work there is attached something that is not right—something that has gone wrong; and I will ferret that out and find fault with it; and *that* will be doing *something!*"

And he kept his word; and everybody said concerning

this fifth brother, "There is certainly something in him: he has a good head; but he does nothing." And by that very means they thought *something* of him !

Now, you see this is only a little story; but it will never end so long as the world lasts.

But what became of the five brothers? Why this is *nothing*, and not *something*.

Listen, it is a capital story.

The eldest brother, he who manufactured bricks, soon became aware of the fact that every brick, however small it might be, produced for him a little coin, though this coin was only copper; and many copper pennies laid one upon the other can be changed into a shining dollar; and wherever one knocks with such a dollar in one's hand, whether at the baker's, or the butcher's, or the tailor's—wherever it may be, the door flies open, and the visitor is welcomed, and gets what he wants. You see that is what comes of bricks. Some of those belonging to the eldest brother certainly crumbled away, or broke in two, but there was a use even for these.

On the high rampart, the wall that kept out the sea, Margaret, the poor woman, wished to build herself a little house. All the faulty bricks were given to her, and a few perfect ones into the bargain, for the eldest brother was a good-natured man, though he certainly did not achieve any thing beyond the manufacture of bricks. The poor woman put together the house for herself It was little and narrow, and the single window was quite crooked. The door was too low, and the thatched roof might have shown better workmanship. But after all, it was a shelter; and from the little house you could look far across the sea, whose waves broke vainly against the protecting rampart on which it was built. The salt billows spurted their spray

over the whole house, which was still standing when he
who had given the bricks for its erection had long been
dead and buried.

The second brother knew better how to build a wall, for
he had served an apprenticeship to it. When he had served
his time and passed his examination, he packed his knapsack and sang the journeyman's song :

" While I am young I'll wander, from place to place I'll roam,
    And everywhere build houses, until I come back home !
    And youth will give me courage, and my true love won't forget:
    Hurrah then for a workman's life ! I'll be a master yet !"

And he carried his idea into effect. When he had come
home and become a master, he built one house after another
in the town. He built a whole street; and when the street
was finished and became an ornament to the place, the
houses built a house for him in return, that was to be his
own. But how can houses build a house? If you ask
them they will not answer you, but people will understand
what is meant by the expression, and say, " Certainly, it
was the street that built his house for him." It was little,
and the floor was covered with clay; but when he danced
with his bride upon this clay floor, it seemed to become
polished oak; and from every stone in the wall sprung
forth a flower, and the room was gay, as if with costliest
paper-hanger's work. It was a pretty house, and in it lived
a happy pair. The flag of the guild fluttered before the
house, and the journeymen and apprentices shouted hurrah !
Yes, he certainly was *something!* And at last he died; and
that was something too.

Now came the architect, the third brother, who had been
at first a carpenter's apprentice, had worn a cap, and
served as an errand-boy, but had afterwards gone to the

academy, and risen to become an architect, and to be called "honored sir." Yes, if the houses of the street had built a house for the brother who had become a bricklayer, the street now received its name from the architect, and the handsomest house in it became his property. *That* was something, and *he* was something; and he had a long title before and after his name. His children were called *genteel* children, and when he died his widow was "a widow of rank," and *that* is something!—and his name always remained at the corner of the street, and lived on in the mouth of every one as the street's name—and *that* was something !

Now came the genius of the family, the fourth brother, who wanted to invent something new and original, and an additional story on the top of it for himself. But the top story tumbled down, and he came tumbling down with it, and broke his neck. Nevertheless he had a splendid funeral, with guild flags and music; poems in the papers, and flowers strewn on the paving-stones in the street; and three funeral orations were held over him, each one longer than the last, which would have rejoiced him greatly, for he always liked it when people talked about him; a monument also was erected over his grave. It was only one story high, but still it was *something*.

Now he was dead, like the other three brothers; but the last, the one who was a critic, outlived them all; and that was quite right, for by this means he got the last word, and it was of great importance to him to have the last word The people always said he had a good head of his own. At last his hour came, and he died, and came to the gates of Paradise. There souls always enter two and two, and he came up with another soul that wanted to get into Paradise too; and who should this be but old dame Margaret, from the house upon the sea-wall.

"I suppose this is done for the sake of contrast, that I and this wretched soul should arrive here at exactly the same time!" said the critic. "Pray, who are you, my good woman?" he asked. "Do you want to get in here too?"

And the old woman curtsied as well as she could: she thought it must be St. Peter himself talking to her.

"I'm a poor old woman of a very humble family," she replied. "I'm old Margaret that lived in the house on the sea-wall."

"Well, and what have you done? what have you accomplished down there?"

"I have really accomplished nothing at all in the world: nothing that I can plead to have the doors here opened to me. It would be a real mercy to allow me to slip in through the gate."

"In what manner did you leave the world?" asked he, just for the sake of saying something; for it was wearisome work standing there and saying nothing.

"Why, I really don't know how I left it. I was sick and miserable during my last years, and could not well bear creeping out of bed, and going out suddenly into the frost and cold. It was a hard winter, but I have got out of it all now. For a few days the weather was quite calm, but very cold, as your honor must very well know. The sea was covered with ice as far as one could look. All the people from the town walked out upon the ice, and I think they said there was a dance there, and skating. There was beautiful music and a great feast there too; the sound came into my poor little room, where I lay ill. And it was towards the evening; the moon had risen beautifully, but it was not yet in its full splendor; I looked from my bed out over the wide sea, and far off, just where the sea and sky join, a strange white cloud came up. I lay looking at the cloud, and I saw a little black spot in the middle of it, that grew larger and larger; and now I knew what it meant, for I am old and experienced, though this token is not often seen. I knew it, and a shuddering came upon me. Twice in my life I have seen the same thing; and I knew there would be an awful tempest, and a spring flood, which would overwhelm the poor people who were now drinking and dancing and rejoicing—young and old, the whole city had issued forth : who was to warn them, if no one saw what was coming yonder, or knew, as I did, what it meant ? I was dreadfully alarmed, and felt more lively than I had done for a long time. I crept out of bed, and got to the window, but could not crawl further, I was so exhausted. But I managed to open the window. I saw the people outside running and jumping about on the ice; I could see the beautiful flags that waved in the wind. I heard the boys shouting 'hurrah !' and the servant men and maids singing. There were all kinds of merriment going on. But the white cloud with the black spot ! I cried out as loud as I could, but no one heard me; I was too far from the people. Soon the storm would burst, and the ice would break, and all who were upon it would be lost without remedy. They could not hear me, and I could not come out to them. Oh ! if· I could only bring them ashore ! Then kind Heaven inspired me with the thought of setting fire to my bed, and rather to let the house burn down, than that all those people should perish so miserably. I succeeded in lighting up a beacon for them. The red flame blazed up on high, and I escaped out of the door, but fell down exhausted on the threshold, and could get no further. The flames rushed out towards me, flickered through the window, and rose high above the roof. All the people on the ice yonder beheld it, and ran as fast as they could, to give aid to a poor old woman who, they thought, was being burned to death. Not one remained behind. I heard them coming; but I also became aware of a rushing sound in the air; I heard a rumbling like the sound of heavy artillery; the spring-flood was lifting the covering of ice, which presently cracked and burst into a thousand fragments. But the people succeeded in reaching the sea-wall—I saved them all! But I fancy I could not bear the cold and the fright, and so I came up here to the gates of Paradise. I am told they are opened to poor creatures like me—and now I have no house left down upon the rampart: not that I think this will give me admission here."

Then the gates of heaven were opened, and the angel led the old woman in. She left a straw behind her, a straw that had been in her bed when she set it on fire to save the lives of many; and this straw had been changed into the purest gold—into gold that grew and grew, and spread out into beauteous leaves and flowers.

" Look, this is what the poor woman brought," said the angel to the critic. " What dost *thou* bring? I know that thou hast accomplished nothing—thou hast not made so much as a single brick. Ah, if thou couldst only return, and effect at least so much as that! Probably the brick, when thou hast made it, would not be worth much; but if it were made with good-will, it would at least be *something*. But thou canst not go back, and I can do nothing for thee !"

Then the poor soul, the old dame who had lived on the dyke, put in a petition for him. She said :

" His brother gave me the bricks and the pieces out of which I built up my house, and that was a great deal for a poor woman like me. Could not all those bricks and pieces be counted as a single brick in his favor? It was an act of mercy. He wants it now : and is not this the very fountain of mercy ?"

Then the angel said :

"Thy brother, whom thou hast regarded as the least among you all, he whose honest industry seemed to thee as the most humble, hath given thee this heavenly gift. Thou shalt not be turned away. It shall be vouchsafed to thee to stand here without the gate, and to reflect, and repent of thy life down yonder ; but thou shalt not be admitted until thou hast in real earnest accomplished *something*."

" I could have said that in better words !" thought the critic, but he did not find fault aloud ; and for him, after all, that was " SOMETHING !"

UNDER THE WILLOW-TREE.

THE region round the little town of Kjöge is very bleak and bare. The town certainly lies by the seashore, which is always beautiful, but just there it might be more beautiful than it is : all around are flat fields, and it is a long way to the forest. But when one is very much at home in a place, one always finds something beautiful, and something that one longs for in the most charming spot in the world that is strange to us. We confess that, by the utmost boundary of the little town, where some humble gardens skirt the streamlet that falls into the sea, it must be a very pretty place in summer ; and this was the opinion of the two children from neighboring houses, who were playing there, and forcing their way through the gooseberry bushes, to get to one another. In one of the gardens stood an elder-tree, and in the other an old willow, and under the latter the children were especially very fond of playing ; they were allowed to play there, though, indeed, the tree stood close beside the stream, and they might easily have fallen into the water. But the eye of God watches over the little ones ; if it did not, they would be badly off. And, moreover, they were very careful with respect to the water; in fact, the boy was so much afraid of it, that they could not lure him into the sea in summer, when the other children were splashing about in the waves. Accordingly, he was famously jeered and mocked at, and had to bear the jeering and mockery as best he could. But once Joanna, the neighbor's little girl, dreamed she was sailing in a boat, and Knud waded out to join her till the water rose, first to his neck, and afterwards closed over his head, so that he disappeared altogether. From the time when little Knud heard of this dream, he would no longer bear the teazing of the other boys. He might go into the water now, he said, for Joanna had dreamed it. He certainly never carried the idea into practice, but the dream was his great guide for all that.

Their parents, who were poor people, often took tea together, and Knud and Joanna played in the gardens and on the high-road, where a row of willows had been planted beside the skirting ditch ; these trees, with their polled tops, certainly did not look beautiful, but they were not put there for ornament, but for use. The old willow-tree in the garden was much handsomer, and therefore children were fond of sitting under it. In the town itself there was a great market-place, and at the time of the fair this place was covered with whole streets of tents and booths, containing silk ribbons, boots, and every thing that a person could wish for. There was great crowding, and generally the weather was rainy; but it did not destroy the fragrance of the honey-cakes and the gingerbread, of which there was a booth quite full; and the best of it was, that the man who kept this booth came every year to lodge during the fair-time in the dwelling of little Knud's father. Consequently there came a present of a bit of gingerbread every now and then, and of course Joanna received her share of the gift. But, perhaps, the most charming thing of all was that the gingerbread dealer knew all sorts of tales, and could even relate histories about his own gingerbread cakes; and one evening, in particular, he told a story about them which made such a deep impression on the children that they never forgot it; and for that reason it is perhaps advisable that we should hear it too, more especially as the story is not long.

"On the shop-board," he said, "lay two gingerbread cakes, one in the shape of a man with a hat, the other of a maiden without a bonnet; both their faces were on the side that was uppermost, for they were to be looked at on that side, and not on the other; and, indeed, most people have a favorable side from which they should be viewed. On the left side the man wore a bitter almond—that was his heart; but the maiden, on the other hand, was honey-cake all over. They were placed as samples on the shop-board, and remaining there a long time, at last they fell in love with one another; but neither told the other, as they should have done if they had expected any thing to come of it.

"'He is a man, and therefore he must speak first,' she thought; but she felt quite contented, for she knew her love was returned.

"His thoughts were far more extravagant, as is always the case with a man. He dreamed that he was a real street boy, that he had four pennies of his own, and that he purchased the maiden, and ate her up. So they lay on the shop-board for weeks and weeks, and grew dry and hard, but the thoughts of the maiden became ever more gentle and maidenly.

" 'It is enough for me that I have lived on the same table with him,' she said, and crack ! she broke in two.

" ' If she had only known my love, she would have kept together a little longer,' he thought.

"And that is the story, and here they are both of them," said the baker in conclusion. "They are remarkable for their curious history, and for their silent love, which never came to any thing. And there they are for you !" and, so saying, he gave Joanna the man who was yet entire, and Knud got the broken maiden ; but the children had been so much impressed by the story that they could not summon courage to eat the lovers up.

On the following day they went out with them to the churchyard, and sat down by the church wall, which is covered, winter and summer, with the most luxuriant ivy as with a rich carpet. Here they stood the two cake figures up in the sunshine among the green leaves, and told the story to a group of other children ; they told them of the silent love which led to nothing. It was called *love* because the story was so lovely, on that they all agreed. But when they turned again to look at the gingerbread pair, a big boy, out of mischief, had **eaten** up the broken maiden. The children cried about this, and afterwards— probably that the poor lover might not be left in the world lonely and desolate—they ate him up too ; but they never never forgot the story.

The children were always together by the elder-tree and under the willow, and the little girl sang the most beautiful songs with a voice that was clear as a bell. Knud, on the other hand, had not a note of music in him, but he knew the words of the song, and that, at least, was something. The people of Kjöge, even to the rich wife of the fancy-shop keeper, stood still and listened when Joanna sang "She has a very sweet voice, that little girl," they said.

Those were glorious days, they could not last forever. The neighbors were neighbors no longer. The little maiden's mother was dead, and the father intended to marry again, in the capital, where he had been promised a living as a messenger, which was to be a very lucrative office. And the neighbors separated regretfully, the children weeping heartily, but the parents promised that they should at least write to one another once a year.

And Knud was bound apprentice to a shoemaker, for the big boy could not be allowed to run wild any longer; and, moreover, he was confirmed.

Ah, how gladly on that day of celebration would he have been in Copenhagen with little Joanna! but he remained in Kjöge, and had never yet been to Copenhagen, though the little town is only five Danish miles distant from the capital; but far across the bay, when the sky was clear, Knud had seen the towers in the distance, and on the day of his confirmation he could distinctly see the golden cross on the principal church glittering in the sun.

Ah, how often his thoughts were with Joanna! Did she think of him? Yes. Towards Christmas there came a letter from her father to the parents of Knud, to say that they were getting on very well in Copenhagen, and especially might Joanna look forward to a brilliant future on the strength of her fine voice. She had been engaged in the theatre in which people sing, and was already earning some money, out of which she sent her dear neighbors of Kjöge a dollar for the merry Christmas Eve. They were to drink her health, she had herself added in a postscript, and in the same postscript there stood further, "A kind greeting to Knud."

The whole family wept: and yet all this was very pleasant; those were joyful tears that they shed. Knud's thoughts had been occupied every day with Joanna; and now he knew that she also thought of him: and the nearer the time came when his apprenticeship would be over, the more clearly did it appear to him that he was very fond of Joanna, and that she must be his wife; and when he thought of this, a smile came upon his lips, and he drew the thread twice as fast as before, and pressed his foot hard against the knee-strap. He ran the awl far into his finger, but he did not care for that. He determined not to play the dumb lover, as the two gingerbread cakes had done: the story should teach him a lesson.

And now he was a journeyman, and his knapsack was packed ready for his journey: at length, for the first time in his life, he was to go to Copenhagen, where a master was already waiting for him. How glad Joanna would be! She was now seventeen years old, and he nineteen.

Already in Kjöge he had wanted to buy a gold ring for her; but he recollected that such things were to be had far better in Copenhagen. And now he took leave of his parents, and on a rainy day, late in the autumn, went forth on foot out of the town of his birth. The leaves were falling down from the trees, and he arrived at his new master's in the metropolis wet to the skin. Next Sunday he was to pay a visit to Joanna's father. The new journeyman's clothes were brought forth, and the new hat from Kjöge was put on, which became Knud very well, for till this time he had only worn a cap. And he found the house he sought, and mounted flight after flight of stairs until he became almost giddy. It was terrible to him to see how people lived piled up one over the other in the dreadful city.

Every thing in the room had a prosperous look, and Joanna's father received him very kindly. To the new wife he was a stranger, but she shook hands with him, and gave him some coffee.

"Joanna will be glad to see you," said the father: "you have grown quite a nice young man. You shall see her presently. She is a girl who rejoices my heart, and, please God, she will rejoice it yet more. She has her own room now, and pays us rent for it." And the father knocked quite politely at the door, as if he were a visitor, and then they went in.

But how pretty every thing was in that room ! such an apartment was certainly not to be found in all Kjöge : the queen herself could not be more charmingly lodged. There were carpets, there were window curtains quite down to the floor, and around were flowers and pictures, and a mirror into which there was almost danger that visitors might step, for it was as large as a door; and there was even a velvet chair.

Knud saw all this at a glance : and yet he saw nothing but Joanna. She was a grown maiden, quite different from what Knud had fancied her, and much more beautiful. In all Kjöge there was not a girl like her. How graceful she was, and with what an odd unfamiliar glance she looked at Knud ! But that was only for a moment, and then she rushed towards him as if she would have kissed him. She did not really do so, but she came very near it. Yes, she was certainly rejoiced at the arrival of the friend of her youth ! The tears were actually in her eyes; and she had much to say, and many questions to put concerning all, from

Knud s parents down to the elder-tree and the willow, which she called Elder-mother and Willow-father, as if they had been human beings; and indeed they might pass as such, 'ust as well as the gingerbread cakes; and of these she spoke too, and of their silent love, and how they had lain upon the shop-board and split in two—and then she laughed very heartily; but the blood mounted into Knud's cheeks, and his heart beat thick and fast. No, she had not grown proud at all. And it was through her—he noticed it well —that her parents invited him to stay the whole evening with them; and she poured out the tea and gave him a cup with her own hands; and afterwards she took a book and read aloud to them, and it seemed to Knud that what she read was all about himself and his love, for it matched so well with his thoughts; and then she sang a simple song, but through her singing it became like a history, and seemed to be the outpouring of her very heart. Yes, certainly she was fond of Knud. The tears coursed down his cheeks— he could not restrain them, nor could he speak a single word : he seemed to himself as if he were struck dumb; and yet she pressed his hand, and said :

" You have a good heart, Knud—remain always as you are now."

That was an evening of matchless delight to Knud; to sleep after it was impossible, and accordingly Knud did **not** sleep.

At parting, Joanna's father had said, " Now, you won't forget us altogether ! Don't let the whole winter go by without once coming to see us again;" and therefore he could very well go again the next Sunday, and resolved to do so. But every evening when working hours were over —and they worked by candlelight there—Knud went out through the town : he went into the street in which Joanna lived, and looked up at her window; it was almost always lit up, and one evening he could see the shadow of her face quite plainly on the curtain—and that was a grand evening for him. His master's wife did not like his galivanting abroad every evening, as she expressed it; and she shook her head; but the master only smiled.

"He is only a young fellow," he said.

But Knud thought to himself: "On Sunday I shall see her, and I shall tell her how completely she reigns in my heart and soul, and that she must be my little wife. I know I am only a poor journeyman shoemaker, but I shall work and strive—yes, I shall tell her so. Nothing comes of silent love : I have learned that from the cakes."

And Sunday came round, and Knud sallied forth; but, unluckily, they were all invited out for that evening, and were obliged to tell him so. Joanna pressed his hand and said :

"Have you ever been to the theatre? You must go once. I shall sing on Wednesday, and if you have time on that evening, I will send you a ticket; my father knows where your master lives."

How kind that was of her ! And on Wednesday at noon he received a sealed paper, with no words written in it; but the ticket was there, and in the evening Knud went to the theatre for the first time in his life. And what did he see? He saw Joanna, and how charming and how beautiful she looked ! She was certainly married to a stranger, but that was all in the play—something that was only make-believe, as Knud knew very well. If it had been real, he thought, she would never have had the heart to send him a ticket that he might go and see it. And all the people shouted and applauded, and Knud cried out "hurrah !"

Even the king smiled at Joanna, and seemed to delight in

her. Ah, how small Knud felt! but then he loved her so dearly, and thought that she loved him too; but it was for the man to speak the first word, as the gingerbread maiden in the child's story had taught him : and there was a great deal for him in that story.

Soon as Sunday came, he went again. He felt as if he were going into a church. Joanna was alone, and received him—it could not have happened more fortunately. "It is well that you are come," she said. "I had an idea of sending my father to you, and I felt a presentiment that you would be here this evening : for I must tell you that I start for France on Friday : I must go there, if I am to become efficient."

It seemed to Knud as if the whole room were whirling round and round with him. He felt as if his heart would presently burst : no tear rose to his eyes, but still it was easy to see how sorrowful he was.

"You honest, faithful soul !" she exclaimed ; and these words of hers loosened Knud's tongue. He told her how constantly he loved her, and that she must become his wife; and as he said this, he saw Joanna change color and turn pale. She let his hand fall, and answered seriously and mournfully :

"Knud, do not make yourself and me unhappy. I shall always be a good sister to you, one in whom you may trust, but I shall never be any thing more." And she drew her white hand over his hot forehead. "Heaven gives us strength for much," she said, "if we only endeavor to do our best."

At that moment the stepmother came into the room ; and Joanna said quickly :

"Knud is quite inconsolable because I am going away. Come, be a man," she continued, and laid her hand upon his shoulder ; and it seemed as if they had been talking of the journey, and nothing else. "You are a child," she added. but now you must be good and reasonable, as you used to be under the willow-tree, when we were both children."

But Knud felt as if the whole world had slid out of its course, and his thoughts were like a loose thread fluttering to and fro in the wind. He stayed, though he could not remember if she had asked him to stay ; and she was kind and good, and poured out his tea for him, and sang to him. It had not the old tone, and yet it was wonderfully beautiful, and made his heart feel ready to burst. And then they parted. Knud did not offer his hand, but she seized it, and said :

"Surely you will shake hands with your sister at parting, old play-fellow !"

And she smiled through the tears that were rolling over her cheeks, and she repeated the word "brother"—and certainly there was good consolation in that—and thus they parted.

She sailed to France, and Knud wandered about the muddy streets of Copenhagen. The other journeymen in the workshop asked him why he went about so gloomily, and told him he should go and amuse himself with them, for he was a young fellow.

And they went with him to the dancing-rooms. He saw many handsome girls there, but certainly not one like Joanna ; and here, where he thought to forget her, she stood more vividly than ever before the eyes of his soul. "Heaven gives us strength for a great deal, if we only try to do our best," she had said ; and holy thoughts came into his mind, and he folded his hands. The violins played, and the girls danced round in a circle ; and he was quite startled, for it seemed to him as if he were in a place to which he ought not to have brought Joanna—for she was there with him, in his heart; and accordingly he went out. He ran through the streets, and passed by the house where she had dwelt: it was dark there, dark everywhere, and empty and lonely. The world went on its course, but Knud pursued his lonely way, unheedingly.

The winter came and the streams were frozen. Every thing seemed to be preparing for a burial. But when spring returned, and the first steamer was to start, a longing seized him to go away, far, far into the world, but not to France. So he packed his knapsack, and wandered far into the German land, from city to city, without rest or peace; and it was not till he came to the glorious old city of Nuremberg that he could master his restless spirit; and in Nuremberg, therefore, he decided to remain.

Nuremberg is a wonderful old city, and looks as if it were cut out of an old picture-book. The streets seem to stretch themselves along just as they please. The houses do not like standing in regular ranks. Gables with little towers, arabesques, and pillars, start out over the pathway, and from the strange peaked roofs water-spouts, formed like dragons or great slim dogs, extend far over the street.

Here in the market-place stood Knud, with his knapsack on his back. He stood by one of the old fountains that are adorned with splendid bronze figures, scriptural and historical, rising up between the gushing jets of water. A pretty servant-maid was just filling her pails, and she gave Knud a refreshing draught; and as her hand was full of roses, she gave him one of the flowers, and he accepted it as a good omen.

From the neighboring church the strains of the organ were sounding: they seemed to him as familiar as the tones of the organ at home at Kjöge ; and he went into the great cathedral. The sunlight streamed in through the stained glass windows, between the two lofty, slender pillars. His spirit became prayerful, and peace returned to his soul.

And he sought and found a good master in Nuremberg, with whom he stayed, and in whose house he learned the German language.

The old moat round the town has been converted into a number of little kitchen-gardens ; but the high walls are standing yet, with their heavy towers. The ropemaker twists his ropes on the gallery or walk built of wood, inside the town wall, where the elder-bushes grow out of the clefts and cracks, spreading their green twigs over the little low houses that stand below ; and in one of these dwelt the master with whom Knud worked ; and over the little garret-window at which Knud sat the elder waved its branches.

Here he lived through a summer and a winter ; but when the spring came again he could bear it no longer. The elder was in blossom, and its fragrance reminded him so of home, that he fancied himself back in the garden at Kjöge ; and therefore Knud went away from his master, and dwelt with another further in the town, over whose house no elder-bush grew.

His workshop was quite close to one of the old stone bridges, by a low water-mill, that rushed and foamed always. Without, rolled the roaring stream, hemmed in by houses, whose old decayed gables looked ready to topple down into the water. No elder grew here—there was not even a flower-pot with its little green plant ; but just opposite the workshop stood a great old willow-tree, that seemed to cling fast to the house, for fear of being carried away by the water, and which stretched forth its branches over the river, just as the willow at Kjöge spread its arms across the streamlet by the gardens there.

Yes, he had certainly gone from the "Elder-mother" to the "Willow-father." The tree here had something, especially on moonlight evenings, that went straight to his heart—and that something was not in the moonlight, but in the old tree itself.

Nevertheless, he could not remain. Why not? Ask the willow-tree, ask the blooming elder! And therefore he bade farewell to his master in Nuremberg, and journeyed onward.

To no one did he speak of Joanna—in his secret heart he hid his sorrow; and he thought of the deep meaning in the old childish story of the two cakes. Now he understood why the man had a bitter almond in his breast—he himself felt the bitterness of it; and Joanna, who was always so gentle and kind, was typified by the honey-cake. The strap of his knapsack seemed so tight across his chest that he could scarcely breathe; he loosened it, but was not relieved. He saw but half the world around him; the other half he carried about him, and within himself. And thus it stood with him.

Not till he came in sight of the high mountains did the world appear freer to him; and now his thoughts were turned without, and tears came into his eyes.

The Alps appeared to him as the folded wings of the earth; how if they were to unfold themselves, and display their variegated pictures of black woods, foaming waters, clouds, and masses of snow? At the last day, he thought, the world will lift up its great wings, and mount upwards towards the sky, and burst like a soap-bubble in the glance of the Highest!

"Ah," sighed he, "that the Last Day were come!"

Silently he wandered through the land, that seemed to him as an orchard covered with soft turf. From the wooden balconies of the houses the girls who sat busy with their lace-making nodded at him; the summits of the mountains glowed in the red sun of the evening; and when he saw the green lakes gleaming among the dark trees, he thought of the coast by the Bay of Kjöge, and there was longing in his bosom, but it was pain no more.

There where the Rhine rolls onward like a great billow, and bursts, and is changed into snow-white, gleaming, cloud-like masses, as if clouds were being created there, with the rainbow fluttering like a loose band above them— there he thought of the water-mill at Kjöge, with its rushing, foaming water.

Gladly would he have remained in the quiet Rhenish town, but here, too, were too many elder-trees and willows, and therefore he journeyed on, over the high, mighty mountains, through shattered walls of rock, and on roads that clung like swallows' nests to the mountain-side. The waters foamed on in the depths, the clouds were below him, and he strode on over thistles, Alpine roses, and snow, in the warm summer sun; and saying farewell to the lands of the North, he passed on under the shade of blooming chestnut-trees, and through vineyards and fields of maize. The mountains were a wall between him and all his recollections; and he wished it to be so.

Before him lay a great glorious city which they called *Milano*, and here he found a German master who gave him work. They were an old pious couple, in whose workship he now labored. And the two old people became quite fond of the quiet journeyman, who said little, but worked all the more, and led a pious Christian life. To himself also it seemed as if Heaven had lifted the heavy burden from his heart.

His favorite pastime was to mount now and then upon the mighty marble church, which seemed to him to have been formed of the snow of his native land, fashioned into roofs, and pinnacles, and decorated open halls : from every corner and every point the white statues smiled upon him. Above him was the blue sky, below him the city and the wide-spreading Lombard plains, and towards the north the high mountains clad with perpetual snow; and he thought of the church of Kjöge, with its red, ivy-covered walls, but he did not long to go thither : here, beyond the mountains, he would be buried.

He had dwelt here a year, and three years had passed away since he left his home, when one day his master took him into the city, not to the circus where riders exhibited, but to the opera, where was a hall worth seeing. There were seven stories, from each of which beautiful silken curtains hung down, and from the ground to the dizzy height of the roof sat elegant ladies, with bouquets of flowers in their hands, as if they were at a ball, and the gentlemen were in full dress, and many of them decorated with gold and silver. It was as bright there as in the brilliant sunshine, and the music rolled gloriously through the building. Every thing was much more splendid than in the theatre at Copenhagen, but then Joanna had been there, and—could it be ! Yes, it was like magic—she was here also ! for the curtain rose, and Joanna appeared, dressed in silk and gold, with a crown upon her head : she sang as he thought none but angels could sing, and came far forward, quite to the front of the stage, and smiled as only Joanna could smile, and looked straight down at Knud. Poor Knud seized his master's hand and called out aloud, "Joanna !" but no one heard but the master, who nodded his head, for the loud music sounded above every thing. "Yes, yes, her name is

Joanna !" said the master, and he drew forth a printed play-bill, and showed Knud her name—for the full name was printed there.

No, it was not a dream ! All the people applauded, and threw wreaths and flowers to her, and every time she went away they called her back, so that she was always going and coming.

In the street the people crowded round her carriage, and drew it away in triumph. Knud was in the foremost row, and shouted as joyously as any; and when the carriage stopped before her brilliantly lighted house, Knud stood close beside the door of the carriage. It flew open, and she stepped out : the light fell upon her dear face, as she smiled, and made a kindly gesture of thanks, and appeared deeply moved. Knud looked straight into her face, and she looked into his, but she did not know him. A man with a star glittering on his breast gave her his arm—and it was whispered about that the two were engaged.

Then Knud went home and packed his knapsack. He was determined to go back to his own home, to the elder and the willow-tree—ah, under the willow-tree ! A whole life is sometimes lived through in a single hour.

The old couple begged him to remain, but no words could induce him to stay. It was in vain they told him that winter was coming, and pointed out that snow had already fallen in the mountains; he said he could march on, with his knapsack on his back, in the wake of the slow-moving carriage, for which they would have to clear a path.

So he went away towards the mountains, and marched up them and down them. His strength was giving way, but still he saw no village, no house; he marched on towards the north. The stars gleamed above him, his feet stumbled, and his head grew dizzy. Deep in the valley stars were shining too, and it seemed as if there were another sky below him. He felt he was ill. The stars below him became more and more numerous, and glowed brighter and brighter, and moved to and fro. It was a little town whose lights beamed there; and when he understood that, he exerted the remains of his strength, and at last reached the shelter of an humble inn.

That night and the whole of the following day he remained there, for his body required rest and refreshment. It was thawing; there was rain in the valley. But early on the second morning came a man with an organ, who played a tune of home; and now Knud could stay no longer. He continued his journey towards the north, marching onward for many days with haste and hurry, as if he were trying to get home before all were dead there; but to no one did he speak of his longing, for no one would have believed in the sorrow of his heart, the deepest a human heart can feel. Such a grief is not for the world, for it is not amusing; nor is it even for friends; and, moreover, he had no friends—a stranger, he wandered through strange lands towards his home in the north.

It was evening. He was walking on the public highroad. The frost began to make itself felt, and the country soon became flatter, containing more field and meadow. By the road-side grew a great willow-tree. Every thing reminded him of home, and he sat down under the tree; he felt very tired, his head began to nod, and his eyes closed in slumber, but still he was conscious that the tree stretched its arms above him; and in his wandering fancy the tree itself appeared to be an old, mighty man—it seemed as if the "Willow-father" himself had taken up his tired son in his arms, and were carrying him back into the land of home, to the bare bleak shore of Kjöge, to the garden of his child hood. Yes, he dreamed it was the willow-tree of Kjöge that had travelled out into the world to seek him, and that now had found him, and had led him back into the little garden by the streamlet; and there stood Joanna, in all her splendor, with the golden crown on her head, as he had seen her last, and she called out "welcome" to him.

And before him stood two remarkable shapes, which looked much more human than he remembered them to have been in his childhood: they had changed also, but they were still the two cakes that turned the right side towards him, and looked very well.

"We thank you," they said to Knud. "You have loosened our tongues, and have taught us that thoughts should be spoken out freely, or nothing will come of them; and now something has indeed come of it—we are betrothed."

Then they went hand in hand through the streets of Kjöge, and they looked very respectable in every way; there was no fault to find with *them*. And they went on, straight towards the church, and Knud and Joanna followed them; they also were walking hand in hand; and the church stood there as it had always stood, with its red walls, on which the green ivy grew; and the great door of the church flew open, and the organ sounded, and they walked up the long aisle of the church. "Our master first," said the cake-couple, and made room for Joanna and Knud, who knelt by the altar, and she bent her head over him, and tears fell from her eyes, but they were icy cold, for it was the ice around her heart that was melting—melting by his strong love; and the tears fell upon his burning cheeks, and he awoke, and was sitting under the old willow-tree in the strange land, in the cold wintry evening: an icy hail was falling from the clouds and beating on his face.

"That was the most delicious hour of my life!" he said,

"and it was but a dream. Oh, let me dream again !" And
he closed his eyes once more, and slept and dreamed.

Towards morning there was a great fall of snow. The
wind drifted the snow over him, but he slept on. The vil-
lagers came forth to go to church, and by the road-side sat
a journeyman. He was dead—frozen to death under the
willow-tree !

THE BEETLE.

The emperor's favorite horse was shod with gold. It
had a golden shoe on each of its feet.

And why was this ?

He was a beautiful creature, with delicate legs, bright
intelligent eyes, and a mane that hung down over his neck
like a veil. He had carried his master through the fire and
smoke of battle, and heard the bullets whistling around
him, had kicked, bitten, and taken part in the fight when
the enemy advanced, and had sprung with his master on
his back over the fallen foe, and had saved the crown of red
gold, and the life of the emperor, which was more valuable
than the red gold ; and that is why the emperor's horse
had golden shoes.

And a beetle came creeping forth.

"First the great ones," said he, "and then the little ones;
but greatness is not the only thing that does it." And so
saying, he stretched out his thin legs.

"And pray what do you want ?" asked the smith.

"Golden shoes, to be sure," replied the beetle.

"Why, you must be out of your senses," cried the smith
"Do you want to have golden shoes too ?"

"Golden shoes? certainly," replied the beetle. "Am I not just as good as that big creature yonder, that is waited on, and brushed, and has meat and drink put before him? Don't I belong to the imperial stable?"

"But *why* is the horse to have golden shoes? Don't you understand that?" asked the smith.

"Understand? I understand that it is a personal slight offered to myself," cried the beetle. "It is done to annoy me, and therefore I am going into the world to seek my fortune."

"Go along!" said the smith.

"You're a rude fellow!" cried the beetle; and then he went out of the stable, flew a little way, and soon afterwards found himself in a beautiful flower-garden, all fragrant with roses and lavender.

"Is it not beautiful here?" asked one of the little lady-birds that flew about with their delicate wings and their red-and-black shields on their backs. "How sweet it is here—how beautiful it is!"

"I'm accustomed to better things," said the beetle. "Do you call *this* beautiful? Why, there is not so much as a dung-heap."

Then he went on, under the shadow of a great stack, and found a caterpillar crawling along.

"How beautiful the world is!" said the caterpillar: "the sun is so warm, and every thing so enjoyable! And when I go to sleep, and die, as they call it, I shall wake up as a butterfly, with beautiful wings to fly with."

"How conceited you are!" exclaimed the stag-beetle. "Fly about as a butterfly, indeed! I've come out of the stable of the emperor, and no one there, not even the emperor's favorite horse—that, by the way, wears my cast-off golden shoes—has any such idea. To have wings to fly! why, we can fly now ;" and he spread his wings and flew away. "I don't want to be annoyed, and yet I am annoyed," he said, as he flew off.

Soon afterwards he fell down upon a great lawn. For awhile he lay there and feigned slumber ; at last he fell asleep in earnest.

Suddenly a heavy shower of rain came falling from the clouds. The beetle woke up at the noise, and wanted to escape into the earth, but could not. He was tumbled over and over ; sometimes he was swimming on his stomach, sometimes on his back, and as for flying, that was out of the question ; he doubted whether he should escape from the place with his life. He therefore remained lying where he was.

When the weather had moderated a little, and the beetle had rubbed the water out of his eyes, he saw something gleaming. It was linen that had been placed there to bleach. He managed to make his way up to it, and crept into a fold of the damp linen. Certainly the place was not so comfortable to lie in as the warm stable ; but there was no better to be had, and therefore he remained lying there for a whole day and a whole night, and the rain kept on during all the time. Towards morning he crept forth : he was very much out of temper about the climate.

On the linen two frogs were sitting. Their bright eyes absolutely gleamed with pleasure.

"Wonderful weather this !" one of them cried. "How refreshing ! And the linen keeps the water together so beautifully. My hind legs seem to quiver as if I were going to swim."

"I should like to know," said the second, "if the swallow, who flies so far round in her many journeys in foreign lands, ever meets with a better climate than this. What delicious dampness ! It is really as if one were lying in a wet ditch. Whoever does not rejoice in this, certainly does not love his fatherland."

" Have you been in the emperor's stable ?" asked the beetle. " There the dampness is warm and refreshing That's the climate for me ; but I cannot take it with me on my journey. Is there never a muck-heap, here in the garden, where a person of rank, like myself, can feel himself at home, and take up his quarters ?"

But the frogs either did not or would not understand him.

" I never ask a question twice !" said the beetle, after he had already asked this one three times without receiving an answer.

Then he went a little further, and stumbled against a fragment of pottery, that certainly ought not to have been lying there ; but as it was once there, it gave a good shelter against wind and weather. Here dwelt several families of earwigs ; and these did not require much, only sociality. The female members of the community were full of the purest maternal affection, and accordingly each one considered her own child the most beautiful and cleverest of all.

" Our son has engaged himself," said one mother. "Dear, innocent boy ! His greatest hope is that he may creep one day into a clergyman's ear. It's very artless and lovable, that ; and being engaged will keep him steady. What joy for a mother !"

" Our son," said another mother, " had scarcely crept out out of the egg, when he was already off on his travels. He's all life and spirits ; he'll run his horns off ! What joy is that for a mother ! Is it not so, Mr. Beetle ?" for she knew the stranger by his horny coat.

"You are both quite right," said he ; so they begged him to walk in ; that is to say, to come as far as he could under the bit of pottery.

"Now, you also see *my* little earwig," observed a third mother and a fourth; "they are lovely little things, and highly amusing. They are never ill-behaved, except when they are uncomfortable in their inside ; but, unfortunately, one is very subject to that at their age."

Thus each mother spoke of her baby ; and the babies talked among themselves, and made use of the little nippers they have in their tails to nip the beard of the beetle.

"Yes, they are always busy about something, the little rogues !" said the mothers ; and they quite beamed with maternal pride ; but the beetle felt bored by that, and therefore he inquired how far it was to the nearest muck-heap.

"That's quite out in the big world, on the other side of the ditch," answered an earwig. "I hope none of my children will go so far, for it would be the death of me."

"But I shall try to go so far," said the beetle ; and he went off without taking formal leave; for that is considered the polite thing to do. And by the ditch he met several friends—beetles, all of them.

"Here we live," they said. "We are very comfortable here. Might we ask you to step down into this rich mud ? You must be fatigued after your journey."

"Certainly," replied the beetle. "I have been exposed to the rain, and have had to lie upon linen, and cleanliness is a thing that greatly exhausts me. I have also pains in one of my wings, from standing in a draught under a fragment of pottery. It is really quite refreshing to be among one's companions once more."

"Perhaps you come from some muck-heap ?" observed the oldest of them.

"Indeed, I come from a much higher place," replied the beetle. "I come from the emperor's stable, where I was born with golden shoes on my feet. I am travelling on a secret embassy. You must not ask me any questions, for I can't betray my secret."

With this the beetle stepped down into the rich mud. There sat three young maiden beetles; and they tittered, because they did not know what to say.

"Not one of them is engaged yet," said their mother; and the beetle maidens tittered again, this time from embarrassment.

"I have never seen greater beauties in the royal stables," exclaimed the beetle, who was now resting himself.

"Don't spoil my girls," said the mother; "and don't talk to them, please, unless you have serious intentions. But of course your intentions are serious, and therefore I give you my blessing."

"Hurrah!" cried all the other beetles together; and our friend was engaged. Immediately after the betrothal came the marriage, for there was no reason for delay.

The following day passed very pleasantly, and the next in tolerable comfort; but on the third it was time to think of food for the wife, and perhaps also for children.

"I have allowed myself to be taken in," said the beetle to himself. "And now there's nothing for it but to take *them* in, in turn."

So said, so done. Away he went, and he stayed away all day. and stayed away all night; and his wife sat there a forsaken widow.

"Oh," said the other beetles, "this fellow whom we received into our family is nothing more than a thorough vagabond. He has gone away, and has left his wife a burden upon our hands."

"Well, then, she shall be unmarried again, and sit here among my daughters," said the mother. "Fie on the villain who forsook her!"

In the mean time the beetle had been journeying on, and had sailed across the ditch on a cabbage-leaf. In the morning two persons came to the ditch. When they saw him, they took him up, and turned him over, looked very learned, especially one of them—a boy.

"Allah sees the black beetle in the black stone and in the black rock. Is not that written in the Koran?" Then he translated the beetle's name into Latin, and enlarged upon the creature's nature and history. The second person, an older scholar, voted for carrying him home. He said they wanted just such good specimens; and this seemed an uncivil speech to our beetle, and in consequence he flew suddenly out of the speaker's hand. As he had now dry wings, he flew a tolerable distance, and reached a hotbed, where a sash of the glass roof was partially open, so he quietly slipped in and buried himself in the warm earth.

"Very comfortable it is here," said he.

Soon after he went to sleep, and dreamed that the emperor's favorite horse had fallen, and had given him his golden shoes, with the promise that he should have two more.

That was all very charming. When the beetle woke up, he crept forth and looked around him. What splendor was in the hothouse! In the background great palm-trees growing up on high; the sun made them look transparent; and beneath them what a luxuriance of green, and of beaming flowers, red as fire, yellow as amber, or white as fresh-fallen snow!

"This is an incomparable plenty of plants," cried the beetle. "How good they will taste when they are decayed!

A capital storeroom this! There must certainly be relations of mine living here. I will just see if I can find any one with whom I may associate. I am proud, certainly, and I am proud of being so." And so he prowled about in the earth, and thought what a pleasant dream that was about the dying horse, and the golden shoes he had inherited.

Suddenly a hand seized the beetle, and pressed him, and turned him round and round.

The gardener's little son and a companion had come to the hotbed, had espied the beetle, and wanted to have their fun with him. First he was wrapped in a vine-leaf, and then put into warm trowsers-pocket. He cribbled and crabbled about there with all his might; but he got a good pressing from the boy's hand for this, which served as a hint to him to keep quiet. Then the boy went rapidly towards the great lake that lay at the end of the garden. Here the beetle was put in an old broken wooden shoe, on which a little stick was placed upright for a mast, and to this mast the beetle was bound with a woollen-thread. Now he was a sailor, and had to sail away.

The lake was not very large, but to the beetle it seemed an ocean; and he was so astonished at its extent, that he fell over on his back and kicked out with his legs.

The little ship sailed away. The current of the water seized it; but whenever it went too far from the shore, one of the boys turned up his trowsers and went in after it, and brought it back to the land. But at length, just as it went merrily out again, the two boys were called away, and very harshly, so that they hurried to obey the summons, ran away from the lake, and left the little ship to its fate. Thus it drove away from the shore, further and further into the open sea: it was terrible work for the beetle, for he could not get away in consequence of being bound to the mast.

Then a fly came and paid him a visit.

"What beautiful weather!" said the fly. "I'll rest here, and sun myself. You have an agreeable time of it."

"You speak without knowing the facts," replied the beetle. "Don't you see that I'm a prisoner."

"Ah! but I'm not a prisoner," observed the fly; and he flew away accordingly.

"Well, now I know the world," said the beetle to himself. "It is an abominable world. I'm the only honest person in it. First, they refuse me my golden shoes; then I have to lie on wet linen, and to stand in the draught; and, to crown all, they fasten a wife upon me. Then when I've taken a quick step out into the world, and found out how one can have it there, and how I wished to have it, one of those human boys comes and ties me up, and leaves me to the mercy of the wild waves, while the emperor's favorite horse prances about proudly in golden shoes. That is what annoys me more than all. But one must not look for sympathy in this world! My career has been very interesting; but what's the use of that, if nobody knows it? The world does not deserve to be made acquainted with my history, for it ought to have given me golden shoes when the emperor's horse was shod, and I stretched out my feet to be shod too. If I had received golden shoes, I should have become an ornament to the stable. Now the stable has lost me, and the world has lost me. It is all over!"

But all was not over yet. A boat, in which there were a few young girls, came rowing up.

"Look, yonder is an old wooden shoe sailing along," said one of the girls.

"There's a little creature bound fast to it," said another.

The boat came quite close to our beetle's ship, and the young girls fished him out of the water. One of them drew a small pair of scissors from her pocket, and cut the woollen thread, without hurting the beetle ; and when she stepped on shore, she put him down on the grass.

"Creep, creep—fly, fly—if thou canst," she said. "Liberty is a splendid thing."

And the beetle flew up, and straight through the open window of a great building; there he sank down, tired and exhausted, exactly on the mane of the emperor's favorite horse, who stood in the stable when he was at home, and the beetle also. The beetle clung fast to the mane, and sat there a short time to recover himself.

"Here I'm sitting on the emperor's favorite horse—sitting on him just like the emperor himself !" he cried. "But what was I saying ? Yes, now I remember. That's a good thought, and quite correct. The smith asked me why the golden shoes were given to the horse. Now I'm quite clear about the answer. They were given to the horse on *my* account."

And now the beetle was in a good temper again.

"Travelling expands the mind rarely," said he.

The sun's rays came streaming into the stable, and shone upon him, and made the place lively and bright.

"The world is not so bad upon the whole," said the beetle ; "but one must know how to take things as they come."

WHAT THE OLD MAN DOES IS ALWAYS RIGHT.

I WILL tell you a story which was told to me when I was a little boy. Every time I thought of the story, it seemed to me to become more and more charming; for it is with stories as with many people—they become better as they grow older.

I take it for granted that you have been in the country, and seen a very old farmhouse with a thatched roof, and mosses and small plants growing wild upon the thatch. There is a stork's nest on the summit of the gable; for we can't do without the stork. The walls of the house are sloping, and the windows are low, and only one of the latter is made so that it will open. The baking-oven sticks out of the wall like a little fat body. The elder-tree hangs over the paling, and beneath its branches, at the foot of the paling, is a pool of water in which a few ducks are disporting themselves. There is a yard-dog, too, who barks at all comers.

Just such a farmhouse stood out in the country ; and in this house dwelt an old couple—a peasant and his wife. Small as was their property, there was one article among it that they could do without—a horse, which made a living out of the grass it found by the side of the high-road. The old peasant rode into the town on this horse ; and often his neighbors borrowed it from him, and rendered the old couple some service in return for the loan of it. But they thought it would be best if they sold the horse, or exchanged it for something that might be more useful to them. But what might this *something* be ?

" You'll know that best, old man," said the wife. " It is fair-day to-day, so ride into town, and get rid of the horse for money, or make a good exchange: whichever you do will be right to me. Ride to the fair."

And she fastened his neckerchief for him, for she could do that better than he could; and she tied it in a double bow, for she could do that very prettily. Then she brushed his hat round and round with the palm of her hand, and gave him a kiss. So he rode away upon the horse that was to be sold or to be bartered for something else. Yes, the old man knew what he was about.

The sun shone hotly down, not a cloud was to be seen in the sky. The road was very dusty, for many people who were all bound for the fair were driving, or riding, or walking upon it. There was no shelter anywhere from the sunbeams.

Among the rest, was a man trudging along, and driving a cow to the fair. The cow was as beautiful a creature as any cow can be.

"She gives good milk, I'm sure," said the peasant. "That would be a very good exchange—the cow for the horse."

"Hallo, you there with the cow!" he said; "I'll tell you what—I fancy a horse costs more than a cow, but don't care for that; a cow would be more useful to me. If you like, we'll exchange."

"To be sure I will," said the man; and they exchanged accordingly.

So that was settled, and the peasant might have turned back, for he had done the business he came to do; but as he had once made up his mind to go to the fair, he determined to proceed, merely to have a look at it; so he went on to the town with his cow.

Leading the animal, he strode sturdily on; and after a time he overtook a man who was driving a sheep. It was a good fat sheep, with a fine fleece on its back.

"I should like to have that fellow," said our peasant to himself. "He would find plenty of grass by our palings, and in the winter we could keep him in the room with us. Perhaps it would be more practical to have a sheep instead of a cow. Shall we exchange?"

The man with the sheep was quite ready, and the bargain was struck. So the peasant went on in the high-road with his sheep.

Soon he overtook another man, who came into the road from a field, carrying a great goose under his arm.

"That's a heavy thing you have there. It has plenty of feathers and plenty of fat, and would look well tied to a string, and paddling in the water at our place. That would be something for my old woman; she could make all kinds of profit out of it. How often she has said, 'If we only had a goose!' Now, perhaps, she can have one; and, if possible, it shall be hers. Shall we exchange? I'll give you my sheep for your goose, and thank you into the bargain."

The other man had not the least objection; and accordingly they exchanged, and our peasant became proprietor of the goose.

By this time he was very near the town. The crowd on the high-road became greater and greater; there was quite a crush of men and cattle. They walked in the road, and close by the palings; and at the barrier they even walked into the toll-man's potato-field, where his one fowl was strutting about, with a string to its leg, lest it should take fright at the crowd, and stray away, and so be lost. This fowl had short tail-feathers, and winked with both its eyes, and looked very cunning. "Cluck, cluck!" said the fowl. What it thought when it said this I cannot tell you; but directly our good man saw it, he thought, "That's the finest fowl I've ever seen in my life ! Why, it's finer than our parson's brood hen. On my word, I should like to have that fowl. A fowl can always find a grain or two, and can almost keep itself. I think it would be a good exchange if I could get that for my goose."

"Shall we exchange ?" he asked the toll-taker.

"Exchange !" repeated the man; "well, that would not be a bad thing."

And so they exchanged; the toll-taker at the barrier kept the goose, and the peasant carried away the fowl.

Now, he had done a good deal of business on his way to the fair, and he was hot and tired. He wanted something to eat, and a glass of brandy to drink; and soon he was in front of the inn. He was just about to step in when the hostler came out, so they met at the door. The hostler was carrying a sack.

"What have you in that sack ?" asked the peasant.

"Rotten apples," answered the hostler; "a whole sackful of them—enough to feed the pigs with."

"Why, that's terrible waste ! I should like to take them to my old woman at home. Last year the old tree by the turf-hole only bore a single apple, and we kept it on the cupboard till it was quite rotten and spoilt. 'It was always property,' my old woman said; but here she could see a quantity of property—a whole sackful. Yes, I shall be glad to show them to her."

"What will you give me for the sackful ?" asked the hostler.

"What will I give? I will give my fowl in exchange."

And he gave the fowl accordingly, and received the apples, which he carried into the guest-room. He leaned the sack carefully by the stove, and then went to the table. But the stove was hot : he had not thought of that. Many guests were present—horse-dealers, ox-herds, and two Englishmen—and the two Englishmen were so rich that their pockets bulged out with gold coins, and almost burst; and they could bet too, as you shall hear.

Hiss-s-s! hiss-s-s! What was that by the stove? The apples were beginning to roast!

"What is that?"

"Why, do you know—," said our peasant.

And he told the whole story of the horse that he had changed for a cow, and all the rest of it, down to the apples.

"Well, your old woman will give it you well when you get home!" said one of the two Englishmen. "There will be a disturbance."

"What?—give me what?" said the peasant. "She will kiss me, and say, 'What the old man does is always right.'"

"Shall we wager?" said the Englishman. "We'll wager coined gold by the ton—a hundred pounds to the hundred-weight!"

"A bushel will be enough," replied the peasant. "I can only set the bushel of apples against it; and I'll throw my-self and my old woman into the bargain—and I fancy that's piling up the measure."

"Done—taken!"

And the bet was made. The host's carriage came up, and the Englishmen got in, and the peasant got in; away they went, and soon they stopped before the peasant's hut.

"Good-evening, old woman."

"Good-evening, old man."

"I've made the exchange."

"Yes, you understand what you're about," said the woman.

And she embraced him, and paid no attention to the stranger guests, nor did she notice the sack.

"I got a cow in exchange for the horse," said he.

"Heaven be thanked!" said she. "What glorious milk we shall have, and butter and cheese on the table! That was a capital exchange!"

"Yes, but I changed the cow for a sheep."

"Ah, that's better still!" cried the wife. "You always think of every thing: we have just pasture enough for a sheep. Ewe's-milk and cheese, and woollen jackets and stockings! The cow cannot give those, and her hairs will only come off. How you think of every thing!"

"But I changed away the sheep for a goose."

"Then this year we shall really have roast goose to eat, my dear old man. You are always thinking of something to give me pleasure. How charming that is! We can let the goose walk about with a string to her leg, and she'll grow fatter still before we roast her."

"But I gave away the goose for a fowl," said the man.

"A fowl? That was a good exchange!" replied the woman. "The fowl will lay eggs and hatch them, and we shall have chickens: we shall have a whole poultry-yard! Oh, that's just what I was wishing for."

"Yes, but I exchanged the fowl for a sack of shrivelled apples."

"What!—I must positively kiss you for that," exclaimed the wife. My dear, good husband! Now, I'll tell you something. Do you know, you had hardly left me this morning, before I began thinking how I could give you something very nice this evening. I thought it should be pancakes with savory herbs. I had eggs, and bacon too; but I wanted herbs. So I went over to the schoolmaster's —they have herbs there, I know—but the schoolmistress is a mean woman, though she looks so sweet. I begged her to lend me a handful of herbs. 'Lend!' she answered me;

WALDEMAR DAA AND HIS DAUGHTERS.

'nothing at all grows in our garden, not even a shrivelled apple. I could not even lend you a shrivelled apple, my dear woman.' But now *I* can lend *her* ten, or a whole sackful. That I'm very glad of; that makes me laugh !" And with that she gave him a sounding kiss.

"I like that !" exclaimed both the Englishmen together " Always going down-hill, and always merry; that's worth the money." So they paid a hundred-weight of gold to the peasant, who was not scolded, but kissed.

Yes, it always pays, when the wife sees and always asserts that her husband knows best, and that whatever he does is right.

You see, that is my story. I heard it when I was a child ; and now you have heard it too, and know that " What the old man does is always right."

— ——— ◆◆◆ ———

THE WIND TELLS ABOUT WALDEMAR DAA AND HIS DAUGHTERS.

WHEN the wind sweeps across the grass the field has a ripple like a pond ; and when it sweeps across the corn the field waves to and fro like a high sea. That is called the wind's dance; but the wind does not dance only, he also tells stories; and how loudly he can sing out of his deep chest, and how different it sounds in the tree-tops in the forest, and through the loopholes and clefts and cracks in walls ! Do you see how the wind drives the clouds up yonder, like a frightened flock of sheep? Do you hear how the wind howls down here through the open valley, like a watchman blowing his horn? With wonderful tones he whistles and screams down the chimney and into the fire-place. The fire crackles and flares up, and shines far into the room, and the little place is warm and snug, and it is pleasant to sit there listening to the sounds. Let the wind speak, for he knows plenty of stories and fairy tales, many more than are known to any of us. Just hear what the wind can tell.

Huh—uh—ush! roar along! That is the burden of the song.

"By the shores of the Great Belt, one of the straits that unite the Cattegat with the Baltic, lies an old mansion with thick red walls," says the Wind. "I know every stone in it; I saw it when it still belonged to the castle of Marsk Stig on the promontory. But it had to be pulled down, and the stone was used again for the walls of a new mansion in another place, the baronial mansion of Borreby, which still stands by the coast.

"I knew them, the noble lords and ladies, the changing races that dwelt there, and now I'm going to tell about Waldemar Daa and his daughters. How proudly he carried himself—he was of royal blood! He could do more than merely hunt the stag and empty the wine-can. 'It *shall* be done,' he was accustomed to say.

"His wife walked proudly in gold-embroidered garments over the polished marble floors. The tapestries were gorgeous, the furniture was expensive and artistically carved. She had brought gold and silver plate with her into the house, and there was German beer in the cellar. Black fiery horses neighed in the stables. There was a wealthy look about the house of Borreby at that time, when wealth was still at home there.

"Four children dwelt there also ; three delicate maidens, Ida, Joanna, and Anna Dorothea : I have never forgotten their names.

"They were rich people, noble people, born in affluence, nurtured in affluence.

"Huh—sh ! roar along !" sang the Wind; and then he continued :

"I did not see here, as in other great noble houses, the high-born lady sitting among her women in the great hall turning the spinning-wheel : here she swept the sounding chords of the cithern, and sang to the sound, but not always old Danish melodies, but songs of a strange land. It was 'live and let live' here ; stranger guests came from far and near, the music sounded, the goblets clashed, and I was not able to drown the noise," said the Wind. "Ostentation, and haughtiness, and splendor, and display, and rule were there, but the fear of the Lord was not there.

"And it was just on the evening of the first day of May," the Wind continued. "I came from the west, and had seen how the ships were being crushed by the waves, with all on board, and flung on the west coast of Jutland. I had hurried across the heath, and over Jutland's wood-girt eastern coast, and over the Island of Fünen, and now I drove over the Great Belt, groaning and sighing.

"Then I lay down to rest on the shore of Seeland, in the neighborhood of the great house of Borreby, where the forest, the splendid oak forest, still rose.

"The young men-servants of the neighborhood were collecting branches and brushwood under the oak-trees ; the largest and driest they could find they carried into the village, and piled them up in a heap, and set them on fire ; and men and maids danced, singing in a circle round the blazing pile.

"I lay quite quiet," continued the Wind ; "but I silently touched a branch, which had been brought by the handsomest of the men-servants, and the wood blazed up brightly, blazed up higher than all the rest ; and now he was the chosen one, and bore the name of the Street-goat, and might choose his Street-lamb first from among the maids ; and there was mirth and rejoicing, greater than I ever heard before in the halls of the rich baronial mansion.

"And the noble lady drove towards the baronial mansion, with her three daughters, in a gilded carriage, drawn by six horses. The daughters were young and fair, three charming blossoms—rose, lily, and pale hyacinth. The mother was a proud tulip, and never acknowledged the salutation of one of the men or maids who paused in their sport to do her honor : the gracious lady seemed a flower that was rather stiff in the stalk.

"Rose, lily, and pale hyacinth ; yes, I saw them all three ! Whose lambkins will they one day become? thought I ; their Street-goat will be a gallant knight, perhaps a prince. Huh—sh ! hurry along ! hurry along !

"Yes, the carriage rolled on with them, and the peasant people resumed their dancing. They rode that summer through all the villages round about. But in the night, when I rose again," said the Wind, " the very noble lady lay down, to rise again no more : that thing came upon her which comes upon all—there is nothing new in that.

"Waldemar Daa stood for a space silent and thoughtful 'The proudest tree can be bowed without being broken,' said a voice within him. His daughters wept, and all the people in the mansion wiped their eyes ; but Lady Daa had driven away—and I drove away, too, and rushed along, huh—sh !" said the Wind.

"I returned again ; I often returned again over the Island of Fünen, and the shores of the Belt, and I sat down by Borreby, by the splendid oak wood ; there the heron made his nest, and wood-pigeons haunted the place, and blue ravens, and even the black stork. It was still spring ; some of them were yet sitting on their eggs, others had already hatched their young. But how they flew up, how they cried ! The axe sounded, blow on blow : the wood was to be felled. Waldemar Daa wanted to build a noble ship, a man-of-war, a three-decker, which the king would be sure to buy ; and therefore the wood must be felled, the landmark of the seamen, the refuge of the birds. The hawk started up and flew away, for its nest was de-stroyed ; the heron and all the birds of the forest became homeless, and flew about in fear and in anger : I could well understand how they felt. Crows and ravens croaked aloud as if in scorn. 'Crack, crack ! the nest cracks, cracks, cracks !'

"Far in the interior of the wood, where the noisy swarm of laborers were working, stood Waldemar Daa and his three daughters ; and all laughed at the wild cries of the birds ; only one, the youngest, Anna Dorothea, felt grieved in her heart ; and when they made preparations to fell a tree that was almost dead, and on whose naked branches the black stork had built his nest, whence the little storks were stretching out their heads, she begged for mercy for the little things, and tears came into her eyes. Therefore the tree with the black stork's nest was left standing. The tree was not worth speaking of.

"There was a great hewing and sawing, and a three-decker was built. The architect was of low origin, but of great pride ; his eyes and forehead told how clever he was, and Waldemar Daa was fond of listening to him, and so was Waldemar's daughter Ida, the eldest, who was now fifteen years old ; and while he built a ship for the father, he was building for himself an airy castle, into which he and Ida were to go as a married couple—which might, indeed, have happened, if the castle with stone walls, and ramparts, and moats had remained. But in spite of his wise head, the architect remained but a poor bird ; and, indeed, what business has a sparrow to take part in a dance of peacocks? Huh—sh ! I careered away, and he careered away, too, for he was not allowed to stay ; and little Ida got over it, because she was obliged to get over it.

"The proud, black horses were neighing in the stable ; they were worth looking at, and accordingly they *were* looked at. The admiral, who had been sent by the king himself to inspect the new ship and take measures for its purchase, spoke loudly in admiration of the beautiful horses.

"I heard all that," said the Wind. "I accompanied the gentlemen through the open door, and strewed blades of straw like bars of gold before their feet. Waldemar Daa wanted to have gold, and the admiral wished for the proud, black horses, and that is why he praised them so much ; but the hint was not taken, and consequently the ship was not bought. It remained on the shore, covered over with boards, a Noah's ark that never got to the water—Huh—sh ! rush away ! away !—and that was a pity.

"In the winter, when the fields were covered with snow, and the water with large blocks of ice that I blew up on to the coast," continued the Wind, "crows and ravens came, all as black as might be, great flocks of them, and alighted on the dead, deserted, lonely ship by the shore, and croaked in hoarse accents of the wood that was no more, of the many pretty birds' nests destroyed, and the little ones left without a home ; and all for the sake of that great bit of lumber, that proud ship that never sailed forth.

"I made the snow-flakes whirl, and the snow lay like a

great lake high around the ship, and drifted over it. I let it hear my voice, that it might know what a storm has to say. Certainly I did my part towards teaching it seaman-ship. Huh—sh! push along.

"And the winter passed away; winter and summer both passed away, and they are still passing away, even as I pass away; as the snow whirls along, and the apple blos-som whirls along, and the leaves fall—away! away! away! and men are passing away, too!

"But the daughters were still young, and little Ida was a rose, as fair to look upon as on the day when the archi-tect saw her. I often seized her long, brown hair, when she stood in the garden by the apple-tree, musing, and not heeding how I strewed blossoms on her hair, and loosened it, while she was gazing at the red sun and the golden sky, through the dark underwood and the trees of the garden.

"Her sister was bright and slender as a lily. Joanna had height and deportment, but was like her mother, rather stiff in the stalk. She was very fond of walking through the great hall, where hung the portraits of her ancestors. The women were painted in dresses of silk and velvet, with a tiny little hat, embroidered with pearls, on their plaited hair. They were handsome women. The gentlemen were represented clad in steel, or in costly cloaks lined with squirrel's skin; they wore little ruffs, and swords at their sides, but not buckled to their hips. Where would Joanna's picture find its place on that wall some day? and how would he look, her noble lord and husband? This is what she thought of, and of this she spoke softly to herself. I heard it, as I swept into the long hall, and turned round to come out again.

"Anna Dorothea, the pale hyacinth, a child of fourteen, was quiet and thoughtful; her great deep blue eyes had a musing look, but the childlike smile still played around her lips; I was not able to blow it away, nor did I wish to do so

"We met in the garden, in the hollow lane, in the field and meadow; she gathered herbs and flowers which she knew would be useful to her father in concocting the drinks and drops he distilled. Waldemar Daa was arrogant and proud, but he was also a learned man, and knew a great deal. That was no secret, and many opinions were expressed concerning it. In his chimney there was fire even in summer-time. He would lock the door of his room, and for days the fire would be poked and raked; but of this he did not talk much—the forces of nature must be conquered in silence; and soon he would discover the art of making the best thing of all—the red gold.

"That is why the chimney was always smoking, therefore the flames crackled so frequently. Yes, I was there, too," said the Wind. "Let it go," I sang down through the chimney: "it will end in smoke, air, coals, and ashes! You will burn yourself! Hu-uh-ush! drive away! drive away! But Waldemar Daa did *not* drive it away."

"The splendid black horses in the stable—what became of them? What became of the old gold and silver vessels in cupboards and chests, the cows in the fields, and the house and home itself? Yes, they may melt, may melt in the golden crucible, and yet yield no gold.

"Empty grew the barns and store-rooms, the cellars and magazines. The servants decreased in number, and the mice multiplied. Then a window broke, and then another, and I could get in elsewhere besides at the door," said the Wind. "'Where the chimney smokes, the meal is being cooked,' the proverb says. But here the chimney smoked that devoured all the meals, for the sake of the red gold.

"I blew through the court-yard gate like a watchman

blowing his horn," the Wind went on, "but no watchman was there. I twirled the weathercock round on the summit of the tower, and it creaked like the snoring of the warder, but no warder was there ; only mice and rats were there Poverty laid the tablecloth ; poverty sat in the wardrobe and in the larder ; the door fell off its hinges, cracks and fissures made their appearance, and I went in and out at pleasure ; and that is how I know all about it.

"Amid smoke and ashes, amid sorrow and sleepless nights, the hair and beard of the master turned gray, and deep furrows showed themselves around his temples ; his skin turned pale and yellow, as his eyes looked greedily for the gold, the desired gold.

"I blew the smoke and ashes into his face and beard : the result of his labor was debt instead of pelf. I sung through the burst window-panes and the yawning clefts in the walls. I blew into the chests of drawers belonging to the daughters, wherein lay the clothes that had become faded and threadbare from being worn over and over again. That was not the song that had been sung at the children's cradle. The lordly life had changed to a life of penury. I was the only one who rejoiced aloud in that castle," said the Wind. "I snowed them up, and they say snow keeps people warm. They had no wood, and the forest from which they might have brought it was cut down. It was a biting frost. I rushed in through loopholes and passages, over gables and roofs, that I might be brisk. They were lying in bed because of the cold, the three high-born daughters ; and their father was crouching under his leathern coverlet. Nothing to bite, nothing to break, no fire on the hearth—there was a life for high-born people ! Hub-sh, let it go ! But that is what my Lord Daa could *not* do--he could *not* let it go.

"'After winter comes spring,' he said. 'After want, good times will come : one must not lose patience ; one must learn to wait ! Now my house and lands are mortgaged, it is indeed high time ; and the gold will soon come. At Easter !'

"I heard how he spoke thus, looking at a spider's web. 'Thou cunning little weaver, thou dost teach me perseverance. Let them tear thy web, and thou wilt begin it again, and complete it. Let them destroy it again, and thou wilt resolutely begin to work again—again ! That is what we must do, and that will repay itself at last.'

"It was the morning of Easter-day. The bells sounded from the neighboring church, and the sun seemed to rejoice in the sky. The master had watched through the night in feverish excitement, and had been melting and cooling, distilling and mixing. I heard him sighing like a soul in despair ; I heard him praying, and I noticed how he held his breath. The lamp was burnt out, but he did not notice it. I blew at the fire of coals, and it threw its red glow upon his ghastly white face, lighting it up with a glare, and his sunken eyes looked forth wildly out of their deep sockets—but they became larger and larger, as though they would burst.

"Look at the alchemic glass ! It glows in the crucible, red-hot, and pure and heavy ! He lifted it with a trembling hand, and cried with a trembling voice, 'Gold ! gold !'

" He was quite dizzy—I could have blown him down," said the Wind; " but I only fanned the glowing coals, and accompanied him through the door to where his daughters sat shivering. His coat was powdered with ashes, and there were ashes in his beard and in his tangled hair. He stood straight up, and held his costly treasure on high, in the brittle glass. ' Found, found !—Gold, gold !' he shouted,

and again held aloft the glass to let it flash in the sunshine;
but his hand trembled, and the alchemic glass fell clattering
to the ground, and broke into a thousand pieces; and the
last bubble of his happiness had burst!   Hu-uh-ush! rushing away!—and I rushed away from the gold-maker's
house.

"Late in autumn, when the days are short, and the mist
comes and strews cold drops upon the berries and leafless
branches, I came back in fresh spirits, rushed through the
air, swept the sky clear, and snapped the dry twigs—which
is certainly no great labor, but yet it must be done.   Then
there was another kind of sweeping clean at Waldemar
Daa's, in the mansion of Borreby.   His enemy, Owe Rainel,
of Basnas, was there with the mortgage of the house and
every thing it contained in his pocket.   I drummed against
the broken window-panes, beat against the old rotten doors,
and whistled through cracks and rifts—huh-sh!   Mr. Owe
Rainel did not like staying there.   Ida and Anna Dorothea
wept bitterly; Joanna stood pale and proud, and bit her
thumb till it bled—but what could that avail?   Owe Rainel
offered to allow Waldemar Daa to remain in the mansion
till the end of his life, but no thanks were given him for his
offer.   I listened to hear what occurred.   I saw the ruined
gentleman lift his head and throw it back prouder than ever,
and I rushed against the house and the old lime-trees with
such force, that one of the thickest branches broke, one
that was not decayed; and the branch remained lying at
the entrance as a broom when any one wanted to sweep the
place out: and a grand sweeping out there was—I thought
it would be so.

"It was hard on that day to preserve one's composure;
but their will was as hard as their fortune.

" There was nothing they could call their own except the clothes they wore : yes, there was one thing more—the alchemist's glass, a new one that had lately been bought, and filled with what had been gathered up from the ground of the treasure which promised so much but never kept its promise. Waldemar Daa hid the glass in his bosom, and taking his stick in his hand, the once rich gentleman passed with his daughters out of the house of Borreby. I blew cold upon his heated cheeks, I stroked his gray beard and his long white hair, and I sang as well as I could—' Huh-sh ! gone away ! gone away !' And that was the end of the wealth and splendor.

" Ida walked on one side of the old man, and Anna Dorothea on the other. Joanna turned round at the entrance—why ? Fortune would not turn because she did so. She looked at the old walls of what had once been the castle of Marsk Stig, and perhaps she thought of his daughters :

<blockquote>

" ' The eldest gave the youngest her hand,
And forth they went to the far-off land.'

</blockquote>

Was she thinking of this old song ? Here were three of them, and their father was with them too. They walked along the road on which they had once driven in their splendid carriage—they walked forth as beggars, with their father, and wandered out into the open field, and into a mud hut, which they rented for a dollar and a half a year—into their new house with the empty rooms and empty vessels. Crows and magpies fluttered above them, and cried, as if in contempt, ' Craw ! craw ! out of the nest ! craw ! craw !' as they had done in the wood at Borreby when the trees were felled.

" Daa and his daughters could not help hearing it. I

blew about their ears, for what use would it be that they should listen ?

"And they went to live in the mud hut on the open field, and I wandered away over moor and field, through bare bushes and leafless forests, to the open waters, the free shores, to other lands—huh-uh-ush !—away, away ! year after year !"

And how did Waldemar Daa and his daughters prosper ? The Wind tells us :

"The one I saw last, yes, for the last time, was Anna Dorothea, the pale hyacinth : then she was old and bent, for it was fifty years afterwards. She lived longer than the rest; she knew all.

"Yonder on the heath, by the Jutland town of Wiborg, stood the fine new house of the canon, built of red bricks with projecting gables ; the smoke came up thickly from the chimney. The canon's gentle lady and her beautiful daughters sat in the bay-window, and looked over the hawthorn hedge of the garden towards the brown heath. What were they looking at ? Their glances rested upon the stork's nest without, and on the hut, which was almost falling in; the roof consisted of moss and houseleek, in so far as a roof existed there at all—the stork's nest covered the greater part of it, and that alone was in proper condition, for it was kept in order by the stork himself.

"That is a house to be looked at, but not to be touched; I must deal gently with it," said the Wind. "For the sake of the stork's nest the hut has been allowed to stand, though it was a blot upon the landscape. They did not like to drive the stork away, therefore the old shed was left standing, and the poor woman who dwelt in it was allowed to stay : she had the Egyptian bird to thank for that; or was it perchance her reward, because she had once interceded for the nest of its black brother in the forest of Borreby? At that time she, the poor woman, was a young child, a pale hyacinth in the rich garden. She remembered all that right well, did Anna Dorothea.

"'Oh! oh!' Yes, people can sigh like the wind moaning in the rushes and reeds 'Oh! oh!' she sighed, "no bells sounded at thy burial, Waldemar Daa! The poor schoolboys did not even sing a psalm when the former lord of Borreby was laid in the earth to rest! Oh, every thing has an end, even misery. Sister Ida became the wife of a peasant. That was the hardest trial that befell our father, that the husband of a daughter of his should be a miserable serf, whom the proprietor could mount on the wooden horse for punishment! I suppose he is under the ground now. And thou, Ida? Alas, alas! it is not ended yet, wretch that I am! Grant me that I may die, kind Heaven!'

"That was Anna Dorothea's prayer in the wretched hut which was left standing for the sake of the stork.

"I took pity on the fairest of the sisters," said the Wind. "Her courage was like that of a man, and in man's clothes she took service as a sailor on board of a ship. She was sparing of words, and of a dark countenance, but willing at her work. But she did not know how to climb; so I blew her overboard before anybody found out that she was a woman, and according to my thinking that was well done!" said the Wind.

"On such an Easter morning as that on which Waldemar Daa had fancied that he had found the red gold, I heard the tones of a psalm under the stork's nest, among the crumbling walls—it was Anna Dorothea's last song.

"There was no window, only a hole in the wall. The

IB AND CHRISTINE MEET THE GIPSY.

sun rose up like a mass of gold, and looked through. What a splendor he diffused ! Her eyes were breaking, and her heart was breaking—but that they would have done, even if the sun had not shone that morning on Anna Dorothea.

"The stork covered her hut till her death. I sang at her grave!" said the Wind. "I sang at her father's grave; I know where his grave is, and where hers is, and nobody else knows it.

"New times, changed times ! The old high-road now runs through cultivated fields; the new road winds among the trim ditches, and soon the railway will come with its train of carriages, and rush over the graves which are forgotten like the names—hu-ush ! passed away, passed away!

"That is the story of Waldemar Daa and his daughters. Tell it better, any of you, if you know how," said the Wind, and turned away—and he was gone.

IB AND CHRISTINE.

Not far from the clear stream Gudenau, in North Jutland, in the forest which extends by its banks and far into the country, a great ridge of land rises and stretches along like a wall through the wood. By this ridge, westward, stands a farmhouse, surrounded by poor land; the sandy soil is seen through the spare rye and wheat-ears that grow upon it. Some years have elapsed since the time of which we speak. The people who lived here cultivated the fields, and moreover kept three sheep, a pig, and two oxen; in fact, they supported themselves quite comfortably, for they had enough to live on if they took things as they came. Indeed, they could have managed to save enough to keep two horses; but, like the other peasants of the neighborhood, they said, "The horse eats itself up"—that is to say, it eats as much as it earns. Jeppe-Jäns cultivated his field in summer. In the winter he made wooden shoes; and then he had an assistant, a journeyman, who understood as well as he himself did how to make the wooden shoes strong, and light, and graceful. They carved shoes and spoons, and that brought in money. It would have been wronging the Jeppe-Jänses to call them poor people.

Little Ib, a boy seven years old, the only child of the family, would sit by, looking at the workmen, cutting at a stick, and occasionally cutting his finger. But one day Ib succeeded so well with two pieces of wood, that they really looked like little wooden shoes; and these he wanted to give to little Christine. And who was little Christine? She was the boatman's daughter, and was graceful and delicate as a gentleman's child; had she been differently dressed, no one would have imagined that she came out of the hut on the neighboring heath. There lived her father, who was a widower, and supported himself by carrying firewood in his great boat out of the forest to the estate of Silkeborg, with its great eel-pond and eel-weir, and sometimes even to the distant little town of Randers. He had no one who could take care of little Christine, and therefore the child was almost always with him in his boat, or in the forest among the heath plants and barberry bushes. Sometimes, when he had to go as far as the town, he would bring little Christine, who was a year younger than Ib, to stay at the Jeppe-Jänses.

Ib and Christine agreed very well in every particular: they divided their bread and berries when they were hungry, they dug in the ground together for treasures, and they ran, and crept, and played about everywhere. And one day they ventured together up the high ridge, **and a long way** into the **forest** ; once they found a few snipes' eggs there, and that was a great event for them.

Ib had never **been on the** heath where Christine's father lived, nor **had he ever been on the** river. But even this was to happen ; for Christine's father once invited him to go with them ; and on the evening before the excursion, he followed the boatman over the heath to the house of the latter.

Next morning early, the two children were sitting high up on the pile of firewood in the boat, eating bread and whistleberries. Christine's father and his assistant **pro**pelled the boat with staves. They had the current with them, and swiftly they glided down the stream, through the lakes it forms in its course, and which sometimes seemed **shut in** by **reeds and** water-plants, though there **was** always room for them **to pass,** and though **the** old trees bent quite **forward over the** water, and the old oaks bent **down** their bare branches, as if they had turned up their **sleeves and** wanted **to show their knotty,** naked arms. Old alder-trees, which the stream **had** washed away from the bank, clung **with their** fibrous **roots** to **the** bottom of the stream, and looked like little wooded islands. The water-lilies rocked themselves on the river. It was a splendid excursion ; and **at last** they came to the great eel-weir, where the **water** rushed through the floodgates ; **and Ib** and Christine thought this was beautiful to behold.

In those days there was no manufactory there, nor **was** there **any town ; only** the old great farmyard, **with its scanty fields, with** few servants and a few head of cattle, **could be seen there ;** and **the** rushing of the water through **the** weir, **and** the cry of the **wild** ducks, were the only **signs of life** in Silkeborg. After the firewood **had** been unloaded, the father of Christine bought a whole bundle of eels and a slaughtered sucking-pig, and all was put into a basket and placed in the stern of the boat. Then they went back again up the stream ; but the wind was favorable, and when the sails were hoisted it was as good as if two horses had been harnessed to the boat.

When they had arrived at a point in the stream where the assistant boatman dwelt, a little way from the bank, the boat was moored, and the two men landed, after exhorting the children to sit still. But the children did not do that ; or at least they obeyed only for a very short time. They must be peeping into the basket in which the eels and the sucking-pig had been placed, and they must needs pull the sucking-pig out, and take it into their hands, and feel and touch it all over ; and as both wanted to hold it at the same time, it came to pass that they let it fall into the water, and the sucking-pig drifted away with the stream—and here was a terrible event !

Ib jumped ashore, and ran a little distance along the bank, and Christine sprang after him.

"Take me with you !" she cried.

And in a few minutes they were deep in the thicket, and could no longer see either the boat or the bank. They ran on a little further, and then Christine fell down on the ground and began to cry ; but Ib picked her up.

"Follow me !" he cried. "Yonder lies the house."

But the house was not yonder. They wandered on and on, over the dry, rustling, last year's leaves, and over fallen branches that crackled beneath their feet. Soon they heard a loud, piercing scream. They stood still and listened, and presently the scream of an eagle sounded through the wood. It was an ugly scream, and they were frightened at it ; but before them, in the thick wood, the most beautiful blueberries grew in wonderful profusion

They were so inviting, that the children could not do otherwise than stop ; and they lingered for some time, eating the blueberries till they had quite blue mouths and blue cheeks. Now again they heard the cry they had heard before.

"We shall get into trouble about the pig," said Christine.

"Come, let us go to our house," said Ib ; "it is here in the wood."

And they went forward. They presently came to a wood, but it did not lead them home ; and darkness came on, and they were afraid. The wonderful stillness that reigned around was interrupted now and then by the shrill cries of the great horrid owl and of the birds that were strange to them. At last they both lost themselves in a thicket. Christine cried, and Ib cried too ; and after they had bemoaned themselves for a time, they threw themselves down on the dry leaves, and went fast asleep.

The sun was high in the heavens when the two children awoke. They were cold ; but in the neighborhood of this resting-place, on the hill, the sun shone through the trees, and there they thought they would warm themselves ; and from there Ib fancied they would be able to see his parents' house. But they were far away from the house in question, in quite another part of the forest. They clambered to the top of the rising ground, and found themselves on the summit of a slope running down to the margin of a transparent lake. They could see fish in great numbers in the pure water illumined by the sun's rays. This spectacle was quite a sudden surprise for them ; but close beside them grew a nut-bush covered with the finest nuts ; and now they picked the nuts, and cracked them, and ate the delicate young kernels, which had only just become perfect. But there was another surprise and another fright in store for them. Out of the thicket stepped a tall old woman; her face was quite brown, and her hair was deep black and shining. The whites of her eyes gleamed like a negro's; on her back she carried a bundle, and in her hand she bore a knotted stick. She was a gipsy. The children did not at once understand what she said. She brought three nuts out of her pocket, and told them that in these nuts the most beautiful, the loveliest things were hidden; for they were wishing-nuts.

Ib looked at her, and she seemed so friendly, that he plucked up courage, and asked her if she would give him the nuts; and the woman gave them to him, and gathered some more for herself, a whole pocketful, from the nut-bush.

And Ib and Christine looked at the wishing-nuts with great eyes.

"Is there a carriage with a pair of horses in this nut?" he asked.

"Yes, there's a golden carriage with two horses," answered the woman.

"Then give me the nut," said little Christine.

And Ib gave it to her, and the strange woman tied it in her pocket-handkerchief for her.

"Is there in this nut a pretty little neckerchief, like the one Christine wears round her neck?" inquired Ib.

"There are ten neckerchiefs in it," answered the woman. "There are beautiful dresses in it, and stockings, and a hat with a veil."

"Then I will have that one too," cried little Christine.

And Ib gave her the second nut also. The third was a little black thing.

"That one you can keep," said Christine; "and it is a pretty one too."

"What is in it?" inquired Ib.

"The best of all things for you," replied the gipsy-woman

And Ib held the nut very tight. The woman promised to lead the children into the right path, so that they might find their way home; and now they went forward, certainly in quite a different direction from the path they should have followed. But that is no reason why we should suspect the gipsy-woman of wanting to steal the children. In the wild wood-path they met the forest bailiff, who knew Ib; and by his help, Ib and Christine both arrived at home, where their friends had been very anxious about them. They were pardoned and forgiven, although they had indeed both deserved "to get into trouble;" firstly, because they had let the sucking-pig fall into the water, and secondly, because they had run away.

Christine was taken back to her father on the heath, and Ib remained in the farmhouse on the margin of the wood by the great ridge. The first thing he did in the evening was to bring forth out of his pocket the little black nut, in which "the best thing of all" was said to be inclosed. He placed it carefully in the crack of the door, and then shut the door so as to break the nut; but there was not much kernel in it. The nut looked as if it were filled with tobacco or black rich earth; it was what we call hollow, or worm-eaten.

"Yes, that's exactly what I thought," said Ib. "How could the very best thing be contained in this little nut? And Christine will get just as little out of her two nuts, and will have neither fine clothes nor the golden carriage."

And winter came on, and the new year began; indeed, several years went by.

Ib was at last to be confirmed; and for that reason he

went during a whole winter to the clergyman, far away in the nearest village, to prepare. About this time the boatman one day visited Ib's parents, and told them that Christine was now going into service, and that she had been really fortunate in getting a remarkably good place, and falling into worthy hands.

"Only think," he said; "she is going to the rich innkeeper's, in the inn at Herning, far towards the west, many miles from here. She is to assist the hostess in keeping the house; and afterwards, if she takes to it well, and stays to be confirmed there, the people are going to adopt her as their own daughter."

And Ib and Christine took leave of one another. People called them "the betrothed;" and at parting the girl showed Ib that she had still the two nuts which he had given her long ago, during their wanderings in the forest; and she told him, moreover, that in a drawer she had carefully kept the little wooden shoes which he had carved as a present for her in their childish days. And thereupon they parted.

Ib was confirmed. But he remained in his mother's house, for he had become a clever maker of wooden shoes, and in summer he looked after the field. He did it all alone, for his mother kept no farm-servant, and his father had died long ago.

Only seldom he got news of Christine from some passing postillion or eel-fisher. But she was well off at the rich innkeeper's; and after she had been confirmed, she wrote a letter to her father, and sent a kind message to Ib and his mother; and in the letter there was mention made of certain linen garments and a fine new gown, which Christine had received as a present from her employers. This was certainly good news.

Next spring there was a knock one day at the door of our Ib's old mother, and behold, the boatman and Christine stepped into the room. She had come on a visit to spend a day : a carriage had to come from the Herning Inn to the next village, and she had taken the opportunity to see her friends once again. She looked as handsome as a real lady, and she had a pretty gown on, which had been well sewn, and made expressly for her. There she stood, in grand array, and Ib was in his working clothes. He could not utter a word : he certainly seized her hand, and held it fast in his own, and was heartily glad; but he could not get his tongue to obey him. Christine was not embarrassed, however, for she went on talking and talking, and, moreover, kissed Ib on his mouth in the heartiest manner.

"Did you know me again directly, Ib?" she asked; but even afterwards, when they were left quite by themselves, and he stood there still holding her hand in his, he could only say :

"You look quite like a real lady, and I am so uncouth. How often I have thought of you, Christine, and of the old times!"

And arm in arm they sauntered up the great ridge, and looked across the stream towards the heath, towards the great hills overgrown with bloom. It was perfectly silent; but by the time they parted it had grown quite clear to him that Christine must be his wife. Had they not, even in their childhood, been called the betrothed pair? To him they seemed to be really engaged to each other, though neither of them had spoken a word on the subject. Only for a few more hours could they remain together, for Christine was obliged to go back into the next village, from whence the carriage was to start early next morning for Herning. Her father and Ib escorted her as far as the village. It was a fair moonlight evening, and when they reached their destination, and Ib still held Christine's hand in his own, he could not make up his mind to let her go. His eyes brightened, but still the words came halting over his lips. Yet they came from the depths of his heart, when he said :

"If you have not become too grand, Christine, and if you can make up your mind to live with me in my mother's house as my wife, we must become a wedded pair some day; but we can wait awhile yet."

"Yes, let us wait for a time, Ib," she replied; and he kissed her lips. "I confide in you, Ib," said Christine; "and I think that I love you—but I will sleep upon it."

And with that they parted. And on the way home Ib told the boatman that he and Christine were as good as betrothed; and the boatman declared he had always expected it would turn out so; and he went home with Ib, and remained that night in the young man's house; but nothing further was said of the betrothal.

A year passed by, in the course of which two letters were exchanged between Ib and Christine. The signature was prefaced by the words, "Faithful till death!" One day the boatman came in to Ib, and brought him a greeting from Christine. What he had further to say was brought out in somewhat hesitating fashion, but it was to the effect that Christine was almost more than prosperous, for she was a pretty girl, courted and loved. The son of the host had been home on a visit; he was employed in the office of some great institution in Copenhagen; and he was very much pleased with Christine, and she had taken a fancy to him : his parents were ready to give their consent, but Christine was very anxious to retain Ib's good opinion; "and so she had thought of refusing this great piece of good fortune," said the boatman.

At first Ib said not a word; but he became as white as the wall, and slightly shook his head. Then he said slowly :

"Christine must not refuse this advantageous offer."

"Then do you write a few words to her," said the boat-man.

And Ib sat down to write; but he could not manage it well : the words would not come as he wished them; and first he altered, and then he tore up the page; but the next morning a letter lay ready to be sent to Christine, and it contained the following words :

"I have read the letter you have sent to your father, and gather from it that you are prospering in all things, and that there is a prospect of higher fortune for you. Ask your heart, Christine, and ponder well the fate that awaits you, if you take me for your husband ; what I possess is but little. Do not think of me, or my position, but think of your own welfare. You are bound to me by no promise, and if in your heart you have given me one, I release you from it. May all treasures of happiness be poured out upon you, Christine. Heaven will console me in its own good time.

"Ever your sincere friend,

"Ib."

And the letter was dispatched, and Christine duly received it.

In the course of that November her banns were published in the church on the heath, and in Copenhagen, where her bridegroom lived; and to Copenhagen she proceeded, under the protection of her future mother-in-law, because the bridegroom could not undertake the journey into Jutland on account of his various occupations. On the journey, Christine met her father in a certain village; and here the two took leave of one another. A few words were men-tioned concerning this fact, but Ib made no remark upon it: his mother said he had grown very silent of late; indeed, he had become very pensive, and thus the three nuts came into his mind which the gipsy-woman had given him long ago, and of which he had given two to Christine. Yes, it seemed right—they were wishing-nuts, and in one of them lay a golden carriage with two horses, and in the other very elegant clothes; all those luxuries would now be Christine's in the capital. Her part had thus come true. And to him, Ib, the nut had offered only black earth. The gipsy-woman had said, this was "the best of all for him." Yes, it was right, that also was coming true. The black earth was the best for him. Now he understood clearly what had been the woman's meaning. In the black earth, in the dark grave, would be the best happiness for him.

And once again years passed by, not very many, but they seemed long years to Ib. The old innkeeper and his wife died, one after the other; the whole of their property, many thousands of dollars, came to the son. Yes, now Christine could have the golden carriage, and plenty of fine clothes.

During the two long years that followed no letter came from Christine; and when her father at length received one from her, it was not written in prosperity, by any means. Poor Christine! neither she nor her husband had understood how to keep the money together; and there seemed to be no blessing with it, because they had not sought it.

And again the weather bloomed and faded. The winter had swept for many years across the heath, and over the ridge beneath which Ib dwelt, sheltered from the rough winds. The spring sun shone bright, and Ib guided the plough across his field, when one day it glided over what appeared to be a fire-stone. Something like a great black ship came out of the ground, and when Ib took it up it proved to be a piece of metal; and the place from which the plough had cut the stone gleamed brightly with ore. It was a great golden armlet of ancient workmanship that he had found. He had disturbed a "Hun's Grave," and discovered the costly treasure buried in it. Ib showed what he had found to the clergyman, who explained its value to him, and then he betook himself to the local judges, who reported the discovery to the keeper of the museum, and recommend d Ib to deliver up the treasure in person.

"You have found in the earth the best thing you could find," said the judge.

"The best thing !" thought Ib. "The very best thing for me, and found in the earth ! Well, if that is the best, the gipsy-woman was correct in what she prophesied to me."

So Ib travelled with the ferry-boat from Aarhus to Copenhagen. To him, who had but once or twice passed beyond the river that rolled by his home, this seemed like a voyage across the ocean. And he arrived in Copenhagen.

The value of the gold he had found was paid over to him ; it was a large sum—six hundred dollars. And Ib of the heath wandered about in the great capital.

On the day on which he had settled to go back with the captain, Ib lost his way in the streets, and took quite a different direction from the one he intended to follow. He had wandered into the suburb of Christianhaven, into a poor little street. Not a human being was to be seen. At last a very little girl came out of one of the wretched houses. Ib inquired of the little one the way to the street which he wanted ; but she looked shyly at him, and began to cry bitterly. He asked her what ailed her, but could not understand what she said in reply. But as they went along the street together, they passed beneath the light of a lamp ; and when the light fell on the girl's face, he felt a strange and sharp emotion, for Christine stood bodily before

him, just as he remembered her from the days of his childhood.

And he went with the little maiden into the wretched
house, and ascended the narrow, crazy staircase, which led
to a little attic chamber in the roof. The air in this chamber was heavy and almost suffocating : no light was burning ; but there was heavy sighing and moaning in one
corner. Ib struck a light with the help of a match. It was
the mother of the child who lay sighing on the miserable
bed.

"Can I be of any service to you ?" asked Ib. "This little
girl has brought me up here, but I am a stranger in this
city. Are there no neighbors or friends whom I could call
to you ?" And he raised the sick woman's head and
smoothed her pillow.

It was Christine of the heath !

For years her name had not been mentioned yonder, for
the mention of her would have disturbed Ib's peace of
mind, and rumor had told nothing good concerning her.
The wealth which her husband had inherited from his parents had made him proud and arrogant. He had given up
his certain appointment, had travelled for half a year in
foreign lands, and on his return had incurred debts, and
yet lived in an expensive fashion. His carriage had bent
over more and more, so to speak, until at last it turned
over completely. The many merry companions and table-
friends he had entertained declared it served him right, for
he had kept house like a madman ; and one morning his
corpse was found in the canal.

The icy hand of death was already on Christine. Her
youngest child, only a few weeks old, expected in prosperity
and born in misery, was already in its grave; and it had
come to this with Christine herself, that she lay, sick to

death and forsaken, in a miserable room, amid a poverty that she might well have borne in her childish days, but which now oppressed her painfully, since she had been accustomed to better things. It was her eldest child, also a little Christine, that here suffered hunger and poverty with her, and whom Ib had now brought home.

"I am unhappy at the thought of dying and leaving the poor child here alone," she said. "Ah, what is to become of the poor thing?" And not a word more could she utter.

And Ib brought out another match, and lighted up a piece of candle he found in the room, and the flame illumined the wretched dwelling. And Ib looked at the little girl, and thought how Christine had looked when she was young; and he felt that for her sake he would be fond of this child, which was as yet a stranger to him. The dying woman gazed at him, and her eyes opened wider and wider —did she recognize him? He never knew, for no further word passed over her lips.

And it was in the forest by the river Gudenau, in the region of the heath. The air was thick and dark, and there were no blossoms on the heath plant; but the autumn tempests whirled the yellow leaves from the wood into the stream, and out over the heath towards the hut of the boatman, in which strangers now dwelt; but beneath the ridge, safe beneath the protection of the high trees, stood the little farm, trimly whitewashed and painted, and within it the turf blazed up cheerily in the chimney; for within was sunlight, the beaming sunlight of a child's two eyes; and the tones of the spring-birds sounded in the words that came from the child's rosy lips; she sat on Ib's knee, and Ib was to her both father and mother, for her own parents were dead, and had vanished from her as a dream vanishes alike from children and grown men. Ib sat in the pretty neat house, for he was a prosperous man, while the mother of the little girl rested in the churchyard at Copenhagen, where she had died in poverty.

Ib had money, and was said to have provided for the uture. He had won gold out of the black earth, and he had a Christine for his own, after all.

———◆·◆———

OLE, THE TOWER-KEEPER.

"IN the world it's always going up and down—and now I can't go up any higher!" So said Ole, the tower-keeper. "Most people have to try both the ups and downs; and, rightly considered, we all get to be watchmen at last, and look down upon life from a height."

Such was the speech of Ole, my friend, the old tower-keeper, a strange, talkative old fellow, who seemed to speak out every thing that came into his head, and who, for all that, had many a serious thought deep in his heart. Yes, he was the child of respectable people, and there were even some who said that he was the son of a privy-councillor, or that he might have been; he had studied, too, and had been assistant teacher and deputy clerk; but of what service was all that to him? In those days he lived in the clerk's house, and was to have every thing in the house, to be at freequarters, as the saying is; but he was still, so to speak, a fine young gentleman. He wanted to have his boots cleaned with patent blacking, and the clerk could only afford ordinary grease; and upon that point they split—one spoke of stinginess, the other of vanity, and the blacking became the black cause of enmity between them, and at last they parted.

This is what he demanded of the world in general—namely, patent blacking—and he got nothing but grease. Accordingly he at last drew back from all men, and became a hermit; but the church tower is the only place in a great city where hermitage, office, and bread can be found together. So he betook himself up thither, and smoked his pipe as he made his solitary rounds. He looked upward and downward, and had his own thoughts, and told in his way of what he read in books and in himself. I often lent him books, good books; and you may know a man by the company he keeps. He loved neither the English governess-novels, nor the French ones, which he called a mixture of empty wind and raisin-stalks: he wanted biographies and descriptions of the wonders of the world. I visited him at least once a year, generally directly after New Year's day, and then he always spoke of this and that which the change of the year had put into his head.

I will tell the story of three of these visits, and will reproduce his own words whenever I can remember them.

First Visit.

Among the books which I had lately lent Ole was one which had greatly rejoiced and occupied him. It was a geological book, containing an account of the boulders.

"Yes, they're rare old fellows, those boulders!" he said; "and to think that we should pass them without noticing them! And over the street pavement, the paving-stones, those fragments of the oldest remains of antiquity, one walks without ever thinking about them. I have done the very thing myself. But now I look respectfully at every paving-stone. Many thanks for the book! It has filled me with thought, and has made me long to read more on the subject. The romance of the earth is, after all, the most wonderful of all romances. It's a pity one can't read the first volume of it, because they're written in a language that we don't understand. One must read in the different strata, in the pebble-stones, for each separate period. Yes, it is a romance, a very wonderful romance, and we all have our place in it. We grope and ferret about, and yet remain where we are, but the ball keeps turning, without emptying the ocean over us; the clod on which we move about holds, and does not let us though. And then it's a story that has been acting for thousands upon thousands of years, and is still going on. My best thanks for the book about the boulders. Those are fellows indeed! they could tell us something worth hearing, if they only knew how to talk. It's really a pleasure, now and then, to become a mere nothing, especially when a man is as highly placed as I am. And then to think that we all, even with patent lacquer, are nothing more than insects of a moment on that anthill the earth, though we may be insects with stars and garters, places and offices! One feels quite a novice beside these venerable million-year-old boulders. On New Year's eve I was reading the book, and had lost myself in it so completely, that I forgot my usual New-Year's diversion, namely, the wild hunt to Amack. Ah, you don't know what that is!

"The journey of the witches on broomsticks is well enough known—that journey is taken on St. John's eve, to the Brocken; but we have a wild journey also, which is national and modern, and that is the journey to Amack on the night of the New Year. All indifferent poets and poetesses, musicians, newspaper writers and artistic notabilities,

I mean those who are no good, ride in the New Year's night through the air to Amack. They sit backwards on their painting brushes or quill-pens, for steel pens won't bear them, they're too stiff. As I told you, I see that every New Year's night, and could mention the majority of the riders by name, but I should not like to draw their enmity upon myself, for they don't like people to talk about their ride to Amack on quill-pens. I've a kind of niece, who is a fish-wife, and who, as she tells me, supplies three respectable newspapers with the terms of abuse and vituperation they use, and she has herself been at Amack as an invited guest; but she was carried out thither, for she does not own a quill-pen, nor can she ride. She has told me all about it. Half of what she said is not true, but the other half gives us information enough. When she was out there, the festivities began with a song : each of the guests had written his own song, for he thought that the best, and it was all one, all the same melody. Then those came march-ing up, in little bands, who are only busy with their mouths. There were ringing bells that sang alternately; and then came the little drummers that beat their tattoo in the family circle ; and acquaintance was made with those who write without putting their names, which here means as much as using grease instead of patent blacking; and then there was the beadle with his boy, and the boy was the worst off, for in gene-ral he gets no notice taken of him ; then, too, there was the good street-sweeper with his cart, who turns over the dust-bin, and calls it "good, very good, remarkably good." And in the midst of the pleasure that was afforded by the mere meeting of these folks, there shot up out of the great dirt-neap at Amack a stem, a tree, an immense flower, a great mushroom, a perfect roof, which formed a sort of warehouse for the worthy company, for in it hung every thing they had given to the world during the Old Year. Out of the tree poured sparks, like flames of fire; these were ideas and thoughts, borrowed from others, which they had used, and which now got free and rushed away like so many fireworks. They played at 'the stick burns,' and the young poets played at 'heart-burns,' and the witlings played off their jests, and the jests rolled away with a thundering sound, as if empty pots were being shattered against the doors. 'It was very amusing!' my niece said; in fact, she said many things that were very malicious but very amusing, but I won't mention them, for a man must be good-natured and not a carping critic. But you will easily perceive that when a man once knows the rights of the journey to Amack, as I know them, it's quite natural that on the New Year's night one should look out to see the wild chase go by. If in the New Year I miss certain persons who used to be there, I am sure to notice others who are new arrivals; but this year I omitted taking my look at the guests. I bowled away on the boulders, rolled back through millions of years, and saw the stones break loose high up in the North, saw them drifting about on icebergs, long before Noah's ark was constructed, saw them sink down to the bottom of the sea, and reappear with a sand-bank, with that one that peered forth from the flood and said, 'This shall be Zealand!' I saw them become the dwelling-place of birds that are unknown to us, and then become the seat of wild chiefs of whom we know nothing, until with their axes they cut their Runic signs into a few of these stones, which then came into the calendar of time. But, as for me, I had gone quite beyond all lapse of time, and had become a cipher and a nothing. Then three or four beautiful falling-stars came down, which cleared the air, and gave my thoughts another direction. You know what a falling-star is, do you not? The learned men are not all clear about it. I have my own ideas about shooting-stars, as the common people in many parts call them, and my idea is this : How often are silent thanksgivings offered up for one who has done a good and noble action ! The thanks are often speechless, but they are not lost for all that. I think these are caught up, and the sunbeams bring the silent, hidden thankfulness over the head of the bene-factor; and if it be a whole people that has been expressing its gratitude through a long lapse of time, the thankfulness appears as a nosegay of flowers, and at length falls in the form of a shooting-star upon the good man's grave. I am always very much pleased when I see a shooting-star, especially in the New Year's night, and then find out for whom the gift of gratitude was intended. Lately a gleam-ing star fell in the southwest, as a tribute of thanksgiving to many, many ! 'For whom was that star intended?' thought I. It fell, no doubt, on the hill by the Bay of Flensberg, where the Danebrog waves over the graves of Schleppegrell, Läslöes, and their comrades. One star also fell in the midst of the land, fell upon Sorö, a flower on the grave of Holberg, the thanks of the year from a great many—thanks for his charming plays.

"It is a great and a pleasant thought to know that a shooting-star falls upon our graves ; on mine certainly none will fall—no sunbeam brings thanks to me, for here there is nothing worthy of thanks. I shall not get the patent lacquer," said Ole; "for my fate on earth is only grease, after all."

Second Visit.

It was New Year's day, and I went up on the tower. Ole spoke of the toasts that were drunk on the transition from the old year into the new, from one grave into the other, as he said. And he told me a story about the glasses, and this story had a very deep meaning. It was this :

" When on the New Year's night the clock strikes twelve, the people at the table rise up, with full glasses in their hands, and drain these glasses, and drink success to the New Year. They begin the year with the glass in their hands; that is a good beginning for topers. They begin the New Year by going to bed, and that's a good beginning for drones. Sleep is sure to play a great part in the New Year, and the glass likewise. Do you know what dwells in the glass ?" asked Ole. "I will tell you—there dwells in the glass, first, health, and then pleasure, then the most complete sensual delight : and misfortune and the bitterest woe dwell in the glass also. Now suppose we count the glasses —of course I count the different degrees in the glasses for different people.

" You see, the *first glass*, that's the glass of health, and in that the herb of health is found growing ; put it up on the beam in the ceiling, and at the end of the year you may be sitting in the arbor of health.

" If you take the *second glass*—from this a little bird soars upwards, twittering in guileless cheerfulness, so that a man may listen to his song and perhaps join in ' Fair is life ! no downcast looks ! Take courage and march onward !'

" Out of the *third glass* rises a little winged urchin who cannot certainly be called an angel-child, for there is goblin blood in his veins, and he has the spirit of a goblin ; not wishing to hurt or harm you, indeed, but very ready to play off tricks upon you. He'll sit at your ear and whisper merry thoughts to you ; he'll creep into your heart and warm you, so that you grow very merry and become a wit, so far as the wits of the others can judge.

"In the *fourth glass* is neither herb, bird, nor urchin : in that glass is the pause drawn by reason, and one may never go beyond that sign.

"Take the *fifth glass*, and you will weep at yourself, you will feel such a deep emotion ; or it will affect you in a different way. Out of the glass there will spring with a bang Prince Carnival, nine times and extravagantly merry : he'll draw you away with him, you'll forget your dignity, if you have any, and you'll forget more than you should or ought to forget. All is dance, song, and sound ; the masks will carry you away with them, and the daughters of vanity, clad in silk and satin, will come with loose hair and alluring charms : but tear yourself away if you can !

"The *sixth glass !* Yes, in that glass sits a demon, in the form of a little, well-dressed, attractive and very fascinating man, who thoroughly understands you, agrees with you in every thing, and becomes quite a second self to you. He has a lantern with him, to give you light as he accompanies you home. There is an old legend about a saint who was allowed to choose one of the seven deadly sins, and who accordingly chose drunkenness, which appeared to him the least, but which led him to commit all the other six. The man's blood is mingled with that of the demon— it is the sixth glass, and with that the germ of all evil shoots up within us ; and each one grows up with a strength like that of the grains of mustard-seed, and shoots up into a tree, and spreads over the whole world ; and most people have no choice but to go into the oven, to be recast in a new form.

"That's the history of the glasses," said the tower-keeper Ole, "and it can be told with lacquer or only with grease ; but I give it you with both !"

Third Visit.

On this occasion I chose the general "moving-day" for my visit to Ole, for on that day it is any thing but agreeable down in the streets in the town ; for they are full of sweepings, shreds, and remnants of all sorts, to say nothing of the cast-off bed straw in which one has to wade about. But this time I happened to see two children playing in this wilderness of sweepings. They were playing at "going to bed," for the occasion seemed especially favorable for this sport : they crept under the straw, and drew an old bit of ragged curtain over themselves by way of coverlet. "It was splendid !" they said ; but it was a little too strong for me, and besides, I was obliged to mount up on my visit.

"It's moving-day to-day," he said ; "streets and houses are like a dust-bin, a large dust-bin ; but I'm content with a cart-load. I may get something good out of that, and I really did get something good out of it, once. Shortly after Christmas I was going up the street ; it was rough weather, wet and dirty ; the right kind of weather to catch cold in. The dustman was there with his cart, which was full, and looked like a sample of streets on moving-day. At the back of the cart stood a fir-tree, quite green still, and with tinsel on its twigs : it had been used on Christmas-eve, and now it was thrown out into the street, and the dustman had stood it up at the back of his cart. It was droll to look at, or you may say it was mournful—all depends on what you think of when you see it ; and I thought about it, and thought this and that of many things that were in the cart : or I might have done so, and that comes to the same thing. There was an old lady's glove too · I wonder what that was thinking of ? Shall I tell you? The glove was lying there, pointing with its little finger at the tree. 'I'm sorry for the tree,' it thought; 'and I was also at the feast, where the chandeliers glittered. My life was, so to speak, a ball-night: a pressure of the hand, and I burst! My memory keeps dwelling upon that, and I have really nothing else to live for!' This is what the glove thought, or what it might have thought. 'That's a stupid affair with yonder fir-tree,' said the potsherds. You see potsherds think every thing is stupid. 'When one is in the dust-cart,' they said, 'one ought not to give one's self airs and wear tinsel. I know that I have been useful in the world, far more useful than such a green stick.' That was a view that might be taken, and I don't think it quite a peculiar one; but for all that the fir-tree looked very well: it was like a little poetry in the dust-heap; and truly there is dust enough in the streets on moving-day. The way is difficult and troublesome then, and I feel obliged to run away out of the confusion; or if I am on the tower, I stay there and look down, and it is amusing enough.

"There are the good people below, playing at 'changing houses.' They toil and tug away with their goods and chattels, and the household goblin sits in an old tub and moves with them; all the little griefs of the lodging and the family, and the real cares and sorrows, move with them out of the old dwelling into the new; and what gain is there for them or for us in the whole affair? Yes, there was written long ago the good old maxim: 'Think on the great moving-day of death!' That is a serious thought; I hope it is not disagreeable to you that I should have touched upon it? Death is the most certain messenger after all, in spite of his various occupations. Yes, Death is the omnibus conductor, and he is the passport writer, and he countersigns our service-book, and he is director of the savings-bank of life. Do you understand me? All the deeds of our life, the great and the little alike, we put into this savings-bank ; and when death calls with his omnibus, and we have to step in, and drive with him into the land of eternity, then on the frontier he gives us our service-book as a pass. As a provision for the journey, he takes this or that good deed we have done, and lets it accompany us ; and this may be very pleasant or very terrific. Nobody has ever escaped this omnibus journey : there is certainly a talk about *one* who was not allowed to go—they call him the Wandering Jew : he has to ride behind the omnibus. If he had been allowed to get in, he would have escaped the clutches of the poets.

"Just cast your mind's eye into that great omnibus. The society is mixed, for king and beggar, genius and idiot, sit side by side : they must go without their property and money ; they have only the service-book and the gift out of the savings-bank with them. But which of our deeds is selected and given to us ? Perhaps quite a little one, one that we have forgotten, but which has been recorded— small as a pea, but the pea can send out a blooming shoot. The poor bumpkin, who sat on a low stool in the corner, and was jeered at and flouted, will perhaps have his worn-out stool given him as a provision ; and the stool may become a litter in the land of eternity, and rise up then as a throne, gleaming like gold, and blooming as an arbor. He who always lounged about, and drank the spiced draught of pleasure, that he might forget the wild things he had done here, will have his barrel given to him on the journey, and will have to drink from it as they go on ; and the drink is bright and clear, so that the thoughts remain pure, and all good and noble feelings are awakened, and he sees and feels what in life he could not or would not see ; and then he has within him the punishment, the *gnawing worm,* which will not die through time incalculable. If on the glasses there stood written '*oblivion,*' on the barrel '*remembrance*' is inscribed.

" When I read a good book, an historical work, I always think at last of the poetry of what I am reading, and of the omnibus of death, and wonder which of the hero's deeds Death took out of the savings-bank for him, and what provisions he got on the journey into eternity. There was once a French king—I have forgotten his name, for the names of good people are sometimes forgotten, even by me, but it will come back some day—there was a king who, during a famine, became the benefactor of his people ; and the people raised to his memory a monument of snow, with the inscription, ' Quicker than this melts didst thou bring help !' I fancy that Death, looking back upon the monument, gave him a single snow-flake as provision, a snow-flake that never melts, and this flake floated over his royal head, like a white butterfly, into the land of eternity. Thus, too, there was a Louis XI.—I have remembered *his* name, for one remembers what is bad—a trait of him often comes into my thoughts, and I wish one could say the story is not true. He had his high lord-constable executed, and he could execute him, right or wrong : but he had the innocent children of the constable, one seven and the other eight years old, placed under the scaffold so that the warm blood of their father spurted over them ; and then he had them sent to the Bastile, and shut up in iron cages, where not even a coverlet was given them to protect them from the cold. And King Louis sent the executioner to them every week, and had a tooth pulled out of the head of each, that they might not be too comfortable ; and the elder of the boys said, 'My mother would die of grief if she knew that my younger brother had to suffer so cruelly ; therefore pull out two of my teeth, and spare him.' The tears came into the hangman's eyes, but the king's will was stronger than the tears ; and every week two little teeth were brought to him on a silver plate ; he had demanded them, and he had them. I fancy that Death took these two teeth out of the savings-bank of life, and gave them to Louis XI., to carry with him on the great journey into the land of immortality : they fly before him like two flames of fire ; they shine and burn, and they bite him, the innocent children's teeth.

"Yes, that's a serious journey, the omnibus ride on the great moving-day ! And when is it to be undertaken ? That's just the serious part of it. Any day, any hour, any minute, the omnibus may draw up. Which of our deeds will Death take out of the savings-bank, and give to us as provision ? Let us think of the moving day that is not marked in the calendar."

<hr />

THE BOTTLE-NECK.

In a narrow, crooked street, among other abodes of poverty, stood an especially narrow and tall house built of timber, which time had knocked about in such fashion that it seemed to be out of joint in every direction. The house was inhabited by poor people, and the deepest poverty was apparent in the garret lodging in the gable, where, in front of the only window, hung an old bent birdcage, which had not even a proper water-glass, but only a bottle-neck reversed, with a cork stuck in the mouth, to do duty for one. An old maid stood by the window : she had hung the cage with green chickweed ; and a little chaffinch hopped from perch to perch, and sang and twittered merrily enough.

"Yes, it's all very well for you to sing," said the bottle-neck ; that is to say, it did not pronounce the words as we can speak them, for a bottle-neck can't speak ; but that's what he thought to himself in his own mind, like when we people talk quietly to ourselves. "Yes, it's all very well for you to sing, you that have all your limbs uninjured. You ought to feel what it's like to lose one's body, and to have only mouth and neck left, and to be hampered with work into the bargain, as in my case ; and then I'm sure you would not sing. But, after all, it is well that there should be somebody at least who is merry. I've no reason to sing, and, moreover, I can't sing. Yes, when I was a whole bottle, I sung out well if they rubbed me with a cork. They used to call me a perfect lark, a magnificent lark ! Ah, when I was out at a picnic with the tanner's family, and his daughter was betrothed ! Yes, I remember it as if it had happened only yesterday. I have gone through a great deal, when I come to recollect. I've been in the fire and the water, have been deep in the black earth, and have mounted higher than most of the others ; and now I'm hanging here, outside the bird-cage, in the air and the sunshine ! Oh, it would be quite worth while to hear my history ; but I don't speak aloud of it, because I can't."

And now the bottle-neck told its story, which was sufficiently remarkable. It told the story to itself, or only thought it in its own mind ; and the little bird sang his song merrily, and down in the street there was driving and hurrying, and every one thought of his own affairs, or

perhaps of nothing at all ; and only the bottle-neck thought.
It thought of the flaming furnace in the manufactory, where
it had been blown into life ; it still remembered that it had
been quite warm, that it had glanced into the hissing furnace, the home of its origin, and had felt a great desire
to leap directly back again ; but that gradually it had become cooler, and had been very comfortable in the place to
which it was taken. It had stood in a rank with a whole
regiment of brothers and sisters, all out of the same furnace ; some of them had certainly been blown into cham-
pagne-bottles, and others into beer-bottles, and that makes
a difference. Later, out in the world, it may well happen
that a beer-bottle may contain the most precious wine, and
a champagne-bottle be filled with blacking ; but even in
decay there is always something left by which people can
see what one has been—nobility is nobility, even when
filled with blacking.

All the bottles were packed up, and our bottle was among
them. At that time it did not think to finish its career as a
bottle-neck, or that it should work its way up to be a bird's
glass, which is always an honorable thing ; for one is of
some consequence, after all. The bottle did not again behold the light of day till it was unpacked with the other
bottles in the cellar of the wine merchant, and rinsed out
for the first time ; and that was a strange sensation. There
it lay, empty and without a cork, and felt strangely unwell,
as if it wanted something, it could not tell what. At last,
it was filled with good, costly wine, and was provided with
a cork, and sealed down. A ticket was placed on it,
marked " first quality ;" and it felt as if it carried off the
first prize at an examination ; for, you see, the wine was
good and the bottle was good. When one is young, that's
the time for poetry ! There was a singing and a sounding

within it, of things which it could not understand—of green, sunny mountains, whereon the grape grows, where many vine-dressers, men and women, sing, and dance, and rejoice. "Ah, how beautiful is life!" There was a singing and sounding to all this in the bottle, as in a young poet's brain ; and many a young poet does not understand the meaning of the song that is within him.

One morning the bottle was bought, for the tanner's apprentice was dispatched for a bottle of wine—" of the best." And now it was put in the provision basket, with ham, and cheese, and sausages ; the finest butter and the best bread were put into the basket, too; the tanner's daughter herself packed it. She was young and pretty ; her brown eyes laughed, and round her mouth played a smile as elegant as that in her eyes. She had delicate hands, beautifully white, and her neck was whiter still ; you saw at once that she was one of the most beautiful girls in the town : and still she was not engaged.

The provision basket was in the lap of the young girl when the family drove out into the forest. The bottle-neck looked out from the folds of the white napkin. There was red wax upon the cork, and the bottle looked straight into the girl's face. It also looked at the young sailor who sat next to the girl. He was a friend of old days, the son of the portrait painter. Quite lately he had passed with honor through his examination as mate, and to-morrow he was to sail away in a ship, far off to a distant land. There had been much talk of this while the basket was being packed ; and certainly the eyes and mouth of the tanner's pretty daughter did not wear a very joyous expression just then.

The young people sauntered through the greenwood, and talked to one another. What were they talking of ? No, the bottle could not hear that, for it was in the provision basket. A long time passed before it was drawn forth; but when that happened, there had been pleasant things going on, for all were laughing, and the tanner's daughter laughed, too; but she spoke less than before, and her cheeks glowed like two roses.

The father took the full bottle and the corkscrew in his hand. Yes, it's a strange thing to be drawn thus, the first time! The bottle-neck could never afterwards forget that impressive moment; and indeed there was quite a convulsion within him when the cork flew out, and a great throbbing as the wine poured forth into the glasses.

"Health to the betrothed pair!" cried the papa; and every glass was emptied to the dregs, and the young mate kissed his beautiful bride.

"Happiness and blessing!" said the two old people, the father and mother; and the young man filled the glasses again.

"Safe return, and a wedding this day next year!" he cried; and when the glasses were emptied he took the bottle, raised it on high, and said, "Thou hast been present at the happiest day of my life, thou shalt never serve another!"

And so saying, he hurled it high into the air. The tanner's daughter did not then think that she should see the bottle fly again; and yet it was to be so. It then fell into the thick reeds on the margin of a little woodland lake; and the bottle-neck could remember quite plainly how it lay there for some time. "I gave them wine, and they gave me marsh-water," he said; "but it was all meant for the best." He could no longer see the betrothed couple and the cheerful old people; but for a long time he could hear them rejoicing and singing. Then at last came two peasant boys, and looked into the reeds; they spied out the bottle, and took it up; and now it was provided for.

At their home, in the wood cottage, the eldest of these brothers, who was a sailor, and about to start on a long voyage, had been the day before to take leave : the mother was just engaged packing up various things he was to take with him on his journey, and which the father was going to carry into the town that evening to see his son once more, and to give him a farewell greeting for the lad's mother and himself. A little bottle of medicated brandy had already been wrapped up in a parcel, when the boys came in with a larger and stronger bottle which they had found. This bottle would hold more than the little one, and they pronounced that the brandy would be capital for a bad digestion, inasmuch as it was mixed with medical herbs. The draught that was now poured into the bottle was not so good as the red wine with which it had once been filled ; these were bitter drops, but even these are sometimes good. The new big bottle was to go, and not the little one ; and so the bottle went travelling again. It was taken on board for Peter Jensen, in the very same ship in which the young mate sailed. But he did not see the bottle ; and, indeed, he would not have known it, or thought it was the same one out of which they had drunk a health to the betrothed pair, and to his own happy return.

Certainly it had no longer wine to give, but still it contained something that was just as good. Accordingly, whenever Peter Jensen brought it out, it was dubbed by his messmates The Apothecary. It contained the best medicine, medicine that strengthened the weak, and it gave liberally so long as it had a drop left. That was a pleasant time, and the bottle sang when it was rubbed with the cork ; and it was called the Great Lark, "Peter Jensen's Lark."

Long days and months rolled on, and the bottle already

stood empty in a corner, when it happened—whether on the passage out or home the bottle could not tell, for it had never been ashore—that a storm arose ; great waves came careering along, darkly and heavily, and lifted and tossed the ship to and fro. The mainmast was shivered, and a wave started one of the planks, and the pumps became useless. It was black night. The ship sank ; but at the last moment, the young mate wrote on a leaf of paper, " God's will be done ! We are sinking !" He wrote the name of his betrothed, and his own name, and that of the ship, and put the leaf in an empty bottle that happened to be at hand : he corked it firmly down, and threw it out into the foaming sea. He knew not that it was the very bottle from which the goblet of joy and hope had once been filled for him ; and now it was tossing on the waves with his last greeting and the message of death.

The ship sank, and the crew sank with her. The bottle sped on like a bird, for it bore a heart, a loving letter, within itself. And the sun rose and set ; and the bottle felt as at the time when it first came into being in the red gleaming oven—it felt a strong desire to leap back into the light.

It experienced calms and fresh storms ; but it was hurled against no rock, and was devoured by no shark ; and thus it drifted on for a year and a day, sometimes towards the north, sometimes towards the south, just as the current carried it. Beyond this, it was its own master ; but one may grow tired even of that.

The written page, the last farewell of the bridegroom to his betrothed, would only bring sorrow if it came into her hands ; but where were the hands, so white and delicate, which had once spread the cloth on the fresh grass in the greenwood, on the betrothal day ? Where was the tanner's daughter? Yes, where was the land, and which land might be nearest to her dwelling? The bottle knew not; it drove onward and onward, and was at last tired of wandering, because that was not in its way; but yet it had to travel until at last it came to land—to a strange land. It understood not a word that was spoken here, for this was not the language it heard spoken before; and one loses a good deal if one does not understand the language.

The bottle was fished out and examined on all sides. The leaf of paper within it was discovered, and taken out, and turned over and over, but the people did not understand what was written thereon. They saw that the bottle must have been thrown overboard, and that something about this was written on the paper, but what were the words? That question remained unanswered, and the paper was put back into the bottle, and the latter was deposited in a great cupboard, in a great room, in a great house.

Whenever strangers came the paper was brought out, and turned over and over, so that the inscription, which was only written in pencil, became more and more illegible, so that at the last no one could see that there were letters on it. And for a whole year more the bottle remained standing in the cupboard; and then it was put into the loft, where it became covered with dust and cobwebs. Ah, how often it thought of the better days, the times when it had poured forth red wine in the greenwood, when it had been rocked on the waves of the sea, and when it had carried a secret, a letter, a parting sigh, safely inclosed in its bosom!

For full twenty years it stood up in the loft; and it might have remained there longer, but that the house was to be rebuilt. The roof was taken off, and then the bottle was noticed, and they spoke about it, but it did not understand their language; for one cannot learn a language by being shut up in a loft, even if one stays there for twenty years.

"If I had been down in the room," thought the bottle, "I might have learned it."

It was now washed and rinsed, and indeed this was requisite. It felt quite transparent and fresh, and as if its youth had been renewed in this its old age ; but the paper it had carried so faithfully had been destroyed in the washing.

The bottle was filled with seeds, though it scarcely knew what they were. It was corked and well wrapped up. No light or lantern was it vouchsafed to behold, much less the sun or the moon ; and yet, it thought, when one goes on a journey one ought to see something ; but though it saw nothing, it did what was most important—it travelled to the place of its destination, and was there uncorked.

"What trouble they have taken over yonder with that bottle !" it heard people say ; "and yet it is most likely broken." But it was not broken.

The bottle understood every word that was now said ; this was the language it had heard at the furnace, and at the wine merchant's, and in the forest, and in the ship, the only good old language it understood; it had come back home, and the language was a salutation of welcome to it. For very joy it felt ready to jump out of people's hands ; hardly did it notice that its cork had been drawn, and that it had been emptied and carried into the cellar, to be placed there and forgotten. There's no place like home, even if it's in a cellar ! It never occurred to the bottle to think how long it would lie there, for it felt comfortable, and accordingly lay there for years. At last the people came down into the cellar to carry off all the bottles, and ours among the rest

Out in the garden there was a great festival. Flaming lamps hung like garlands, and paper lanterns shone transparent, like great tulips. The evening was lovely, the weather still and clear, the stars twinkled ; it was the time of the new moon, but in reality the whole moon could be seen as a bluish-gray disk with a golden rim round half its surface, which was a very beautiful sight for those who had good eyes.

The illumination extended even to the most retired of the garden walks ; at least so much of it, that one could find one's way there. Among the leaves of the hedges stood bottles, with a light in each ; and among them was also the bottle we know, and which was destined one day to finish its career as a bottle-neck, a bird's drinking-glass. Every thing here appeared lovely to our bottle, for it was once more in the greenwood, amid joy and feasting, and heard song and music, and the noise and murmur of a crowd, especially in that part of the garden where the lamps blazed and the paper lanterns displayed their many colors. Thus it stood, in a distant walk certainly, but that made it the more important ; for it bore its light, and was at once ornamental and useful, and that is as it should be : in such an hour one forgets twenty years spent in a loft, and it is right one should do so.

There passed close to it a pair, like the pair who had walked together long ago in the wood, the sailor and the tanner's daughter ; the bottle seemed to experience all that over again. In the garden were walking not only the guests, but other people who were allowed to view all the splendor; and among these latter came an old maid who seemed to stand alone in the world. She was just thinking, like the bottle, of the greenwood, and of a young betrothed pair—of a pair which concerned her very nearly, a pair in which she had an interest, and of which she had been a part, in the happiest hour of her life—the hour one never forgets, if one should become ever so old a maid. But she did not know our bottle, nor did the bottle recognize the old maid : it is thus we pass each other in the world, meeting again and again, as these two met, now that they were together again in the same town.

From the garden the bottle was dispatched once more to the wine merchant's, where it was filled with wine, and sold to the aëronaut, who was to make an ascent in his balloon on the following Sunday. A great crowd had assembled to witness the sight ; military music had been provided, and many other preparations had been made. The bottle saw every thing, from a basket in which it lay next to a live rabbit, which latter was quite bewildered because he knew he was to be taken up into the air, and let down again in a parachute ; but the bottle knew nothing of the " up " or the " down ;" it only saw the balloon swelling up bigger and bigger, and at last, when it could swell no more, beginning to rise, and to grow more and more restless. The ropes that held it were cut, and the huge machine floated aloft with the aëronaut and the basket containing the bottle and the rabbit, and the music sounded, and all the people cried, " Hurrah !"

" This is a wonderful passage, up into the air !" thought the bottle; " this is a new way of sailing ; at any rate, up here we cannot strike upon any thing."

Thousands of people gazed up at the balloon, and the old maid looked up at it also ; she stood at the open window of the garret, in which hung the cage with the little chaffinch, who had no water-glass as yet, but was obliged to be content with an old cup. In the window stood a myrtle in a pot; and it had been put a little aside that it might not fall out, for the old maid was leaning out of the window to look, and she distinctly saw the aëronaut in the balloon, and how he let down the rabbit in the parachute, and then drank to the health of all the spectators, and at length hurled the bottle high in the air. She never thought that this was the identical bottle which she had already once seen thrown aloft in honor of her and of her friend on the day of rejoicing in the greenwood, in the time of her youth.

The bottle had no respite for thought; for it was quite startled at thus suddenly reaching the highest point in its career. Steeples and roofs lay far, far beneath, and the people looked like mites.

But now it began to descend with a much more rapid fall than that of the rabbit; the bottle threw somersaults in the air, and felt quite young, and quite free and unfettered; and yet it was half full of wine, though it did not remain so long. What a journey! The sun shone on the bottle, all the people were looking at it, the balloon was already far away, and soon the bottle was far away too; for it fell upon a roof and broke; but the pieces had got such an impetus that they could not stop themselves, but went jumping and rolling on till they came down in the court-yard and lay there in smaller pieces yet; the bottle-neck only managed to keep whole, and that was cut off as clean as if it had been done with a diamond.

"That would do capitally for a bird-glass," said the cellerman; but they had neither bird nor cage; and to expect them to provide both, because they had found a bottle-neck that might be made available for a glass, would have been expecting too much: but the old maid in the garret, perhaps it might be useful to her; and now the bottle-neck was taken up to her, and was provided with a cork. The part that had been uppermost was now turned downwards, as often happens when changes take place; fresh water was poured into it, and it was fastened to the cage of the little bird, which sung and twittered right merrily.

"Yes, it's very well for you to sing," said the bottle-neck; and it was considered remarkable for having been in the balloon—for that was all they knew of its history. Now it hung there as a bird-glass, and heard the murmuring and noise of the people in the street below, and also the words of the old maid in the room within. An old friend had just come to visit her, and they talked—not of the bottle-neck, but about the myrtle in the window.

"No, you certainly must not spend a dollar for your daughter's bridal wreath," said the old maid. "You shall have a beautiful little nosegay from me, full of blossoms. Do you see how splendidly that tree has come on? yes, that has been raised from a spray of the myrtle you gave me on the day after my betrothal, and from which I was to have made my own wreath when the year was past; but that day never came! The eyes closed that were to have been my joy and delight through life. In the depths of the sea he sleeps sweetly, my dear one! The myrtle has become an old tree, and I am become a yet older woman; and when it faded at last, I took the last green shoot and planted it in the ground, and it has become a great tree; and now at length the myrtle will serve at the wedding—as a wreath for your daughter."

There were tears in the eyes of the old maid. She spoke of the beloved of her youth, of their betrothal in the wood; many thoughts came to her, but the thought never came, that quite close to her, before the very window, was a re membrance of those times; the neck of the bottle which had shouted for joy when the cork flew out with a bang on the betrothal day. But the bottle-neck did not recognize her, for he was not listening to what the old maid said—and still that was because he was thinking of her.

GOOD-HUMOR.

My father left me the best inheritance; to wit--good humor. And who was my father? Why, that has nothing to do with the humor. He was lively and stout, round and fat; and his outer and inner man were in direct contradiction to his calling. And pray what was he by profession and calling in civil society? Yes, if this were to be written down and printed in the very beginning of a book, it is probable that many when they read it would lay the book aside, and say, "It looks so uncomfortable—I don't like any thing of that sort." And yet my father was neither a horse slaughterer nor an executioner; on the contrary, his office placed him at the head of the most respectable gentry of the town; and he held his place by right, for it was his right place. He had to go first before the bishop even, and before the princes of the blood. He always went first—for he was the driver of the hearse !

There, now it's out ! And I will confess that when people saw my father sitting perched up on the omnibus of death, dressed in his long, wide, black cloak, with his black-bordered three-cornered hat on his head—and then his face, exactly as the sun is drawn, round and jocund—it was difficult for them to think of the grave and of sorrow. The face said, "It doesn't matter, it doesn't matter; it will be better than one thinks."

You see, I have inherited my good-humor from him, and also the habit of going often to the churchyard, which is a good thing to do if it be done in the right spirit; and then I take in the *Intelligencer*, just as he used to do.

I am not quite young. I have neither wife, nor children,

nor a library; but, as aforesaid, I take in the *Intelligencer*, and that's my favorite newspaper, as it was also my father's. It is very useful, and contains every thing that a man needs to know—such as who preaches in the church and in the new books. And then what a lot of charity, and what a number of innocent, harmless verses are found in it ! Advertisements for husbands and wives, and requests for interviews—all quite simple and natural. Certainly, one may live merrily and be contentedly buried if one takes in the *Intelligencer*. And, as a concluding advantage, by the end of his life a man will have such a capital store of paper, that he may use it as a soft bed, unless he prefers to rest upon wood-shavings.

The newspaper and my walk to the churchyard were always my most exciting occupations — they were like bathing-places for my good-humor.

The newspaper every one can read for himself. But please come with me to the churchyard ; let us wander there where the sun shines and the trees grow green. Each of the narrow houses is like a closed book, with the back placed uppermost, so that one can only read the title and judge what the book contains, but can tell nothing about it ; but I know something of them. I heard it from my father, or found it out myself. I have it all down in my record that I wrote out for my own use and pleasure : all that lie here, and a few more too, are chronicled in it.

Now we are in the churchyard.

Here, behind this white railing, where once a rose-tree grew—it is gone now, but a little evergreen from the next grave stretches out its green fingers to make a show—there rests a very unhappy man; and yet, when he lived, he was in what they call a good position. He had enough to live upon, and something over; but worldly cares, or to speak more correctly, his artistic taste, weighed heavily upon him. If in the evening he sat in the theatre to enjoy himself thoroughly, he would be quite put out if the machinist had put too strong a light into one side of the moon, or if the sky-pieces hung down over the scenes when they ought to have hung behind them, or when a palm-tree was introduced into a scene representing the Berlin Zoological Gardens, or a cactus in a view of the Tyrol, or a beech-tree in the far north of Norway. As if that was of any consequence. Is it not quite immaterial? Who would fidget about such a trifle? It's only make-believe, after all, and every one is expected to be amused. Then sometimes the public applauded too much to suit his taste, and sometimes too little. "They're like wet wood this evening," he would say; "they won't kindle at all!" And then he would look round to see what kind of people they were; and sometimes he would find them laughing at the wrong time, when they ought not to have laughed, and that vexed him; and he fretted, and was an unhappy man, and at last fretted himself into his grave.

Here rests a very happy man. That is to say, a very grand man. He was of high birth, and that was lucky for him, for otherwise he would never have been any thing worth speaking of; and nature orders all that very wisely, so that it's quite charming when we think of it. He used to go about in a coat embroidered back and front, and appeared in the saloons of society just like one of those costly, pearl-embroidered bell-pulls, which have always a good, thick, serviceable cord behind them to do the work. He likewise had a good stout cord behind him, in the shape of a substitute, who did his duty, and who still continues to do it behind another embroidered bell-pull. Every thing is so nicely managed, it's enough to put one into a good-humor.

Here rests—well, it's a very mournful reflection—here rests a man who spent sixty-seven years considering how he should get a good idea. The object of his life was to say a good thing, and at last he felt convinced in his own mind that he had got one, and was so glad of it that he died of pure joy at having caught an idea at last. Nobody derived any benefit from it, and no one even heard what the good thing was. Now, I can fancy that this same good thing won't let him live quiet in his grave; for let us suppose that it is a good thing which can only be brought out at breakfast if it is to make an effect, and that he, according to the received opinion concerning ghosts, can only rise and walk at midnight. Why, then the good thing would not suit the time, and the man must carry his good idea down with him again. What an unhappy man he must be!

Here rests a remarkably stingy woman. During her lifetime she used to get up at night and mew, so that the neighbors might think she kept a cat—she was so remarkably stingy.

Here is a maiden of another kind. When the canary bird of the heart begins to chirp, reason puts her fingers in her ears. The maiden was going to be married, but—well, it's an every-day story, and we will let the dead rest.

Here sleeps a widow who carried melody in her mouth and gall in her heart. She used to go out for prey in the families round about; and the prey she hunted was her neighbors' faults, and she was an indefatigable hunter.

Here's a family sepulchre. Every member of this family held so firmly to the opinions of the rest, that if all the world, and the newspapers into the bargain, said of a certain thing it is so and so, and the little boy came home from school and said, "I've learned it thus and thus," they declared his opinion to be the only true one, because he oc-

longed to the family.   And it is an acknowledged fact that if the yard-cock of the family crowed at midnight, they would declare it was morning, though the watchmen and all the clocks in the city were crying out that it was twelve o'clock at night.

The great poet Goethe concludes his "Faust" with the words "may be continued;" and our wanderings in the churchyard may be continued too.   If any of my friends, or my non-friends, go on too fast for me, I go out to my favorite spot and select a mound, and bury him or her here—bury that person who is yet alive; and there those I bury must stay till they come back as new and improved characters. I inscribe their life and their deeds, looked at in my fashion, in my record; and that's what all people ought to do.   They ought not to be vexed when any one goes on ridiculously, but bury him directly, and maintain their good-humor, and keep to the *Intelligencer*, which is often a book written by the people with its hand guided.

When the time comes for me to be bound with my history in the boards of the grave, I hope they will put up as my epitaph, "A good-humored one."   And that's my story.

A LEAF FROM THE SKY.

High up yonder, in the thin clear air, flew an angel with a flower from the heavenly garden.   As he was kissing the flower, a very little leaf fell down into the soft soil in the midst of the wood, and immediately took root, and sprouted, and sent forth shoots among the other plants.

" A funny kind of slip that," said the plants.

And neither thistle nor stinging-nettle would recognize the stranger.

"That must be a kind of garden plant," said they.

And they sneered; and the plant was despised by them as being a thing out of the garden.

"Where are you coming?" cried the lofty thistles, whose leaves are all armed with thorns.

"You give yourself a good deal of space. That's all nonsense—we are not here to support you!" they grumbled.

And winter came, and snow covered the plant; but the plant imparted to the snowy covering a lustre as if the sun was shining upon it from below as from above. When spring came, the plant appeared as a blooming object, more beautiful than any production of the forest.

And now appeared on the scene the botanical professor, who could show what he was in black and white. He inspected the plant and tested it, but found it was not included in his botanical system; and he could not possibly find out to what class it belonged.

"That must be some subordinate species," he said. "I don't know it. It's not included in any system."

"Not included in any system!" repeated the thistles and the nettles.

The great trees that stood round about saw and heard it; but they said not a word, good or bad, which is the wisest thing to do for people who are stupid.

There came through the forest a poor innocent girl. Her heart was pure, and her understanding was enlarged by faith. Her whole inheritance was an old Bible; but out of its pages a voice said to her, "If people wish to do us evil, remember how it was said of Joseph. They imagined evil in their hearts, but God turned it to good. If we suffer wrong—if we are misunderstood and despised—then we may recall the words of Him who was purity and goodness itself, and who forgave and prayed for those who buffeted Him and nailed Him to the cross." The girl stood still in front of the wonderful plant, whose great leaves exhaled a sweet and refreshing fragrance, and whose flowers glittered like a colored flame in the sun; and from each flower there came a sound as though it concealed within itself a deep fount of melody that thousands of years could not exhaust. With pious gratitude the girl looked on this beautiful work of the Creator, and bent down one of the branches towards herself to breathe in its sweetness; and a light arose in her soul. It seemed to do her heart good; and gladly would she have plucked a flower, but she could not make up her mind to break one off, for it would soon fade if she did so. Therefore the girl only took a single leaf, and laid it in her Bible at home; and it lay there quite fresh, always green, and never fading.

Among the pages of the Bible it was kept; and, with the Bible, it was laid under the young girl's head when, a few weeks afterwards, she lay in her coffin, with the solemn calm of death on her gentle face, as if the earthly remains bore the impress of the truth that she now stood before her Creator.

But the wonderful plant still bloomed without in the forest. It was almost like a tree to look upon; and all the birds of passage bowed before it.

"That's giving itself foreign airs now," said the thistles and the burdocks; "we never behave like that here."

And the black snails actually spat at the flower.

Then came the swineherd. He was collecting thistles and shrubs, to burn them for the ashes. The wonderful plant was placed bodily in his bundle.

"It shall be made useful," he said; and so said, so done.

But soon afterwards, the king of the country was troubled with a terrible depression of spirits. He was busy and industrious, but that did him no good. They read him deep and learned books, and then they read from the lightest and most superficial that they could find; but it was of no use. Then one of the wise men of the world, to whom they had applied, sent a messenger to tell the king that there was one remedy to give him relief and to cure him. He said:

"In the king's own country there grows in a forest a plant of heavenly origin. Its appearance is thus and thus. It cannot be mistaken."

"I fancy it was taken up in my bundle, and burnt to ashes long ago," said the swineherd; "but I did not know any better."

"You didn't know any better! Ignorance of ignorances!"

And those words the swineherd might well take to himself, for they were meant for him, and for no one else.

Not another leaf was to be found; the only one lay in the coffin of the dead girl, and no one knew any thing about that.

And the king himself, in his melancholy, wandered out to the spot in the wood.

"Here is where the plant stood," he said; "it is a sacred place."

And the place was surrounded with a golden railing, and a sentry was posted there.

The botanical professor wrote a long treatise upon the heavenly plant. For this he was gilded all over, and this gilding suited him and his family very well. And indeed that was the most agreeable part of the whole story. But the king remained as low-spirited as before; but that he had always been, at least so the sentry said.

THE DUMB BOOK.

By the high-road in the forest lay a lonely peasant's hut, the road went right through the farmyard. The sun shone down, and all the windows were open. In the house was bustle and movement ; but in the garden, in an arbor of blossoming elder, stood an open coffin. A dead man had been carried out here, and he was to be buried this morning Nobody stood by the coffin and looked sorrowfully at the dead man; no one shed a tear for him : his face was covered with a white cloth, and under his head lay a great thick book, whose leaves consisted of whole sheets of blotting-paper, and on each leaf lay a faded flower. It was a complete herbarium, gathered by him in various places; it was to be buried with him, for so he had wished it. With each flower a chapter in his life was associated.

"Who is the dead man?" we asked ; and the answer was :

"The Old Student. They say he was once a brisk lad, and studied the old languages, and sang, and even wrote poems. Then something happened to him that made him turn his thoughts to brandy, and take to it; and when at last he had ruined his health, he came out here into the country, where somebody paid for his board and lodging He was as gentle as a child, except when the dark mood came upon him; but when it came he became like a giant, and then ran about in the woods like a hunted stag; but when we once got him home again, and prevailed with him so far that he opened the book with the dried plants, he often sat whole days, and looked sometimes at one plant and sometimes at another, and at times the tears rolled over his cheeks : Heaven knows what he was thinking of. But he begged us to put the book into the coffin, and now he lies there, and in a little while the lid will be nailed down, and he will have his quiet rest in the grave."

The face-cloth was raised, and there was peace upon the features of the dead man, and a sunbeam played upon it; a swallow shot with arrowy flight into the arbor, and turned rapidly, and twittered over the dead man's head.

What a strange feeling it is—and we have doubtless all experienced it—that of turning over old letters of the days of our youth ! a new life seems to come up with them, with all its hopes and sorrows. How many persons with whom we were intimate in those days are, as it were, dead to us ! and yet they are alive, but for a long time we have not thought of them—of them whom we then thought to hold fast for ages, and with whom we were to share sorrow and joy.

Here the withered oak-leaf in the book reminded the owner of the friend, the school-fellow, who was to be a friend for life : he fastened the green leaf in the student's cap in the greenwood, when the bond was made " for life:" where does he live now ? The leaf is preserved, but the friendship has perished ! And here is a foreign hothouse plant, too delicate for the gardens of the North ; the leaves almost seem to keep their fragrance still. She gave it to him, the young lady in the nobleman's garden. Here is the water-rose, which he plucked himself, and moistened with salt tears—the roses of the sweet waters. And here is a nettle—what tale may its leaves have to tell ? What were his thoughts when he plucked it and kept it ? Here is a lily of the valley, from the solitudes of the forest. Here's an evergreen from the flower-pot of the tavern ; and here's a naked sharp blade of grass.

The blooming elder waves its fresh fragrant blossoms over the dead man's head, and the swallow flies past again. "Pee-wit! pee-wit!" And now the men come with nails and hammers, and the lid is laid over the dead man, that his head may rest upon the dumb book—vanished and scattered!

THE JEWISH GIRL.

AMONG the children in a charity school sat a little Jewish girl. She was a good, intelligent child, the quickest in all the school; but she had to be excluded from one lesson, for she was not allowed to take part in the Scripture lesson, for it was a Christian school.

In that hour the girl was allowed to open the geography book, or to do her sum for the next day; but that was soon done; and when she had mastered her lesson in geography, the book indeed remained open before her, but the little one read no more in it; she listened silently to the words of the Christian teacher, who soon became aware that she was listening more intently than almost any of the other children.

"Read your book, Sara," the teacher said, in mild reproof; but her dark beaming eye remained fixed upon him; and once when he addressed a question to her, she knew how to answer better than any of the others could have done. She had heard and understood, and had kept his words in her heart.

When her father, a poor, honest man, first brought the girl to the school, he had stipulated that she should be excluded from the lessons on the Christian faith. But it would have caused disturbance, and perhaps might have awakened discontent in the minds of the others, if she had been sent from the room during the hours in question, and consequently she stayed ; but this could not go on any longer.

The teacher betook himself to the father, and exhorted him either to remove his daughter from the school, or to consent that Sara should become a Christian.

"I can no longer be a silent spectator of the gleaming eyes of the child, and her deep and earnest longing for the words of the Gospel," said the teacher.

Then the father burst into tears.

"I know but little of the commandment given to my fathers," he said ; "but Sara's mother was steadfast in the faith, a true daughter of Israel, and I vowed to her as she lay dying that our child should never be baptized. I must keep my vow, for it is even as a covenant with God Himself."

And accordingly the little Jewish maiden quitted the Christian school.

Years have rolled on.

In one of the smallest provincial towns there dwelt, as a servant in a humble household, a maiden who held the Mosaic faith. Her hair was black as ebony, her eye dark as night, and yet full of splendor and light, as is usual with the daughters of Israel. It was Sara. The expression in the countenance of the now grown-up maiden was still that of the child sitting upon the school-room bench and listening with thoughtful eyes to the words of the Christian teacher.

Every Sunday there pealed from the church the sounds of the organ and the song of the congregation. The strains penetrated into the house where the Jewish girl, industrious and faithful in all things, stood at her work.

"Thou shalt keep holy the Sabbath-day," said a voice within her, the voice of the Law ; but her Sabbath-day was a working day among the Christians, and that seemed unfortunate to her. But then the thought arose in her soul: "Doth God reckon by days and hours ?" And when this thought grew strong within her, it seemed a comfort that on the Sunday of the Christians the hour of prayer remained undisturbed; and when the sound of the organ and the songs of the congregation sounded across to her as she stood in the kitchen at her work, then even that place seemed to become a sacred one to her. Then she would read in the Old Testament, the treasure and comfort of her people, and it was only in this one she could read ; for she kept faithfully in the depths of her heart the words the teacher had spoken when she left the school, and the promise her father had given to her dying mother, that she should never receive Christian baptism, or deny the faith of her ancestors. The New Testament was to be a sealed book to her; and yet she knew much of it, and the Gospel echoed faintly among the recollections of her youth.

One evening she was sitting in a corner of the living-room. Her master was reading aloud; and she might listen to him, for it was not the Gospel that he read, but an old story-book, therefore she might stay. The book told of a Hungarian knight who was taken prisoner by a Turkish pasha, who caused him to be yoked with his oxen to the plough, and driven with blows of the whip till the blood came, and he almost sank under the pain and ignominy he endured. The faithful wife of the knight at home parted with all her jewels, and pledged the castle and land. The knight's friends amassed large sums, for the ransom demanded was almost unattainably high : but it was collected at last, and the knight was freed from servitude and misery.

Sick and exhausted, he reached his home. But soon another summons came to war against the foes of Christianity: the knight heard the cry, and he could stay no longer, for he had neither peace nor rest. He caused himself to be lifted on his war-horse; and the blood came back to his cheek, his strength appeared to return, and he went forth to battle and to victory. The very same pasha who had yoked him to the plough became his prisoner, and was dragged to his castle. But not an hour had passed when the knight stood before the captive pasha, and said to him:

"What dost thou suppose awaiteth thee?"

"I know it," replied the Turk. "Retribution."

"Yes, the retribution of the Christian!" resumed the knight. "The doctrine of Christ commands us to forgive our enemies, and to love our fellow-man, for it teaches us that God is love. Depart in peace, depart to thy home: I will restore thee to thy dear ones; but in future be mild and merciful to all who are unfortunate."

Then the prisoner broke out into tears, and exclaimed:

"How could I believe in the possibility of such mercy! Misery and torment seemed to await me, they seemed inevitable; therefore I took poison, which I secretly carried about me, and in a few hours its effects will slay me. I must die—there is no remedy! But before I die, do thou expound to me the teaching which includes so great a measure of love and mercy, for it is great and godlike! Grant me to hear this teaching, and to die a Christian!" And his prayer was fulfilled.

That was the legend which the master read out of the old story-book. All the audience listened with sympathy and pleasure; but Sara, the Jewish girl, sitting alone in her corner, listened with a burning heart; great tears came into her gleaming black eyes, and she sat there with a gentle and lowly spirit as she had once sat on the school bench, and felt the grandeur of the Gospel ; and the tears rolled down over her cheeks.

But again the dying words of her mother rose up within her :

"Let not my daughter become a Christian," the voice cried ; and together with it arose the word of the law: "Thou shalt honor thy father and thy mother."

"I am not admitted into the community of the Christians," she said; "they abuse me for being a Jew girl—our neighbor's boys hooted me last Sunday, when I stood at the open church-door, and looked in at the flaming candles on the altar, and listened to the song of the congregation. Ever since I sat upon the school bench I have felt the force of Christianity, a force like that of a sunbeam, which streams into my soul, however firmly I may shut my eyes against it. But I will not pain thee in thy grave, O my mother, I will not be unfaithful to the oath of my father, I will not read the Bible of the Christians. I have the religion of my people, and to that will I hold!"

And years rolled on again.

The master died. His widow fell into poverty ; and the servant girl was to be dismissed. But Sara refused to leave the house: she became the staff in time of trouble, and kept the household together, working till late in the night to earn the daily bread through the labor of her hands; for no relative came forward to assist the family, and the widow became weaker every day, and lay for months together on the bed of sickness. Sara worked hard, and in the intervals sat kindly ministering by the sick-bed: she was gentle and pious, an angel of blessing in the poverty-stricken house.

"Yonder on the table lies the Bible," said the sick woman to Sara. "Read me something from it, for the night appears to be so long—oh, so long!—and my soul thirsts for the word of the Lord."

And Sara bowed her head. She took the book, and folded her hands over the Bible of the Christians, and opened it, and read to the sick woman. Tears stood in her eyes, which gleamed and shone with ecstasy, and light shone in her heart.

" Oh, my mother," she whispered to herself ; " thy child may not receive the baptism of the Christians, or be admitted into the congregation—thou hast willed it so, and I shall respect thy command : we will remain in union together on earth; but beyond this earth there is a higher union, even union in God ! He will be at our side, and lead us through the valley of death. It is He that descendeth upon the earth when it is athirst, and covers it with fruitfulness. I understand it—I know not how I came to learn the truth; but it is through Him, through Christ !"

And she started as she pronounced the sacred name, and there came upon her a baptism as of flames of fire, and her frame shook, and her limbs tottered, so that she sank down fainting, weaker even than the sick woman by whose couch she had watched.

" Poor Sara !" said the people; " she is overcome with night watching and toil !"

They carried her out into the hospital for the sick poor. There she died; and from thence they carried her to the grave, but not to the churchyard of the Christians, for yonder was no room for the Jewish girl; outside, by the wall, her grave was dug.

But God's sun, that shines upon the graves of the Christians, throws its beams also upon the grave of the Jewish girl beyond the wall; and when the psalms are sung in the churchyard of the Christians, they echo likewise over her lonely resting-place; and she who sleeps beneath is included in the call to the resurrection, in the name of Him who spake to his disciples :

"John baptized you with water, but I will baptize you with the Holy Ghost !"

<hr>

THE THORNY ROAD OF HONOR.

An old story yet lives of the "Thorny Road of Honor," of a marksman, who indeed attained to rank and office, but only after a lifelong and weary strife against difficulties. Who has not, in reading this story, thought of his own strife, and of his own numerous "difficulties?" The story is very closely akin to reality; but still it has its harmonious explanation here on earth, while reality often points beyond the confines of life to the regions of eternity. The history of the world is like a magic-lantern that displays to us, in light pictures upon the dark ground of the present, how the benefactors of mankind, the martyrs of genius, wandered along the thorny road of honor.

From all periods, and from every country, these shining pictures display themselves to us; each only appears for a few moments, but each represents a whole life, sometimes a whole age, with its conflicts and victories. Let us contemplate here and there one of the company of martyrs— the company which will receive new members until the world itself shall pass away.

We look down upon a crowded amphitheatre. Out of the

"Clouds" of Aristophanes, satire and humor are pouring down in streams upon the audience; on the stage, Socrates, the most remarkable man in Athens, he who had been the shield and defence of the people against the thirty tyrants, is held up mentally and bodily to ridicule—Socrates, who saved Alcibiades and Xenophon in the turmoil of battle, and whose genius soared far above the gods of the ancients. He himself is present; he has risen from the spectator's bench, and has stepped forward, that the laughing Athenians may well appreciate the likeness between himself and the caricature on the stage : there he stands before them, towering high above them all.

Thou juicy, green, poisonous hemlock, throw thy shadow over Athens—not thou, olive-tree of fame !

Seven cities contended for the honor of giving birth to Homer—that is to say, they contended after his death ! Let us look at him as he was in his lifetime. He wanders on foot through the cities, and recites his verses for a livelihood; the thought for the morrow turns his hair gray ! He, the great seer, is blind, and painfully pursues his way—the sharp thorn tears the mantle of the king of poets. His song yet lives, and through that alone live all the heroes and gods of antiquity.

One picture after another springs up from the east, from the west, far removed from each other in time and place, and yet each one forming a portion of the thorny road of honor, on which the thistle indeed displays a flower, but only to adorn the grave.

The camels pass along under the palm-trees; they are richly laden with indigo and other treasures of price, sent by the ruler of the land to him whose songs are the delight of the people, the fame of the country : he whom envy and falsehood have driven into exile has been found, and the caravan approaches the little town in which he has taken refuge. A poor corpse is carried out of the town-gate, and the funeral procession causes the caravan to halt. The dead man is he whom they have been sent to seek—Firdusi—who has wandered the thorny road of honor even to the end.

The African, with blunt features, thick lips, and woolly hair, sits on the marble steps of the palace in the capital of Portugal, and begs : he is the submissive slave of Camoens, and but for him, and for the copper coins thrown to him by the passers-by, his master, the poet of the " Lusiad," would die of hunger. Now, a costly monument marks the grave of Camoens.

There is a new picture.

Behind the iron grating a man appears, pale as death, with long unkempt beard.

" I have made a discovery," he says, " the greatest that has been made for centuries; and they have kept me locked up here for more than twenty years !"

Who is the man ?

" A madman," replies the keeper of the madhouse. " What whimsical ideas these lunatics have ! He imagines that one can propel things by means of steam. It is Solomon de Cares, the discoverer of the power of steam, whose theory, expressed in dark words, is not understood by Richelieu—and he dies in the madhouse !"

Here stands Columbus, whom the street boys used once to follow and jeer, because he wanted to discover a new world—and he *has* discovered it. Shouts of joy greet him from the breasts of all, and the clash of bells sounds to celebrate his triumphant return; but the clash of the bells of envy soon drowns the others. The discoverer of a world, he who lifted the American gold land from the sea, and gave it to his king—he is rewarded with iron chains. He wishes that these chains may be placed in his coffin, for they witness of the world, and of the way in which a man's contemporaries reward good service.

One picture after another comes crowding on; the thorny path of honor and of fame is over-filled.

Here in dark night sits the man who measured the mountains in the moon; he who forced his way out into the endless space, among stars and planets; he, the mighty man who understood the spirit of nature, and felt the earth moving beneath his feet—Galileo. Blind and deaf he sits —an old man thrust through with the spear of suffering, and amid the torments of neglect, scarcely able to lift his foot—that foot with which, in the anguish of his soul, when men denied the truth, he stamped upon the ground with the exclamation, " *Yet* it moves !"

Here stands a woman of childlike mind, yet full of faith and inspiration; she carries the banner in front of the combating army, and brings victory and salvation to her fatherland. The sound of shouting arises, and the pile flames up : they are burning the witch, Joan of Arc. Yes, and a future century jeers at the white lily. Voltaire, the satyr of human intellect, writes " *La Pucelle.*"

At the *Thing* or assembly at Viborg, the Danish nobles burn the laws of the king—they flame up high, illuminating the period and the lawgiver, and throw a glory into the dark prison-tower, where an old man is growing gray and bent. With his finger he marks out a groove in the stone table. It is the popular king who sits there, once the ruler of three kingdoms, the friend of the citizen and the peasant : it is Christian the Second. Enemies wrote his history. Let us remember his improvements of seven and twenty years, if we cannot forget his crime.

A ship sails away, quitting the Danish shores; a man leans against the mast, casting a last glance towards the Island Hueen. It is Tycho Brahé. He raised the name of Denmark to the stars, and was rewarded with injury, loss, nd sorrow. He is going to a strange country.

"The vault of heaven is above me everywhere," he says, "and what do I want more?" And away sails the famous Dane, the astronomer, to live honored and free in a strange land.

"Ay, free, if only from the unbearable sufferings of the body!" comes in a sigh through time, and strikes upon our ear. What a picture! Griffenfeldt, a Danish Prometheus, bound to the rocky island of Munkholm.

We are in America, on the margin of one of the largest rivers; an innumerable crowd has gathered, for it is said that a ship is to sail against wind and weather, bidding defiance to the elements; the man who thinks he can solve the problem is named Robert Fulton. The ship begins its passage, but suddenly it stops. The crowd begins to laugh and whistle and hiss—the very father of the man whistles with the rest.

"Conceit! Foolery!" is the cry. "It has happened just as he deserved : put the crack-brain under lock and key!"

Then suddenly a little nail breaks, which had stopped the machine for a few moments; and now the wheels turn again, he floats break the force of the waters, and the ship continues its course—and the beam of the steam-engine short ens the distance between far lands from hours into minutes.

O human race, canst thou grasp the happiness of such a minute of consciousness, this penetration of the soul by its mission, the moment in which all dejection, and every wound —even those caused by thy own fault—is changed into health and strength and clearness—when discord is converted to harmony—the minute in which men seem to recognize the manifestation of the heavenly grace in one man, and feel how this one imparts it to all?

Thus the thorny path of honor shows itself as a glory, surrounding the earth with its beams : thrice happy he who is chosen to be a wanderer there, and, without merit of his own, to be placed between the builder of the bridge and the earth, between Providence and the human race !

On mighty wings the spirit of history floats through the ages, and shows—giving courage and comfort, and awakening gentle thoughts—on the dark nightly background, but in gleaming pictures, the thorny path of honor; which does not, like a fairy tale, end in brilliancy and joy here on earth, but stretches out beyond all time, even into eternity !

———◆•◆———

THE OLD GRAVESTONE.

In a little provincial town, in the time of the year when people say "the evenings are drawing in," there was one evening quite a social gathering in the home of a father of a family. The weather was still mild and warm. The lamp gleamed on the table; the long curtains hung down in folds before the open windows, by which stood many flower-pots; and outside, beneath the dark blue sky, was the most beautiful moonshine. But they were not talking about this. They were talking about the old great stone which lay below in the courtyard, close by the kitchen door, and on which the maids often laid the cleaned copper kitchen utensils that

they might dry in the sun, and where the children were
fond of playing. It was, in fact, an old gravestone.

"Yes," said the master of the house, "I believe the stone
comes from the old convent churchyard; for from the church
yonder, the pulpit, the memorial boards, and the gravestones
were sold. My father bought the latter, and they were cut
in two to be used as paving-stones; but that old stone was
kept back, and has been lying in the courtyard ever since."

"One can very well see that it is a gravestone," observed
the eldest of the children ; "we can still decipher on it an
hour-glass and a piece of an angel ; but the inscription
which stood below it is quite effaced, except that you may
read the name of *Preben*, and a great *S* close behind it, and
a little further down the name of *Martha*. But nothing
more can be distinguished, and even that is only plain when
it has been raining, or when we have washed the stone."

"On my word, that must be the gravestone of Preben
Schwane and his wife !"

These words were spoken by an old man ; so old, that he
might well have been the grandfather of all who were present in the room.

"Yes, they were one of the last pairs that were buried
in the old churchyard of the convent. They were an honest old couple. I can remember them from the days of my
boyhood. Every one knew them, and every one esteemed
them. They were the oldest pair here in the town. The
people declared that they had more than a tubful of gold ;
and yet they went about very plainly dressed, in the
coarsest stuffs, but always with splendidly clean linen.
They were a fine old pair, Preben and Martha ! When
both of them sat on the bench at the top of the steep stone
stairs in front of the house, with the old linden-tree spreading its branches above them, and nodded at one in their

kind gentle way, it seemed quite to do one good. They were very kind to the poor ; they fed them and clothed them ; and there was judgment in their benevolence, and true Christianity. The old woman died first : that day is still quite clear before my mind. I was a little boy, and had accompanied my father over there, and we were just there when she fell asleep. The old man was very much moved, and wept like a child. The corpse lay in the room next to the one where we sat ; and he spoke to my father and to a few neighbors who were there, and said how lonely it would be now in his house, and how good and faithful she (his dead wife) had been, how many years they had wandered together through life, and how it had come about that they came to know each other and to fall in love. I was, as I have told you, a boy, and only stood by and listened to what the others said ; but it filled me with quite a strange emotion to listen to the old man, and to watch how his cheeks gradually flushed red when he spoke of the days of their courtship, and told how beautiful she was, and how many little innocent pretexts he had invented to meet her. And then he talked of the wedding-day, and his eyes gleamed ; he seemed to talk himself back into that time of joy. And yet she was lying in the next room—dead— an old woman ; and he was an old man, speaking of the past days of hope ! Yes, yes, thus it is ! Then I was but a child, and now I am old—as old as Preben Schwane was then. Time passes away, and all things change. I can very well remember the day when she was buried, and how Preben Schwane walked close behind the coffin. A few years before the couple had caused their gravestone to be prepared, and their names to be engraved on it, with the inscription, all but the date. In the evening the stone was taken to the churchyard, and laid over the grave ; and the year afterwards it was taken up, that old Preben Schwane might be laid to rest beside his wife. They did not leave behind them any thing like the wealth people had attributed to them : what there was went to families distantly related to them—to people of whom until then one had known nothing. The old wooden house, with the seat at the top of the steps, beneath the lime-tree, was taken down by the corporation ; it was too old and rotten to be left standing. Afterwards, when the same fate befell the convent church, and the graveyard was levelled, Preben's and Martha's tombstone was sold, like every thing else, to any one who would buy it ; and that is how it has happened that this stone was not hewn in two, as many another has been, but that it still lies below in the yard as a scouring-bench for the maids, and a plaything for the children. The high-road now goes over the resting-place of old Preben and his wife. No one thinks of them any more."

And the old man who had told all this shook his head scornfully.

" Forgotten ! Every thing will be forgotten !" he said.

And then they spoke in the room of other things ; but the youngest child, a boy with great serious eyes, mounted up on a chair behind the window-curtains, and looked out into the yard, where the moon was pouring its radiance over the old stone—the old stone that had always appeared to him so tame and flat, but which lay there now like a great leaf out of a book of chronicles. All that the boy had heard about old Preben and his wife seemed concentrated in the stone ; and he gazed at it, and looked at the pure bright moon and up into the clear air, and it seemed as though the countenance of the Creator was beaming over His world.

"Forgotten! Every thing will be forgotten!" was repeated in the room.

But in that moment an invisible angel kissed the boy's forehead, and whispered to him :

"Preserve the seed-corn that has been intrusted to thee, that it may bear fruit. Guard it well! Through thee, my child, the obliterated inscription on the old tombstone shall be chronicled in golden letters to future generations! The old pair shall wander again arm in arm through the streets, and smile, and sit with their fresh healthy faces under the lime-tree on the bench by the steep stairs, and nod at rich and poor. The seed-corn of this hour shall ripen in the course of time to a blooming poem. The beautiful and the good shall not be forgotten ; it shall live on in legend and in song."

<hr>

THE OLD BACHELOR'S NIGHTCAP.

There is a street in Copenhagen that has this strange name—"Hysken Sträde." Whence comes this name, and what is its meaning ? It is said to be German ; but injustice has been done to the Germans in this matter, for it would have to be "Häuschen," and not "Hysken." For here stood, once upon a time, and indeed for a great many years, a few little houses, which were principally nothing more than wooden booths, just as we see now in the market-places at fair-time. They were, perhaps, a little larger, and had windows ; but the panes consisted of horn or bladder, for glass was then too expensive to be used in every house. But then we are speaking of a long time ago—so long since, that grandfather and great-grandfather,

when they talked about them, used to speak of them as
" the old times "—in fact, it is several centuries ago.

The rich merchants in Bremen and Lubeck carried on
trade with Copenhagen. They did not reside in the town
themselves, but sent their clerks, who lived in the wooden
booths in the Häuschen Street, and sold beer and spices.
The German beer was good, and there were many kinds of
it, as there were, for instance, Bremen, and Prussinger, and
Sons beer, and even Brunswick mumm ; and quantities of
spices were sold—saffron, and aniseed, and ginger, and especially pepper. Yes, pepper was the chief article here,
and so it happened that the German clerks got the nick-
name " pepper gentry ;" and there was a condition made
with them in Lubeck and in Bremen, that they would not
marry at Copenhagen, and many of them became very old.
They had to care for themselves, and to look after their
own comforts, and to put out their own fires—when they
had any ; and some of them became very solitary old boys,
with eccentric ideas and eccentric habits. From them, all
unmarried men, who have attained a certain age, are called
in Denmark " pepper gentry ;" and this must be understood
by all who wish to comprehend this history.

The " pepper gentleman " becomes a butt for ridicule, and
is continually told that he ought to put on his nightcap,
and draw it down over his eyes, and do nothing but sleep
The boys sing,

> " Cut, cut wood !
> Poor bachelor so good.
> Go, take your nightcap, go to rest,
> For 'tis the nightcap suits you best !"

Yes, that's what they sing about the " pepperer "—thus they
make game of the poor bachelor and his nightcap, and turn

it into ridicule, just because they know very little about either. Ah, that kind of nightcap no one should wish to earn ! And why not ?—We shall hear :

In the old times the " Housekin Street" was not paved, and people stumbled out of one hole into another, as in a neglected by-way; and it was narrow too. The booths leaned side by side, and stood so close together that in the summer-time a sail was often stretched from one booth to its opposite neighbor, on which occasion the fragrance of pepper, saffron, and ginger became doubly powerful. Behind the counters young men were seldom seen. The clerks were generally old boys; but they did not look like what we should fancy them, namely, with wig, and nightcap, and plush small-clothes, and with waistcoat and coat buttoned up to the chin. No, grandfather's great-grandfather may look like that, and has been thus portrayed, but the " pepper gentry" had no superfluous means, and accordingly did not have their portraits taken ; though, indeed, it would be interesting now to have a picture of one of them, as he stood behind the counter or went to church on holy-days. His hat was high-crowned and broad-brimmed, and sometimes one of the youngest clerks would mount a feather. The woollen shirt was hidden behind a broad linen collar, the close jacket was buttoned up to the chin, and the cloak hung loose over it ; and the trowsers were tucked in to the broad-toed shoes, for the clerks did not wear stockings. In their girdles they sported a dinner-knife and spoon, and a larger knife was placed there also for the defence of the owner; and this weapon was often very necessary. Just so was Anthony, one of the oldest clerks, clad on high-days and holy-days, except that, instead of a high-crowned hat, he wore a low bonnet, and under it a knitted cap (a regular nightcap), to which he had grown so accustomed that it was always on his head ; and he had two of them—night caps, of course. The old fellow was a subject for a painter. He was as thin as a lath, had wrinkles clustering round his eyes and mouth, and long bony fingers, and bushy gray eyebrows: over the left eye hung quite a tuft of hair, and that did not look very handsome, though it made him very noticeable. People knew that he came from Bremen; but that was not his native place, though his master lived there. His own native place was in Thuringia, the town of Eisenach, close by the Wartburg. Old Anthony did not speak much of this, but he thought of it all the more.

The old clerks of the Häuschen Street did not often come together. Each one remained in his booth, which was closed early in the evening; and then it looked dark enough in the street: only a faint glimmer of light forced its way through the little horn-pane in the roof; and in the booth sat, generally on his bed, the old bachelor, his German hymn-book in his hand, singing an evening psalm in a low voice; or he went about in the booth till late into the night, and busied himself about all sorts of things. It was certainly not an amusing life. To be a stranger in a strange land is a bitter lot : nobody cares for you, unless you happen to get in anybody's way.

Often when it was dark night outside, with snow and rain, the place looked very gloomy and lonely. No lamps were to be seen, with the exception of one solitary light hanging before the picture of the Virgin that was fastened against the wall. The plash of the water against the neighboring rampart at the castle wharf could be plainly heard. Such evenings are long and dreary, unless people devise some employment for themselves. There is not always packing or unpacking to do, nor can the scales be polished or paper bags be made continual'y; and, failing these, peo-

ple should devise other employment for themselves. And
that is just what old Anthony did; for he used to mend his
clothes and put pieces on his boots. When he at last
sought his couch, he used from habit to keep his nightcap
on. He drew it down a little closer; but soon he would
push it up again, to see if the light had been properly extinguished. He would touch it, press the wick together,
and then lie down on the other side, and draw his nightcap
down again; but then a doubt would come upon him, if
every coal in the little firepan below had been properly
deadened and put out—a tiny spark might have been left
burning, and might set fire to something and cause damage.
And therefore he rose from his bed, and crept down the ladder, for it could scarcely be called a stair. And when he
came to the firepan not a spark was to be discovered, and
he might just go back again. But often, when he had gone
half the way back, it would occur to him that the shutters
might not be securely fastened ; yes, then his thin legs
must carry him down-stairs once more. He was cold, and
his teeth chattered in his mouth when he crept back again
to bed; for the cold seems to become doubly severe when it
knows it cannot stay much longer. He drew up the
coverlet closer around him, and pulled down the nightcap
lower over his brows, and turned his thoughts away from
trade and from labors of the day. But that did not procure
him agreeable entertainment; for now old thoughts came
and put up their curtains, and these curtains have sometimes pins in them, with which one pricks one's self, and one
cries out " Oh !" and they prick into one's flesh and burn
so, that the tears sometimes come into one's eyes; and that
often happened to old Anthony—hot tears. The largest
pearls streamed forth, and fell on the coverlet or on the
floor, and then they sounded as if one of his heartstrings

had broken. Sometimes again they seemed to rise up in flame, illuminating a picture of life that never faded out of his heart. If he then dried his eyes with his nightcap, the tears and the picture were indeed crushed, but the source of the tears remained, and welled up afresh from his heart. The pictures did not come up in the order in which the scenes had occurred in reality, for very often the most painful would come together; then again the most joyful would come, but these had the deepest shadows of all.

The beech-woods of Denmark are acknowledged to be fine, but the woods of Thuringia arose far more beautiful in the eyes of Anthony. More mighty and more venerable seemed to him the old oaks around the proud knightly castle, where the creeping plants hung down over the stony blocks of the rock ; sweeter there bloomed the flowers of the apple-tree than in the Danish land. This he remem bered very vividly. A glittering tear rolled down over his cheek; and in this tear he could plainly see two children playing—a boy and a girl. The boy had red cheeks, and yellow curling hair, and honest blue eyes. He was the son of the merchant Anthony—it was himself. The little girl had brown eyes and black hair, and had a bright clever look. She was the burgomaster's daughter Molly. The two were playing with an apple. They shook the apple, and heard the pips rattling in it. Then they cut the apple in two, and each of them took a half; they divided even the pips, and ate them all but one, which the little girl proposed that they should lay in the earth.

"Then you shall see," she said, " what will come out. It will be something you don't at all expect. A whole apple-tree will come out, but not directly."

And she put the pip in a flower-pot, and both were very busy and eager about it. The boy made a hole in the earth with his finger, and the little girl dropped the pip in it, and they both covered it with earth.

"Now, you must not take it out to-morrow to see if it has struck root," said Molly. "That won't do at all. I did it with my flowers; but only twice. I wanted to see if they were growing—and I didn't know any better then—and the plants withered."

Anthony took away the flower-pot, and every morning, the whole winter through, he looked at it; but nothing was to be seen but the black earth. At length, however, the spring came, and the sun shone warm again; and two little green leaves came up out of the pot.

"Those are for me and Molly," said the boy. "That's beautiful—that's marvellously beautiful!"

Soon a third leaf made its appearance. Whom did that represent? Yes, and there came another, and yet another. Day by day and week by week they grew larger, and the plant began to take the form of a real tree. And all this was now mirrored in a single tear, which was wiped away and disappeared; but it might come again from its source in the heart of old Anthony.

In the neighborhood of Eisenach a row of stony mountains rises up. One of these mountains is round in outline, and lifts itself above the rest, naked and without tree, bush, or grass. It is called the Venus Mount. In this mountain dwells Lady Venus, one of the deities of the heathen times. She is also called Lady Holle; and every child in and around Eisenach has heard about her. She it was who ured Tannhauser, the noble knight and minstrel, from the circle of the singers of the Wartburg into her mountain.

Little Molly and Anthony often stood by this mountain: and once Molly said:

"You may knock and say, 'Lady Holle, open the door—Tannhauser is here!'"

But Anthony did not dare. Molly, however, did it, though she only said the words, "Lady Holle, Lady Holle!" aloud and distinctly; the rest she muttered so indistinctly that Anthony felt convinced she had not really said any thing; and yet she looked as bold and saucy as possible—as saucy as when she sometimes came round him with other little girls in the garden, and all wanted to kiss him because he did not like to be kissed and tried to keep them off; and she was the only one who dared to kiss him in spite of his resistance.

"*I* may kiss him!" she would say proudly.

That was her vanity; and Anthony submitted, and thought no more about it.

How charming and how teasing Molly was! It was said that Lady Holle in the mountain was beautiful also, but that her beauty was like that of a tempting fiend. The greatest beauty and grace was possessed by Saint Elizabeth, the patron of the country, the pious Princess of Thuringia, whose good actions have been immortalized in many places in legends and stories. In the chapel her picture was hanging, surrounded by silver lamps; but it was not in the least like Molly.

The apple-tree which the two children had planted grew year by year, and became taller and taller—so tall, that it had to be transplanted into the garden, into the fresh air, where the dew fell and the sun shone warm. And the tree developed itself strongly, so that it could resist the winter. And it seemed as if, after the rigor of the cold season was past, it put forth blossoms in spring for very joy. In the autumn it brought two apples—one for Molly and one for Anthony. It could not well have produced less.

The tree had grown apace, and Molly grew like the tree. She was as fresh as an apple-blossom; but Anthony was not long to behold this flower. All things change! Molly's father left his old home, and Molly went with him, far away. Yes, in our time steam has made the journey they took a matter of a few hours, but then more than a day and a night were necessary to go so far eastward from Eisenach to the furthest border of Thuringia, to the city which is still called Weimar.

And Molly wept, and Anthony wept; but all their tears melted into one, and this tear had the rosy, charming hue of joy. For Molly told him she loved him—loved him more than all the splendors of Weimar.

One, two, three years went by, and during this period two letters were received. One came by a carrier, and a traveller brought the other. The way was long and difficult, and passed through many windings by towns and villages.

Often had Molly and Anthony heard of Tristram and Iseult, and often had the boy applied the story to himself and Molly, though the name Tristram was said to mean "born in tribulation," and that did not apply to Anthony, nor would he ever be able to think, like Tristram, "She has forgotten me." But, indeed, Iseult did not forget her faithful knight; and when both were laid to rest in the earth, one on each side of the church, the linden-trees grew from their graves over the church roof, and there encountered each other in bloom. Anthony thought that was beautiful, but mournful; but it could not become mournful between him and Molly: and he whistled a song of the old minne-singer, Walter of the Vogelverde:

> "Under the lindens
> Upon the heath."

And especially that passage appeared charming to him :

> " From the forest, down in the vale,
>   Sang her sweet song to the nightingale."

This song was often in his mouth, and he sang and whistled it in the moonlight nights, when he rode along the deep hollow way on horseback to get to Weimar and visit Molly. He wished to come unexpectedly, and he came unexpectedly.

He was made welcome with full goblets of wine, with jovial company, fine company, and a pretty room and a good bed were provided for him; and yet his reception was not what he had dreamt and fancied it would be. He could not understand himself—he could not understand the others : but *we* can understand it. One may be admitted into a house and associate with the family without becoming one of them. One may converse together as one would converse in a post-carriage, and know one another as people know each other on a journey, each incommoding the other and wishing that either one's self or the good neighbor were away. Yes, this was the kind of thing Anthony felt.

" I am an honest girl," said Molly ; " and I myself will tell you what it is. Much has changed since we were children together—changed inwardly and outwardly. Habit and will have no power over our hearts. Anthony, I should not like to have an enemy in you, now that I shall soon be far away from here. Believe me, I entertain the best wishes for you; but to feel for you what I know now one may feel for a man, has never been the case with me. You must reconcile yourself to this. Farewell, Anthony !"

And Anthony bade her farewell. No tear came into his eye, but he felt that he was no longer Molly's friend. Hot iron and cold iron alike take the skin from our lips, and we have the same feeling when we kiss it : and he kissed him-self into hatred as into love.

Within twenty-four hours Anthony was back in Eisenach, though certainly the horse on which he rode was ruined.

"What matter !" he said : "I am ruined too ; and I will destroy every thing that can remind me of her, or of Lady Holle, or Venus the heathen woman ! I will break down the apple-tree and tear it up by the roots, so that it never shall bear flower or fruit more !"

But the apple-tree was not broken down, though he him-self was broken down, and bound on a couch by fever. What was it that raised him up again? A medicine was presented to him which had strength to do this—the bitterest of medicines, that shakes up body and spirit together. An-thony's father ceased to be the richest of merchants. Heavy days—days of trial—were at the door ; misfortune came rolling into the house like great waves of the sea. The father became a poor man. Sorrow and suffering took away his strength. Then Anthony had to think of some-thing else besides nursing his love-sorrows and his anger against Molly. He had to take his father's place—to give orders, to help, to act energetically, and at last to go out into the world and earn his bread.

Anthony went to Bremen. There he learned what poverty and hard-living meant ; and these sometimes make the heart hard, and sometimes soften it, even too much.

How different the world was, and how different the people from what he had supposed them to be in his childhood ! What were the minne-singer's songs to him now ?—an echo, a vanishing sound ! Yes, that is what he thought some-times ; but again the songs would sound in his soul, and his heart became gentle.

"God's will is best !" he would say then. "It is well

that I was not permitted to keep Molly's heart—that she did not remain true to me. What would it have led to now, when fortune has turned away from me? She quitted me before she knew of this loss of prosperity, or had any notion of what awaited me. That was a mercy of Providence towards me. Every thing has happened for the best. It was not her fault—and I have been so bitter, and have shown so much rancor towards her!"

And years went by. Anthony's father was dead, and strangers lived in the old house. But Anthony was destined to see it again. His rich employer sent him on commercial journeys, and his duty led him into his native town of Eisenach. The old Wartburg stood unchanged on the mountain, with "the monk and the nun" hewn out in stone. The great oaks gave to the scene the outlines it had possessed in his childish days. The Venus Mount glimmered gray and naked over the valley. He would have been glad to cry, "Lady Holle, Lady Holle, unlock the door, and I shall enter and remain in my native earth!"

That was a sinful thought, and he blessed himself to drive it away. Then a little bird out of the thicket sang clearly, and the old minne-song came into his mind :

> "From the forest, down in the vale,
> Sang her sweet song the nightingale."

And here in the town of his childhood, which he thus saw again through tears, much came back into his remembrance. The paternal house stood as in the old times; but the garden was altered, and a field-path led over a portion of the old ground, and the apple-tree that he had not broken down stood there, but outside the garden, on the further side of the path. But the sun threw its rays on the apple-tree as in the old days, the dew descended gently upon it as then, and it bore such a burden of fruit that the branches were bent down towards the earth.

"That flourishes!" he said. "The tree can grow!"

Nevertheless, one of the branches of the tree was broken Mischievous hands had torn it down towards the ground; for now the tree stood by the public way

"They break its blossoms off without a feeling of thankfulness—they steal its fruit and break the branches. One might say of the tree as has been said of some men—'It was not sung at his cradle that it should come thus.' How brightly its history began, and what has it come to? Forsaken and forgotten—a garden tree by the hedge, in the field, and on the public way! There it stands unprotected, plundered, and broken! It has certainly not died, but in the course of years the number of blossoms will diminish; at last the fruit will cease altogether; and at last—at last all will be over!"

Such were Anthony's thoughts under the tree; such were his thoughts during many a night in the lonely chamber of the wooden house in the distant land—in the Häuschen Street in Copenhagen, whither his rich employer, the Bremen merchant, had sent him, first making it a condition that he should not marry.

"Marry! Ha, ha!" he laughed bitterly to himself.

Winter had set in early; it was freezing hard. Without, a snow-storm was raging, so that every one who could do so remained at home; thus, too, it happened that those who lived opposite to Anthony did not notice that for two days his house had not been unlocked, and that he did not show himself; for who would go out unnecessarily in such weather?

They were gray, gloomy days; and in the house, whose windows were not of glass, twilight only alternated with dark night. Old Anthony had not left his bed during the two days, for he had not the strength to rise; he had for a long time felt in his limbs the hardness of the weather. Forsaken by all, lay the old bachelor, unable to help himself. He could scarcely reach the water-jug that he had placed by his bedside, and the last drop it contained had been consumed. It was not fever, nor sickness, but old age that had struck him down. Up yonder, where his couch was placed, he was overshadowed as it were by continual night. A little spider, which, however, he could not see, busily and cheerfully span its web around him, as if it were weaving a little crape banner that should wave when the old man closed his eyes.

The time was very slow, and long, and dreary. Tears he had none to shed, nor did he feel pain. The thought of Molly never came into his mind. He felt as if the world and its noise concerned him no longer—as if he were lying outside the world, and no one were thinking of him. For a moment he felt a sensation of hunger—of thirst. Yes, he felt them both. But nobody came to tend him—nobody He thought of those who had once suffered want; of Saint Elizabeth, as she had once wandered on earth; of her, the saint of his home and of his childhood, the noble Duchess of Thuringia, the benevolent lady who had been accustomed to visit the lowliest cottages, bringing to the inmates refreshment and comfort. Her pious deeds shone bright upon his soul. He thought of her as she had come to distribute words of comfort, binding up the wounds of the afflicted, giving meat to the hungry; though her stern husband had chidden her for it. He thought of the legend told of her, how she had been carrying the full basket containing food and wine, when her husband, who watched her footsteps, came forth and asked angrily what she was carrying, whereupon she answered, in fear and trembling, that the basket contained roses which she had plucked in the garden; how he had torn away the white cloth from the basket, and a miracle had been performed for the pious lady ; for bread, and wine, and every thing in the basket had been transformed into roses !

Thus the saint's memory dwelt in Anthony's quiet mind; thus she stood bodily before his downcast face, before his warehouse in the simple booth in the Danish land. He uncovered his head, and looked into her gentle eyes, and every thing around him was beautiful and roseate. Yes, the roses seemed to unfold themselves in fragrance. There came to him a sweet, peculiar odor of apples, and he saw a blooming apple-tree, which spread its branches above him —it was the tree which Molly and he had planted together.

And the tree strewed down its fragrant leaves upon him, cooling his burning brow. The leaves fell upon his parched lips, and were like strengthening bread and wine; and they fell upon his breast, and he felt reassured and calm, and inclined to sleep peacefully.

" Now I shall sleep," he whispered to himself. " Sleep is refreshing. To-morrow I shall be upon my feet again, and strong and well—glorious, wonderful ! That apple-tree, planted in true affection, now stands before me in heavenly radiance—"

And he slept.

The day afterwards—it was the third day that his shop had remained closed—the snow-storm had ceased, and a neighbor from the opposite house came over towards the booth where dwelt old Anthony, who had not yet shown himself. Anthony lay stretched upon his bed—dead—with his old cap clutched tightly in his two hands ! They did not put that cap on his head in his coffin, for he had a new white one.

Where were now the tears that he had wept? What had become of the pearls? They remained in the nightcap—and the true ones do not come out in the wash—they were preserved in the nightcap, and in time forgotten; but the old thoughts and the old dreams still remained in the "bachelor's nightcap." Don't wish for such a cap for yourself. It would make your forehead very hot, would make your pulse beat feverishly, and conjure up dreams which appear like reality. The first who wore that identical cap afterwards felt all that at once, though it was half a century afterwards; and that man was the burgomaster himself, who, with his wife and eleven children, was well and firmly established, and had amassed a very tolerable amount of wealth. He was immediately seized with dreams of unfortunate love, of bankruptcy, and of heavy times.

"Hallo! how the nightcap burns!" he cried out, and tore it from his head.

And a pearl rolled out, and another, and another, and they sounded and glittered.

"This must be gout," said the burgomaster. "Something dazzles my eyes!"

They were tears, shed half a century before by old Anthony from Eisenach.

Every one who afterwards put that nightcap upon his head had visions and dreams which excited him not a little. His own history was changed into that of Anthony, and became a story; in fact, many stories. But some one else may tell *them*. We have told the first. And our last word is—don't wish for "The Old Bachelor's Nightcap."

THE MARSH KING'S DAUGHTER.

The storks tell their little ones very many stories, all of the moor and the marsh. These stories are generally adapted to the age and capacity of the hearers. The youngest are content if they are told " Kribble-krabble, plurre-murre" as a story, and find it charming; but the older ones want something with a deeper meaning, or at any rate something relating to the family. Of the two oldest and longest stories that have been preserved among the storks, we are only acquainted with one, namely, that of Moses, who was exposed by his mother on the banks of the Nile, and whom the king's daughter found, and who afterwards became a great man and a prophet. That history is very well known.

The second is not known yet, perhaps, because it is quite an inland story. It has been handed down from mouth to mouth, from stork-mamma to stork-mamma, for thousands of years, and each of them has told it better and better ; and now *we'll* tell it best of all.

The first stork pair who told the story had their summer residence on the wooden house of the Viking, which lay by the wild moor in Wendsyssel; that is to say, if we are to speak out of the abundance of our knowledge, hard by the great moor in the circle of Hjörring, high up by the Skagen, the northern point of Jutland. The wilderness there is still a great wide moor-heath, about which we can read in the official description of districts. It is said that in old times there was here a sea, whose bottom was upheaved; now the moorland extends for miles on all sides, surrounded

THE KING OF EGYPT'S RECOVERY.

by damp meadows, and unsteady shaking swamp, and turfy moor, with blueberries and stunted trees. Mists are almost always hovering over this region, which seventy years ago was still inhabited by wolves. It is certainly rightly called the " wild moor;" and one can easily think how dreary and lonely it must have been, and how much marsh and lake there was here a thousand years ago. Yes, in detail, exactly the same things were seen then that may yet be beheld. The reeds had the same height, and bore the same kind of long leaves and bluish-brown feathery plumes that they bear now; the birch stood there, with its white bark and its fine loosely-hanging leaves, just as now; and as regards the living creatures that dwelt here—why, the fly wore its gauzy dress of the same cut that it wears now; and the favorite colors of the stork were white picked out with black, and red stockings. The people certainly wore coats of a different cut to those they now wear; but whoever stepped out on the shaking moorland, be he huntsman or follower, master or servant, met with the same fate a thousand years ago that he would meet with to-day. He sank and went down to the " marsh king," as they called him, who ruled below in the great moorland empire. They also called him " gungel king;" but we like the name " marsh king" better, and by that we'll call him, as the storks did. Very little is known of the marsh king's rule; but perhaps that is a good thing.

In the neighborhood of the moorland, hard by the great arm of the German Ocean and the Cattegat, which is called the Lümfjorden, lay the wooden house of the Viking, with its stone water-tight cellars, with its tower and its three projecting stories. On the roof the stork had built his nest; and stork-mamma there hatched the eggs, and felt sure that her hatching would come to something.

One evening stork-papa stayed out very long; and when he came home he looked very bustling and important.

"I've something very terrible to tell you," he said to the stork-mamma.

"Let that be," she replied. "Remember that I'm hatching the eggs, and you might agitate me, and I might do them a mischief."

"You must know it," he continued. "She has arrived here—the daughter of our host in Egypt—she has dared to undertake the journey here—and she's gone!"

"She who came from the race of the fairies? Oh, tell me all about it! You know I can't bear to be kept long in suspense when I'm hatching eggs."

"You see, mother, she believed in what the doctor said, and you told me true. She believed that the moor-flowers would bring healing to her sick father, and she has flown here in swan's plumage, in company with the other swan-princesses, who come to the North every year to renew their youth. She has come here, and she is gone!"

"You are much too long-winded!" exclaimed the stork-mamma, "and the eggs might catch cold. I can't bear being kept in such suspense!"

"I have kept watch," said the stork-papa; "and to-night, when I went into the reeds—there where the marsh ground will bear me—three swans came. Something in their flight seemed to say to me, 'Look out! That's not altogether swan; it's only swan's feathers!' Yes, mother, you have a feeling of intuition, just as I have; you know whether a thing is right or wrong."

"Yes, certainly," she replied; "but tell me about the princess. I'm sick of hearing of the swan's feathers."

"Well, you know that in the middle of the moor there is something like a lake," continued stork-papa. "You can see one corner of it if you raise yourself a little. There, by the reeds and the green mud lay a great alder stump; and on this the three swans sat, flapping their wings and looking about them. One of them threw off her plumage, and I immediately recognized her as our house princess from Egypt! There she sat, with no covering but her long black hair. I heard her tell the others to pay good heed to the swan's plumage, while she dived down into the water to pluck the flowers which she fancied she saw growing there. The others nodded, and picked up the empty feather dress and took care of it. 'I wonder what they will do with it?' thought I; and perhaps she asked herself the same question. If so, she got an answer—a very practical answer—for the two rose up and flew away with her swan's plumage. 'Do thou dive down,' they cried; 'thou shalt never see Egypt again! Remain thou here in the moor!' And so saying, they tore the swan's plumage into a thousand pieces, so that the feathers whirled about like a snow-storm; and away they flew—the two faithless princesses!"

"Why, that is terrible!" said stork-mamma. "I can't bear to hear any more of it. But now tell me what happened next."

"The princess wept and lamented aloud. Her tears fell fast on the alder stump, and the latter moved; for it was not a regular alder stump, but the marsh king—he who lives and rules in the depths of the moor! I myself saw it—how the stump of the tree turned round, and ceased to be a tree stump; long, thin branches grew forth from it like arms. Then the poor child was terribly frightened, and sprang up to flee away. She hurried across to the green slimy ground; but that cannot even carry me, much less her. She sank immediately, and the alder stump dived down too; and it was he who drew her down. Great

11*

black bubbles rose up out of the moor-slime, and the last trace of both of them vanished when these burst. Now the princess is buried in the wild moor, and never more will she bear away a flower to Egypt. Your heart would have burst, mother, if you had seen it."

"You ought not to tell me any thing of the kind at such a time as this," said stork-mamma; "the eggs might suffer by it. The princess will find some way of escape; some one will come to help her. If it had been you or I, or one of our people, it would certainly have been all over with us."

"But I shall go and look every day to see if any thing happens," said stork-papa.

And he was as good as his word.

A long time had passed, when at last he saw a green stalk shooting up out of the deep moor-ground. When it reached the surface, a leaf spread out and unfolded itself broader and broader; close by it, a bud came out. And one morning, when stork-papa flew over the stalk, the bud opened through the power of the strong sunbeams, and in the cup of the flower lay a beautiful child—a little girl— looking just as if she had risen out of the bath. The little one so closely resembled the princess from Egypt, that at the first moment the stork thought it must be the princess herself; but, on second thoughts, it appeared more probable that it must be the daughter of the princess and of the marsh king; and that also explained her being placed in the cup of the water-lily.

"But she cannot possibly be left lying there," thought stork-papa; "and in my nest there are so many persons already. But stay, I have a thought. The wife of the Viking has no children, and how often has she not wished for a little one! People always say, 'The stork has brought a little one;' and I will do so in earnest this

time. I shall fly with the child to the Viking's wife.
What rejoicing there will be yonder!"

And the stork lifted the little girl out of the flower-cup,
flew to the wooden-house, picked a hole with his beak in
the bladder-covered window, laid the charming child on the
bosom of the Viking's wife, and then hurried up to the
stork-mamma, and told her what he had seen and done;
and the little storks listened to the story, for they were
big enough to do so now.

"So you see," he concluded, "the princess is not dead,
for she must have sent the little one up here; and now that
is provided for too."

"Ah, I said it would be so, from the very beginning!"
said the stork-mamma; "but now think a little of your own
family. Our travelling time is drawing on; sometimes I
feel quite restless in my wings already. The cuckoo and
the nightingale have started; and I heard the quails saying that they were going too, so soon as the wind was
favorable. Our young ones will behave well at the exer-
cising, or I am much deceived in them."

The Viking's wife was extremely glad when she woke
next morning and found the charming infant lying in her
arms. She kissed and caressed it; but it cried violently,
and struggled with its arms and legs, and did not seem
rejoiced at all. At length it cried itself to sleep; and as
it lay there still and tranquil, it looked exceedingly beautiful. The Viking's wife was in high glee: she felt light in
body and soul; her heart leapt within her; and it seemed
to her as if her husband and his warriors, who were absent,
must return quite as suddenly and unexpectedly as the
little one had come.

Therefore she and the whole household had enough to do
in preparing every thing for the reception of her lord. The

long colored curtains of tapestry, which she and her maids
had worked, and on which they had woven pictures of their
idols, Odin, Thor, and Freya, were hung up ; the slaves
polished the old shields, that served as ornaments ; and
cushions were placed on the benches, and dry wood laid on
the fireplace in the midst of the hall, so that the flames
might be fanned up at a moment's notice. The Viking's
wife herself assisted in the work, so that towards evening
she was very tired, and went to sleep quickly and lightly.

When she awoke towards morning, she was violently
alarmed, for the infant had vanished ! She sprang from
her couch, lighted a pine-torch, and searched all round
about ; and, behold, in the part of the bed where she had
stretched her feet, lay, not the child, but a great ugly frog !
She was horror-struck at the sight, and seized a heavy stick
to kill the frog ; but the creature looked at her with such
strange, mournful eyes, that she was not able to strike the
blow. Once more she looked round the room—the frog
uttered a low, wailing croak, and she started, sprang from
the couch, and ran to the window and opened it. At that
moment the sun shone forth, and flung its beams through
the window on the couch and on the great frog ; and suddenly it appeared as though the frog's great mouth contracted
and became small and red, and its limbs moved and stretched
and became beautifully symmetrical, and it was no longer
an ugly frog which lay there, but her pretty child !

" What is this ?" she said. " Have I had a bad dream ?
Is it not my own lovely cherub lying there ?"

And she kissed and hugged it ; but the child struggled
and fought like a little wild-cat.

Not on this day nor on the morrow did the Viking return,
although he certainly was on his way home ; but the wind
was against him, for it blew towards the south, favorably

for the storks. A good wind for one is a contrary wind for another.

When one or two more days and nights had gone, the Viking's wife clearly understood how the case was with her child, and that a terrible power of sorcery was upon it. By day it was charming as an angel of light, though it had a wild, savage temper ; but at night it became an ugly frog, quiet and mournful, with sorrowful eyes. Here were two natures changing inwardly as well as outwardly with the sunlight. The reason of this was, that by day the child had the form of its mother, but the disposition of its father ; while, on the contrary, at night the paternal descent became manifest in its bodily appearance, though the mind and heart of the mother then became dominant in the child. Who might be able to loosen this charm that wicked sorcery had worked ?

The wife of the Viking lived in care and sorrow about it ; and yet her heart yearned towards the little creature, of whose condition she felt she should not dare tell her husband on his return ; for he would probably, according to the custom which then prevailed, expose the child on the public highway, and let whoever listed take it away. The good Viking woman could not find it in her heart to allow this, and she therefore determined that the Viking should never see the child except by daylight.

One morning the wings of storks were heard rushing over the roofs ; more than a hundred pairs of those birds had rested from their exercise during the previous night, and now they soared aloft, to travel southwards.

" All males here, and ready," they cried ; " and the wives and children too."

" How light we feel !" screamed the young storks in chorus : " it seems to be creeping all over us, down into our very toes, as if we were filled with frogs. Ah, how charming it is, travelling to foreign lands!"

"Mind you keep close to us during your flight," said the papa and mamma. "Don't use your beaks too much, for that tires the chest."

And the storks flew away.

At the same time the sound of the trumpets rolled across the heath, for the Viking had landed with his warriors; they were returning home, richly laden with spoil from the Gallic coast, where the people, as in the land of the Britons, sang in frightened accents :

"Deliver us from the wild Northmen!"

And life and tumultuous joy came with them into the Viking's castle on the moorland. The great mead-tub was brought into the hall, the pile of wood was set ablaze, horses were killed, and a great feast was to begin. The officiating priest sprinkled the slaves with warm blood : the fire crackled, the smoke rolled along beneath the roof: but they were accustomed to that. Guests were invited, and received handsome gifts : all feuds and all malice were forgotten. And the company drank deep, and threw the bones of the feast in each other's faces, and this was considered a sign of good-humor. The bard, a kind of minstrel, but who was also a warrior, and had been on the expedition with the rest, sang them a song, in which they heard all their warlike deeds praised, and every thing remarkable specially noticed. Every verse ended with the burden :

"Goods and gold, friends and foes will die; every man must one day die;
   But a famous name will never die!"

And with that they beat upon their shields, and hammered the table in glorious fashion with bones and knives.

The Viking's wife sat upon the high seat in the open hall. She wore a silken dress, and golden armlets, and great amber beads : she was in her costliest garb. And the bard mentioned her in his song, and sang of the rich treasure she had brought her rich husband. The latter was delighted with the beautiful child, which he had seen in the daytime in all its loveliness; and the savage ways of the little creature pleased him especially. He declared that the girl might grow up to be a stately heroine, strong and determined as a man. She would not wink her eyes when a practised hand cut off her eyebrows with a sword by way of a jest.

The full mead-barrel was emptied, and a fresh one brought in; for these were people who liked to enjoy all things plentifully. The old proverb was indeed well known, which says, "The cattle know when they should quit the pasture, but a foolish man knoweth not the measure of his own appetite." Yes, they knew it well enough; but one *knows* one thing, and one *does* another. They also knew that "even the welcome guest becomes wearisome when he sitteth long in the house;" but for all that they sat still, for pork and mead are good things; and there was high carousing, and at night the bondmen slept among the warm ashes, and dipped their fingers in the fat grease and licked them. Those were glorious times !

Once more in the year the Viking sallied forth, though the storms of autumn already began to roar : he went with his warriors to the shores of Britain, for he declared that was but an excursion across the water; and his wife stayed at home with the little girl. And thus much is certain, that the poor lady soon got to love the frog with its gentle eyes and its sorrowful sighs, almost better than the pretty child that bit and beat all around her.

The rough damp mist of autumn, which devours the leaves of the forest, had already descended upon thicket and heath. "Birds featherless," as they called the snow, flew in thick masses, and winter was coming on fast. The sparrows took possession of the storks' nests, and talked about the absent proprietors according to their fashion; but these—the stork pair, with all the young ones—what had become of them?

The storks were now in the land of Egypt, where the sun sent forth warm rays, as it does here on a fine midsummer day. Tamarinds and acacias bloomed in the country all around; the crescent of Mahomet glittered from the cupolas of the temples, and on the slender towers sat many a stork pair resting after the long journey. Great troops divided the nests, built close together on venerable pillars and in fallen temple-arches of forgotten cities. The date-palm lifted up its screen as if it would be a sunshade; the grayish-white pyramids stood like masses of shadow in the clear air of the far desert, where the ostrich ran his swift career, and the lion gazed with his great grave eyes at the marble sphinx which lay half buried in the sand. The waters of the Nile had fallen, and the whole river-bed was crowded with frogs, and this spectacle was just according to the taste of the stork family. The young storks thought it was optical illusion, they found every thing so glorious.

"Yes, it's delightful here ; and it's always like this in our warm country," said the stork-mamma; and the young ones felt quite frisky on the strength of it.

"Is there any thing more to be seen ?" they asked. "Are we to go much further into the country ?"

"There's nothing further to be seen," answered stork-mamma. "Behind this delightful region there are luxuriant forests, whose branches are interlaced with one another, while prickly climbing plants close up the paths—only the elephant can force a way for himself with his great feet; and the snakes are too big, and the lizards too quick for us. If you go into the desert, you'll get your eyes full of sand when there's a light breeze, but when it blows great guns you may get into the middle of a pillar of sand. It is best to stay here, where there are frogs and locusts. I shall stay here, and you shall stay too."

And there they remained. The parents sat in the nest on the slender minaret, and rested, and yet were busily employed smoothing and cleaning their feathers, and whetting their beaks against their red stockings. Now and then they stretched out their necks, and bowed gravely, and lifted their heads, with their high foreheads and fine smooth feathers, and looked very clever with their brown eyes. The female young ones strutted about in the juicy reeds, looked slyly at the other young storks, made acquaintances, and swallowed a frog at every third step, or rolled a little snake to and fro in their bills, which they thought became them well, and, moreover, tasted nice. The male young ones began a quarrel, beat each other with their wings, struck with their beaks, and even pricked each other till the blood came. And in this way sometimes one couple was betrothed, and sometimes another, of the young ladies and gentlemen, and that was just what they wanted, and their chief object in life : then they took to a new nest, and began new quarrels, for in hot countries people are generally hot-tempered and passionate. But it was pleasant for all that, and the old people especially were much rejoiced, for all that young people do seems to suit them well. There was sunshine every day, and every day plenty to eat, and nothing to think of but pleasure. But in the rich castle at the Egyptian host's, as they called him, there was no pleasure to be found.

The rich mighty lord reclined on his divan, in the midst of the great hall of the many-colored walls, looking as if he were sitting in a tulip: but he was stiff and powerless in all his limbs, and lay stretched out like a mummy. His family and servants surrounded him, for he was not dead, though one could not exactly say that he was alive. The healing moor-flower from the North, which was to have been found and brought home by her who loved him best, never appeared. His beauteous young daughter, who had flown in the swan's plumage over sea and land, to the far North, was never to come back. "She is dead!" the two returning swan-maidens had said, and they had concocted a complete story, which ran as follows :

"We three together flew high in the air : a hunter saw us, and shot his arrow at us; it struck our young companion and friend; and slowly, singing her farewell song, she sank down, a dying swan, into the woodland lake. By the shore of the lake, under a weeping birch-tree, we laid her in the cold earth. But we had our revenge. We bound fire under the wings of the swallow who had her nest beneath the huntsman's thatch ; the house burst into flames, the huntsman was burnt in the house, and the glare shone over the sea as far as the hanging birch beneath which she sleeps. Never will she return to the land of Egypt."

And then the two wept. And when stork-papa heard the story, he clapped with his beak, so that it could be heard a long way off.

"Treachery and lies !" he cried. "I should like to run my beak deep into their chests."

"And perhaps break it off," interposed the stork-mamma; "and then you would look well. Think first of yourself, and then of your family, and all the rest does not concern you."

"But to-morrow I shall seat myself at the edge of the open cupola, when the wise and learned men assemble, to consult on the sick man's state : perhaps they may come a little nearer the truth."

And the learned and wise men came together and spoke a great deal, out of which the stork could make no sense—and it had no result, either for the sick man or for the daughter in the swampy waste. But for all that, we may listen to what the people said, for we have to listen to a great deal of talk in the world.

But then it's an advantage to hear what went before, what has been said; and in this case we are well informed, for we know just as much about it as stork-papa.

"Love gives life ! the highest love gives the highest life ! Only through love can his life be preserved." That is what they all said, and the learned men said it was very cleverly and beautifully spoken.

"That is a beautiful thought !" stork-papa said immediately.

"I don't quite understand it," stork-mamma replied : "and that's not my fault, but the fault of the thought. But let it be as it will, I've something else to think of."

And now the learned men had spoken of love to this one and that one, and of the difference between the love of one's neighbor and love between parents and children, of the love of plants for the light, when the sunbeam kisses the ground and the germ springs forth from it—every thing was so fully and elaborately explained that it was quite impossible for stork-papa to take it in, much less to repeat it. He felt quite weighed down with thought, and half shut his eyes, and the whole of the following day he stood thoughtfully on one leg : it was quite heavy for him to carry, all that learning.

But one thing stork-papa understood. All, high and low, had spoken out of their inmost hearts, and said that it was a great misfortune for thousands of people, yes, for the whole country, that this man was lying sick, and could not get well, and that it would spread joy and pleasure abroad if he should recover. But where grew the flower that could restore him to health? They had all searched for it, consulted learned books, the twinkling stars, the weather and the wind; they had made inquiries in every by-way of which they could think; and at length the wise men and the learned men had said, as we have already told, that " Love begets life—will restore a father's life;" and on this occasion they had surpassed themselves, and said more than they understood. They repeated it, and wrote down as a recipe, " Love begets life." But how was the thing to be prepared according to the recipe? that was a point they could not get over. At last they were decided upon the point that help must come by means of the princess, through her who clave to her father with her whole soul; and at last a method had been devised whereby help could be procured in this dilemma. Yes, it was already more than a year ago since the princess had sallied forth by night, when the brief rays of the new moon were waning : she had gone out to the marble sphinx, had shaken the dust from her sandals, and gone onward through the long passage which leads into the midst of one of the great pyramids, where one of the mighty kings of antiquity, surrounded by pomp and treasure, lay swathed in mummy-cloths. There she was to incline her ear to the breast of the dead king; for thus, said the wise men, it should be made manifest to her where she might find life and health for her father. She had fulfilled all these injunctions, and had seen in a vision that she was to bring home from the deep lake in the north ern moorland—the very place had been accurately described to her—the lotos-flower which grows in the depths of the waters, and then her father would regain health and strength.

And therefore she had gone forth in the swan's plumage out of the land of Egypt to the open heath, to the woodland moor. And the stork-papa and stork-mamma knew all this ; and now we also know it more accurately than we knew it before. We know that the marsh king had drawn her down to himself, and know that to her loved ones at home she is dead forever. One of the wisest of them said, as the stork-mamma said too, "She will manage to help her-self ;" and at last they quieted their minds with that, and resolved to wait and see what would happen, for they knew of nothing better that they could do.

"I should like to take away the swan's feathers from the two faithless princesses," said the stork-papa ; "then, at any rate, they will not be able to fly up again to the wild moor, and do mischief. I'll hide the two swan-feather suits up there, till somebody has occasion for them."

"But where do you intend to hide them?" asked stork-mamma.

"Up in our nest in the moor," answered he. "I and our young ones will take turns in carrying them up yonder, on our return, and if that should prove too difficult for us, there are places enough on the way where we can conceal them till our next journey. Certainly, one suit of swan's feathers would be enough for the princess, but two are always better. In those northern countries, no one can have too many wraps."

"No one will thank you for it," quoth stork-mamma ;

"but you're the master. Except at breeding-time, I have nothing to say."

In the Viking's castle by the wild moor, whither the storks bent their flight when the spring approached, they had given the little girl the name of Helga ; but this name was too soft for a temper like that which was associated with her beauteous form. Every month this temper showed itself in sharper outlines ; and in the course of years—during which the storks made the same journey over and over again, in autumn to the Nile, in spring back to the moorland lake—the child grew to be a great girl ; and before people were aware of it, she was a beautiful maiden in her sixteenth year. The shell was splendid, but the kernel was harsh and hard ; and she was hard, as indeed were most people in those dark, gloomy times. It was a pleasure to her to splash about with her white hands in the blood of the horse that had been slain in sacrifice. In her wild mood she bit off the neck of the black cock the priest was about to offer up ; and to her father she said in perfect seriousness :

" If thy enemy should pull down the roof of thy house, while thou wert sleeping in careless safety ; if I felt it or heard it, I would not wake thee even if I had the power. I should never do it, for my ears still tingle with the blow that thou gavest me years ago—thou ! I have never forgotten it."

But the Viking took her words in jest ; for, like all others, he was bewitched with her beauty, and he knew not how temper and form changed in Helga. Without a saddle, she sat upon a horse, as if she were part of it, while it rushed along in full career ; nor would she spring from the horse when it quarrelled and fought with other horses. Often she would throw herself in her clothes from the high shore into the sea, and swim to meet the Viking when his boat steered near home ; and she cut the longest lock of her hair, and twisted it into a string for her bow.

"Self-achieved is well-achieved," she said.

The Viking's wife was strong of character and of will, according to the custom of the times ; but, compared to her daughter, she appeared as a feeble, timid woman ; for she knew that an evil charm weighed heavily upon the unfortunate child.

It seemed as if, out of mere malice, when her mother stood on the threshold, or came out into the yard, Helga would often seat herself on the margin of the well, and wave her arms in the air ; then suddenly she would dive into the deep well, when her frog-nature enabled her to dive and rise, down and up, until she climbed forth again like a cat, and came back into the hall dripping with water, so that the green leaves strewn upon the ground floated and turned in the streams that flowed from her garments.

But there was one thing that imposed a check upon Helga, and that was the evening twilight. When that came she was quiet and thoughtful, and would listen to reproof and advice; and then a secret feeling seemed to draw her towards her mother. And when the sun sank, and the usual transformation of body and spirit took place in her, she would sit quiet and mournful, shrunk to the shape of the frog, her body indeed much larger than that of the animal whose likeness she took, and for that reason much more hideous to behold; for she looked like a wretched dwarf with a frog's head and webbed fingers. Her eyes then assumed a very melancholy expression. She had no voice, and could only utter a hollow croaking that sounded like the stifled sob of a dreaming child. Then the Viking's wife took her on her lap, and forgot the ugly form as she looked into the mournful eyes, and said :

"I could almost wish that thou wert always my poor dumb frog-child; for thou art only the more terrible when thy nature is veiled in a form of beauty."

And the Viking woman wrote Runic characters against sorcery and spells of sickness, and threw them over the wretched child; but she could not see that they worked any good.

"One can scarcely believe that she was ever so small that she could lie in the cup of a water-lily," said stork-papa, "now she's grown up the image of her Egyptian mother. Ah, we shall never see that poor lady again ! Probably she did not know how to help herself, as you and the learned men said. Year after year I have flown to and fro, across and across the great moorland, and she has never once given a sign that she was still alive. Yes, I may as well tell you, that every year, when I came here a few days before you, to repair the nest and attend to various matters, I spent a whole night in flying to and fro over the lake, as if I had been an owl or a bat, but every time in vain. The two suits of swan feathers which I and the young ones dragged up here out of the land of the Nile have consequently not been used : we had trouble enough with them to bring them hither in three journeys; and now they lie down here in the nest, and if it should happen that a fire broke out, and the wooden house were burned, they would be destroyed."

"And our good nest would be destroyed too," said stork-mamma; "but you think less of that than of your plumage stuff and of your moor-princess. You'd best go down into the mud and stay there with her. You're a bad father to your own children, as I said already when I hatched our first brood. I only hope neither we nor our children will get an arrow in our wings through that wild girl. Helga doesn't know in the least what she does. I wish she would only remember that we have lived here longer than she, and that we have never forgotten our duty, and have given our toll every year, a feather, an egg, and a young one, as it was right we should do. Do you think I can now wander about in the courtyard and everywhere, as I was wont in former days, and as I still do in Egypt, where I am almost the playfellow of the people, and that I can press into pot and kettle as I can yonder? No, I sit up here and am angry at her, the stupid chit! And I am angry at you too. You should have just left her lying in the water-lily, and she would have been dead long ago."

"You are much better than your words," said stork-papa. "I know you better than you know yourself."

And with that he gave a hop, and flapped his wings heavily twice, stretched out his legs behind him, and flew away, or rather sailed away, without moving his wings He had already gone some distance, when he gave a great *flap!* The sun shone upon his grand plumage, and his head and neck were stretched forth proudly. There was power in it, and dash!

"After all, he's handsomer than any of them," said stork-mamma to herself; "but I won't tell him so."

Early in that autumn the Viking came home, laden with booty, and bringing prisoners with him. Among these was a young Christian priest, one of those who contemned the gods of the North.

Often in those later times there had been a talk, in hall and chamber, of the new faith that was spreading far and wide in the South, and which, by means of Saint Ansgarius, had penetrated as far as Hedeby on the Schlei. Even Helga had heard of this belief in One who, from love to men and for their redemption, had sacrificed His life ; but with her all this had, as the saying is, gone in at one ear and come out at the other. It seemed as if she only understood the meaning of the word " love," when she crouched in the corner of the chamber in the form of a miserable frog ; but the Viking's wife had listened to the mighty history that was told throughout the lands, and had felt strangely moved thereby.

On their return from the voyage, the men told of the splended temples, of their hewn stones, raised for the worship of Him whose worship is love. Some massive vessels, made with cunning art, of gold, had been brought home among the booty, and each one had a peculiar fragrance ; for they were incense vessels, which had been swung by Christian priests before the altar.

In the deep cellars of the Viking's house the young priest had been immured, his hands and feet bound with strips of bark. The Viking's wife declared that he was beautiful as Bulder to behold, and his misfortune touched her heart; but Helga declared that it would be right to tie ropes to his heels, and fasten him to the tails of wild oxen. And she exclaimed :

"Then I would let loose the dogs—hurrah ! over the moor and across the swamp ! That would be a spectacle for the gods ! And yet finer would it be to follow him in his career."

But the Viking would not suffer him to die such a death : he purposed to sacrifice the priest on the morrow, on the death-stone in the grove, as a despiser and foe of the high gods.

For the first time a man was to be sacrificed here.

Helga begged, as a boon, that she might sprinkle the image of the god and the assembled multitude with the blood of the priest. She sharpened her glittering knife, and when one of the great savage dogs, of whom a number were running about near the Viking's abode, ran by her, she thrust the knife into his side, "merely to try its sharpness," as she said. And the Viking's wife looked mournfully at the wild, evil-disposed girl; and when the night came on and the maiden exchanged beauty of form for gentleness of soul, she spoke in eloquent words to Helga of the sorrow that was deep in her heart.

The ugly frog, in its monstrous form, stood before her, and fixed its brown eyes upon her face, listening to her words, and seeming to comprehend them with human intelligence.

"Never, not even to my lord and husband, have I allowed my lips to utter a word concerning the sufferings I have to undergo through thee," said the Viking's wife; "my heart is full of woe concerning thee : more powerful and greater than I ever fancied it, is the love of a mother ! But love never entered into thy heart—thy heart that is like the wet, cold moorland plants."

Then the miserable form trembled, and it was as though these words touched an invisible bond between body and soul, and great tears came into the mournful eyes.

"Thy hard time will come," said the Viking's wife; "and it will be terrible to me too. It had been better if thou hadst been set out by the high-road, and the night wind had lulled thee to sleep."

And the Viking's wife wept bitter tears, and went away full of wrath and bitterness of spirit, vanishing behind the curtain of furs that hung loose over the beam and divided the hall.

The wrinkled frog crouched in the corner alone. A deep silence reigned around; but at intervals a half-stifled sigh escaped from its breast, from the breast of Helga. It seemed as though a painful new life were arising in her inmost heart. She came forward and listened; and stepping forward again, grasped with her clumsy hands the heavy pole that was laid across before the door. Silently and laboriously she pushed back the pole, silently drew back the bolt, and took up the flickering lamp which stood in the ante-chamber of the hall. It seemed as if a strong hidden will gave her strength. She drew back the iron bolt from the closed cellar-door, and crept in to the captive. He was asleep; and when he awoke and saw the hideous form, he shuddered as though he had beheld a wicked apparition. She drew her knife, cut the bonds that confined his hands and feet, and beckoned him to follow her.

He uttered some holy names, and made the sign of the cross; and when the form remained motionless at his side, he said :

"Who art thou ? Whence this animal shape that thou bearest, while yet thou art full of gentle mercy ?"

The frog-woman beckoned him to follow, and led him through corridors shrouded with curtains, into the stables, and there pointed to a horse. He mounted on its back ; but she also sprang up before him, holding fast by the horse's mane. The prisoner understood her meaning, and in a rapid trot they rode on a way which he would never have found, on to the open heath.

He thought not of her hideous form, but felt how the mercy and loving-kindness of the Almighty were working by means of this monstrous apparition; he prayed pious prayers, and sang songs of praise. Then she trembled. Was it the power of song and of prayer that worked in her, or was she shuddering at the cold morning twilight that was approaching? What were her feelings? She raised herself up, and wanted to stop the horse and to alight; but the Christian priest held her back with all his strength, and sang a pious song, as if that would have the power to loosen the charm that turned her into the hideous semblance of a frog. And the horse galloped on more wildly than ever; the sky turned red, the first sunbeam pierced through the clouds, and as the flood of light came streaming down, the frog changed its nature. Helga was again the beautiful maiden with the wicked, demoniac spirit. He held a beautiful maiden in his arms, but was horrified at the sight: he swung himself from the horse, and compelled it to stand. This seemed to him a new and terrible sorcery; but Helga likewise leaped from the saddle, and stood on the ground. The child's short garment reached only to her knee. She plucked the sharp knife from her girdle, and quick as lightning she rushed in upon the astonished priest.

"Let me get at thee!" she screamed; "let me get at thee, and plunge this knife in thy body! Thou art pale as straw, thou beardless slave!"

She pressed in upon him. They struggled together in a hard strife, but an invisible power seemed given to the Christian captive. He held her fast; and the old oak-tree beneath which they stood came to his assistance; for its root, which projected over the ground, held fast the maiden's feet that had become entangled in it. Quite close to them gushed a spring; and he sprinkled Helga's face and neck with the fresh water, and commanded the unclean spirit to come forth, and blessed her in the Christian fashion; but the water of faith has no power when the well spring of faith flows not from within.

And yet the Christian showed his power even now, and opposed more than the mere might of a man against the evil that struggled within the girl. His holy action seemed to overpower her: she dropped her hands, and gazed with frightened eyes and pale cheeks upon him who appeared to her a mighty magician, learned in secret arts; he seemed to her to speak in a dark Runic tongue, and to be making cabalistic signs in the air. She would not have winked had he swung a sharp knife or a glittering axe against her; but she trembled when he signed her with the sign of the cross on her brow and her bosom, and she sat there like a tamed bird with bowed head.

Then he spoke to her in gentle words of the kindly deed she had done for him in the past night, when she came to him in the form of the hideous frog, to loosen his bonds, and to lead him out to life and light; and he told her that she too was bound in closer bonds than those that had confined him, and that she should be released by his means. He would take her to Hedeby (Schleswig), to the holy Ansgarius, and yonder in the Christian city the spell that bound her would be loosed. But he would not let her sit before him on the horse, though of her own accord she offered to do so.

"Thou must sit behind me, not before me," he said. "Thy magic beauty hath a power that comes of evil, and I fear it; and yet I feel that the victory is sure to him who hath faith."

And he knelt down and prayed fervently. It seemed as though the woodland scenes were consecrated as a holy church by his prayer. The birds sang as though they belonged to the new congregation, the wild-flowers smelt sweet as incense; and while he spoke, the horse that had carried them both in headlong career stood still before the tall bramble-bushes, and plucked at them, so that the ripe juicy berries fell down upon Helga's hands, offering them selves for her refreshment.

Patiently she suffered the priest to lift her on the horse, and sat like a somnambulist, neither completely asleep nor wholly awake. The Christian bound two branches together with bark, in the form of a cross, which he held up high as they rode through the forest. The wood became thicker as they went on, and at last became a trackless wilderness.

The wild sloe grew across the way, so that they had to ride round the bushes. The bubbling spring became not a stream but a standing marsh, round which likewise they were obliged to lead the horse. There was strength and refreshment in the cool forest breeze; and no small power lay in the gentle words, which were spoken in faith and in Christian love, from a strong inward yearning to lead the poor lost one into the way of light and life.

They say the rain-drops can hollow the hard stone, and the waves of the sea can smooth and round the sharp edges of the rocks. Thus did the dew of mercy, that dropped upon Helga, smooth what was rough, and penetrate what was hard in her. The effects did not yet appear, nor was she aware of them herself ; but doth the seed in the bosom of earth know, when the refreshing dew and the quickening sunbeams fall upon it, that it hath within itself the power of growth and blossoming ? As the song of the mother penetrates into the heart of the child, and it babbles the words after her, without understanding their import, until they afterwards engender thought, and come forward in due time clearer and more clearly, so here also did the Word work, that is powerful to create.

They rode forth from the dense forest, across the heath, and then again through pathless roads; and towards evening they encountered a band of robbers.

"Where hast thou stolen that beauteous maiden?" cried the robbers; and they seized the horse's bridle, and dragged the two riders from its back. The priest had no weapon save the knife he had taken from Helga; and with this he tried to defend himself. One of the robbers lifted his axe to slay him, but the young priest sprang aside and eluded the blow, which struck deep into the horse's neck, so that the blood spurted forth, and the creature sank down on the ground. Then Helga seemed suddenly to wake from her long reverie, and threw herself hastily upon the gasping animal. The priest stood before her to protect and defend her, but one of the robbers swung his iron hammer over the Christian's head, and brought it down with such a crash that the blood and brains were scattered around, and the priest sank to the earth, dead.

Then the robbers seized beautiful Helga by her white arms and her slender waist; but the sun went down, and its last ray disappeared at that moment, and she was changed into the form of a frog. A white-green mouth spread over half her face, her arms became thin and slimy, and broad hands with webbed fingers spread out upon them like fans. Then the robbers were seized with terror, and let her go. She stood, a hideous monster, among them; and as it is the nature of the frog to do, she hopped up high, and disappeared in the thicket. Then the robbers saw that this must be a bad prank of the spirit Loke, or the evil power of magic, and in great affright they hurried away from the spot.

The full moon was already rising. Presently it shone with splendid radiance over the earth, and poor Helga crept forth from the thicket in the wretched frog's shape. She stood still beside the corpse of the priest and the carcase of the slain horse. She looked at them with eyes that appeared to weep, and from the frog-mouth came forth a croaking like the voice of a child bursting into tears. She leant first over the one, then over the other, brought water in her hollow hand, which had become larger and more capacious by the webbed skin, and poured it over them; but dead they were, and dead they would remain, she at last understood. Soon wild beasts would come and tear their dead bodies; but no, that must not be! so she dug up the earth as well as she could, in the endeavor to prepare a grave for them. She had nothing to work with but a stake and her two hands encumbered with the webbed skin that grew between the fingers, and which were torn by the labor, so that the blood flowed over them. At last she saw that her endeavors would not succeed. Then she brought water and washed the dead man's face, and covered it with fresh green leaves; she brought green boughs and laid them upon him, scattering dead leaves in the spaces between. Then she brought the heaviest stones she could carry, and laid them over the dead body, stopping up the interstices with moss. And now she thought the grave hill would be strong and secure. The night had passed away in this difficult work—the sun broke through the clouds, and beautiful Helga stood there in all her loveliness, with bleeding hands, and with the first tears flowing that had ever bedewed her maiden cheeks.

Then in this transformation it seemed as if two natures were striving within her. Her whole frame trembled, and she looked around, as if she had just awoke from a troubled dream. Then she ran towards the slender tree, clung to it for support, and in another moment she had climbed the summit of the tree, and held fast. There she sat like a squirrel, and remained the whole day long in the silent solitude of the wood, where every thing is quiet, and, as they say, dead. Butterflies fluttered around in sport, and in the neighborhood were several ant-hills, each with its hundreds of busy little occupants moving briskly to and fro. In the air danced a number of gnats, swarm upon swarm, and hosts of burning flies, ladybirds, gold-beetles, and other little winged creatures; the worm crept forth from the damp ground, the moles came out; but except these, all was silent around—silent, and, as people say, dead—for they speak of things as they understand them. No one noticed Helga, but some flocks of crows, that flew screaming about the top of the tree on which she sat; the birds hopped close **up** to her on the twigs with **a** pert curiosity; but when the glance of her eye fell upon them, it was **a** signal for their flight. But they could not understand her—nor, indeed, could she understand herself.

When the evening twilight came **on, and the** sun was sinking, the time of her transformation roused **her to** fresh activity. She glided down from the **tree, and as** the last sunbeam vanished she stood in the wrinkled form of the frog, with the torn webbed-skin on her hands; but her eyes now gleamed with a splendor of beauty that had scarcely been theirs when she wore her garb **of** loveliness, for they were a pair of pure, pious, maidenly eyes that shone out of the frog-face. They bore witness of depth of feeling, of the gentle human heart; and the beauteous eyes overflowed **in** tears, weeping precious drops that lightened the heart.

On the sepulchral mound she had raised there yet lay the cross of boughs, the last work of him who slept beneath. Helga lifted up the cross, in pursuance of a sudden thought that came upon her. She planted it upon the burial mound, **over** the priest and the dead horse. The sorrowful remembrance of him called fresh tears into her eyes; and in this tender frame **of** mind she marked the same sign in the sand around the **grave; and as she wrote the sign** with both her hands, the webbed-skin fell from them like a torn glove ; and when she washed her hands in the woodland spring, and gazed in wonder at their snowy whiteness, she again made the holy sign in the air between herself and the dead man ; then her lips trembled, the holy name that had been preached to her during the ride from the forest came to her mouth, and she pronounced it audibly.

Then the frog-skin fell from her, and she was once more the beauteous maiden. But her head sank wearily, her tired limbs required rest, and she fell into a deep slumber.

Her sleep, however, was short. Towards midnight she awoke. Before her stood the dead horse, beaming and full of life, which gleamed forth from his eyes and from his wounded neck ; close beside the creature stood the murdered Christian priest, "more beautiful than Bulder," the Viking woman would have said ; and yet he seemed to stand in a flame of fire.

Such gravity, such an air of justice, such a piercing look shone out of his great mild eyes, that their glance seemed to penetrate every corner of her heart. Beautiful Helga trembled at the look, and her remembrance awoke as though she stood before the tribunal of judgment. Every good deed that had been done for her, every loving word that had been spoken, seemed endowed with life ; she understood that it had been love that kept her here during the days of trial, during which the creature formed of dust and spirit, soul and earth, combats and struggles ; she acknowledged that she had only followed the leading of temper, and had done nothing for herself ; every thing had been given her, every thing had happened as it were by the interposition of Providence. She bowed herself humbly, confessing her own deep imperfection in the presence of the Power that can read every thought of the heart—and then the priest spoke:

"Thou daughter of the moorland," he said, "out of the earth, out of the moor, thou camest; but from the earth thou shalt arise. I come from the land of the dead. Thou, too, shalt pass through the deep valleys into the beaming mountain region, where dwell mercy and completeness. I cannot lead thee to Hedeby, that thou mayst receive Christian baptism; for, first, thou must burst the veil of waters over the deep moorland, and draw forth the living source of thy being and of thy birth; thou must exercise thy faculties in deeds before the consecration can be given thee."

And he lifted her upon the horse, and gave her a golden censer similar to the one she had seen in the Viking's castle. The open wound in the forehead of the slain Christian shone like a diadem. He took the cross from the grave and held it aloft. And now they rode through the air, over the rustling wood, over the hills where the old heroes lay buried, each on his dead war-horse; and the iron figures rose up and galloped forth, and stationed themselves on the summits of the hills. The golden hoop on the forehead of each gleamed in the moonlight, and their mantles floated in the night breeze. The dragon that guards buried treasures likewise lifted up his head and gazed after the riders. The gnomes and wood-spirits peeped forth from beneath the hills and from between the furrows of the fields, and flitted to and fro with red, blue, and green torches, like the sparks in the ashes of a burnt paper.

Over woodland and heath, over river and marsh they fled away, up to the wild moor; and over this they hovered in wide circles. The Christian priest held the cross aloft; it gleamed like gold; and from his lips dropped pious prayers. Beautiful Helga joined in the hymns he sang, like a child joining in its mother's song. She swung the censer, and a wondrous fragrance of incense streamed forth thence, so

that the reeds and grass of the moor burst forth into blos
som. Every germ came forth from the deep ground. All
that had life lifted itself up. A veil of water-lilies spread
itself forth like a carpet of wrought flowers, and upon this
carpet lay a sleeping woman, young and beautiful. Helga
thought it was her own likeness she saw upon the mirror of
the calm waters. But it was her mother whom she beheld,
the moor king's wife, the princess from the banks of the
Nile.

The dead priest commanded that the slumbering woman
should be lifted upon the horse; but the horse sank under
the burden, as though its body had been a cloth fluttering
in the wind. But the holy sign gave strength to the airy
phantom, and then the three rode from the moor to the firm
land.

Then the cock crowed in the Viking's castle, and the
phantom shapes dissolved and floated away in air; but
mother and daughter stood opposite each other.

"Am I really looking at my own image from beneath the
deep waters?" asked the mother.

"Is it myself that I see reflected on the clear mirror?"
exclaimed the daughter.

And they approached one another, and embraced. The
heart of the mother beat quickest, and she understood the
quickening pulses.

"My child! thou flower of my own heart! my lotus-
flower of the deep waters!"

And she embraced her child anew, and wept; and the
tears were as a new baptism of life and love to Helga.

"In the swan's plumage came I hither," said the mother;
"and here also I threw off my dress of feathers. I sank
through the shaking moorland, far down into the black
slime, which closed like a wall around me. But soon I felt

a fresher stream; a power drew me down, deeper and ever deeper. I felt the weight of sleep upon my eyelids; I slumbered, and dreams hovered round me. It seemed to me that I was again in the pyramid in Egypt, and yet the waving willow trunk that had frightened me up in the moor was ever before me. I looked at the clefts and wrinkles in the stem, and they shone forth in colors, and took the form of hieroglyphics: it was the case of the mummy at which I was gazing; at last the case burst, and forth stepped the thousand-year-old king, the mummied form, black as pitch, shining black as the wood-snail or the fat mud of the swamp; whether it was the marsh king or the mummy of the pyramids I knew not. He seized me in his arms, and I felt as if I must die. When I returned to consciousness a little bird was sitting on my bosom, beating with its wings, and twittering and singing. The bird flew away from me up towards the heavy, dark covering; but a long green band still fastened him to me. I heard and understood his longing tones : ' Freedom ! Sunlight ! to my father !' Then I thought of my father and the sunny land of my birth, my life, and my love; and I loosened the band and let the bird soar away home to the father. Since that hour I have dreamed no more. I have slept a sleep, a long and heavy sleep, till within this hour ; harmony and incense awoke me and set me free."

The green band from the heart of the mother to the bird's wings, where did it flutter now ? whither had it been wafted ? Only the stork had seen it. The band was the green stalk, the bow at the end, the beauteous flower, the cradle of the child that had now bloomed into beauty, and was once more resting on its mother's heart.

And while the two were locked in each other's embrace, the old stork flew around them in smaller and smaller circles, and at length shot away in swift flight towards his nest, whence he brought out the swan-feather suits he had preserved there for years, throwing one to each of them; and the feathers closed around them, so that they soared up from the earth in the semblance of two white swans.

"And now we will speak with one another," quoth stork-papa, "now we understand each other, though the beak of one bird is differently shaped from that of another. It happens more than fortunately that you came to-night. To-morrow we should have been gone—mother, myself, and the young ones ; for we're flying southward. Yes, only look at me ! I am an old friend from the land of the Nile, and mother has a heart larger than her beak. She always declared the princess would find a way to help herself ; and I and the young ones carried the swan's feathers up here. But how glad I am ! and how fortunate that I'm here still ! At dawn of day we shall move hence, a great company of storks. We'll fly first, and do you follow us ; thus you cannot miss your way ; moreover, I and the youngsters will keep a sharp eye upon you."

"And the lotus-flower which I was to bring with me," said the Egyptian princess, "she is flying by my side in the swan's plumage ! I bring with me the flower of my heart ; and thus the riddle has been read. Homeward ! homeward !"

But Helga declared she could not quit the Danish land before she had once more seen her foster-mother, the affectionate Viking woman. Every beautiful recollection, every kind word, every tear that her foster-mother had wept for her, rose up in her memory, and in that moment she almost felt as if she loved the Viking woman best of all.

"Yes, we must go to the Viking's castle," said stork-papa ; "mother and the youngsters are waiting for us there. How they will turn up their eyes and flap their wings! Yes, you see mother doesn't speak much—she's short and dry, but she means all the better. I'll begin clapping at once, that they may know we are coming." And stork-papa clapped in first-rate style, and they all flew away towards the Viking's castle.

In the castle every one was sunk in deep sleep. The Viking's wife had not retired to rest until it was late. She was anxious about Helga, who had vanished with a Christian priest three days before : she knew Helga must have assisted him in his flight, for it was the girl's horse that had been missed from the stables ; but how all this had been effected was a mystery to her. The Viking woman had heard of the miracles told of the Christian priest, and which were said to be wrought by him and by those who believed in his words and followed him. Her passing thoughts formed themselves into a dream, and it seemed to her that she was still lying awake on her couch, and that deep darkness reigned without. The storm drew near : she heard the sea roaring and rolling to the east and to the west, like the waves of the North Sea and the Cattegat. The immense snake, which was believed to surround the span of the earth in the depths of the ocean, was trembling in convulsions ; she dreamed that the night of the fall of the gods had come—Ragnarok, as the heathen called the last day, when every thing was to pass away, even the great gods themselves. The war-trumpet sounded, and the gods rode over the rainbow, clad in steel, to fight the last battle. The winged Valkyrs rode before them, and the dead warriors closed the train. The whole firmament was ablaze with northern lights, and yet the darkness seemed to predominate. It was a terrible hour.

And close by the terrified Viking woman Helga seemed

to be crouching on the floor in the hideous frog-form, trembling and pressing close to her foster-mother, who took her on her lap, and embraced her affectionately, hideous though she was. The air resounded with the blows of clubs and swords, and with the hissing of arrows, as if a hailstorm were passing across it. The hour was come when earth and sky were to burst, the stars to fall, and all things to oe swallowed up in Surtur's sea of fire; but she knew that there would be a new heaven and a new earth, that the cornfields then would wave where now the ocean rolled over the desolate tracts of sand, and that the unutterable God would reign; and up to Him rose Bulder the gentle, the affectionate, delivered from the kingdom of the dead. He came; the Viking woman saw him, and recognized his countenance; it was that of the captive Christian priest. "White Christian!" she cried aloud, and with these words she pressed a kiss upon the forehead of the hideous frog-child. Then the frog-skin fell off, and Helga stood revealed in all her beauty, lovely and gentle as she had never appeared, and with beaming eyes. She kissed her foster-mother's hands, blessed her for all the care and affection lavished during the days of bitterness and trial, for the thought she had awakened and cherished in her, for naming the name, which she repeated, "White Christian; and beauteous Helga arose in the form of a mighty swan, and spread her white wings with a rushing like the sound of a troop of birds of passage winging their way through the air.

. The Viking woman woke; and she heard the same noise without still continuing. She knew it was the time for the storks to depart, and that it must be those birds whose wings she heard. She wished to see them once more, and to bid them farewell as they set forth on their journey. Therefore she rose from her couch, and stepped out upon the threshold, and on the top of the gable she saw stork ranged behind stork, and around the castle, over the high trees, flew bands of storks wheeling in wide circles ; but opposite the threshold where she stood, by the well where Helga had often sat and alarmed her with her wildness, sat two white swans gazing at her with intelligent eyes. And she remembered her dream, which still filled her soul as if it were reality. She thought of Helga in the shape of a swan, and of the Christian priest ; and suddenly she felt her heart rejoice within her.

The swans flapped their wings and arched their necks, as if they would send her a greeting, and the Viking's wife spread out her arms towards them, as if she felt all this ; and smiled through her tears, and then stood sunk in deep thought.

Then all the storks arose, flapping their wings and clapping with their beaks, to start on their voyage towards the South.

" We will not wait for the swans," said stork-mamma : " if they want to go with us they had better come. We can't sit here till the plovers start. It is a fine thing, after all, to travel in this way, in families, not like the finches and partridges, where the male and female birds fly in separate bodies, which appears to me a very unbecoming thing. What are yonder swans flapping their wings for ?"

" Well, every one flies in his own fashion," said stork-papa : " the swans in an oblique line, the cranes in a triangle, and the plovers in a snake's line."

" Don't talk about snakes while we are flying up here," said stork-mamma. " It only puts ideas into the children's heads which can't be gratified."

" Are those the high mountains of which I heard tell ?" asked Helga, in the swan's plumage.

"They are storm-clouds driving on beneath us," replied her mother.

"What are yonder white clouds that rise so high?" asked Helga again.

"Those are the mountains covered with perpetual snow which you see yonder," replied her mother.

And they flew across the lofty Alps towards the blue Mediterranean.

"Africa's land! Egypt's strand!" sang, rejoicingly, in her swan's plumage, the daughter of the Nile, as from the lofty air she saw her native land looming in the form of a yellowish wavy stripe of shore.

And all the birds caught sight of it, and hastened their flight.

"I can scent the Nile mud and wet frogs," said stork-mamma; "I begin to feel quite hungry. Yes; now you shall taste something nice; and you will see the maraboo bird, the crane, and the ibis. They all belong to our family, though they are not nearly so beautiful as we. They give themselves great airs, especially the ibis. He has been quite spoilt by the Egyptians, for they make a mummy of him and stuff him with spices. I would rather be stuffed with live frogs, and so would you, and so you shall. Better have something in one's inside while one is alive than to be made a fuss with after one is dead. That's my opinion, and I am always right."

"Now the storks are come," said the people in the rich house on the banks of the Nile, where the royal lord lay in the open hall on the downy cushions, covered with a leopard skin, not alive and yet not dead, but waiting and hoping for the lotus-flower from the deep moorland in the far North. Friends and servants stood around his couch.

And into the hall flew two beauteous swans. They had

come with the storks. They threw off their dazzling white plumage, and two lovely female forms were revealed, as like each other as two dewdrops. They bent over the old, pale, sick man, they put back their long hair, and while Helga bent over her grandfather, his white cheeks reddened, his eyes brightened, and life came back to his wasted limbs. The old man rose up cheerful and well; and daughter and grand-daughter embraced him joyfully, as if they were giving him a morning greeting after a long, heavy dream.

And joy reigned through the whole house, and likewise in the stork's nest, though there the chief cause was certainly the good food, especially the numberless frogs, which seemed to spring up in heaps out of the ground; and while the learned men wrote down hastily, in flying characters, a sketch of the history of the two princesses, and of the flower of health that had been a source of joy for the home and the land, the stork pair told the story to their family in their own fashion, but not till all had eaten their fill, otherwise the youngsters would have found something more interesting to do than to listen to stories.

" Now, at last, you will become something," whispered stork-mamma; " there's no doubt about that."

" What should I become ?" asked stork-papa. " What have I done ? Nothing at all !"

" You have done more than the rest ! But for you and the youngsters the two princesses would never have seen Egypt again, or have effected the old man's cure. You will turn out something ! They must certainly give you a doctor's degree, and our youngsters will inherit it, and so will their children after them, and so on. You already look like an Egyptian doctor; at least in my eyes."

" I cannot quite repeat the words as they were spoken,"

said stork-papa, who had listened from the roof to the report of these events, made by the learned men, and was now telling it again to his own family. "What they said was so confused, it was so wise and learned, that they immediately received rank and presents—even the head cook received an especial mark of distinction—probably for the soup."

"And what did you receive?" asked stork-mamma. "Surely they ought not to forget the most important person of all, and you are certainly he! The learned men have done nothing throughout the whole affair but used their tongues; but you will doubtless receive what is due to you."

Late in the night, when the gentle peace of sleep rested upon the now happy house, there was one who still watched. It was not stork-papa, though he stood upon one leg, and slept on guard—it was Helga who watched. She bowed herself forward over the balcony, and looked into the clear air, gazed at the great gleaming stars, greater and purer in their lustre than she had ever seen them in the North, and yet the same orbs. She thought of the Viking woman in the wild moorland, of the gentle eyes of her foster-mother, and of the tears which the kind soul had wept over the poor frog-child that now lived in splendor under the gleaming stars, in the beauteous spring air on the banks of the Nile. She thought of the love that dwelt in the breast of the heathen woman, the love that had been shown to a wretched creature, hateful in human form, and hideous in its transformation. She looked at the gleaming stars, and thought of the glory that had shone upon the forehead of the dead man, when she flew with him through the forest and across the moorland; sounds passed through her memory, words she had heard pronounced as they rode onward, and when she was borne wandering and trembling through the air, words from the great fountain of love that embraces all human kind.

Yes, great things had been achieved and won! Day and night beautiful Helga was absorbed in the contemplation of the great sum of her happiness, and stood in the contemplation of it like a child that turns hurriedly from the giver to gaze on the splendors of the gifts it has received. She seemed to lose herself in the increasing happiness, in contemplation of what might come, of what would come. Had she not been borne by miracle to greater and greater bliss? And in this idea she one day lost herself so completely, that she thought no more of the Giver. It was the exuberance of youthful courage, unfolding its wings for a bold flight! Her eyes were gleaming with courage, when suddenly a loud noise in the courtyard below recalled her thoughts from their wandering flight. There she saw two great ostriches running round rapidly in a narrow circle. Never before had she seen such creatures—great clumsy things they were, with wings that looked as if they had been clipped, and the birds themselves looking as if they had suffered violence of some kind; and now for the first time she heard the legend which the Egyptians tell of the ostrich.

Once, they say, the ostriches were a beautiful, glorious race of birds, with strong large wings; and one evening the larger birds of the forest said to the ostrich, "Brother, shall we fly to-morrow, *God willing,* to the river to drink?" And the ostrich answered, "I will." At daybreak, accordingly, they winged their flight from thence, flying first up on high, towards the sun, that gleamed like the eye of God —higher and higher, the ostrich far in advance of all the other birds. Proudly the ostrich flew straight towards the light, boasting of his strength, and not thinking of the

Giver, or saying, "Good willing!" Then suddenly the avenging angel drew aside the veil from the flaming ocean of sunlight, and in a moment the wings of the proud bird were scorched and shrivelled up, and he sank miserably to the ground. Since that time, the ostrich has never again been able to raise himself in the air, but flees timidly along the ground, and runs round in a narrow circle. And this is a warning for us men, that in all our thoughts and schemes, in all our doings and devices, we should say, "God willing." And Helga bowed her head thoughtfully and gravely, and looked at the circling ostrich, noticing its timid fear, and its stupid pleasure at sight of its own great shadow cast upon the white sunlit wall. And seriousness struck its roots deep into her mind and heart. A rich life in present and future happiness was given and won. And what was yet to come? The best of all, "*God willing.*"

In early spring, when the storks flew again towards the North, beautiful Helga took off her golden bracelet, and scratched her name upon it; and beckoning to the stork-father, she placed the golden hoop around his neck, and begged him to deliver it to the Viking woman, so that the latter might see that her adopted daughter was well, and had not forgotten her.

"That's heavy to carry," thought the stork-papa, when he had the golden ring round his neck; "but gold and honor are not to be flung into the street. The stork brings good fortune; they'll be obliged to acknowledge that over yonder."

"You lay gold and I lay eggs," said the stork-mamma. "But with you it's only once in a way, whereas I lay eggs every year; but neither of us is appreciated—that's very disheartening."

"Still one has one's inward consciousness, mother," replied stork-papa.

"But you can't hang that round your neck," stork-mamma retorted ; "and it won't give you a good wind or a good meal."

The little nightingale, singing yonder in the tamarind-tree, will soon be going north too.   Helga the fair had often heard the sweet bird sing up yonder by the wild moor; now she wanted to give it a message to carry, for she had learned the language of birds when she flew in the swan's plumage ; she had often conversed with stork and with swallow, and she knew the nightingale would understand her.   So she begged the little bird to fly to the beech-wood, on the peninsula of Jutland, where the grave-hill had been reared with stones and branches, and begged the nightingale to persuade all other little birds that they might build their nests around the place, so that the song of birds should resound over that sepulchre for evermore.   And the nightingale flew away—and time flew away.

In autumn the eagle stood upon the pyramid and saw a stately train of rich laden camels approaching, and richly attired armed men on foaming Arab steeds, shining white as silver, with pink trembling nostrils, and great thick manes hanging down almost over their slender legs. Wealthy guests, a royal prince of Arabia, handsome as a prince should be, came into the proud mansion on whose roof the stork's nest now stood empty : those who had inhabited the nest were away now, in the far north ; but they would soon return.   And, indeed, they returned on that very day that was so rich in joy and gladness.   Here a marriage was celebrated, and fair Helga was the bride, shining in jewels and silk.   The bridegroom was the young Arab prince, and bride and bridegroom sat together at the upper end of the table, between the mother and grandfather.

But her gaze was not fixed upon the bridegroom, with

his manly sun-browned cheeks, round which a black beard curled; she gazed not at his dark fiery eyes, that were fixed upon her—but far away at a gleaming star that shone down from the sky.

Then strong wings were heard beating the air. The storks were coming home, and however tired the old stork pair might be from the journey, and however much they needed repose, they did not fail to come down at once to the balustrades of the verandah; for they knew what feast was being celebrated. Already on the frontier of the land they had heard that Helga had caused their figures to be painted on the wall—for did they not belong to her history?

"That's very pretty and suggestive," said the stork-papa.

"But it's very little," observed stork-mamma. "They could not possibly have done less."

And when Helga saw them, she rose and came on to the verandah, to stroke the backs of the storks. The old pair waved their heads and bowed their necks, and even the youngest among the young ones felt highly honored by the reception.

And Helga looked up to the gleaming star, which seemed to glow purer and purer; and between the star and herself there floated a form, purer than the air, and visible through it: it floated quite close to her. It was the spirit of the dead Christian priest; he too was coming to her wedding feast—coming from heaven.

"The glory and brightness yonder outshines every thing that is known on earth!" he said.

And fair Helga begged so fervently, so beseechingly, as she had never yet prayed, that it might be permitted her to gaze in there for one single moment, that she might be allowed to cast but a single glance into the brightness that beamed in the kingdom.

Then he bore her up amid splendor and glory. Not only around her, but within her, sounded voices and beamed a brightness that words cannot express.

" Now we must go back; thou wilt be missed," he said.

" Only one more look !" she begged. " But one short minute more !"

" We must go back to the earth. The guests will all depart."

" Only one more look—the last."

And Helga stood again in the verandah; but the marriage lights without had vanished, and the lamps in the hall were extinguished, and the storks were gone—nowhere a guest to be seen—no bridegroom—all seemed to have been swept away in those few short minutes !

Then a great dread came upon her. Alone she went through the empty great hall into the next chamber. Strange warriors slept yonder. She opened a side door which led into her own chamber; and, as she thought to step in there, she suddenly found herself in the garden; but yet it had not looked thus here before—the sky gleamed red—the morning dawn was come.

Three minutes only in heaven and a whole night on earth had passed away !

Then she saw the storks again. She called to them spoke their language; and stork-papa turned his head towards her, listened to her words, and drew near.

" You speak our language," he said ; " what do you wish ? Why do you appear here—you, a strange woman ?"

" It is I—it is Helga—dost thou not know me ? Three minutes ago we were speaking together yonder in the verandah !"

"That's a mistake," said the stork ; "you must have dreamt all that !"

"No, no !" she persisted. And she reminded him of the Viking's castle, and of the great ocean, and of the journey hither.

Then stork-papa winked with his eyes, and said:

"Why, that's an old story, which I heard from the time of my great-grandfather. There certainly was here in Egypt a princess of that kind from the Danish land, but she vanished on the evening of her wedding-day, many hundred years ago, and never came back ! You may read about it yourself yonder on the monument in the garden; there you'll find swans and storks sculptured, and at the top you are yourself in white marble !"

And thus it was. Helga saw it, and understood it, and sank on her knees.

The sun burst forth in glory; and as, in time of yore, the frog-shape had vanished in its beams, and the beautiful form had stood displayed, so now in the light a beauteous form, clearer, purer than air—a beam of brightness—flew up into heaven !

The body crumbled to dust ; and a faded lotus-flower lay on the spot where Helga had stood.

"Well, that's a new ending to the story," said stork-papa. "I had certainly not expected it. But I like it very well."

"But what will the young ones say to it ?" said stork-mamma.

"Yes, certainly, that's the important point," replied he.

THE LAST DREAM OF THE OLD OAK-TREE.

A CHRISTMAS TALE.

In the forest, high up on the steep shore, hard by the open sea-coast, stood a very old oak-tree. It was exactly three hundred and sixty-five years old, but that long time was not more for the tree than just as many days would be to us men. We wake by day and sleep through the night, and then we have our dreams : it is different with the tree, which keeps awake through three seasons of the year, and does not get its sleep till winter comes. Winter is its time for rest, its night after the long day which is called spring, summer, and autumn.

On many a warm summer day the ephemera, the fly that lives but for a day, had danced around his crown—had lived, enjoyed, and felt happy; and then rested for a moment in quiet bliss the tiny creature, on one of the great fresh oak-leaves; and then the tree always said:

"Poor little thing ! Your whole life is but a single day ! How very short ! It's quite melancholy !"

"Melancholy ! Why do you say that ?" the ephemera would then always reply. "It is wonderfully bright, warm, and beautiful all around me, and that makes me rejoice !"

"But only one day, and then it's all done !"

"Done !" repeated the ephemera. "What's the meaning of *done?* Are you *done*, too ?"

"No ; I shall perhaps live for thousands of your days, and my day is whole seasons long ! It's something so long, that you can't at all manage to reckon it out."

"No ? then I don't understand you You say you have

thousands of my days; but I have thousands of moments, in which I can be merry and happy. Does all the beauty of this world cease when you die ?"

"No," replied the Tree; "it will certainly last much longer—far longer than I can possibly think."

"Well, then, we have the same time, only that we reckon differently."

And the Ephemera danced and floated in the air, and re-joiced in her delicate wings of gauze and velvet, and rejoiced in the balmy breezes laden with the fragrance of meadows and of wild-roses and elder-flowers, of the garden hedges, wild thyme, and mint, and daisies ; the scent of these was all so strong that the Ephemera was almost intoxicated. The day was long and beautiful, full of joy and of sweet feeling, and when the sun sank low the little fly felt very agreeably tired of all its happiness and enjoyment. The delicate wings would not carry it any more, and quietly and slowly it glided down upon the soft grass-blade, nodded its head as well as it could nod, and went quitely to sleep— and was dead.

"Poor little Ephemera !" said the Oak. "That was a terribly short life !"

And on every summer day the same dance was repeated, the same question and answer, and the same sleep. The same thing was repeated through whole generations of ephemera, all of them felt equally merry and equally happy.

The Oak stood there awake through the spring morning, the noon of summer, and the evening of autumn ; and its time of rest, its night, was coming on apace. Winter was approaching.

Already the storms were singing their "good-night, good night !" Here fell a leaf and there fell a leaf.

"We'll rock you, and dandle you ! Go to sleep, go to

sleep !   We sing you to sleep, we shake you to sleep, but it does you good in your old twigs, does it not?   They seem to crack for very joy !   Sleep sweetly, sleep sweetly !   It's your three hundred and sixty-fifth night.   Properly speak- ing, you're only a stripling as yet !   Sleep sweetly !   The clouds strew down snow, there will be quite a coverlet, warm and protecting, around your feet.   Sweet sleep to you, and pleasant dreams !"

And the Oak-Tree stood there, denuded of all its leaves, to sleep through the long winter, and to dream many a dream, always about something that had happened to it— just as in the dreams of men.

The great Oak had once been small—indeed, an acorn had been its cradle.   According to human computation, it was now in its fourth century.   It was the greatest and best tree in the forest ; its crown towered far above all the other trees, and could be descried from afar across the sea, so that it served as a landmark to the sailors : the tree had no idea how many eyes were in the habit of seeking it.   High up in its green summit the wood-pigeon built her nest, and the cuckoo sat in its boughts, and sang his song ; and in autumn, when the leaves looked like thin plates of copper, the birds of passage came and rested there, before they flew away across the sea ; but now it was winter, and the tree stood there leafless, so that every one could see how gnarled and crooked the branches were that shot forth from its trunk.   Crows and rooks came and took their seat by turns in the boughs, and spoke of the hard times which were beginning, and of the difficulty of getting a living in winter.

It was just at the holy Christmas time, when the tree dreamed its most glorious dream.

The tree had a distinct feeling of the festive time, and

fancied he heard the bells ringing from the churches all around ; and yet it seemed as if it were a fine summer's day, mild and warm. Fresh and green he spread out his mighty crown ; the sunbeams played among the twigs and the leaves ; the air was full of the fragrance of herbs and blossoms ; gay butterflies chased each other to and fro. The ephemeral insects danced as if all the world were created merely for them to dance and be merry in. All that the tree had experienced for years and years, and that had happened around him, seemed to pass by him again, as in a festive pageant. He saw the knights of ancient days ride by with their noble dames on gallant steeds, with plumes waving in their bonnets and falcons on their wrists. The hunting-horn sounded, and the dogs barked. He saw hostile warriors in colored jerkins and with shining weapons, with spear and halbert, pitching their tents and striking them again. The watch-fires flamed up anew, and men sang and slept under the branches of the tree. He saw loving couples meeting near his trunk, happily, in the moonshine ; and they cut the initials of their names in the gray-green bark of his stem. Once—but long years had rolled by since then—citherns and Æolian harps had been hung up on his boughs by merry wanderers; and now they hung there again, and once again they sounded in tones of marvellous sweetness. The wood-pigeons cooed, as if they were telling what the tree felt in all this, and the cuckoo called out to tell him how many summer days he had yet to live.

Then it appeared to him as if new life were rippling down into the remotest fibre of his root, and mounting up into his highest branches, to the tops of the leaves. The tree felt that he was stretching and spreading himself, and through his root he felt that there was life and motion even in the ground itself. He felt his strength increase, he grew higher, his stem shot up unceasingly, and he grew more and more, his crown became fuller, and spread out ; and in proportion as the tree grew, he felt his happiness increase, and his joyous hope that he should reach even higher—quite up to the warm brilliant sun.

Already had he grown high above the clouds, which floated past beneath his crown like dark troops of passage-birds, or like great white swans. And every leaf of the tree had the gift of sight, as if it had eyes wherewith to see; the stars became visible in broad daylight, great and sparkling; each of them sparkled like a pair of eyes, mild and clear.   They recalled to his memory well-known gentle eyes, eyes of children, eyes of lovers who had met beneath his boughs.

It was a marvellous spectacle, and one full of happiness and joy !   And yet amid all this happiness the tree felt a longing, a yearning desire that all other trees of the wood beneath him, and all the bushes, and herbs, and flowers, might be able to rise with him, that they too might see this splendor, and experience this joy.   The great majestic oak was not quite happy in his happiness, while he had not them all, great and little, about him; and this feeling of yearning trembled through his every twig, through his every leaf, warmly and fervently as through a human heart.

The crown of the tree waved to and fro, as if he sought something in his silent longing, and he looked down.   Then he felt the fragrance of thyme, and soon afterwards the more powerful scent of honeysuckle and violets ; and he fancied he heard the cuckoo answering him.

Yes, through the clouds the green summits of the forest came peering up, and under himself the Oak saw the other trees, as they grew and raised themselves aloft.   Bushes and herbs shot up high, and some tore themselves up bodily by the roots to rise the quicker. The birch was the quickest of all.   Like a white streak of lighthing, its slender stem shot upwards in a zigzag line, and the branches spread around it like green gauze and like banners; the whole woodland natives, even to the brown-plumed rushes, grew up with the rest, and the birds came too, and sang; and on the grass blade that fluttered aloft like a long silken ribbon into the air, sat the grasshopper cleaning his wings with his leg; the May beetles hummed, and the bees murmured, and every bird sang in his appointed manner ; all was song and sound of gladness up into the high heaven.

"But the little blue flower by the water-side, where is that ?" said the Oak; "and the purple bell-flower and the daisy ?" for, you see, the old Oak-Tree wanted to have them all about him.

"We are here—we are here !" was shouted and sung in reply.

"But the beautiful thyme of last summer—and in the last year there was certainly a place here covered with lilies of the valley ! and the wild apple-tree that blossomed so splendidly ! and all the glory of the wood that came year by year—if that had only just been born, it might have been here now !"

"We are here, we are here !" replied voices still higher in the air.   It seemed as if they had flown on before.

"Why, that is beautiful, indescribably beautiful !" exclaimed the old Oak-Tree, rejoicingly.   "I have them all around me, great and small; not one has been forgotten ! How can so much happiness be imagined ?   How can it be possible ?"

"In heaven, in the better land, it can be imagined, and it is possible !" the reply sounded through the air.

And the old tree, who grew on and on, felt how his roots were tearing themselves free from the ground.

"That's right, that's better than all?" said the tree. "Now no fetters hold me! I can fly up now, to the very highest, in glory and in light! And all my beloved ones are with me, great and small—all of them, all!"

That was the dream of the old Oak-Tree; and while he dreamt thus a mighty storm came rushing over land and sea—at the holy Christmas-tide. The sea rolled great billows towards the shore; there was a cracking and crashing in the tree—his root was torn out of the ground in the very moment while he was dreaming that his root freed itself from the earth. He fell. His three hundred and sixty-five years were now as the single day of the ephemera.

On the morning of the Christmas festival, when the sun rose, the storm had subsided. From all the churches sounded the festive bells, and from every hearth, even from the smallest hut, arose the smoke in blue clouds, like the smoke from the altars of the druids of old at the feast of thanks-offerings. The sea became gradually calm, and on board a great ship in the offing, that had fought successfully with the tempest, all the flags were displayed, as a token of joy suitable to the festive day.

"The tree is down—the old Oak-Tree, our landmark on the coast!" said the sailors. "It fell in the storm of last night. Who can replace it? No one can."

This was the funeral oration, short but well meant, that was given to the tree, which lay stretched on the snowy covering on the sea-shore; and over its prostrate form sounded the notes of a song from the ship, a carol of the joys of Christmas, and of the redemption of the soul of man by His blood, and of eternal life.

"Sing, sing aloud, this blessed morn—
It is fulfilled—and He is born:
Oh, joy without compare!
Hallelujah! Hallelujah!"

Thus sounded the old psalm-tune, and every one on board the ship felt lifted up in his own way, through the song and the prayer, just as the old tree had felt lifted up in its last, its most beauteous dream in the Christmas night.

THE BELL-DEEP.

"Ding-dong! ding-dong!" It sounds up from the "bell-deep," in the Odense-Au. Every child in the old town of Odense, on the island of Fünen, knows the Au, which washes the gardens round about the town, and flows on under the wooden bridges from the dam to the water-mill. In the Au grow the yellow water-lilies and brown feathery reeds; the dark velvety flag grows there, high and thick; old, decayed willows, slanting and tottering, hang far out over the stream beside the monks' meadow and by the bleaching-ground; but opposite there are gardens upon gardens, each different from the rest, some with pretty flowers and bowers like little dolls' pleasure-grounds, often displaying only cabbage and other kitchen plants; and here and there the gardens cannot be seen at all, for the great elder-trees that spread themselves out by the bank, and hang far out over the streaming waters, which are deeper here and there than an oar can fathom. Opposite the old nunnery is the deepest place, which is called the "bell-deep," and there dwells the old water-spirit, the "Au-mann." This spirit sleeps through the day while the sun shines down upon the water ; but in starry and moonlit nights he shows himself. He is very old : grandmother says that she has heard her own grandmother tell of him; he is said to lead a solitary life, and to have nobody with whom he can converse save the great old church-bell. Once the bell hung in the church tower; but now there is no trace left of the tower or of the church, which was called St. Alban's.

"Ding-dong ! ding-dong !" sounded the bell, when the tower still stood there; and one evening, while the sun was setting, and the bell was swinging away bravely, it broke loose and came flying down through the air, the brilliant metal shining in the ruddy beam.

"Ding-dong ! ding-dong ! Now I'll retire to rest !" sang the bell, and flew down into the Odense-Au where it is deepest; and that is why the place is called the "bell-deep." But the bell got neither rest nor sleep. Down in the Au-mann's haunt it sounds and rings, so that the tones sometimes pierce upward through the waters; and many people maintain that its strains forebode the death of some one ; but that is not true, for then the bell is only talking with the Au-mann, who is now no longer alone.

And what is the bell telling ? It is old, very old, as we have already observed; it was there long before grandmother's grandmother was born; and yet it is but a child in comparison with the Au-mann, who is an old quiet personage, an oddity, with his hose of eel-skin, and his scaly jacket with the yellow lilies for buttons, and a wreath of reed in his hair and seaweed in his beard; but he looks very pretty for all that.

What the bell tells ? To repeat it all would require years and days; for year by year it is telling the old stories, sometimes short ones, sometimes long ones, according to its whim; it tells of old times, of the dark, hard, times, thus:

"In the church of St. Alban, the monk mounted up into the tower. He was young and handsome, but thoughtful exceedingly. He looked through the loophole out upon the Odense-Au, when the bed of the water was yet broad, and the monks' meadow was still a lake; he looked out over it, and over the rampart, and over the nuns' hill opposite, where the convent lay, and the light gleamed forth from the nun's cell; he had known the nun right well, and he thought of her, and his heart beat quicker as he thought. Ding-dong! ding-dong!"

Yes, this was the story the bell told.

"Into the tower came also the dapper man-servant of the bishop; and when I, the bell, who am made of metal, rang hard and loud, and swung to and fro, I might have beaten out his brains. He sat down close under me, and played with two little sticks as if they had been a stringed instrument; and he sang to it. 'Now I may sing it out aloud, though at other times I may not whisper it. I may sing of every thing that is kept concealed behind lock and bars. Yonder it is cold and wet. The rats are eating her up alive! Nobody knows of it! Nobody hears of it! Not even now, for the bell is ringing and singing its loud ding-dong, ding-dong!'

"There was a king in those days; they called him Canute. He bowed himself before bishop and monk; but when he offended the free peasants with heavy taxes and hard words, they seized their weapons and put him to flight like a wild beast. He sought shelter in the church, and shut gate and door behind him. The violent band surrounded the church; I heard tell of it. The crows, ravens, and magpies started up in terror at the yelling and shouting that sounded around. They flew into the tower and out again, they looked down upon the throng below, and they also looked into the windows of the church, and screamed out aloud what they saw there. King Canute knelt before the altar in prayer, his brothers Eric and Benedict stood by him as a guard with drawn swords; but the king's servant, the treacherous Blake, betrayed his master; the throng in front of the church knew where they could hit the king, and one of them flung a stone through a pane of glass, and the king lay there dead ! The cries and screams of the savage horde and of the birds sounded through the air, and I joined it also; for I sang ' Ding-dong ! ding-dong !'

" The church-bell hangs high and looks far around, and sees the birds around it, and understands their language; the wind roars in upon it through windows and loopholes; and the wind knows every thing, for he gets it from the air, which encircles all things, and the church-bell under-stands his tongue, and rings it out into the world, ' Ding-dong ! ding-dong !'

" But it was too much for me to hear and to know; I was not able any longer to ring it out. I became so tired, so heavy, that the beam broke, and I flew out into the gleam-ing Au where the water is deepest, and where the Au-mann lives solitary and alone; and year by year I tell him what I have heard and what I know. Ding-dong ! ding-dong !"

Thus it sounds complainingly out of the bell-deep in the Odense-Au : that is what grandmother told us.

But the schoolmaster says that there was not any bell that rung down there, for that it could not do so : and that no Au-mann dwelt yonder, for there was no Au-mann at all ! And when all the other church-bells are sounding sweetly, he says that it is not really the bells that are sounding, but that it is the air itself which sends forth the notes ; and grandmother said to us that the bell itself said it was the air who told it him ; consequently they are agreed on that point, and this much is sure. "Be cautious, cautious, and take good heed to thyself," they both say.

The air knows every thing. It is around us, it is in us, it talks of our thoughts and of our deeds, and it speaks longer of them than does the bell down in the depths of the Odense-Au where the Au-mann dwells ; it rings it out into the vault of heaven, far, far out, forever and ever, till the heaven bells sound "Ding-dong ! ding-dong !"

⚬•⚬

THE PUPPET SHOWMAN.

On board the steamer was an elderly man with such a merry face that, if it did not belie him, he must have been the happiest fellow in creation. And, indeed, he declared he was the happiest man ; I heard it out of his own mouth. He was a Dane, a travelling theatre director. He had all his company with him in a large box, for he was proprietor of a puppet-show. His inborn cheerfulness, he said, had been *purified* by a Polytechnic candidate, and the experiment had made him completely happy. I did not at first understand all this, but afterwards he explained the whole story to me, and here it is. He told me:

"It was in the little town of Slagelse I gave a representation in the hall of the posting-house, and had a brilliant audience, entirely a juvenile one, with the exception of two respectable matrons. All at once a person in black, of student-like appearance, came into the room and sat down ; he laughed aloud at the telling-parts, and applauded quite

appropriately. That was quite an unusual spectator for
me !   I felt anxious to know who he was, and I heard
he was a candidate for the Polytechnic Institution in Copenhagen, who had been sent out to instruct the folks in the
provinces.   Punctually at eight o'clock my performance
closed ; for children must go early to bed, and a manager
must consult the convenience of his public. At nine o'clock
the candidate commenced his lecture, with experiments,
and now I formed part of *his* audience. It was wonderful
to hear and to see. The greater part of it was beyond my
scope ; but still it made me think that if we men can find
out so much, we must be surely intended to last longer than
the little span until we are hidden away in the earth.
They were quite miracles in a small way that he showed,
and yet every thing flowed as naturally as water ! At the
time of Moses and the prophets such a man would have
been received among the sages of the land ; in the middle
ages they would have burned him at a stake. All night
long I could not go to sleep. And the next evening, when
I gave another performance, and the candidate was again
present, I felt fairly overflowing with humor. I once heard
from a player that when he acted a lover he always thought
of one particular lady among the audience ; he only played
for her, and forgot all the rest of the house ; and now
the Polytechnic candidate was my ' she,' my only auditor,
for whom alone I played. ·And when the performance was
over, all the puppets were called before the curtain, and the
Polytechnic candidate invited me into his room to take a glass
of wine ; and he spoke of my comedies and I of his science;
and I believe we were both equally pleased. But I had the
best of it, for there was much in what he did of which he
could not always give me an explanation. For instance,
that a piece of iron that falls through a spiral should become

THE BEAR PLAYING AT SOLDIERS WITH THE CHILDREN.

magnetic. Now, how does that happen? The spirit comes upon it; but whence does it come? It is as with people in this world; they are made to tumble through the spiral of this world, and the spirit comes upon them, and there stands a Napoleon, or a Luther, or a person of that kind. 'The whole world is a series of miracles,' said the candidate; 'but we are so accustomed to them that we call them every-day matters.' And he went on explaining things to me until my skull seemed lifted up over my brain, and I declared that if I were not an old fellow I would at once visit the Polytechnic Institution, that I might learn to look at the sunny side of the world, though I am one of the happiest of men. 'One of the happiest!' said the candidate, and he seemed to take real pleasure in it. 'Are you happy?' 'Yes,' I replied, 'and they welcome me in all the towns where I come with my company; but I certainly have *one* wish, which sometimes lies like lead, like an Alp, upon my good-humor: I should like to become a real theatrical manager, the director of a real troupe of men and women!' 'I see,' he said, 'you would like to have life breathed into your puppets, so that they might be real actors, and you their director; and would you then be quite happy?' He did not believe it; but I believed it, and we talked it over all manner of ways without coming any nearer to an agreement; but we clanked our glasses together, and the wine was excellent. There was some magic in it, or I should certainly have become tipsy. But that did not happen; I retained my clear view of things, and somehow there was sunshine in the room, and sunshine beamed out of the eyes of the polytechnic candidate. It made me think of the old stories of the gods, in their eternal youth, when they still wandered upon earth and paid visits to the mortals; and I said so to him, and he smiled, and I could have sworn he was one of the ancient gods in disguise, or that, at any rate, he belonged to the family ! and certainly he must have been something of the kind, for my highest wish was to have been fulfilled, the puppets were to be gifted with life, and I was to be director of a real company. We drank to my success, and clinked our glasses. He packed all my dolls into a box, bound the box on my back, and then let me fall through a spiral. I heard myself tumbling, and then I was lying on the floor—I know that quite well—and the whole company sprang out of the box. The spirit had come upon all of us: all the puppets had become distinguished artists, so they said themselves, and I was the director. All was ready for the first representation; the whole company wanted to speak to me, and the public also. The dancing lady said the house would fall down if she did not keep it up by standing on one leg; for she was the great genius, and begged to be treated as such. The lady who acted the queen wished to be treated off the stage as a queen, or else she should get out of practice. The man who was only employed to deliver a letter gave himself just as many airs as the first lover, for he declared the little ones were just as important as the great ones, and that all were of equal consequence, considered as an artistic whole. The hero would only play parts composed of nothing but points; for those brought him down the applause. The prima donna would only play in a red light; for she declared that a blue one did not suit her complexion. It was like a company of flies in a bottle; and I was in the bottle with them, for I was the director. My breath stopped and my head whirled round; I was as miserable as a man can be. It was quite a novel kind of men among whom I now found myself. I only wished I had them all in the box again, and that I had never been a di rector at all; so I told them roundly that after all they were nothing but puppets; and then they killed me. I found myself lying on my bed in my room; and how I got there, and how I got away at all from the polytechnic candidate, he may perhaps know, for I don't. The moon shone upon the floor where the box lay open, and the dolls all in a confusion together—great and small all scattered about; but I was not idle. Out of bed I jumped, and into the box they had all to go, some on their heads, some on their feet, and I shut down the lid and seated myself upon the box. 'Now you'll just have to stay there,' said I, 'and I shall beware how I wish you flesh and blood again.' I felt quite light; my good-humor had come back, and I was the happiest of mortals. The polytechnic student had fully purified me. I sat as happy as a king, and went to sleep on the box. The next morning—strictly speaking it was noon, for I slept wonderfully late that day—I was still sitting there, happy and conscious that my former wish had been a foolish one. I inquired for the polytechnic candidate, but he was gone, like the Greek and Roman gods; and from that time I've been the happiest of men. I am a happy director: none of my company ever grumble, nor my public either, for they are always merry. I can put my pieces together just as I please. I take out of every comedy what pleases me best, and no one is angry at it. Pieces that are neglected now-a-days by the great public, but which it used to run after thirty years ago, and at which it used to cry till the tears ran down its cheeks, these pieces I now take up; I put them before the little ones, and the little ones cry just as papa and mamma used to cry thirty years ago; but I shorten them, for the youngsters don't like a long palaver; what they want is something mournful, but quick."

THE PIGS.

CHARLES DICKENS once told us about a pig, and since that time we are in a good humor if we only hear one grunt. St. Anthony took the pig under his protection; and when we think of the prodigal son we always associate with him the idea of feeding swine; and it was in front of a pig-sty that a certain carriage stopped in Sweden, about which I am going to talk. The farmer had his pig-sty built out towards the high-road, close by his house, and it was a wonderful pig-sty. It was an old state carriage. The seats had been taken out and the wheels taken off, and so the body of the old coach lay on the ground, and four pigs were shut up inside it. I wonder if these were the first that had ever been there? That point could not certainly be determined; but that it had been a real state coach every thing bore witness, even to the damask rag that hung down from the roof; every thing spoke of better days.

"Humph! humph!" said the occupants, and the coach creaked and groaned; for it had come to a mournful end. "The beautiful has departed," it sighed—or at least it might have done so.

We came back in autumn. The coach was there still, but the pigs were gone. They were playing the grand lords out in the woods. Blossoms and leaves were gone from all the trees, and storm and rain ruled, and gave them neither peace nor rest; and the birds of passage had flown. "The beautiful has departed! This was the glorious greenwood, but the song of the birds and the warm sunshine are gone! gone!" Thus said the mournful voice that creaked in the lofty branches of the trees, and it sounded like a deep-drawn sigh, a sigh from the bosom of the wild-rose tree, and of him who sat there; it was the rose-king. Do you know him? He is all beard, the finest reddish-green beard; he is easily recognized. Go up to the wild-rose bushes, and when in autumn all the flowers have faded from them, and only the wild hips remain, you will often find under them a great red-green moss-flower; and that is the rose-king. A little green leaf grows up out of his head, and that's his feather. He is the only man of his kind on the rose-bush; and he it was who sighed.

"Gone! gone! The beautiful is gone! The roses have faded, and the leaves fallen down! It's wet here! it's boisterous here! The birds who used to sing are dumb, and the pigs go out hunting for acorns, and the pigs are the lords of the forest!"

The nights were cold and the days were misty; but, for all that, the raven sat on the branch and sang, "Good! good!" Raven and crow sat on the high bough; and they had a large family, who all said, "Good! good!" and the majority is always right.

Under the high trees, in the hollow, was a great puddle, and here the pigs reclined, great and small. They found the place so inexpressibly lovely! "Oui! oui!" they all exclaimed. That was all the French they knew, but even that was something; and they were so clever and so fat!

The old ones lay quite still, and reflected; the young ones were very busy, and were not quiet a moment. One little porker had a twist in his tail like a ring, and this ring was his mother's pride; she thought all the rest were looking at the ring, and thinking only of the ring: but that they were not doing; they were thinking of themselves and of what was useful, and what was the use of the wood

They had always heard that the acorns they ate grew at the roots of the trees, and accordingly they had grubbed up the ground; but there came quite a little pig—it's always the young ones who come out with their new-fangled notions—who declared that the acorns fell down from the branches, for one had just fallen down on his head, and the idea had struck him at once; afterwards he had made observations, and now was quite certain on the point. The old ones put their heads together. "Umph!" they said, "umph! The glory has departed: the twittering of the birds is all over: we want fruit; whatever is good to eat is good, and we eat every thing."

"Oui! oui!" chimed in all the rest.

But the mother now looked at her little porker, the one with the ring in his tail. "One must not overlook the beautiful," she said. "Good! good!" cried the crow, and flew down from the tree to try and get an appointment as nightingale; for some one must be appointed; and the crow obtained the office directly.

"Gone! gone!" sighed the rose-king. "All the beautiful is gone!"

It was boisterous, it was gray, cold, and windy; and through the forest and over the field swept the rain in long dark streaks. Where is the bird who sang, where are the flowers upon the meadow, and the sweet berries of the wood! Gone! gone!

Then a light gleamed from the forester's house. It was lit up like a star, and threw its long ray among the trees. A song sounded forth out of the house! Beautiful children played there around the old grandfather. He sat with the Bible on his knee, and read of the Creator and of a better world, and spoke of spring that would return, of the forest that would array itself in fresh green, of the roses that would bloom, the nightingale that would sing, and of the beautiful that would reign in its glory again.

But the rose-king heard it not, for he sat in the cold, damp weather, and sighed, "Gone! gone!" And the pigs were the lords of the forest, and the old mother-sow looked proudly at her little porker with the twist in his tail. "There is always somebody who has a soul for the beautiful!" she said.

A STORY FROM THE SAND-DUNES.

THIS is a story from the sand-dunes or sand-hills of Jutland; though it does not begin in Jutland, the northern peninsula, but far away in the south, in Spain. The ocean is the high-road between the nations—transport thyself thither in thought to sunny Spain. There it is warm and beautiful, there the fiery pomegranate blossoms flourish among the dark laurels; from the mountains a cool refreshing wind blows down upon and over the orange-gardens, over the gorgeous Moorish halls with their golden cupolas and colored walls: through the streets go children in procession, with candles and with waving flags, and over them, lofty and clear, rises the sky with its gleaming stars. There is a sound of song and of castanets, and youths and maidens join in the dance under the blooming acacias, while the mendicant sits upon the hewn marble stone, refreshing himself with the juicy melon, and dreamily enjoying life. The whole is like a glorious dream. And there was a newly-married couple who completely gave themselves up to its charm; moreover, they possessed the good things of this life, health and cheerfulness of soul, riches and honor.

"We are as happy as it is possible to be," exclaimed the young couple, from the depths of their hearts. They had indeed but one step more to mount in the ladder of happiness, in the hope that God would give them a child; a son like them in form and in spirit.

The happy child would be welcomed with rejoicing, would be tended with all care and love, and enjoy every advantage that wealth and ease possessed by an influential family could give.

And the days went by like a glad festival.

"Life is a gracious gift of Providence, an almost inappreciable gift!" said the young wife, "and yet they tell us that fulness of joy is found only in the future life, forever and ever. I cannot compass the thought."

"And perhaps the thought arises from the arrogance of men," said the husband. "It seems a great pride to believe that we shall live forever, that we shall be as gods. Were these not the words of the serpent, the origin of falsehood?"

"Surely you do not doubt the future life?" exclaimed the young wife; and it seemed as if one of the first shadows flitted over the sunny heaven of her thoughts.

"Faith promises it, and the priests tell us so!" replied the man; "but amid all my happiness, I feel that it is arrogance to demand a continued happiness, another life after this. Has not so much been given us in this state of existence, that we ought to be, that we *must* be, contented with it?"

"Yes, it has been given to *us*," said the young wife, "but to how many thousands is not this life one scene of hard trial! How many have been thrown into this world, as if only to suffer poverty and shame and sickness and misfortune! If there were no life after this, every thing on earth would be too unequally distributed, and the Almighty would not be justice itself."

"Yonder beggar," replied the man, "has his joys which seem to him great, and which rejoice him as much as the king is rejoiced in the splendor of his palace. And then, do you not think that the beast of burden, which suffers blows and hunger, and works itself to death, suffers from its heavy fate? The dumb beast might likewise demand a future life, and declare the decree unjust that does not admit it into a higher place of creation."

"HE has said, 'In my Father's house are many mansions,'" replied the young wife : "heaven is immeasurable, as the love of our Maker is immeasurable. Even the dumb beast is His creature; and I firmly believe that no life will be lost, but that each will receive that amount of happiness which he can enjoy, and which is sufficient for him."

"This world is sufficient for me !" said the man, and he threw his arms round his beautiful, amiable wife, and then smoked his cigarette on the open balcony, where the cool air was filled with the fragrance of oranges and pinks. The sound of music and the clatter of castanets came up from the road, the stars gleamed above, and two eyes full of affection, the eyes of his wife, looked on him with the undying glance of love.

"Such a moment," he said, "makes it worth while to be born, to fall, and to disappear !" and he smiled. The young wife raised her hand in mild reproach, and the shadow passed away from her world, and they were happy—quite happy.

Every thing seemed to work together for them. They advanced in honor, in prosperity, and in joy. There was a change, indeed, but only a change of place ; not in enjoyment of life and of happiness. The young man was sent by his sovereign as ambassador to the court of Russia. This was an honorable office, and his birth and his acquirements gave him a title to be thus honored. He possessed a great fortune, and his wife had brought him wealth equal to his own, for she was the daughter of a rich and respected merchant. One of this merchant's largest and finest ships was to be dispatched during that year to Stockholm, and it was arranged that the dear young people, the daughter and the son-in-law, should travel in it to St. Petersburg. And all the arrangements on board were princely—rich carpets for the feet, and silk and luxury on all sides.

In an old heroic song, "The King's Son of England," it says, "Moreover, he sailed in a gallant ship, and the anchor was gilded with ruddy gold, and each rope was woven through with silk." And this ship involuntarily rose in the mind of him who saw the vessel from Spain, for here was the same pomp, and the same parting thought naturally arose—the thought:

> "God grant that we all in joy
> Once more may meet again."

And the wind blew fairly seaward from the Spanish shore, and the parting was to be but a brief one, for in a few weeks the voyagers would reach their destination; but when they came out upon the high seas, the wind sank, the sea became calm and shining, the stars of heaven gleamed brightly, and they were festive evenings that were spent in the sumptuous cabin.

At length the voyagers began to wish for wind, for a favoring breeze; but the breeze would not blow, or, if it did arise, it was contrary. Thus weeks passed away, two full months; and then at last the fair wind blew—it blew from the southwest The ship sailed on the high seas between Scotland and Jutland, and the wind increased just as in the old song of " The King's Son of England :"

> " And it blew a storm, and the rain came down,
> And they found not land nor shelter,
> And forth they threw their anchor of gold,
> As the wind blew westward, towards Denmark."

This all happened a long, long while ago. King Christian VII. then sat on the Danish throne, and he was still a young man. Much has happened since that time, much has changed or has been changed. Sea and moorland have been converted into green meadows, heath has become arable land, and in the shelter of the West Jute huts grow apple-trees and rose bushes, though they certainly require to be sought for, as they bend beneath the sharp west wind. In Western Jutland one may go back in thought to the old times, further back than the days when Christian VII. bore rule. As it did then, in Jutland, the brown heath now also extends for miles, with its " Huns' Graves," its aerial spectacles, and its crossing, sandy, uneven roads ; westward, where large rivulets run into the bays, extend marshes and meadow-land, girdled with lofty sand-hills, which, like a row of Alps, raise their peaked summits towards the sea, only broken by the high clayey ridges, from which the waves, year by year, bite out huge mouthfuls, so that the impending shores fall down as if by the shock of an earthquake. Thus it is there to-day, and thus it was many, many years ago, when the happy pair were sailing in the gorgeous ship

It was in the last days of September, a Sunday, and sunny weather ; the chiming of the church-bells in the bay of Nissum was wafted along like a chain of sounds. The churches there are erected almost entirely of hewn boulder stones, each like a piece of rock; the North Sea might foam over them, and they would not be overthrown. Most of them are without steeples, and the bells are hung between two beams in the open air. The service was over, and the congregation thronged out into the churchyard, where then, as now, not a tree nor a brush was to be seen; not a single flower had been planted there, nor had a wreath been laid upon the graves. Rough mounds show where the dead had been buried, and rank grass, tossed by the wind, grows thickly over the whole churchyard. Here and there a grave had a monument to show, in the shape of a half-decayed block of wood rudely shaped into the form of a coffin, the said block having been brought from the forest of West Jutland; but the forest of West Jutland is the wild sea itself, where the inhabitants find the hewn beams and planks and fragments which the breakers cast ashore. The wind and the sea-fog soon destroy the wood. One of these blocks had been placed by loving hands on a child's grave, and one of the women, who had come out of the church, stepped towards it. She stood still in front of it, and let her glance rest on the discolored memorial. A few moments afterwards her husband stepped up to her. Neither of them spoke a word, but he took her hand, and they wandered across the brown heath, over moor and meadow, towards the sand-hills; for a long time they thus walked silently side by side.

"That was a good sermon to-day," the man said at length. "If we had not God to look to, we should have nothing!"

"Yes," observed the woman, "He sends joy and sorrow, and He has a right to send them. To-morrow our little boy would have been five years old, if we had been allowed to keep him."

"You will gain nothing by fretting, wife," said the man, "The boy is well provided for. He is there whither we pray to go."

And they said nothing more, but went forward to their house among the sand-hills. Suddenly, in front of one of the houses where the sea-grass did not keep the sand down with its twining roots, there arose what appeared to be a column of smoke rising into the air. A gust of wind swept in among the hills, whirling the particles of sand high in the air. Another, and the strings of fish hung up to dry flapped and beat violently against the wall of the hut; and then all was still again, and the sun shone down hotly.

Man and wife stepped into the house. They had soon taken off their Sunday clothes, and emerging again, they hurried away over the dunes, which stood there like huge waves of sand suddenly arrested in their course, while the sand-weeds and the dune-grass, with its bluish stalks, spread a changing color over them. A few neighbors came up, and helped one another to draw the boats higher up on the sand. The wind now blew more sharply than before; it was cutting and cold: and when they went back over the sand-hills, sand and little pointed stones blew into their faces. The waves reared themselves up with their white crowns of foam, and the wind cut off their crests, flinging the foam far around.

The evening came on. In the air was a swelling roar, moaning and complaining like a troop of despairing spirits, that sounded above the hoarse rolling of the sea; for the fisher's little hut was on the very margin. The sand rattled against the window-panes, and every now and then came a violent gust of wind, that shook the house to its foundations. It was dark, but towards midnight the moon would rise.

The air became clearer, but the storm swept in all its gigantic force over the perturbed sea. The fisher-people had long gone to bed, but in such weather there was no chance of closing an eye. Presently there was a knocking at the window, and the door was opened, and a voice said :

"There's a great ship fast stranded on the outermost reef."

In a moment the fish-people had sprung from their couch, and hastily arrayed themselves.

The moon had risen, it was light enough to make the surrounding objects visible, to those who could open their eyes for the blinding clouds of sand. The violence of the wind was terrible ; and only by creeping forward between the gusts was it possible to pass among the sand-hills ; and now the salt spray flew up from the sea like down, while the ocean foamed like a roaring cataract towards the beach. It required a practiced eye to descry the vessel out in the offing. The vessel was a noble brig. The billows now lifted it over the reef, three or four cables' length out of the usual channel. It drove towards the land, struck against the second reef, and remained fixed.

To render assistance was impossible ; the sea rolled fairly in upon the vessel, making a clean breach over her. Those on shore fancied they heard the cries of help from on board, and could plainly descry the busy useless efforts made by the stranded crew. Now a wave came rolling onward, falling like a rock upon the bowsprit, and tearing it from the brig. The stern was lifted high above the flood. Two people were seen to embrace and plunge together into the sea; in a moment more, and one of the largest waves that rolled towards the sand-hills threw a body upon the shore. It was a woman, and appeared quite dead, said the sailors; but some women thought they discerned signs of life in her, and the stranger was carried across the sand-hills into the fisherman's hut. How beautiful and fair she was ! certainly she must be a great lady.

They laid her upon the humble bed that boasted not a yard of linen, but there was a woollen coverlet, and that would keep the occupant warm.

Life returned to her, but she was delirious, and knew nothing of what had happened, or where she was; and it was better so, for every thing she loved and valued lay buried in the sea. It was with her ship as with the vessel in the song of "The King's Son of England."

> "Alas, it was a grief to see
> How the gallant ship sank speedily."

Portions of wreck and fragments of wood drifted ashore, and they were all that remained of what had been the ship The wind still drove howling over the coast. For a few moments the strange lady seemed to rest; but she awoke in pain, and cries of anguish and fear came from her lips. She opened her wonderfully beautiful eyes, and spoke a few words, but none understood her.

And behold, as a reward for the pain and sorrow she had undergone, she held in her arms a new-born child, the child that was to have rested upon a gorgeous couch, surrounded by silken curtains, in the sumptuous home. It was to have been welcomed with joy to a life rich in all the goods of the earth; and now Providence had caused it to be born in this humble retreat, and not even a kiss did it receive from its mother.

The fisher's wife laid the child upon the mother's bosom, and it rested on a heart that beat no more, for she was dead. The child who was to be nursed by wealth and fortune, was cast into the world, washed by the sea among the sand-hills, to partake the fate and heavy days of the poor. And here again comes into our mind the old song of the English king's son, in which mention is made of the customs prevalent at that time, when knights and squires plundered those who had been saved from shipwreck.

The ship had been stranded some distance south of Nissum Bay. The hard, inhuman days in which, as we have stated, the inhabitants of the Jutland shores did evil to the shipwrecked, were long past. Affection and sympathy and self-sacrifice for the unfortunate were to be found, as they are to be found in our own time, in many a brilliant example. The dying mother and the unfortunate child would have found succor and help wherever the wind blew them; but nowhere could they have found more earnest care than in the hut of the poor fisher-wife, who had stood but yesterday, with a heavy heart, beside the grave which covered her child, which would have been five years old that day, if God had spared it to her.

No one knew who the dead stranger was, or could even form a conjecture. The pieces of wreck said nothing on the subject.

Into the rich house in Spain no tidings penetrated of the fate of the daughter and the son-in-law. They had not arrived at their destined post, and violent storms had raged during the past weeks. At last the verdict was given, "Foundered at sea—all lost."

But in the sand-hills near Hunsby, in the fisherman's hut, lived a little scion of the rich Spanish family.

Where Heaven sends food for two, a third can manage to make a meal, and in the depths of the sea is many a dish of fish for the hungry.

And they called the boy Jürgen.

"It must certainly be a Jewish child," the people said, "it looks so swarthy."

"It might be an Italian or a Spaniard," observed the clergyman.

But to the fisherwoman these three nations seemed all the same, and she consoled herself with the idea that the child was baptized as a Christian.

The boy throve. The noble blood in his veins was warm, and he became strong on his homely fare. He grew apace in the humble house, and the Danish dialect spoken by the West Jutes became his language. The pomegranate seed from Spanish soil became a hardy plant on the coast of West Jutland. Such may be a man's fate! To this home he clung with the roots of his whole being. He was to have experience of cold and hunger, and the misfortunes and hardships that surrounded the humble; but he tasted also of the poor man's joys.

Childhood has sunny heights for all, whose memory gleams through the whole after-life. The boy had many opportunities for pleasure and play. The whole coast, for miles and miles, was full of playthings; for it was a mosaic of pebbles, red as coral, yellow as amber, and others again white and rounded like birds' eggs; and all smoothed and prepared by the sea. Even the bleached fish-skeletons, the water-plants dried by the wind, seaweed, white, gleaming, and long linen-like bands, waving among the stones, all these seemed made to give pleasure and amusement to the eye and the thoughts; and the boy had an intelligent mind —many and great faculties lay dormant in him. How readily he retained in his mind the stories and songs he heard, and how neat-handed he was! With stones and mussel-shells he put together pictures and ships with which one could decorate the room; and he could cut out his thoughts wonderfully on a stick, his foster-mother said, though the boy was still so young and little! His voice sounded sweetly ; every melody flowed at once from his lips. Many chords were attuned in his heart which might have sounded out into the world, if he had been placed elsewhere than in the fisherman's hut by the North Sea.

One day another ship was stranded there. Among other things, a chest of rare flower-bulbs floated ashore. Some were put into the cooking-pots, for they were thought to be eatable, and others lay and shrivelled in the sand, but they did not accomplish their purpose, or unfold the richness of color whose germ was within them. Would it be better with Jürgen? The flower-bulbs had soon played their part, but he had still years of apprenticeship before him.

Neither he nor his friends remarked in what a solitary and uniform way one day succeeded another ; for there was plenty to do and to see. The sea itself was a great lesson-book, unfolding a new leaf every day, such as calm and storm, breakers and waifs. The visits to the church were festal visits. But among the festal visits in the fisherman's house, one was particularly distinguished. It was repeated twice in the year, and was, in fact, the visit of the brother of Jürgen's foster-mother, the eel-breeder from Zjaltring, upon the neighborhood of the "Bow Hill." He used to come in a cart painted red, and filled with eels. The cart was covered and locked like a box, and painted all over with blue and white tulips. It was drawn by two dun oxen, and Jürgen was allowed to guide them.

The eel-breeder was a witty fellow, a merry guest, and brought a measure of brandy with him. Every one received a small glassful, or a cupful when there was a scarcity of glasses : even Jürgen had as much as a large thimbleful, that he might digest the fat eel, the eel-breeder said, who always told the same story over again; and when his hearers laughed, he immediately told it over again to the same audience. As, during his childhood, and even later, Jürgen used many expressions from this story of the eel-breeder's, and made use of it in various ways, it is as well that we should listen to it too. Here it is:

"The eels went into the bay; and the mother-eel said to her daughters, who begged leave to go a little way up the bay, 'Don't go too far: the ugly eel-spearer might come and snap you all up.' But they went too far; and of eight daughters only three came back to the eel-mother, and these wept and said, 'We only went a little way before the door, and the ugly eel-spearer came directly, and stabbed five of our party to death.' 'They'll come again,' said the mother-eel. 'Oh no,' exclaimed the daughters, 'for he skinned them, and cut them in two, and fried them.' 'Oh, they'll come again,' the mother-eel persisted. 'No,' replied the daughters, 'for he ate them up.' 'They'll come again,' repeated the mother-eel. 'But he drank brandy after them,' continued the daughters. 'Ah, then they'll never come back,' said the mother, and she burst out crying, 'It's the brandy that buries the eels.'

"And therefore," said the eel-breeder, in conclusion, "it is always right to take brandy after eating eels."

And this story was the tinsel-thread, the most humorous recollection of Jürgen's life. *He* likewise wanted to go a little way outside the door, and up the bay—that is to say, out into the world in a ship; and his mother said, like the eel-breeder, "There are so many bad people—eel-spearers!" But he wished to go a little way past the sand-hills, a little way into the dunes, and he succeeded in doing so. Four merry days, the happiest of his childhood, unrolled themselves, and the whole beauty and splendor of Jutland, all the joy and sunshine of his home, were concentrated in these. He was to go to a festival—though it was certainly a burial feast.

A wealthy relative of the fisherman's family had died. The farm lay deep in the country, eastward, and a point towards the north, as the saying is. Jürgen's foster-parents were to go, and he was to accompany them from the dunes, across heath and moor. They came to the green meadows where the river Skjärn rolls its course, the river of many eels, where mother-eels dwell with their daughters, who are caught and eaten up by wicked people. But men were said sometimes to have acted no better towards their own fellow-men; for had not the knight, Sir Bugge, been murdered by wicked people? and though he was well spoken of, had he not wanted to kill the architect, as the legend tells us, who had built for him the castle, with the thick walls and tower, where Jürgen and his parents now stood, and where the river falls into the bay? The wall on the ramparts still remained, and red crumbling fragments lay strewn around. Here it was that Sir Bugge, after the architect had left him, said to one of his men, "Go thou after him, and say, 'Master, the tower shakes.' If he turns round, you are to kill him, and take from him the money I paid him; but if he does not turn round, let him depart in peace." The man obeyed, and the architect never turned round, but called back, "The tower does not shake in the least, but one day there will come a man from the west, in a blue cloak, who will cause it to shake!" And indeed so it chanced, a hundred years later; for the North Sea broke in, and the tower was cast down, but the man who then possessed the castle, Prebjörn Gyldenstjerne, built a new castle higher up, at the end of the meadow, and that stands to this day, and is called Nörre Vosborg.

Past this castle went Jürgen and his foster-parents. They had told him its story during the long winter evenings, and now he saw the lordly castle, with its double moat, and trees, and bushes; the wall, covered with ferns, rose within the moat; but most beautiful of all were the lofty lime-trees, which grew up to the highest windows, and filled the air with sweet fragrance. In a corner of the garden, towards the northwest, stood a great bush, full of blossoms, like winter snow amid the summer's green: it was a juniper-bush, the first that Jürgen had seen thus in bloom. He never forgot it, nor the lime-tree: the child's soul treasured up these remembrances of beauty and fragrance to gladden the old man.

From Nörre Vosborg, where the juniper blossomed, the way went more easily; for they encountered other guests who were also bound for the burial, and were riding in wagons. Our travellers had to sit all together on a little box at the back of the wagon, but even this was preferable to walking, they thought. So they pursued their journey in the wagon across the rugged heath. The oxen which drew the vehicle slipped every now and then, where a patch of fresh grass appeared amid the heather. The sun shone warm, and it was wonderful to behold how in the far distance something like smoke seemed to be rising; and yet this smoke was clearer than the mist; it was transparent, and looked like rays of light rolling and dancing afar over the heath.

"That is Lokeman driving his sheep," said some one; and this was enough to excite the fancy of Jürgen. It seemed to him as if they were now going to enter fairyland, though every thing was still real.

How quiet it was! Far and wide the heath extended around them like a beautiful carpet. The heather bloomed; the juniper-bushes and the fresh oak-saplings stood up like nosegays from the earth. An inviting place for a frolic, if it were not for the number of poisonous adders of which the travellers spoke, as they did also of the wolves which formerly infested the place, from which circumstance the region was still called the Wolfsborg region. The old man who guided the oxen related how, in the lifetime of his father, the horses had to sustain many a hard fight with the wild beasts that were now extinct ; and how he himself, when he went out one morning to bring in the horses, had found one of them standing with its fore-feet on a wolf it had killed, after the savage beast had torn and lacerated the legs of the brave horse.

The journey over the heath and the deep sand was only too quickly accomplished. They stopped before the house of mourning, where they found plenty of guests within and without. Wagon after wagon stood ranged in a row, and horses and oxen went out to crop the scanty pasture. Great sand-hills, like those at home in the North Sea, rose behind the house, and extended far and wide. How had they come here, miles into the interior of the land, and as large and high as those on the coast ? The wind had lifted and carried them hither, and to them also a history was attached.

Psalms were sung, and a few of the old people shed tears ; beyond this, the guests were cheerful enough, as it appeared to Jürgen, and there was plenty to eat and drink. Eels there were of the fattest, upon which brandy should be poured to bury them, as the eel-breeder said ; and certainly his maxim was here carried out.

Jürgen went to and fro in the house. On the third day he felt quite at home, like as in the fisherman's hut on the sand-hills where he had passed his early days. Here on the heath there was certainly an unheard-of wealth, for the flowers and blackberries and bilberries were to be found in plenty, so large and sweet, that when they were crushed beneath the tread of the passers-by, the heath was colored with their red juice.

Here was a Hun's grave, and yonder another. Columns of smoke rose into the still air ; it was a heath-fire, he was told, that shone so splendidly in the dark evening.

Now came the fourth day, and the funeral festivities were to conclude, and they were to go back from the land-dunes to the sand-dunes.

"Ours are the best," said the old fisherman, Jürgen's foster-father ; "these have no strength."

And they spoke of the way in which the sand-dunes had come into the country, and it seemed all very intelligible. This was the explanation they gave :

A corpse had been found on the coast, and the peasants had buried it in the churchyard ; and from that time the sand began to fly, and the sea broke in violently. A wise man in the parish advised them to open the grave and to look if the buried man was not lying sucking his thumb ; for if so, he was a man of the sea, and the sea would not rest until it had got him back. So the grave was opened, and he really was found with his thumb in his mouth. So they laid him upon a cart and harnessed two oxen before it ; and, as if stung by an adder, the oxen ran away with the man of the sea over heath and moorland to the ocean ; and then the sand ceased flying inland, but the hills that had been heaped up still remained there. All this Jürgen heard and treasured in his memory from the happiest days of his childhood, the days of the burial-feast. How glorious it was to get out into strange regions, and to see strange people ! And he was to go further still. He was not yet fourteen years old when he went out in a ship to see what the world could show him : bad weather, heavy seas, malice, and hard men—these were his experiences, for he became a ship-boy

There were cold nights, and bad living, and blows to be endured; then he felt as if his noble Spanish blood boiled within him, and bitter wicked words seethed up to his lips; but it was better to gulp them down, though he felt as the eel must feel when it is flayed and cut up, and put into the frying-pan.

"I shall come again!" said a voice within him. He saw the Spanish coast, the native land of his parents. He even saw the town where they had lived in happiness and prosperity; but he knew nothing of his home or race, and his race knew just as little about him.

The poor ship-boy was not allowed to land; but on the last day of their stay he managed to get ashore. There were several purchases to be made, and he was to carry them on board.

There stood Jürgen in his shabby clothes, which looked as if they had been washed in the ditch and dried in the chimney: for the first time he, the inhabitant of the dunes, saw a great city. How lofty the houses seemed, and how full of people were the streets! some pushing this way, some that—a perfect maelstrom of citizens and peasants, monks and soldiers—a calling and shouting, and jingling of bell-harnessed asses and mules, and the church-bells chiming between song and sound, hammering and knocking, all going on at once. Every handicraft had its home in the basements of the houses or in the lanes; and the sun shone so hotly, and the air was so close, that one seemed to be in an oven full of beetles, cockchafers, bees, and flies, all humming and murmuring together. Jürgen hardly knew where he was or which way he went. Ther he saw just in front of him the mighty portal of the cathe dral; the lights were gleaming in the dark aisles, and a fragrance of incense was wafted towards him. Even tho poorest beggar ventured up the steps into the temple. The sailor with whom Jürgen went, took his way through the church; and Jürgen stood in the sanctuary. Colored pictures gleamed from their golden ground. On the altar stood the figure of the Virgin with the child Jesus, surrounded by lights and flowers; priests in festive garb were chanting, and choir-boys, beautifully attired, swung the silver censer. What splendor, what magnificence did he see here! It streamed through his soul and overpowered him; the church and the faith of his parents surrounded him, and touched a chord in his soul, so that the tears overflowed his eyes.

From the church they went to the market-place. Here a quantity of provisions were given him to carry. The way to the harbor was long, and, tired and overpowered by various emotions, he rested for a few moments before a splendid house, with marble pillars, statues, and broad staircases. Here he rested his bundle against the wall. Then a liveried porter came out, lifted up a silver-headed cane, and drove him away—him, the grandson of the house. But no one there knew that, and he just as little as any one. And afterwards he went on board again, and there were hard words and cuffs, little sleep and much work; such were his experiences. They say that it is well to suffer in youth, if age brings something to make up for it.

His time of servitude on shipboard had expired, and the vessel lay once more at Ringkjöbing, in Jutland: he came ashore and went home to the sand-dunes by Hunsby; but his foster-mother had died while he was away on his voyage.

A hard winter followed that summer. Snow-storms swept over land and sea, and there was a difficulty in getting about. How variously things were distributed in the world! here biting cold and snow-storms, while in the Spanish land there was burning sunshine and oppressive heat. And yet, when here at home there came a clear frosty day, and Jürgen saw the swans flying in numbers from the sea towards the land, and across to Vosborg, it appeared to him that people could breathe most freely here; and here too was a splendid summer! In imagination he saw the heath bloom and grow purple with rich, juicy berries, and saw the elder-trees and the lime-trees at Vosborg in blossom. He determined to go there once more.

Spring came on, and the fishery began. Jürgen was an active assistant in this; he had grown in the last year, and was quick at work. He was full of life, he understood how to swim, to tread water, to turn over and tumble in the flood. They often warned him to beware of the troops of dog-fish, which could seize the best swimmer, and draw him down and devour him; but such was not Jürgen's fate.

At the neighbor's on the dune was a boy named Martin, with whom Jürgen was very friendly, and the two took service in the same ship to Norway, and also went together to Holland; and they had never had any quarrel; but a quarrel can easily come, for when a person is hot by nature, he often uses strong gestures, and that is what Jürgen did one day on board when they had a quarrel about nothing at all. They were sitting behind the cabin door, eating out of a delf plate which they had placed between them. Jürgen held his pocket-knife in his hand, and lifted it against Martin, and at the same time became ashy pale in the face, and his eyes had an ugly look. Martin only said—

"Ah! ha! you are one of that sort, who are fond of using the knife!"

Hardly were the words spoken, when Jürgen's hand sank down. He answered not a syllable, but went on eating, and afterwards walked away to his work. When they were resting again, he stepped up to Martin, and said—

"You may hit me in the face! I have deserved it. But I feel as if I had a pot in me that boiled over."

"There let the thing rest," replied Martin; and after that they were almost doubly as good friends as before; and when afterwards they got back to the dunes and began telling their adventures, this was told among the rest; and Martin said that Jürgen was certainly passionate, but a good fellow for all that.

They were both young and strong, well-grown and stalwart; but Jürgen was the cleverer of the two.

In Norway the peasants go into the mountains, and lead out the cattle there to pasture. On the west coast of Jutland, huts have been erected among the sand-hills; they are built of pieces of wreck, and roofed with turf and heather. There are sleeping-places around the walls, and here the fisher-people live and sleep during the early spring. Every fisherman has his female helper, his manager, as she is called, whose business consists in baiting the hooks, preparing the warm beer for the fishermen when they come ashore, and getting their dinners cooked when they come back into the hut tired and hungry. Moreover, the managers bring up the fish from the boat, cut them open, prepare them, and have generally a great deal to do.

Jürgen, his father, and several other fishermen and their managers inhabited the same hut; Martin lived in the next one.

One of the girls, Else by name, had known Jürgen from childhood: they were glad to see each other, and in many things were of the same mind; but in outward appearance they were entirely opposite; for he was brown, whereas she was pale and had flaxen hair, and eyes as blue as the sea in sunshine.

One day as they were walking together, and Jürgen held her hand in his very firmly and warmly, she said to him:

"Jürgen, I have something weighing upon my heart! Let me be your manager, for you are like a brother to me, whereas Martin, who has engaged me—he and I are lovers —but you need not tell that to the rest."

And it seemed to Jürgen as if the loose sand were giving way under his feet. He spoke not a word, but only nodded his head, which signified " yes." More was not required; but suddenly he felt in his heart that he detested Martin; and the longer he considered of this—for he had never thought of Else in this way before—the more did it become clear to him that Martin had stolen from him the only being he loved ; and now it was all at once plain to him, that Else was the being in question.

When the sea is somewhat disturbed, and the fishermen come home in their great boat, it is a sight to behold how they cross the reefs. One of the men stands upright in the bow of the boat, and the others watch him, sitting with the oars in their hands. Outside the reef they appear to be rowing, not towards the land, but backing out to sea, till the man standing in the boat gives them the sign that the great wave is coming which is to float them across the reef ; and accordingly the boat is lifted—lifted high in the air, so that its keel is seen from the shore ; and in the next minute the whole boat is hidden from the eye; neither mast nor keel nor people can be seen, as though the sea had devoured them; but in a few moments they emerge like a great-sea animal climbing up the waves, and the oars move as if the creature had legs. The second and the third reef are passed in the same manner; and now the fishermen jump into the water; every wave helps them, and pushes the boat well forward, till at length they have drawn it beyond the range of the breakers.

A wrong order given in front of the reef—the slightest hesitation—and the boat must founder.

"Then it would be all over with me, and Martin too!" This thought struck Jürgen while they were out at sea, where his foster-father had been taken alarmingly ill. The fever had seized him. They were only a few oars' strokes from the reef, and Jürgen sprang from his seat, and stood up in the bow.

"Father—let me come!" he said; and his eye glanced towards Martin, and across the waves : but while every oar bent with the exertions of the rowers, as the great wave came towering towards them, he beheld the pale face of his father, and dare not obey the evil impulse that had seized him. The boat came safely across the reef to land, but the evil thought remained in his blood, and roused up every little fibre of bitterness which had remained in his memory since he and Martin had been comrades. But he could not weave the fibres together, nor did he endeavor to do so. He felt that Martin had despoiled him, and this was enough to make him detest his former friend. Several of the fishermen noticed this, but not Martin, who continued obliging and talkative—the latter a little too much.

Jürgen's adopted father had to keep his bed, which became his death-bed, for in the next week he died; and now Jürgen was installed as heir in the little house behind the sand-hills. It was but a little house, certainly, but still it was something, and Martin had nothing of the kind.

"You will not take sea-service again, Jürgen?" observed one of the old fishermen. "You will always stay with us, now."

But this was not Jürgen's intention, for he was just thinking of looking about him a little in the world. The eel-breeder of Zjaltring had an uncle in Alt-Skage, who was a fisherman, but at the same time a prosperous merchant, who had ships upon the sea; he was said to be a good old man, and it would not be amiss to enter his service. Alt-Skage lies in the extreme north of Jutland, as far removed form the Hunsby dunes as one can travel in that country; and this is just what pleased Jürgen, for he did not want to remain till the wedding of Martin and Else, which was to be celebrated in a few weeks.

The old fisherman asserted that it was foolish now to quit the neighborhood; for that Jürgen had a home, and Else would probably be inclined to take him rather than Martin.

Jürgen answered so much at random, that it was not easy to understand what he meant; but the old man brought Else to him, and she said, "You have a home now; that ought to be well considered."

And Jürgen thought of many things.

The sea has heavy waves, but there are heavier waves in the human heart. Many thoughts, strong and weak, thronged through Jürgen's brain; and he said to Else,

"If Martin had a house like mine, whom would you rather have?"

"But Martin has no house, and cannot get one."

"But let us suppose he had one."

"Why, then, I would certainly take Martin, for that's what my heart tells me; but one can't live upon that."

And Jürgen thought of these things all night through. Something was working within him, he could not understand what it was, but he had a thought that was stronger than his love for Else; and so he went to Martin, and what he said and did there was well considered. He let the house to Martin on the most liberal terms, saying that he wished to go to sea again, because it pleased him to do so. And Else kissed him on the mouth when she heard that, for she loved Martin best.

In the early morning Jürgen purposed to start. On the evening before his departure, when it was already growing late, he felt a wish to visit Martin once more ; he started, and among the dunes the old fisher met him, who was angry at his going. The old man made jokes about Martin, and declared there must be some magic about that fellow, " of whom all the girls were so fond." Jürgen paid no heed to this speech, but said farewell to the old man, and went on towards the house where Martin dwelt. He heard loud talking within. Martin was not alone, and this made Jürgen waver in his determination, for he did not wish to encounter Else ; and on second consideration, he thought it better not to hear Martin thank him again, and therefore turned back.

On the following morning, before break of day, he fastened his knapsack, took his wooden provision-box in his hand, and went away among the sand-hills towards the coast path. The way was easier to traverse than the heavy sand-road, and moreover shorter ; for he intended to go in the first instance to Zjaltring, by Bowberg, where the eel-breeder lived, to whom he had promised a visit.

The sea lay pure and blue before him, and mussel-shells and sea-pebbles, the playthings of his youth, crunched under his feet. While he was thus marching on, his nose suddenly began to bleed : it was a trifling incident, but little things can have great significances. A few large drops of blood fell upon one of his sleeves. He wiped them off and stopped the bleeding, and it seemed to him as if this had cleared and lightened his brain. In the sand the sea-eringa was blooming here and there. He broke off a stalk and stuck it in his hat; he determined to be merry and of good cheer, for he was going into the wide world—"a little way outside the door, in front of the bay," as the young eels had said. "Beware of bad people, who will catch you and flay you, cut you in two, and put you in the frying-pan!" he repeated in his mind, and smiled, for he thought he should find his way through the world—good courage is a strong weapon.

The sun already stood high when he approached the narrow entrance to Nissum Bay. He looked back, and saw a couple of horsemen galloping a long distance behind him, and they were accompanied by other people. But this concerned him nothing.

The ferry was on the opposite side of the bay. Jürgen called to the ferryman; and when the latter came over with the boat, Jürgen stepped in; but before they had gone half-way across, the men whom he had seen riding so hastily behind him, hailed the ferryman, and summoned him to return in the name of the law. Jürgen did not understand the reason of this, but he thought it would be best to turn back, and therefore himself took an oar and returned. The moment the boat touched the shore, the men sprang on board, and, before he was aware, they had bound his hands with a rope.

"Thy wicked deed will cost thee thy life," they said. "It is well that we caught thee."

He was accused of nothing less than murder. Martin had been found dead, with a knife thrust through his neck. One of the fishermen had (late on the previous evening) met Jürgen going towards Martin's house; and this was not the first time Jürgen had raised his knife against Martin

—so they knew that he was the murderer. The town in which the prison was built was a long way off, and the wind was contrary for going there; but not half an hour would be required to get across the bay, and a quarter of an hour would bring them from thence to Nörre Vosborg, a great castle with walls and ditches. One of Jürgen's captors was a fisherman, a brother of the keeper of the castle; and he declared it might be managed that Jürgen should for the present be put into the dungeon at Vosborg, where Long Martha the gipsy had been shut up till her execution.

No attention was paid to the defence made by Jürgen; the few drops of blood upon his shirt-sleeves bore heavy witness against him. But Jürgen was conscious of innocence; and as there was no chance of immediately righting himself, he submitted to his fate.

The party landed just at the spot where Sir Bugge's castle had stood and where Jürgen had walked with his foster-parents after the burial-feast, during the four happiest days of his childhood. He was led by the old path over the meadow to Vosborg; and again the elder blossomed and the lofty lindens smelt sweet, and it seemed but yesterday that he had left the spot.

In the two wings of the castle a staircase leads down to a spot below the entrance, and from thence there is access to a low vaulted cellar. Here Long Martha had been imprisoned, and hence she had been led away to the scaffold. She had eaten the hearts of five children, and had been under the delusion that if she could obtain two more, she would be able to fly and to make herself invisible. In the midst of the cellar roof was a little narrow air-hole, but no window. The blooming lindens could not waft a breath of comforting fragrance into that abode, where all was dark and mouldy. Only a rough bench stood in the prison; but "a good conscience is a soft pillow," and consequently Jürgen could sleep well.

The thick oaken door was locked, and secured on the outside by an iron bar; but the goblin of superstition can creep through a key-hole into the baron's castle just as into the fisherman's hut; and wherefore should he not creep in here, where Jürgen sat thinking of Long Martha and her evil deeds? Her last thought on the night before her execution had filled this space; and all the magic came into Jürgen's mind which tradition asserted to have been practised there in the old times, when Sir Schwanwedel dwelt there. All this passed through Jürgen's mind, and made him shudder; but a sunbeam—a refreshing thought from without—penetrated his heart even here; it was the remembrance of the blooming elder and the fragrant lime-trees.

He was not left there long. They carried him off to the town of Ringkjöbing, where his imprisonment was just as hard.

Those times were not like ours. Hard measure was dealt out to the " common" people; and it was just after the days when farms were converted into knights' estates, on which occasions coachmen and servants were often made magistrates, and had it in their power to sentence a poor man, for a small offence, to lose his property and to corporal punishment. Judges of this kind were still to be found ; and in Jutland, far from the capital and from the enlightened well-meaning head of the government, the law was still sometimes very loosely administered ; and the smallest grievance that Jürgen had to expect was that his case would be protracted.

Cold and cheerless was his abode—and when would this

state of things end? He had innocently sunk into misfortune and sorrow—that was his fate. He had leisure now to ponder on the difference of fortune on earth, and to wonder why this fate had been allotted to him; and he felt sure that the question would be answered in the next life—the existence that awaits us when this is over. This faith had grown strong in him in the poor fisherman's hut; that which had never shone into his father's mind, in all the richness and sunshine of Spain, was vouchsafed as a light of comfort in his poverty and distress—a sign of mercy from God that never deceives.

The spring storms began to blow. The rolling and moaning of the North Sea could be heard for miles inland when the wind was lulled ; for then it sounded like the rushing of a thousand wagons over a hard road with a mine beneath. Jürgen, in his prison, heard these sounds, and it was a relief to him. No melody could have appealed so directly to his heart as did these sounds of the sea—the rolling sea, the boundless sea, on which a man can be borne across the world before the wind, carrying his own house with him wherever he is driven, just as the snail carries its home even into a strange land.

How he listened to the deep moaning, and how the thought arose in him—"Free ! free ! How happy to be free, even without shoes and in ragged clothes !" Sometimes, when such thoughts crossed his mind, the fiery nature rose within him, and he beat the wall with his clenched fists.

Weeks, months, and a whole year had gone by, when a vagabond—Niels, the thief, called also the horse couper—was arrested ; and now the better times came, and it was seen what wrong Jürgen had endured.

In the neighborhood of Ringkjöbing, at a beer-house, Niels, the thief, had met Martin on the afternoon before

Jürgen's departure from home and before the murder. A few glasses were drunk—not enough to cloud any one's brain, but yet enough to loosen Martin's tongue ; and he began to boast, to say that he had obtained a house, and intended to marry ; and when Niels asked where he intended to get the money, Martin shook his pocket proudly, and said :

"The money is there, where it ought to be."

This boast cost him his life ; for when he went home, Niels went after him, and thrust a knife through his throat, to rob the murdered man of the expected gold, which did not exist.

This was circumstantially explained; but for us it is enough to know that Jürgen was set at liberty. But what amends did he get for having been imprisoned a whole year, and shut out from all communion with men? They told him he was fortunate in being proved innocent, and that he might go. The burgomaster gave him two dollars for travelling expenses, and many citizens offered him provisions and beer—there were still good men, not all "grind and flay." But the best of all was, that the merchant Brönne Skjagen, the same into whose service Jürgen intended to go a year since, was just at that time on business in the town of Ringkjöbing. Brönne heard the whole story ; and the man had a good heart, and understood what Jürgen must have felt and suffered. He therefore made up his mind to make it up to the poor lad, and convince him that there were still kind folks in the world.

So Jürgen went forth from the prison as if to Paradise, to find freedom, affection, and trust. He was to travel this road now ; for no goblet of life is all bitterness : no good man would pour out such measure to his fellow-man, and how should He do it, who is love itself?

"Let all that be buried and forgotten," said Brönne the merchant. "Let us draw a thick line through last year: and we will even burn the calendar. And in two days we'll start for dear, friendly, peaceful Skjagen. They call Skjagen an out-of-the-way corner; but it's a good warm chimney-corner, and its windows open towards every part of the world."

That was a journey!—it was like taking fresh breath—out of the cold dungeon air into the warm sunshine! The heath stood blooming in its greatest pride, and the herd-boy sat on the Hun's grave and blew his pipe, which he had carved for himself out of the sheep's bone. Fata Morgana, the beautiful aerial phenomenon of the desert, showed itself with hanging gardens and swaying forests, and the wonderful cloud phenomenon, called here the "Lokeman driving his flock," was seen likewise.

Up through the land of the Wendels, up towards Skjagen, they went, from whence the men with the long beards (the Longobardi, or Lombards) had emigrated in the days when, in the reign of King Snio, all the children and the old people were to have been killed, till the noble Dame Gambaruk proposed that the young people had better emigrate. All this was known to Jürgen—thus much knowledge he had; and even if he did not know the land of the Lombards beyond the high Alps, he had an idea how it must be there, for in his boyhood he had been in the south, in Spain. He thought of the southern fruits piled up there; of the red pomegranate blossoms; of the humming, murmuring, and toiling in the great beehive of a city he had seen: but, after all, home is best; and Jürgen's home was Denmark.

At length they reached "Wendelskaju," as Skjagen is called in the old Norwegian and Icelandic writings. Then already Old Skjagen, with the western and eastern town, ex tended for miles, with sand-hills and arable land, as far as the lighthouse near the "Skjagenzweig." Then, as now, the houses were strewn among wind-raised sand-hills—a desert where the wind sports with the sand, and where the voices of the seamen and the wild swans strike harshly on the ear. In the southwest, a mile from the sea, lies Old Skjagen; and here dwelt merchant Brönne, and here Jürgen was henceforth to dwell. The great house was painted with tar; the smaller buildings had each an overturned boat for a roof; the pig-sty had been put together of pieces of wreck. There was no fence here, for indeed there was nothing to fence in; but long rows of fishes were hung upon lines, one above the other, to dry in the wind. The whole coast was strewn with spoilt herrings; for there were so many of those fish, that a net was scarcely thrown into the sea before they were caught by cartloads; there were so many, that often they were thrown back into the sea, or left to lie on the shore.

The old man's wife and daughter, and his servants too, came rejoicingly to meet him. There was a great pressing of hands, and talking, and questioning. And the daughter, what a lovely face and bright eyes she had!

The interior of the house was roomy and comfortable. Fritters that a king would have looked upon as a dainty dish, were placed on the table; and there was wine from the vineyard of Skjagen—that is, the sea; for there the grapes come ashore ready pressed and prepared in barrels and in bottles.

When the mother and daughter heard who Jürgen was, and how innocently he had suffered, they looked at him in a still more friendly way; and the eyes of the charming Clara were the friendliest of all. Jürgen found a happy home in Old Skjagen. It did his heart good; and his heart had been sorely tried, and had drunk the bitter goblet of love, which softens or hardens according to circumstances. Jürgen's heart was still soft—it was young, and there was still room in it; and therefore it was well that Mistress Clara was going in three weeks in her father's ship to Christiansand, in Norway, to visit an aunt, and to stay there the whole winter.

On the Sunday before her departure they all went to church, to the holy communion. The church was large and handsome, and had been built centuries before by Scotchmen and Hollanders; it lay at a little distance from the town. It was certainly somewhat ruinous, and the road to it was heavy, through the deep sand; but the people gladly went through the difficulties to get to the house of God, to sing psalms and hear the sermon. The sand had heaped itself up round the walls of the church ; but the graves were kept free from it.

It was the largest church north of the Limfjord. The Virgin Mary, with the golden crown on her head and the child Jesus in her arms, stood lifelike upon the altar; the holy apostles had been carved in the choir; and on the wall hung portraits of the old burgomasters and councillors of Skjagen; the pulpit was of carved work. The sun shone brightly into the church, and its radiance fell on the polished brass chandelier, and on the little ship that hung from the vaulted roof.

Jürgen felt as if overcome by a holy, child-like feeling, like that which possessed him when, as a boy, he had stood in the splendid Spanish cathedral; but here the feeling was different, for he felt conscious of being one of the congregation.

After the sermon followed the holy communion. He partook of the bread and wine, and it happened that he knelt beside Mistress Clara; but his thoughts were so fixed upon heaven and the holy service, that he did not notice his neighbor until he rose from his knees, and then he saw tears rolling down her cheeks.

Two days later she left Skjagen and went to Norway. He stayed behind, and made himself useful in the house and in the business. He went out fishing, and at that time fish were more plentiful and larger than now. Every Sunday when he sat in the church, and his eye rested on the statue of the Virgin on the altar, his glance rested for a time on the spot where Mistress Clara had knelt beside him, and he thought of her, how hearty and kind she had been to him.

And so the autumn and the winter time passed away. There was wealth here, and a real family life; even down to the domestic animals, who were all well kept. The kitchen glittered with copper and tin and white plates, and from the roof hung hams and beef, and winter stores in plenty. All this is still to be seen in many rich farms of the west coast of Jutland: plenty to eat and drink, clean decorated rooms, clever heads, happy tempers, and hospitality prevail there as in an Arab tent.

Never since the famous burial-feast had Jürgen spent such a happy time; and yet Mistress Clara was absent, except in the thoughts and memory of all.

In April a ship was to start for Norway, and Jürgen was to sail in it. He was full of life and spirits, and looked so jovial that Dame Brönne declared it did her good to see him.

"And it's a pleasure to see you too, old wife," said the old merchant. "Jürgen has brought life into our winter evenings, and into you too, mother. You look younger this year, and you seem well and bonny. But then you were

once the prettiest girl in Wiborg, and that's saying a great
deal, for I have always found the Wiborg girls the prettiest
of any."

Jürgen said nothing to this, but he thought of a certain
maiden of Skjagen ; and he sailed to visit that maiden, for
the ship steered to Christiansand, in Norway, and a favoring wind bore it rapidly to that town.

One morning merchant Brönne went out to the lighthouse
that stands far away from Old Skjagen : the coal-fire had
long gone out, and the sun was already high when he
mounted the tower. The sand-banks extend under the water a
whole mile from the shore. Outside these banks many ships
were seen that day ; and with the help of his telescope the old
man thought he descried his own vessel, the "Karen Brönne."

Yes, surely, there she was ; and the ship was sailing up
with Jürgen and Clara on board. The church and the
lighthouse appeared to them as a heron and a swan rising
from the blue waters. Clara sat on deck, and saw the sand-
hills gradually looming forth ; if the wind held she might
reach her home in about an hour—so near were they to
home and its joys—so near were they to death and its ter-
rors. For a plank in the ship gave way, and the water
rushed in. The crew flew to the pumps, and attempted to
stop the leak. A signal of distress was hoisted ; but they
were still a full mile from the shore. Fishing-boats were in
sight, but they were still far distant. The wind blew shore-
ward, and the tide was in their favor too ; but all was in-
sufficient, for the ship sank. Jürgen threw his right arm
about Clara, and pressed her close to him.

With what a look she gazed in his face ! As he threw
himself in God's name into the water with her, she uttered
a cry ; but still she felt safe, certain that he would not let
her sink.

And now, in the hour of terror and danger, Jürgen experienced what the old song told:

> "And written it stood, how the brave king's son
> Embraced the bride his valor had won."

How rejoiced he felt that he was a good swimmer! He worked his way onward with his feet and with one hand, while with the other he tightly held the young girl. He rested upon the waves, he trod the water, he practised all the arts he knew, so as to reserve strength enough to reach the shore. He heard how Clara uttered a sigh, and felt a convulsive shudder pass through her, and he pressed her to him closer than ever. Now and then a wave rolled over her; and he was still a few cables' length from the land, when help came in the shape of an approaching boat. But under the water—he could see it clearly—stood a white form gazing at him; a wave lifted him up, and the form approached him: he felt a shock, and it grew dark, and every thing vanished from his gaze.

On the sand-reef lay the wreck of a ship: the sea washed over it; the white figure-head leant against an anchor, the sharp iron extended just to the surface. Jürgen had come in contact with this, and the tide had driven him against it with double force. He sank down fainting with his load; but the next wave lifted him and the young girl aloft again.

The fishermen grasped them, and lifted them into the boat. The blood streamed down over Jürgen's face; he seemed dead, but he still clutched the girl so tightly that they were obliged to loosen her by force from his grasp. And Clara lay pale and lifeless in the boat that now made for the shore.

All means were tried to restore Clara to life; but she was dead! For some time he had been swimming onward with a corpse, and had exerted himself to exhaustion for one who was dead.

Jürgen was still breathing. The fishermen carried him into the nearest house upon the sand-hills. A kind of surgeon who lived there, and was at the same time a smith and a general dealer, bound up Jürgen's wounds in a temporary way, till a physician could be got next day from the nearest town.

The brain of the sick man was affected. In delirium he uttered wild cries; but on the third day he lay quiet and exhausted on his couch, and his life seemed to hang by a thread, and the physician said it would be best if this string snapped.

"Let us pray that God may take him to Himself; he will never be a sane man again!"

But life would not depart from him—the thread would not snap; but the thread of memory broke : the thread of all his mental power had been cut through ; and, what was most terrible, a body remained—a living healthy body—that wandered about like a spectre.

Jürgen remained in the house of the merchant Brönne.

"He contracted his illness in his endeavor to save our child," said the old man, "and now he is our son."

People called Jürgen imbecile; but that was not the right expression. He was like an instrument in which the strings are loose and will sound no more; only at times for a few minutes they regained their power, and then they sounded anew : old melodies were heard, snatches of song ; pictures unrolled themselves, and then disappeared again in the mist, and once more he sat staring before him, without a thought. We may believe that he did not suffer, but his dark eyes lost their brightness, and looked only like black clouded glass.

"Poor imbecile Jürgen!" said the people.

He it was whose life was to have been so pleasant that it would be "presumption and pride" to expect or believe in a higher existence hereafter. All his great mental faculties had been lost; only hard days, pain, and disappointment had been his lot. He was like a rare plant torn from its native soil, and thrown upon the sand, to wither there. And was the image, fashioned in God's likeness, to have no better destination? Was it to be merely the sport of chance? No. The all-loving God would certainly repay him in the life to come, for what he had suffered and lost here. "The Lord is good to all ; and His mercy is over all His works." These words from the Psalms of David, the old pious wife of the merchant repeated in patience and hope, and the prayer of her heart was that Jürgen might soon be summoned to enter into the life eternal.

In the churchyard where the sand blows across the walls, Clara lay buried. It seemed as if Jürgen knew nothing of this—it did not come within the compass of his thoughts, which comprised only fragments of a past time. Every Sunday he went with the old people to church, and sat silent there with vacant gaze. One day, while the Psalms were being sung, he uttered a deep sigh, and his eyes gleamed : they were fixed upon the altar, upon the place where he had knelt with his friend who was dead. He uttered her name, and became pale as death, and tears rolled over his cheeks.

They led him out of the church; and he said to the bystanders that he was well, and had never been ill : he, the heavily afflicted, the waif cast forth upon the world, remembered nothing of his sufferings. And the Lord our Creator is wise and full of loving-kindness—who can doubt it ?

In Spain, where the warm breezes blow over the Moorish cupola, among the orange-trees and laurels, where song and the sound of castagnettes are always heard, sat in the sumptuous house a childish old man, the richest merchant in the place, while children marched in procession through the streets, with waving flags and lighted tapers. How much of his wealth would the old man not have given to be able to press his children to his heart—his daughter, or her child, that had perhaps never seen the light in this world, far less a Paradise !

" Poor child !"

Yes, poor child—a child still, and yet more than thirty years old; for to that age Jürgen had attained in Old Skjagen.

The drifting sand had covered the graves in the church-yard quite up to the walls of the church; but yet the dead must be buried among their relations and loved ones who had gone before them. Merchant Brönne and his wife now rested here with their children, under the white sand.

It was spring-time, the season of storms. The sand-hills whirled up in clouds, and the sea ran high, and the flocks of birds flew like clouds in the storms, shrieking across the dunes; and shipwreck followed shipwreck on the reefs of " Skjagenzweig," from towards the Hunsby dunes. One evening Jürgen was sitting alone in the room. Suddenly his mind seemed to become clearer, and a feeling of unrest came upon him, which in his younger years had often driven him forth upon the heath and the sand-hills.

" Home ! home !" he exclaimed. No one heard him. He went out of the house towards the dunes. Sand and stones blew into his face and whirled around him. He went on further and further towards the church : the sand lay high around the walls, half over the windows ; but the heap had been shovelled away from the door, and the entrance was free and easy to open : and Jürgen went into the church.

The storm went howling over the town of Skjagen Within the memory of man the sea had not run so high—a terrible tempest ! but Jürgen was in the temple of God, and while black night reigned without, a light arose in his soul, a light that was never to be extinguished ; he felt the heavy stone which seemed to weigh upon his head burst asunder. He thought he heard the sound of the organ, but it was the storm and the moaning of the sea. He sat down on one of the seats ; and behold, the candles were lighted up one by one; a richness was displayed such as he had only seen in the church in Spain; and all the pictures of the old councillors were endued with life, and stepped forth from the walls against which they had stood for centuries, and seated themselves in the entrance of the church. The gates and doors flew open, and in came all the dead people, festively clad, and sat down to the sound of beautiful music, and filled the seats in the church. Then the psalm-tune rolled forth like a sounding sea; and his old foster-parents from the Hunsby dunes were here, and the old merchant Brönne and his wife; and at their side, close to Jürgen, sat their friendly, lovely daughter Clara, who gave her hand to Jürgen, and they both went to the altar, where they had once knelt together, and the priest joined their hands and united them together for life. Then the sound of music was heard again, wonderful, like a child's voice full of joy and expectation, and it swelled on to an organ's sound, to a tempest of full, noble sounds, lovely and elevating to hear, and yet strong enough to burst the stone tombs.

And the little ship that hung down from the roof of the choir came down, and became wonderfully large and beautiful, with silken sails and golden yards, "and every rope wrought through with silk," as the old song said. The married pair went on board, and the whole congregation with them, for there was room and joyfulness for all. And the walls and arches of the church bloomed like the juniper and the fragrant lime-trees, and the leaves and branches waved and distributed coolness; then they bent and parted, and the ship sailed through the midst of them, through the sea, and through the air; and every church taper became a star, and the wind sang a psalm-tune, and all sang with the wind :

" In love, to glory—no life shall be lost. Full of blessedness and joy. Hallelujah !"

And these words were the last that Jürgen spoke in this world. The thread snapped that bound the immortal soul, and nothing but a dead body lay in the dark church, around which the storm raged, covering it with loose sand.

The next morning was Sunday, and the congregation and their pastor went forth to the service. The road to church had been heavy ; the sand made the way almost impassable ; and now, when they at last reached their goal, a great hill of sand was piled up before the entrance, and the church itself was buried. The priest spoke a short prayer, and said that God had closed the door of this house, and the congregation must go and build a new one for Him elsewhere.

So they sang a psalm under the open sky, and went back to their homes.

Jürgen was nowhere to be found in the town of Skijagen, or in the dunes, however much they sought for him. It was thought that the waves, which had rolled far up on the sand, had swept him away.

His body lay buried in a great sepulchre, in the church

itself. In the storm the Lord's hand had thrown a handful of earth on his grave; and the heavy mound of sand lay upon it, and lies there to this day.

The whirling sand had covered the high vaulted passages; white-thorn and wild-rose trees grew over the church, over which the wanderer now walks; while the tower, standing forth like a gigantic tombstone over a grave, is to be seen for miles around: no king has a more splendid tombstone. No one disturbs the rest of the dead; no one knew of this, and we are the first who know of this grave—the storm sang the tale to me among the sand-hills.

THE BISHOP OF BÖRGLUM AND HIS WARRIORS.

Our scene is in Northern Jutland, in the so-called "wild moor." We hear what is called the "Wester-wow-wow"—the peculiar roar of the North Sea as it breaks against the western coast of Jutland. It rolls and thunders with a sound that penetrates for miles into the land; and we are quite near the roaring. Before us rises a great mound of sand—a mountain we have long seen, and towards which we are wending our way, driving slowly along through the deep sand. On this mountain of sand is a lofty old building—the convent of Börglum. In one of its wings (the larger one) there is still a church. And at this convent we now arrive in the late evening hour; but the weather is clear in the bright June night around us. The eye can range far, far over field and moor to the bay of Aalborg, over heath and meadow, and far across the dark-blue sea.

Now we are there, and roll past between barns and other farm-buildings; and at the left of the gate we turn aside to the old Castle Farm, where the lime-trees stand in lines along the walls, and, sheltered from the wind and weather, grow so luxuriantly that their twigs and leaves almost conceal the windows.

We mount the winding staircase of stone, and march through the long passages under the heavy roof-beams. The wind moans very strangely here, both within and without. It is hardly known how, but people say—yes, people say a great many thing when they are frightened or want to frighten others—they say that the old dead choir-men glide silently past us into the church, where Mass is sung. They can be heard in the rushing of the storm, and their singing brings up strange thoughts in the hearers—thoughts of the old times into which we are carried back.

On the coast a ship is stranded; and the bishop's warriors are there, and spare not those whom the sea has spared. The sea washes away the blood that has flowed from cloven skulls. The stranded goods belong to the bishop, and there is a store of goods here. The sea casts up tubs and barrels filled with costly wine for the convent cellar; and in the convent is already good store of beer and mead. There is plenty in the kitchen—dead game and poultry, hams and sausages; and fat fish swim in the ponds without.

The Bishop of Börglum is a mighty lord. He has great possessions, but still he longs for more—every thing must bow before the mighty Olaf Glob. His rich cousin at Thyland is dead, and his widow is to have the rich inheritance. But how comes it that one relation is always harder towards another than even strangers would be? The widow's husband had possessed all Thyland, with the exception of the

Church property. Her son was not at home. In his boy-hood he had already started on a journey, for his desire was to see foreign lands and strange people. For years there had been no news of him. Perhaps he had long been laid in the grave, and would never come back to his home to rule where his mother then ruled.

"What has a woman to do with rule?" said the bishop.

He summoned the widow before a court; but what did he gain thereby? The widow had never been disobedient to the law, and was strong in her just rights.

Bishop Olaf, of Börglum, what dost thou purpose? What writest thou on yonder smooth parchment, sealing it with thy seal, and intrusting it to the horsemen and servants who ride away—far away—to the city of the Pope?

It is the time of falling leaves and of stranded ships, and soon icy winter will come.

Twice had icy winter returned before the bishop welcomed the horsemen and servants back to their home. They came from Rome with a papal decree—a ban, or bull, against the widow who had dared to offend the pious bishop. "Cursed be she, and all that belongs to her. Let her be expelled from the congregation and the Church. Let no man stretch forth a helping hand to her, and let friends and relations avoid her as a plague and a pestilence!"

"What will not bend must break," said the Bishop of Börglum.

All forsake the widow; but she holds fast to her God. He is her helper and defender.

One servant only—an old maid—remained faithful to her; and, with the old servant, the widow herself followed the plough; and the crop grew, though the land had been cursed by the Pope and the bishop.

"Thou child of hell, I will yet carry out my purpose!"

cried the Bishop of Börglum. "Now will I lay the hand of the Pope upon thee, to summon thee before the tribunal that shall condemn thee!"

Then did the widow yoke the two last oxen that remained to her to a wagon, and mounted upon the wagon, with her old servant, and travelled away across the heath out of the Danish land. As a stranger she came into a foreign country, where a strange tongue was spoken and where new customs prevailed. Further and further she journeyed, to where green hills rise into mountains, and the vine clothes their sides. Strange merchants drive by her, and they look anxiously after their wagons laden with merchandise. They fear an attack from the armed followers of the robber-knights. The two poor women, in their humble vehicle drawn by two black oxen, travel fearlessly through the dangerous sunken road and through the darksome forest. And now they were in Franconia. And there met them a stalwart knight, with a train of twelve followers. He paused, gazed at the strange vehicle, and questioned the women as to the goal of their journey and the place whence they came. Then one of them mentioned Thyland, in Denmark, and spoke of her sorrows—of her woes—which were soon to cease; for so Divine Providence had willed it. For the stranger knight is the widow's son. He seized her hand, he embraced her, and the mother wept. For years she had not been able to weep, but had only bitten her lips till the blood started.

It is the time of falling leaves and of stranded ships, and soon will icy winter come.

The sea rolled wine-tubs to the shore for the bishop's cellar. In the kitchen the deer roasted on the spit before the fire. At Börglum it was warm and cheerful in the heated rooms, while cold winter raged without, when a piece of news was brought to the bishop : "Jens Glob, of Thyland, has come back, and his mother with him." Jens Glob laid a complaint against the bishop, and summoned him before the temporal and the spiritual court.

"That will avail him little," said the bishop. "Best leave off thy efforts, knight Jens."

Again it is the time of falling leaves, of stranded ships—icy winter comes again, and the "white bees" are swarming, and sting the traveller's face till they melt.

"Keen weather to-day," say the people, as they step in.

Jens Glob stands so deeply wrapped in thought that he singes the skirt of his wide garment.

"Thou Börglum bishop," he exclaims, "I shall subdue thee after all ! Under the shield of the Pope, the law cannot reach thee ; but Jens Glob shall reach thee !"

Then he writes a letter to his brother-in-law, Olaf Hase, in Sallingland, and prays that knight to meet him on Christmas Eve, at Mass, in the church at Widberg. The bishop himself is to read the Mass, and consequently will journey from Börglum to Thyland ; and this is known to Jens Glob.

Moorland and meadow are covered with ice and snow. The marsh will bear horse and rider, the bishop with his priests and armed men. They ride the shortest way, through the waving reeds, where the wind moans sadly.

Blow thy brazen trumpet, thou trumpeter clad in foxskin ! it sounds merrily in the clear air. So they ride on over heath and moorland—over what is the garden of Fata Morgana in the hot summer, though now icy, like all the country—towards the church of Widberg.

The wind is blowing his trumpet too—blowing it harder and harder. He blows up a storm—a terrible storm—that increases more and more. Towards the church they ride, as fast as they may through the storm. The church stands firm, but the storm careers on over field and moorland, over land and sea.

Börglum's bishop reaches the church; but Olaf Hase will scarce do so, hard as he may ride. He journeys with hi warriors on the further side of the bay, to help Jens Glob,. now that the bishop is to be summoned before the judgment seat of the Highest.

The church is the judgment-hall ; the altar is the council-table. The lights burn clear in the heavy brass candelabra. The storm reads out the accusation and the sentence, roaming in the air over moor and heath, and over the rolling waters. No ferry-boat can sail over the bay in such weather as this.

Olaf Hase makes halt at Ottesworde. There he dismisses his warriors, presents them with their horses and harness, and gives them leave to ride home and greet his wife. He intends to risk his life alone in the roaring waters ; but they are to bear witness for him that it is not his fault if Jens Glob stands without re-enforcement in the church at Widberg. The faithful warriors will not leave him, but follow him out into the deep waters. Ten of them are carried away; but Olaf Hase and two of the youngest men reach the further side. They have still four miles to ride.

It is past midnight. It is Christmas. The wind has abated. The church is lighted up; the gleaming radiance shines through the window-frames, and pours out over meadow and heath. The Mass has long been finished, silence reigns in the church, and the wax is heard dropping from the candles to the stone pavement. And now Olaf Hase arrives.

In the forecourt Jens Glob greets him kindly, and says :

" I have just made an agreement with the bishop."

"Sayest thou so?" replied Olaf Hase. "Then neither thou nor the bishop shall quit this church alive."

And the sword leaps from the scabbard, and Olaf Hase deals a blow that makes the panel of the church-door, which Jens Glob hastily closes between them, fly in fragments.

"Hold, brother! First hear what the agreement was that I made. I have slain the bishop and his warriors and priests. They will have no word more to say in the matter, nor will I speak again of all the wrong that my mother has endured."

The long wicks of the altar-lights glimmer red; but there is a redder gleam upon the pavement, where the bishop lies with cloven skull, and his dead warriors around him, in the quiet of the holy Christmas night.

And four days afterwards the bells toll for a funeral in the convent of Börglum. The murdered bishop and the slain warriors and priests are displayed under a black canopy, surrounded by candelabra decked with crape. There lies the dead man, in the black cloak wrought with silver; the crosier in the powerless hand that was once so mighty. The incense rises in clouds, and the monks chant the funeral hymn. It sounds like a wail—it sounds like a sentence of wrath and condemnation that must be heard far over the land, carried by the wind—sung by the wind—the wail that sometimes is silent, but never dies; for ever again it rises in song, singing even into our own time this legend of the Bishop of Börglum and his hard nephew. It is heard in the dark night by the frightened husbandman, driving by in the heavy sandy road past the convent of Börglum. It is heard by the sleepless listener in the thickly-walled rooms at Börglum. And not only to the ear of superstition is the sighing and the tread of hurrying feet audible in the long echoing passages leading to the convent-door that has long been locked. The door still seems to open, and the lights seem to flame in the brazen candlesticks; the fragrance of incense arises; the church gleams in its ancient splendor; and the monks sing and say the Mass over the slain bishop, who lies there in the black silver-embroidered mantle, with the crozier in his powerless hand; and on his pale proud forehead gleams the red wound like fire, and there burn the worldly mind and the wicked thoughts.

Sink down into his grave—into oblivion—ye terrible shapes of the times of old!

Hark to the raging of the angry wind, sounding above the rolling sea. A storm approaches without, calling aloud for human lives. The sea has not put on a new mind with the new time. This night it is a horrible pit to devour up lives, and to-morrow, perhaps, it may be a glassy mirror— even as in the old time that we have buried. Sleep sweetly, if thou canst sleep!

Now it is morning.

The new time flings sunshine into the room. The wind still keeps up mightily. A wreck is announced—as in the old time.

During the night, down yonder by Löken, the little fishing village with the red-tiled roofs—we can see it up here from the window—a ship has come ashore. It has struck, and is fast imbedded in the sand; but the rocket apparatus has thrown a rope on board, and formed a bridge from the wreck to the mainland; and all on board were saved, and reached the land, and were wrapped in warm blankets; and to-day they are invited to the farm at the convent of Börglum. In comfortable rooms they encounter hospitality and friendly faces. They are addressed in the language of their country, and the piano sounds for them with melodies of their native land ; and before these have died away, and the chord has been struck, the wire of thought, that reaches to the land of the sufferers, announces that they are rescued. Then their anxieties are dispelled; and at even they join in the dance at the feast given in the great hall at Börglum. Waltzes and Styrian dances are given, and Danish popular songs, and melodies of foreign lands in these modern times.

Blessed be thou, new time ! Speak thou of summer and of purer gales ! Send thy sunbeams gleaming into our hearts and thoughts ! On thy glowing canvas let them be painted—the dark legends of the rough hard times that are past !

♦♦♦

THE SNOW-MAN.

"It's so wonderfully cold that my whole body crackles !" said the Snow-Man. "This is a kind of wind that can blow life into one; and how the gleaming one up yonder is staring at me !" He meant the sun, which was just about to set. "It shall not make *me* wink—I shall manage to keep the pieces."

He had two triangular pieces of tile in his head instead of eyes. His mouth was made of an old rake, and consequently was furnished with teeth.

He had been born amid the joyous shouts of the boys, and welcomed by the sound of sledge-bells and the slashing of whips.

The sun went down, and the full moon rose, round, large, clear, and beautiful in the blue air.

"There it comes again from the other side," said the

Snow-Man. He intended to say the sun is showing himself again. "Ah! I have cured him of staring. Now let him hang up there and shine, that I may see myself. If I only knew how I could manage to move from this place, I should like so much to move. If I could, I would slide along yonder on the ice, just as I see the boys slide; but I don't understand it; I don't know how to run."

"Away! away!" barked the old Yard-Dog. He was quite hoarse, and could not pronounce the genuine "bow, wow." He had got the hoarseness from the time when he was an indoor dog, and lay by the fire. "The sun will teach you to run! I saw that last winter, in your predecessor, and before that in *his* predecessor. Away! away! —and away they all go."

"I don't understand you, comrade," said the Snow-Man. "That thing up yonder is to teach me to run?" He meant the moon. "Yes, it was running itself when I saw it a little while ago, and now it comes creeping from the other side."

"You know nothing at all," retorted the Yard-Dog. "But then you've only just been patched up. What you see yonder is the moon, and the one that went before was the sun. It will come again to-morrow, and will teach you to run down into the ditch by the wall. We shall soon have a change of weather; I can feel that in my left hind leg, for it pricks and pains me : the weather is going to change."

"I don't understand him," said the Snow-Man; "but I have a feeling that he's talking about something disagreeable. The one who stared so just now, and whom he called the sun, is not my friend. I can feel that, too."

"Away! away!" barked the Yard-Dog; and he turned round three times, and then crept into his kennel to sleep.

The weather really changed. Towards morning, a thick damp fog lay over the whole region; later there came a wind, an icy wind. The cold seemed quite to seize upon one ; but when the sun rose, what splendor ! Trees and bushes were covered with hoar-frost, and looked like a complete forest of coral, and every twig seemed covered with gleaming white buds. The many delicate ramifications, concealed in summer by the wreath of leaves, now made their appearance : it seemed like a lace-work, gleaming white. A snowy radiance sprang from every twig. The birch waved in the wind—it had life, like the rest of the trees in summer. It was wonderfully beautiful. And when the sun shone, how it all gleamed and sparkled, as if diamond dust had been strewn everywhere, and big diamonds had been dropped on the snowy carpet of the earth ! or one could imagine that countless little lights were gleaming, whiter than even the snow itself.

"That is wonderfully beautiful," said a young girl, who came with a young man into the garden. They both stood still near the Snow-Man, and contemplated the glittering trees. "Summer cannot show a more beautiful sight," said she ; and her eyes sparkled.

"And we can't have such a fellow as this in summer-time," replied the young man, and he pointed to the Snow-Man. "He is capital."

The girl laughed, nodded at the Snow-Man, and then danced away over the snow with her friend—over the snow that cracked and crackled under her tread as if she were walking on starch.

"Who are those two ?" the Snow-Man inquired of the Yard-Dog. "You've been longer in the yard than I. Do you know them ?"

"Of course I know them," replied the Yard-Dog. "She

has stroked me, and he has thrown me a meat-bone. I don't bite those two."

"But what are they?" asked the Snow-man.

"Lovers!" replied the Yard-Dog. "They will go to live in the same kennel, and gnaw at the same bone. Away! away!"

"Are they the same kind of beings as you and I?" asked the Snow-Man.

"Why, they belong to the master," retorted the Yard-Dog. "People certainly know very little who were only born yesterday. I can see that in you. I have age, and information. I know every one here in the house, and I know a time when I did not lie out here in the cold, fastened to a chain. Away! away!"

"The cold is charming," said the Snow-Man. "Tell me, tell me. But you must not clank with your chain, for it jars within me when you do that."

"Away! away!" barked the Yard-Dog. "They told me I was a pretty little fellow: then I used to lie in a chair covered with velvet, up in master's house, and sit in the lap of the mistress of all. They used to kiss my nose, and wipe my paws with an embroidered handkerchief. I was called 'Ami—dear Ami—sweet Ami.' But afterwards I grew too big for them, and they gave me away to the housekeeper. So I came to live in the basement story. You can look into that from where you are standing, and you can see into the room where I was master; for I was master at the housekeeper's. It was certainly a smaller place than up-stairs, but I was more comfortable, and was not continually taken hold of and pulled about by children, as I had been. I received just as good food as ever, and even better. I had my own cushion, and there was a stove, the finest thing in the world at this season. I went under the stove, and could lie down quite beneath it. Ah ! I still dream of that stove. Away ! away !"

"Does a stove look so beautiful ?" asked the Snow-Man. "Is it at all like me ?"

"It's just the reverse of you. It's as black as a crow, and has a long neck and brazen drum. It eats firewood, so that the fire spurts out of its mouth. One must keep at its side, or under it, and there one is very comfortable. You can see it through the window from where you stand."

And the Snow-Man looked and saw a bright polished thing with a brazen drum, and the fire gleamed from the lower part of it. The Snow-Man felt quite strangely : an odd emotion came over him, he knew not what it meant, and could not account for it ; but all people who are not snow-men know the feeling.

" And why did you leave her ?" asked the Snow-Man, for it seemed to him that the stove must be of the female sex. "How could you quit such a comfortable place ?"

"I was obliged," replied the Yard-Dog. "They turned me out of doors, and chained me up here. I had bitten the youngest young master in the leg, because he kicked away the bone I was gnawing. 'Bone for bone,' I thought. They took that very much amiss, and from that time I have been fastened to a chain and have lost my voice. Don't you hear how hoarse I am? Away ! away ! I can't talk any more like other dogs. Away ! away ! that was the end of the affair."

But the Snow-Man was no longer listening to him. He was looking in at the housekeeper's basement lodging, into the room where the stove stood on its four legs, just the same size as the Snow-Man himself.

" What a strange crackling within me !" he said. "Shall I ever get in there? It is an innocent wish, and our inno cent wishes are certain to be fulfilled. I must go in there and lean against her, even if I have to break through the window."

"You will never get in there," said the Yard-Dog ; "and if you approach the stove you'll melt away—away !"

"I am as good as gone," replied the Snow-Man. "I think I am breaking up."

The whole day the Snow-Man stood looking in through the window. In the twilight hour the room became still more inviting : from the stove came a mild gleam, not like the sun nor like the moon ; no, it was only as the stove can glow when he has something to eat. When the room-door opened, the flame started out of his mouth ; this was a habit the stove had. The flame fell distinctly on the white face of the Snow-Man, and gleamed red upon his bosom.

"I can endure it no longer," said he ; "how beautiful it looks when it stretches out its tongue !"

The night was long ; but it did not appear long to the Snow-Man, who stood there lost in his own charming reflections, crackling with the cold.

In the morning the window-panes of the basement lodging were covered with ice. They bore the most beautiful ice-flowers that any snow-man could desire ; but they concealed the stove. The window-panes would not thaw ; he could not see the stove, which he pictured to himself as a lovely female being. It crackled and whistled in him and around him ; it was just the kind of frosty weather a snow-man must thoroughly enjoy. But he did not enjoy it ; and, indeed, how could he enjoy himself when he was stove-sick ?

"That's a terrible disease for a Snow-Man," said the Yard-Dog. "I have suffered from it myself, but I got over it. Away ! away !" he barked ; and he added, "The weather is going to change."

And the weather did change; it began to thaw.

The warmth increased, and the Snow-Man decreased. He said nothing, and made no complaint—and that's an infallible sign.

One morning he broke down. And behold, where he had stood, something like a broomstick remained sticking up out of the ground. It was the pole round which the boys had built him up.

"Ah, now I can understand why he had such an intense longing," said the Yard-Dog. "Why, there's a shovel for cleaning out the stove fastened to the pole. The Snow-Man had a stove-rake in his body, and that's what moved within him. Now he has got over that too. Away! away!"

And soon they had got over the winter.

"Away! away!" barked the hoarse Yard-Dog; but the girls in the house sang:

> "Green thyme! from your house come out;
> Willow, your woolly fingers stretch out;
> Lark and cuckoo cheerfully sing,
> For in February is coming the spring.
> And with the cuckoo I'll sing too,
> Come thou, dear sun, come out, cuckoo!"

And nobody thought any more of the Snow-Man.

TWO MAIDENS.

Have you ever seen a maiden? I mean what our paviors call a maiden, a thing with which they ram down the paving-stones in the roads. A maiden of this kind is made altogether of wood, broad below, and girt round with iron rings; at the top she is narrow, and has a stick passed across through her waist; and this stick forms the arms of the maiden.

In the shed stood two maidens of this kind. They had their place among shovels, hand-carts, wheelbarrows, and measuring-tapes; and to all this company the news had come that the maidens were no longer to be called "maidens," but "hand-rammers;" which word was the newest and the only correct designation among the paviors for the thing we all know from the old times by the name of "the maiden."

Now, there are among us human creatures certain individuals who are known as "emancipated women;" as, for instance, principals of institutions, dancers who stand professionally on one leg, milliners, and sick-nurses; and with this class of emancipated women, the two maidens in the shed associated themselves. They were "maidens" among the pavior folk, and determined not to give up this honorable appellation, and let themselves be miscalled rammers.

"Maiden is a human name, but hand-rammer is a *thing*, and we won't be called *things*—that's insulting us."

"My lover would be ready to give up his engagement," said the youngest, who was betrothed to a pavior's hammer; and the hammer is the thing which drives great piles into the earth, like a machine, and therefore does on a large scale what ten maidens effect in a smaller way. "He wants to marry me as a maiden, but whether he would have me, were I a hand-rammer, is a question; so I won't have my name changed."

"And I," said the elder one, "would rather have both my arms broken off."

But the wheelbarrow was of a different opinion; and the wheelbarrow was looked upon as of some consequence, for he considered himself a quarter of a coach, because he went about upon one wheel.

"I must submit to your notice," he said, "that the name 'maiden' is common enough, and not nearly so refined as 'hand-rammer,' or 'stamper,' which latter has also been proposed, and through which you would be introduced into the category of seals; and only think of the great stamp of state, which impresses the royal seal that gives effect to the laws!   No, in your case I would surrender my maiden name."

"No, certainly not!" exclaimed the elder. "I am too old for that."

"I presume you have never heard of what is called 'European necessity?'" observed the honest measuring tape. "One must be able to adapt one's self to time and circumstances, and if there is a law that the 'maiden' is to be called 'hand-rammer,' why, she must be called 'hand-rammer,' and no pouting will avail, for every thing has its measure."

"No, if there must be a change," said the younger, "I should prefer to be called 'Missy,' for that reminds one a little of maidens."

"But I would rather be chopped to chips," said the elder.

At last they all went to work. The maidens rode—that is, they were put in a wheelbarrow, and that was a distinction; but still they were called "hand-rammers."   "Mai—!" they said, as they were bumped upon the pavement. 'Mai—!" and they were very nearly pronouncing the whole word "maiden;" but they broke off short, and swallowed the last syllable; for after mature deliberation they considered it beneath their dignity to protest. But they always called each other "maiden," and praised the good old days in which every thing had been called by its right name, and those who were maidens were called maidens. And they remained as they were; for the hammer really broke off his engagement with the younger one, for nothing would suit him but he must have a maiden for his bride.

THE FARMYARD COCK AND THE WEATHERCOCK.

THERE were two Cocks—one on the dunghill, the other on the roof. Both were conceited; but which of the two effected most? Tell us your opinion; but we shall keep our own, nevertheless.

The poultry-yard was divided by a partition of boards from another yard, in which lay a manure-heap, whereon lay and grew a great Cucumber, which was fully conscious of being a forcing-bed plant.

"That's a privilege of birth," the Cucumber said to herself. "Not all can be born cucumbers; there must be other kinds too. The fowls, the ducks, and all the cattle in the neighboring yard are creatures too. I now look up to the Yard-Cock on the partition. He certainly is of much greater consequence than the Weathercock, who is so highly placed, and who can't even creak, much less crow; and he has neither hens nor chickens, and thinks only of himself, and perspires verdigris. But the Yard-Cock—he's something like a cock! His gait is like a dance, his crowing is music; and wherever he comes, it is known directly. What a trumpeter he is! If he would only come in here |

Even if he were to eat me up, stalk and all, it would be a blissful death," said the Cucumber.

In the night the weather became very bad. Hens, chickens, and even the Cock himself sought shelter. The wind blew down the partition between the two yards with a crash; the tiles came tumbling down, but the weathercock sat firm. He did not even turn round; he could not turn round, and yet he was young and newly cast, but steady and sedate. He had been "born old," and did not at all resemble the birds that fly beneath the vault of heaven, such as the sparrows and the swallows. He despised those, considering them piping birds of trifling stature—ordinary song-birds. The pigeons, he allowed, were big and shining, and gleamed like mother-o'-pearl, and looked like a kind of weathercocks; but then they were fat and stupid, and their whole endeavor was to fill themselves with food. "Moreover, they are tedious things to converse with," said the Weathercock.

The birds of passage had also paid a visit to the Weathercock, and told him tales of foreign lands, of airy caravans, and exciting robber stories; of encounters with birds of prey; and that was interesting for the first time, but the Weathercock knew that afterwards they always repeated themselves, and that was tedious. "They are tedious, and all is tedious," he said. "No one is fit to associate with, and one and all of them are wearisome and stupid."

"The world is worth nothing," he cried. "The whole thing is a stupidity."

The Weathercock was what is called "used up;" and that quality would certainly have made him interesting in the eyes of the Cucumber if she had known it; but she had only eyes for the Yard-Cock, who had now actually come into her own yard.

The wind had blown down the plank, but the storm had passed over.

"What do you think of *that* crowing?" the Yard-Cock inquired of his hens and chickens. "It was a little rough —the elegance was wanting."

And hens and chickens stepped upon the muck-heap, and the Cock strutted to and fro on it like a knight.

"Garden plant!" he cried out to the Cucumber; and in this one word she understood his deep feeling, and forgot that he was pecking at her and eating her up—a happy death!

And the hens came, and the chickens came, and when one of them runs the rest run also; and they clucked and chirped, and looked at the Cock, and were proud that he was of their kind.

"Cock-a-doodle-doo!" he crowed. "The chickens will grow up large fowls if I make a noise in the poultry-yard of the world."

And hens and chickens clucked and chirped, and the Cock told them a great piece of news:

"A cock can lay an egg; and do you know what there is in that egg? In that egg lies a basilisk. No one can stand the sight of a basilisk. Men know that, and now you know it too—you know what is in me, and what a cock of the world I am."

And with this the Yard-Cock flapped his wings, and made his comb swell up, and crowed again; and all of them shuddered—all the hens and the chickens; but they were proud that one of their people should be such a cock of the world. They clucked and chirped, so that the Weathercock heard it; and he heard it, but he never stirred.

"It's all stupid stuff!" said a voice within the Weathercock. "The Yard-Cock does not lay eggs, and I am too lazy to lay any. If I liked, I could lay a wind-egg; but the world is not worth a wind-egg. And now I don't like even to sit here any longer."

And with this the Weathercock broke off; but he did not kill the Yard-Cock, though he intended to do so, as the hens declared. And what does the moral say?—"Better to crow than to be 'used up' and break off."

THE PEN AND INKSTAND.

In the room of a poet, where his inkstand stood upon the table, it was said, "It is wonderful what can come out of an inkstand. What will the next thing be? It is wonderful!"

"Yes, certainly," said the Inkstand. "It's extraordinary—that's what I always say," he exclaimed to the pen and to the other articles on the table that were near enough to hear. "It is wonderful what a number of things can come out of me. It's quite incredible. And I really don't myself know what will be the next thing, when that man begins to dip into me. One drop out of me is enough for half a page of paper; and what cannot be contained in half a page? From me all the works of the poet go forth—all these living men, whom people can imagine they have met—all the deep feeling, the humor, the vivid pictures of nature. I myself don't understand how it is, for I am not acquainted with nature, but it certainly is in me. From me all these things have gone forth, and from me proceed the troops of charming maidens, and of brave knights on prancing steeds, and all the lame and the blind, and I don't know what more—I assure you I don't think of any thing."

"There you are right," said the Pen; "you don't think at all ; for if you did, you would comprehend that you only furnish the fluid. You give the fluid, that I may exhibit upon the paper what dwells in me, and what I would bring to the day. It is the pen that writes. No man doubts that; and, indeed, most people have about as much insight into poetry as an old inkstand."

"You have but little experience," replied the Inkstand. "You've hardly been in service a week, and are already half worn out. Do you fancy you are the poet? You are only a servant; and before you came I had many of your sorts, some of the goose family, and others of English manufacture. I know the quill as well as the steel pen. Many have been in my service, and I shall have many more when *he* comes—the man who goes through the motions for me, and writes down what he derives from me. I should like to know what will be the next thing he'll take out of me."

"Inkpot !" exclaimed the Pen.

Late in the evening the poet came home. He had been to a concert, where he had heard a famous violinist, with whose admirable performances he was quite enchanted. The player had drawn a wonderful wealth of tone from the instrument : sometimes it had sounded like tinkling water-drops, like rolling pearls, sometimes like birds twittering in chorus, and then again it went swelling on like the wind through the fir-trees. The poet thought he heard his own heart weeping, but weeping melodiously, like the sound of woman's voice. It seemed as though not only the strings sounded, but every part of the instrument. It was a wonderful performance ; and difficult as the piece was, the bow seemed to glide easily to and fro over the strings, and it looked as though every one might do it. The violin seemed to sound of itself, and the bow to move of itself—these two appeared to do every thing; and the audience forgot the master who guided them and breathed soul and spirit into them. The master was forgotten; but the poet remembered him, and named him, and wrote down his thoughts concerning the subject:

"How foolish it would be of the violin and the bow to boast of their achievements. And yet we men often commit this folly—the poet, the artist, the laborer in the domain of science, the general—we all do it. We are only the instruments which the Almighty uses : to Him alone be the honor ! We have nothing of which we should be proud."

Yes, that is what the poet wrote down. He wrote it in the form of a parable, which he called "The Master and the Instrument."

"That is what you get, madam," said the Pen to the Inkstand, when the two were alone again. "Did you not hear him read aloud what I have written down?"

"Yes, what I gave you to write," retorted the Inkstand. "That was a cut at you, because of your conceit. That you should not even have understood that you were being quizzed ! I gave you a cut from within me—surely I must know my own satire !"

"Ink-pipkin !" cried the Pen.

"Writing-stick !" cried the Inkstand.

And each of them felt a conviction that he had answered well ; and it is a pleasing conviction to feel that one has given a good answer—a conviction on which one can sleep; and accordingly they slept upon it. But the poet did not sleep. Thoughts welled up from within him, like the tones from the violin, falling like pearls, rushing like the storm-wind through the forests. He understood his own heart in these thoughts, and caught a ray from the Eternal Master.

To *Him* be all the honor !

THE CHILD IN THE GRAVE.

THERE was mourning in the house, sorrow in every heart. The youngest child, a boy four years old, the joy and hope of his parents, had died. There still remained to them two daughters, the elder of whom was about to be confirmed—good, charming girls both; but the child that one has lost always seems the dearest; and here it was the youngest, and a son. It was a heavy trial. The sisters mourned as young hearts can, and were especially moved at the sight of their parents' sorrow. The father was bowed down, and the mother completely struck down by the great grief. Day and night she had been busy about the sick child, and had tended, lifted, and carried it; she had felt how it was a part of herself. She could not realize that the child was dead, and that it must be laid in a coffin and sleep in the ground. She thought God *could not* take this child from her; and when it was so, nevertheless, and there could be no more doubt on the subject, she said in her feverish pain:

"God did not know it. He has heartless servants here on earth, who do according to their own liking, and hear not the prayers of a mother."

In her grief she fell away from God, and then there came dark thoughts, thoughts of death, of everlasting death, that man was but dust in the dust, and that with this life all was ended. But these thoughts gave her no stay, nothing on which she could take hold; and she sank into the fathomless abyss of despair.

In her heaviest hours she could weep no more, and she thought not of the young daughters who were still left to her. The tears of her husband fell upon her forehead, but she did not look at him. Her thoughts were with the dead child; her whole thought and being were fixed upon it, to call back every remembrance of the little one, every innocent childish word it had uttered.

The day of the funeral came. For nights before the mother had not slept; but in the morning twilight she now slept, overcome by weariness; and in the mean time the coffin was carried into a distant room, and there nailed down, that she might not hear the blows of the hammer.

When she awoke and wanted to see her child, the husband said:

"We have nailed down the coffin. It was necessary to do so."

"When God is hard towards me, how should men be better?" she said, with sobs and groans.

The coffin was carried to the grave. The disconsolate mother sat with her young daughters. She looked at her daughters, and yet did not see them, for her thoughts were no longer busy at the domestic hearth. She gave herself up to her grief, and grief tossed her to and fro as the sea tosses a ship without compass or rudder. So the day of the funeral passed away, and similar days followed, of dark, wearying pain. With moist eyes and mournful glances, the sorrowing daughters and the afflicted husband looked upon her who would not hear their words of comfort; and, indeed, what words of comfort could they speak to her, when they themselves were heavily bowed down?

It seemed as though she knew sleep no more; and yet he would now have been her best friend, who would have strengthened her body, and poured peace into her soul. They persuaded her to seek her couch, and she lay still there, like one who slept. One night her husband was listening, as he often did, to her breathing, and fully believed that she had now found rest and relief. He folded his arms and prayed, and soon sank into a deep healthy sleep ; and thus he did not notice that his wife rose, threw on her clothes, and silently glided from the house, to go where her thoughts always lingered—to the grave which held her child. She stepped through the garden of the house, and over the fields, where a path led to the church yard. No one saw her on her walk—she had seen nobody, for her eyes were fixed upon the one goal of her journey.

It was a lovely starlight night ; the air was still mild ; it was in the beginning of September. She entered the churchyard, and stood by the little grave, which looked like a great nosegay of fragrant flowers. She sat down, and bowed her head low over the grave, as if she could have seen her child through the intervening earth, her little boy, whose smile rose so vividly before her—the gentle expression of whose eyes, even on the sick-bed, she could never forget. How eloquent had that glance been, when she had bent over him, and seized his delicate hand, which he had no longer strength to raise ! As she had sat by his crib, so she now sat by his grave, but here her tears had free course, and fell thick upon the grave.

"Thou wouldst gladly go down and be with thy child," said a voice quite close to her, a voice that sounded so clear and deep, it went straight to her heart. She looked up ; and near her stood a man wrapped in a black cloak, with a hood drawn closely down over his face. But she glanced keenly up, and saw his face under his hood. It was stern, but yet awakened confidence, and his eyes beamed with the radiance of youth.

"Down to my child !" she repeated ; and a despairing supplication spoke out of her words.

"Darest thou follow me," asked the form. "I am Death'

And she bowed her head in acquiescence. Then suddenly it seemed as though all the stars were shining with the radiance of the full moon; she saw the varied colors of the flowers on the grave, and the covering of earth was gradually withdrawn like a floating drapery; and she sank down, and the apparition covered her with a black cloak; night closed around her, the night of death, and she sank deeper than the sexton's spade can penetrate; and the churchyard was as a roof over her head.

A corner of the cloak was removed, and she stood in a great hall which spread wide and pleasantly around. It was twilight. But in a moment her child appeared, and was pressed to her heart, smiling at her in greater beauty than he had ever possessed. She uttered a cry, but it was inaudible. A glorious swelling strain of music sounded in the distance, and then near to her, and then again in the distance: never had such tones fallen on her ear; they came from beyond the great dark curtain which separated the hall from the great land of eternity beyond.

"My sweet darling mother," she heard her child say. It was the well-known, much-loved voice, and kiss followed kiss in boundless felicity; and the child pointed to the dark curtain.

"It is not so beautiful on earth. Do you see, mother—do you see them all? Oh, that is happiness!"

But the mother saw nothing which the child pointed out—nothing but the dark night. She looked with earthly eyes, and could not see as the child saw, which God had called to Himself. She could hear the sounds of the music, but she heard not the word—*the Word* in which she was to believe.

"Now I can fly, mother—I can fly with all the other happy children into the presence of the Almighty. I would fain fly; but, if you weep as you are weeping now, I might be lost to you—and yet I would go so gladly. May I not fly? And you will come to me soon—will you not, dear mother?"

"Oh, stay! stay!" entreated the mother. "Only one moment more—only once more I should wish to look at thee, and kiss thee, and press thee in my arms."

And she kissed and fondled the child. Then her name was called from above—called in a plaintive voice. What might this mean?

"Hearest thou?" asked the child. "It is my father who calls thee."

And in a few moments deep sighs were heard, as of weeping children.

"They are my sisters," said the child. "Mother, you surely have not forgotten them?"

And then she remembered those she had left behind. A great terror came upon her. She looked out into the night, and above her dim forms were flitting past. She seemed to recognize a few more of these. They floated through the Hall of Death towards the dark curtain, and there they vanished. Would her husband and her daughters thus flit past? No, their sighs and lamentations still sounded from above: —and she had been nearly forgetting them for the sake of him who was dead!

"Mother, now the bells of heaven are ringing," said the child. "Mother, now the sun is going to rise."

And an overpowering light streamed in upon her. The child had vanished, and she was borne upwards. It became cold round about her, and she lifted up her head, and saw that she was lying in the churchyard, on the grave of her child.

But the Lord had been a stay unto her feet, in a dream,

and a light to her spirit; and she bowed her knees and prayed for forgiveness that she had wished to keep back a soul from its immortal flight, and that she had forgotten her duties towards the living who were left to her.

And when she had spoken those words, it was as if her heart were lightened. Then the sun burst forth, and over her head a little bird sang out, and the church-bells sounded for early service. Every thing was holy around her, and her heart was chastened. She acknowledged the goodness of God, she acknowledged the duties she had to perform, and eagerly she went home. She bent over her husband, who still slept; her warm devoted kiss awakened him, and heartfelt words of love came from the lips of both. And she was gentle and strong, as a wife can be; and from her came the consoling words:

" God's will is always the best."

Then her husband asked her:

"From whence hast thou all at once derived this strength —this feeling of consolation?"

And she kissed him, and kissed her children, and said:

"They came from God, through the child in the grave."